W9-BRI-200

"A book by Christina Dodd is like a glass of champagne…sparkling and sinfully delicious."
—LISA KLEYPAS

"A star in any genre! Dodd writes with power and passion—and always leaves me satisfied!"—J. R. WARD

"Christina Dodd keeps getting better and better."
—DEBBIE MACOMBER

"A master."—KRISTIN HANNAH

Praise for
Thigh High

"An extraordinarily good read . . . gripping, with a no-holds-barred lovemaking that definitely brings the heat level high. . . . The most engaging thing about *Thigh High* is its characters. . . . By the end of the story I felt as if I knew them all—and I hated saying good-bye!"　　　　　　　—Romance Readers at Heart

"Dodd has penned another terrific story with a hero and heroine you'll fall in love with and littered with wonderful secondary characters and enough fast-moving twists and turns and sizzling hot sensuality to keep you turning pages until the final word."
　　　　　　　—Romance Novel TV

"Christina Dodd is a master. . . . *Thigh High* is a winner I highly recommend."　　　—Romance Reviews Today

"Charming and likable characters . . . make this an enjoyable read."　　　　　　　—Fresh Fiction

"Graced with an endearingly quirky cast of secondary characters and a wonderfully matched pair of protagonists, whose sexual chemistry is as hot and steamy as summer in New Orleans, Dodd's latest is funny, sexy, and entertaining."　　　　　　　—*Booklist*

continued . . .

"I can't wait to see what Ms. Dodd has in store because if *Thigh High* is any indication, we'll be in for a treat."
—Romance Junkies

"Dodd's latest hero is like a heat-seeking missile: Once he's set on a course, he's hard to shake. Making this damaged and obsessive hero likable despite his arrogance demonstrates Dodd's wonderful gift for characterization. The offbeat characters and undeniable charm of New Orleans make this romp a joy to experience!" —*Romantic Times* (top pick, 4½ stars)

"A humorous over-the-top wild spin of the Big Easy starring two likable protagonists. . . . Fans will enjoy Christina Dodd's amusing romantic dance around New Orleans." —*Midwest Book Review*

Raves for Christina Dodd

"Dodd delivers a high-octane, blowout finale. . . . This romantic suspense novel is a delicious concoction that readers will be hard-pressed not to consume in one gulp." —*Publishers Weekly*

"Dodd's latest sparkling romantic suspense novel is another of her superbly sexy literary confections expertly spiced with sassy wit and featuring a beguiling cast of wonderfully entertaining characters."—*Booklist*

"Sure to heat up the night." —Romance Junkies

"Dodd brings her unique sense of plotting, character, humor, and surprise to this wonderful tale. You'll relish every word, cherish each poignant moment and ingenious plot twist, sigh deeply and eagerly await the sequel. Dodd is clever, witty, and sexy."

—*Romantic Times*

"Dodd adds humor, sizzling sensuality, and a cast of truly delightful secondary characters to produce a story that will not disappoint." —*Library Journal*

"Strong and likable characters make this an enjoyable read. Ms. Dodd peppers the story with interesting secondary personalities, which adds to the reading pleasure." —The Best Reviews

"Sexy and witty, daring and delightful."
—*New York Times* bestselling author Teresa Medeiros

"A master romantic storyteller."
—*New York Times* bestselling author Kristin Hannah

"Christina Dodd keeps getting better and better."
—*New York Times* bestselling author Debbie Macomber

"Treat yourself to a fabulous book—anything by Christina Dodd!"
—*New York Times* bestselling author Jill Barnett

Christina Dodd's
Contemporary Romantic Suspense

Trouble in High Heels
Tongue in Chic
Thigh High

Christina Dodd's Paranormal
Darkness Chosen Series

Scent of Darkness
Touch of Darkness
Into the Shadow
Into the Flame

Christina Dodd

Danger in a Red Dress

A SIGNET BOOK

SIGNET

Published by New American Library, a division of
Penguin Group (USA) Inc., 375 Hudson Street,
New York, New York 10014, USA
Penguin Group (Canada), 90 Eglinton Avenue East, Suite 700, Toronto,
Ontario M4P 2Y3, Canada (a division of Pearson Penguin Canada Inc.)
Penguin Books Ltd., 80 Strand, London WC2R 0RL, England
Penguin Ireland, 25 St. Stephen's Green, Dublin 2,
Ireland (a division of Penguin Books Ltd.)
Penguin Group (Australia), 250 Camberwell Road, Camberwell, Victoria 3124,
Australia (a division of Pearson Australia Group Pty. Ltd.)
Penguin Books India Pvt. Ltd., 11 Community Centre, Panchsheel Park,
New Delhi - 110 017, India
Penguin Group (NZ), 67 Apollo Drive, Rosedale, North Shore 0632,
New Zealand (a division of Pearson New Zealand Ltd.)
Penguin Books (South Africa) (Pty.) Ltd., 24 Sturdee Avenue,
Rosebank, Johannesburg 2196, South Africa

Penguin Books Ltd., Registered Offices:
80 Strand, London WC2R 0RL, England

First published by Signet, an imprint of New American Library,
a division of Penguin Group (USA) Inc.

First Printing, March 2009
10 9 8 7 6 5 4 3 2 1

Copyright © Christina Dodd, 2009
All rights reserved

Ⓟ REGISTERED TRADEMARK—MARCA REGISTRADA

Printed in the United States of America

Without limiting the rights under copyright reserved above, no part of this
publication may be reproduced, stored in or introduced into a retrieval
system, or transmitted, in any form, or by any means (electronic, mechanical,
photocopying, recording, or otherwise), without the prior written permission
of both the copyright owner and the above publisher of this book.

PUBLISHER'S NOTE
This is a work of fiction. Names, characters, places, and incidents either are the
product of the author's imagination or are used fictitiously, and any
resemblance to actual persons, living or dead, business establishments,
events, or locales is entirely coincidental.
    The publisher does not have any control over and does not assume any
responsibility for author or third-party Web sites or their content.

If you purchased this book without a cover you should be aware that this book
is stolen property. It was reported as "unsold and destroyed" to the publisher
and neither the author nor the publisher has received any payment for this
"stripped book."

The scanning, uploading, and distribution of this book via the Internet or via
any other means without the permission of the publisher is illegal and
punishable by law. Please purchase only authorized electronic editions, and
do not participate in or encourage electronic piracy of copyrighted materials.
Your support of the author's rights is appreciated.

For Monty McAllister, for no particular reason.
Nope. None. No reason. Not one.

And for Donna McAllister,
for being so welcoming and generous
with your time, help and friendship.

ACKNOWLEDGMENTS

Danger in a Red Dress winds up not one but two series for me: the Fortune Hunters, with the wonderful Manly brothers, and the Lost Texas Hearts, with the heartbreaking and heartwarming Prescott family. As I look back on so many years and so many stories, I'm thankful for the inspiration and the help I've received. I want to offer my appreciation to everyone at NAL: Leslie Gelbman for her creative guidance; the editorial department, especially the astute Kara Cesare; the art department led by Anthony Ramondo; publicity with Craig Burke and Michele Langley, and of course, the spectacular Penguin sales department. Thank you all.

I especially want to thank my fans, who have patiently waited to read Gabriel's story, and nagged ever so politely. Sarah and Santa, this one's for you.

ONE

Hannah Grey couldn't remember when she'd enjoyed a funeral more.

She sat in the back pew of the Methodist church; the service had been lovely, the elderly man in the coffin was content to be there, and best of all, Mr. Donald Dresser's neglectful family had been discomfited by the praise lavished on him. His offspring, grandchildren, and great-grandchildren had looked uncomfortable, bored, or pious, depending on their ages and personalities, and Hannah hoped they hated every squirming minute of listening to the minister praise Mr. Dresser for his bravery in combat, his innate business sense, and his devotion to his community—qualities that none of them had inherited.

Now, while the Dresser family shuffled past the coffin, then into the vestibule to accept condolences, Hannah stood, shrugged into her long black coat, and walked up the aisle. She looked down at Mr. Dresser, dressed in his World War II uniform, his arthritis-twisted fingers crossed over his chest. He looked good. Stern. He had been a cantankerous old son of a bitch, but he had had his reasons. As he had told Hannah on a daily basis, *I'm sick and tired of being alive when all my friends are dead, my kids are worthless, and the only use I have for a pretty young nurse like you is to help me piss.*

She was fiercely glad he was at peace, but she wiped a tear away as she whispered, "Godspeed, old man. Godspeed."

She turned away, fumbling with her gloves, and walked to the vestibule. The mourners were gone, but Jeff Dresser stood alone, waiting for her.

He was fifty, handsome, well-dressed, and attractive— at least, he thought he was attractive. Big difference.

"On behalf of the family, we'd like to thank you for your care of our father. You're the first home-care nurse who could stick it out for more than two weeks, and we've sent your final wages to the agency." He handed her a plain white envelope. "But here's a bonus for you, with our gratitude."

She looked at the envelope. Looked at him. Noted that even at his father's funeral, when she was covered from head to foot in all-concealing black winter clothes, the fading playboy couldn't resist looking her over. "Thank you, Jeff. I'm sorry that your father had to die in such pain, but I loved hearing the stories of his life. He was very interesting."

She had Jeff's attention now. "He talked to you? He

told you the stories of his life? By God, that's more than he would ever do with us!"

"All I had to do was ask."

He stiffened, hearing the rebuke.

She tucked the envelope into her coat pocket and turned away. "Goodbye."

He muttered something quietly resentful, and strode past her and out the door.

So this was it. The end of another job. Time to go back to the placement agency.

Another man, about Jeff's age, but imposing, stood holding the church door open, and the cold February air filled the foyer. "Miss Grey? Do you remember me?"

She shook his outstretched hand. "Of course." Stephen Burkhart had been Mr. Dresser's attorney. The two men had spent hours cloistered in the study, and during his visits, he had been pleasant, respectful of the limitations she placed on her patient, and watchful. Very watchful.

"Miss Grey," he said, "there'll be a reading of the will at my office at four. Mr. Dresser asked that you attend."

"Because . . . because Mr. Dresser left me an inheritance?" She smiled and sighed, recalling the previous occasion she'd received a bequest from a patient, and how much Mr. Coleman's family had resented even that small amount. When she thought about how much the Dressers anticipated getting their hands on the old man's sizable fortune, she almost wished Mr. Dresser hadn't bothered. "He was worried about what he called my lack of resources," she explained. "I told him once I paid off my student loans, I'd be in the clear, and I meant it. I wasn't hinting."

"You knew Mr. Dresser better than that. He was not the type to respond to hints." Mr. Burkhart placed his hand on her shoulder. "Be at my office at four."

Hannah paused in the door of the conference room of Burkhart, Burkhart and Gargano, attorneys at law, and found herself facing a long polished wood table, a nervous Kayla Thomas of Teignmouth's Opportunity Council, sixteen surly members of the Dresser family, and a stern-faced Stephen Burkhart.

"Steve, did the old man give a bequest to the nurse, too? My God, did he leave money to every single person he ever met?" Donald Jr. swung toward Kayla Thomas. "He already gave a bundle to the Opportunity Council this year, and now she's here with her hand out."

Kayla flushed. "I am here because Mr. Burkhart asked me to be here."

Mr. Burkhart met Donald Jr.'s resentful gaze. "It's a clean will which makes Mr. Dresser's intentions clear."

Hannah slid into the nearest chair. The legal assistant followed her in, shut the door behind her, seated herself, and prepared to take dictation.

Mr. Burkhart announced, "Mr. Dresser originally had my father prepare his last will and testament, and five months ago asked me to help him amend it."

The Dresser family muttered and shifted.

Mr. Burkhart ignored them. "On his behalf, I scheduled a screening of his mental health at the Hartford

Mental Clinic. Once the soundness of his mind was established, we discussed his wishes, then wrote his will, as follows." Unfolding the stiff papers, he read, " 'I, Donald Dresser, of Teignmouth, New Hampshire, do hereby make, publish, and declare this to be my last will and testament, hereby expressly revoking all wills and codicils heretofore made by me. . . .' "

As Mr. Burkhart worked his way through the formalities, Hannah observed the Dresser family. Donald Jr. and his wife looked impatient. Jeff leaned forward, his gimlet gaze fixed on the attorney. Mr. Dresser's only daughter, Cynthia, chewed her thumbnail.

Kayla Thomas braced herself against the table.

They were all anticipating . . . something, and Hannah felt the same suspense that gripped them tighten her nerves.

" 'To Miss Hannah Grey, I leave fifty thousand dollars in recognition of her kind and faithful service, with best wishes for her future.' "

Hannah's breath stopped in her chest.

Fifty thousand dollars?

She had never had a father. Her mother had supported them on a legal assistant's salary, but there had been medical bills. Now for the first time in Hannah's life, she had a financial cushion, and the relief left her gasping—and facing sixteen pairs of accusing Dresser eyes.

Mr. Burkhart continued. " 'To my family, I leave a chance to redeem themselves. To each of my descendants currently living, I leave fifty thousand dollars—' "

An audible gasp rose from the Dressers.

Mr. Burkhart soldiered on. "And the chance to work at Dresser Insurance under the supervision of the board of directors now in place.' "

Cynthia came to her feet. "I don't believe this!"

Donald Jr. rapped sharply on the table with his knuckles. "Who has control of Dad's fortune?"

Mr. Burkhart read, " 'To the Opportunity Council of Teignmouth, New Hampshire, I leave the bulk of my fortune, to be supervised and dispensed by Kayla Thomas, a young woman whose acumen I've grown to respect—' "

Now all the members of the Dresser family were on their feet, shouting at Mr. Burkhart, at the white-faced Kayla Thomas, and at one another, while Hannah watched first in horror, then in amazement, then in amusement. She knew this wasn't the place or the time, not so soon after Mr. Dresser's funeral, yet as she observed Cynthia stomp her foot, Donald Jr. pound on the table, and Jeff gesture like a windmill, the amusement grew.

The fifty thousand dollars that seemed like such a fortune to her was an insult to these people, income for a month, spending money at the gambling tables, a tight budget for a shopping trip.

Damn the old man. He had set this up. He had known this would happen. No wonder the visits from the lawyer had left him with rosy cheeks and glittering eyes. He had anticipated a furor of epic proportions, and she knew that somewhere in the great beyond, he was rubbing his hands and laughing.

And she . . . she couldn't help it. She laughed, too.

As if that was a signal, silence fell, and the Dresser family focused on her.

"What did you do to earn that fifty thousand, Miss Grey?" Jeff asked. "What kind of services did you render to the old man that made him fifty thousand dollars' worth of grateful?"

Hannah's merriment died an ugly death. "I do not indulge in sex with my patients, if that's what you're insinuating. Certainly not with your father, frail as he was."

Jeff snorted. "No man is that frail. Not Dad, for sure."

"Jeff, that's enough," Mr. Burkhart said. "During my visits, Miss Grey showed herself to be a nurse of upright character. She did not sleep with your father."

"Are you kidding?" Jeff gestured wildly at Hannah. "Look at her, sitting there with her innocent expression and a body that won't end, and fifty thousand dollars of our money. You can't tell me she didn't do the old man to death."

A cold anger sprang from deep inside of Hannah.

"Jeff." Donald Jr. had himself under control again. "Shut up. We'll fight the will. The old man was obviously insane."

At the insult to Mr. Dresser, Hannah's anger grew, crawling along her nerves, encasing them in ice.

"You heard Burkhart. You heard about the screening of Dad's mental health. Do you really think Burkhart didn't close all the loopholes?" Jeff gestured at Mr. Burkhart with the same vigor he'd used on Hannah. "This little slut managed to screw the old guy stupid, and now she's *laughing* at us." He turned on Hannah again. "Didn't you? Didn't you screw him stupid?"

Under his insulting, denigrating assault, Hannah's discipline shattered. "Mr. Dresser was never stupid." She swept the family with a scornful gaze, then returned her attention to Jeff. "I took care of his . . . needs. I met his . . . requirements. I was his . . . friend . . . when he needed one. Make of that what you will." She knew exactly what they *would* make of that.

Mr. Burkhart used his fingers to cut his own throat, to tell her to shut up.

She would not. What difference did it make if she lost the inheritance before she had it? She was in a glorious rage, slapping the smarmy Jeff down with every word, letting Donald Jr. and Cynthia know the father they'd neglected had been alive and in need of attention.

She stood up and smiled coldly. "When you think about it, fifty thousand for my services is cheap. I kept Mr. Dresser busy so the rest of you could enjoy your last days of reckless indulgence. I hope you take benefit from your employment at Dresser Insurance. Working for your living should be an interesting experience for you all." With a grand sense of satisfaction, she opened the door and swept from the conference room.

"Come back here," Jeff yelled. "Don't you dare turn your back on me!"

She walked steadily down the corridor.

Behind her, Jeff continued to shout.

The rest of the family picked up the volume.

Hannah walked on, her gaze fixed on the elevator at the end of the hall.

Putting her hand in her pocket, she found the envelope Jeff Dresser had given her earlier. The bonus the Dresser family had given her in gratitude for her care of their deceased patriarch.

She got into the elevator and punched the button for the first floor.

Jeff stalked toward her, fists clenched.

Before he could reach her, the doors closed in his face.

She could almost hear Mr. Dresser's voice. *The little asshole.*

She pulled the envelope out of her pocket. She broke the seal, looked at the check . . . and laughed on the edge of hysteria.

"Really. You shouldn't have," she said aloud.

The Dresser family's gratitude came to twenty-five dollars.

TWO

Five months later

In the elegant entry of the Teignmouth Country Club, Carrick Manly stopped in front of the mirror. He looked himself over and smoothed his dark hair, ruffled by the spring breeze. He was six one, broad shouldered, and dressed in an understated black suit with a crisp white shirt and dull gold tie. When a man had a background like his, when he sported distinctive green eyes, he had to seem understated. He had to look conservative. He had to be *careful*.

Satisfied with his appearance, he stepped into the doorway of the elegant smoking room.

Collinson met him before he had crossed the threshold. "Good day, Mr. Manly, you'll want your copy of the *Wall Street Journal*." Hushed, reserved, and ageless, Collinson was the perfect majordomo for the exclusive men's club.

"Of course." Carrick took the proffered paper,

tucked it under his arm, and assessed the posture and mood of each and every man inside. It was a skill he'd developed and honed during the slim years.

The club looked as it had for a hundred fifty years: dark paneling, high windows, overstuffed leather chairs, newspapers scattered on the end tables. The low buzz of male conversation and the clink of glasses filled the air.

Mathew Davis was smirking at the glowing tip of his cigar. Carrick had heard rumors of a successful insider stock deal; obviously they were true.

Headphones on, Judge Warner Edgerly watched a DVD on his handheld, a heated flush climbing up his shiny forehead. He must be reviewing porn again.

Jeff Dresser sat at the bar hunched over a gin and tonic. Dresser looked hangdog and irritated, and anything that made the pompous jackass unhappy must be good news.

Carrick slid into a seat next to Harold Grindle, the nosiest old gossip in New England. "What's the problem with Jeff Dresser?" he murmured.

"What?" Harold shouted.

Carrick leaned forward and turned up the volume on Harold's hearing aid. Still quietly, he asked, "I said, what's the problem with Jeff Dresser?"

"Oh." Harold lowered his voice, too. "Haven't you heard?" With a sly grin that relished each of Jeff's tribulations, he reported the tale of Donald Dresser Sr.'s death and the details of his will.

When he had finished, Carrick whistled softly. "So the Dressers are working at the insurance firm?"

"The members of the board of directors are tearing out their hair. The stock is descending with each passing day. As a preventive measure, they've fired a few of the most worthless progeny"—Harold's rheumy old eyes glistened—"*including* Cynthia."

"No!"

"She's threatening to sue, but Burkhart assures me her claim will never stand up in court. I asked him about the scandal concerning old Donald's private nurse. He clammed up about that, but *I* heard she slept with the old man to the tune of five hundred thousand dollars."

Carrick's eyebrows shot up disbelievingly. "The old man must have gone senile, then, because when I knew him, he hadn't an ounce of weakness in him."

Harold drew back, offended. "I only report what I've heard." He turned off his hearing aid, and loudly, he huffed, "Upstart!"

Ah, yes. The first insult of the day.

Sauntering over to the bar, Carrick took a seat two stools down from Dresser. "Gin and tonic," he told the bartender.

He hated gin and tonics, but he wasn't going to drink it, anyway. He was merely ordering up a little camaraderie.

He placed the *Wall Street Journal* on the polished cherrywood bar and scanned the headlines, then turned with a well-feigned start. "I didn't see you there, Mr. Dresser. How's Ryan?"

Ryan Dresser was the asshole who had made Carrick's life hell after Nathan Manly crashed his multibillion-dollar business, walked with the money to South America or Thailand or wherever the hell he'd gone, and left Carrick and his mother destitute and humiliated.

"Ryan? Oh, he's fine. Twenty-six years old and absolutely good for nothing. Every one of my children is good for nothing." Jeff Dresser was slurring his words, drunk at two o'clock in the afternoon.

This just got better and better.

"But Ryan's got all that money behind him. How can he be good for nothing?"

Dresser shot him a glance that told Carrick he wasn't so drunk he didn't recognize sarcasm when he heard it.

The bartender slid the drink across to Carrick, who lifted it in a swift and distracting salute. "Here's to the oil companies. Long may they reign."

"I suppose you've heard the story." Dresser glanced behind him resentfully. "They've all heard the story, and they haven't stopped chuckling yet."

Carrick wisely kept quiet.

"Even that damn girl laughed. Laughed right in our faces!" Dresser shoved his glass back at the bartender, who refilled and returned it.

Carrick played dumb. "What damn girl, sir?"

"Miss Hannah Grey, RN. Dad's nurse." Dresser tipped the drink down his throat. "He gave that bitch fifty thousand for a blow job."

"Must have been a good blow job." Carrick spun his icy glass on the bar.

"Wide blue eyes, hair so blond it's platinum, an

innocent face, and a body that will not quit. Yeah, I imagine it was a hell of a blow job." Dresser smiled a nasty smile. "Burkhart claimed she was an upright character. You should have seen the look on his face when she admitted she'd done it!"

"She admitted to a blow job? In front of the lawyer?"

"She didn't say a blow job. She said she and Dad were . . . *friends*, in just that tone of voice. Sexy, but not bright." Dresser smirked. "The family brought suit to stop the execution of the will."

"How did that go?" Obviously not well, but Carrick liked making the patronizing bastard admit it.

"The will is clean. That damn Burkhart made sure of that. But I got revenge on Hannah Grey. I filed a suit with the state of New Hampshire. Her nursing certificate is suspended pending investigation, and her placement agency dropped her."

An idea brewed in Carrick's mind. "So Hannah Grey can't work in the state of New Hampshire, and she's living off the inheritance from your father. That won't keep her for long."

"Even better, she has no other resources, and it's been five months since she's held a job." The open malice in Dresser's face made Carrick almost sorry for Miss Hannah Grey. "I may be broke, I may be working for my living, but by God, she knows now she can't play games with me and get away with it."

There was nothing more to be learned from Jeff Dresser, so Carrick stood. "Give Ryan my regards, and tell him if I need insurance, I'll definitely keep him in mind."

Dresser rocked back on his stool as if Carrick had struck him—which he had, in a cunning show of gamesmanship.

Carrick took a few steps away, then turned back. "About this Hannah Grey. I imagine you see her occasionally."

"Occasionally." Hostility etched Dresser's voice. "Why?"

"I'll bet she's too embarrassed to look you in the eyes."

"Embarrassed? Are you kidding? That little witch smiles at me and lifts her chin."

So Hannah Grey was Carrick's kind of woman; she kept her eyes on the purse, and wasn't squeamish about doing what had to be done to get it.

"Good," Carrick said. "Good. That's all I needed to know."

THREE

Hannah sat in the small shop, Buzz Beans, her hands wrapped around her warm cup of French roast, stared at the screen of her laptop, and moaned softly.

Behind her, Sophia was cleaning the tables in the quiet neighborhood coffee shop. "Another rejection?" It wasn't so much a question as a statement.

"If I don't get a job pretty soon, I'm going to have to change my name, hitchhike to New York, and become a musical star."

"You can't sing or dance." Sophia was the kid sister of Hannah's best high school friend, and she knew all too well how Hannah sounded with a karaoke machine.

"Stop crushing my dreams."

Sophia glanced toward the counter and lowered her voice. "How about a cheese pierogi? We made extras this morning and—"

"I'm fine. Thank you." Hannah smiled at the young barista, trying to convey her appreciation while holding onto her pride.

"Yeah, but . . . Mr. Nowak has been bitching because you're here every morning, buy one cup of coffee without any add-ins, and use his free Internet for two hours. Then you do it again in the afternoon. You know what a grump he is when he shouts."

"So he's been listening to Jeff Dresser." Who, for all that he'd lost a lot of influence in this town, hadn't yet been counted out as a mover and shaker.

"Yeah." Sophia was squirming. "But I thought if you made a purchase—"

Hannah smiled at Sophia and said loudly, "When you've got a minute, Sophia, could I get a cheese pierogi and coffee?" Because she couldn't afford the cheese pierogi, but she definitely couldn't afford Internet hookup.

Mr. Nowak looked up from his paper, his sharp dark eyes fixed with hostile intent on Hannah. "Sophia, you keep cleaning. I'll do it."

Man, Hannah had announced she'd been one old man's *friend*, and Mr. Nowak thought she could corrupt his helper. She waited patiently while he warmed the pierogi and fixed her coffee.

The brief illusion of security Mr. Dresser's inheritance had offered had ended abruptly with her flash of temper. She had thought she might lose the inheritance. Instead, she'd lost the possibility of holding a job.

Five months ago, fifty thousand dollars had seemed like a fortune. Now, even with frugal living, the legal bills to fight for her nursing certificate and the lack of income had reduced her fifty thousand dollars to twenty-two thousand. And with Jeff Dresser using his influence to slow the investigation of misconduct, she was going to have to do something besides the work she knew and loved. Retail, probably, which she'd done in high school, and thoroughly hated.

"Here," Mr. Nowak said. "I won't charge you for the coffee."

Maybe he wasn't so bad after all. . . .

Then he smiled at her in that knowing way.

"I insist on paying." She pushed the cup back toward him, because she'd seen that smile before, more times in the last five months than she wanted to remember, and on more men's faces than she could bear to think about. And she was not giving this disgusting little troll of a man sex for a cup of coffee. Or for his free Internet. Or for fifty thousand dollars, either.

His smile disappeared. "You come here every day—"

The door chimed as someone came in.

Mr. Nowak's voice swelled. "Buying your cup of coffee, using my Internet, when everyone in this town knows you are a slut."

Hannah stiffened in humiliation and anger.

He continued. "Everyone in this *state* knows you got money from poor old Mr. Dresser by—"

A strange man spoke beside her. "Is there a problem here?"

Mr. Nowak pointed a finger at Hannah. "She tried to steal from me. She tried to steal a . . . a . . ."

"I'd be very careful, Mr. Nowak," Hannah said steadily. "Very careful."

His gaze shifted to Sophia, then back to Hannah, then to the stranger. Hannah could almost see him thinking of the gossip if he brought charges, and he shriveled like a three-day-old party balloon. "Go on. Take the food. Take the coffee. Get out and don't come back. You . . . you . . ."

"Wait." The stranger held up his hand. "If she was stealing from you, you should have her arrested. Shoplifting is a serious crime. But you can't just bandy that charge around. That's defamation of character. She could sue."

The last person to stand up for her had been old Mr. Dresser himself. Now, in astonishment, Hannah turned to look at the stranger.

He was a fine-looking piece of man flesh: over six foot, whipcord thin, broad shoulders, dark hair, distinctive green eyes, her age or a little older. And he dressed like a wealthy businessman, in a conservative black suit with a dull gold tie.

"She could sue, but she wouldn't win," Mr. Nowak blustered.

"She's a beautiful young woman," the stranger said. "Juries always sympathize with a beautiful young woman."

"You're a *lawyer*," Mr. Nowak said in revulsion.

The stranger shrugged.

Mr. Nowak started to say something ill advised, then with hard-won control changed his mind. "Sophia, come and take his order." He disappeared into the back room.

Sophia whipped around the counter and washed her hands, smiling brightly all the time. "What can I get you, sir?"

"I'll have a medium Earl Grey tea, hot, with a splash of milk." He looked down at Hannah. "I know it's ridiculous, but I learned to drink it that way when I was a kid. If you sit with me, I promise not to crook my pinkie." And he smiled.

Hannah stood there, awestruck by his straight white teeth, his long black lashes, the dimple in his cheek.

"Wow," Sophia said out loud.

Grabbing her cup, Hannah said, "I drink coffee. Black." She winced. *Scintillating, Hannah.*

"That is so much more sensible." He took the tea Sophia placed on the counter. "Let me pay for Miss . . . ?" He looked an inquiry at Hannah.

"Grey. Hannah Grey."

"Let me pay for Miss Grey's order, also. I don't want the manager to come back when I'm gone and make trouble."

"He's the owner," Sophia said.

At the same time, Hannah said, "I can pay for it."

"He's the owner? All the more reason." He smiled at Sophia, whose jaw dropped at the gorgeous sight. Then he turned to Hannah. "Miss Grey, my mother is from one of the founding families in Maine. She lives in a hundred-fifty-year-old mansion on the coast, and as far as I can tell, she's never left the twentieth century. She would kick my rear if she ever heard I let a lady buy her own coffee. So please spare my mother—she has arthritis and simply getting around is an effort."

With indecent eagerness, Sophia said, "Really? Arthritis? What a coincidence. Hannah is a home-care nurse who specializes in arthritis cases. She's the best!" She made eyes at Hannah, and used little shooing motions with her hands.

She was right. Hannah knew she was right. An arthritis patient? In Maine? Hannah couldn't afford to let this opportunity slip through her fingers. She looked right into the stranger's eyes and said, "If you should ever need help with your mother, I *am* the best, and I'm between cases."

"My mother won't hear of a nurse, but she's definitely getting to the point where I'm going to have to insist. . . ." He quirked an eyebrow, appealing to Hannah's understanding.

She felt squeamish. She didn't lie well, not even lies of omission. Her nursing certificate had been suspended. She should tell him that. She should, but if she didn't get a job soon . . .

He sighed heavily. "One of us should be ashamed of ourselves."

She jumped. He already knew? "What? Who?"

"Me, of course. I'm leading you on." He shook his head as if disgusted by his own deception. "Mother has other problems, more serious than merely arthritis. She's diabetic, has a heart condition, and she can't or won't control it or her weight. She's agoraphobic—she hasn't stepped foot out of our house since my father walked out fifteen years ago. She's under investigation by the government, which has put a huge amount of pressure on her, and I'm afraid she's starting to crack. "

"Investigation?" Hannah said tentatively.

"My father is Nathan Manly." He spoke stoically.

"Oh." Everyone in New England knew the name and the disgrace attached to it. Fifteen years ago, Nathan Manly had destroyed his multibillion-dollar company, stolen the capital, and fled to parts unknown, humiliating his wife and leaving his family without funds. His illegitimate sons (rumors claimed there were a dozen and the number climbed every time the story was told) were abandoned, too. Best of all, Nathan Manly and his money had never been found, lending the Manly scandal the status of legend.

"I knew I recognized you. From TV!" Sophia almost leaped across the counter. "You're *Carrick* Manly!"

He smiled at her excitement. "Don't hold it against me," he said wryly.

"I would never do that." Sophia backed up and leaned against the wall, her knees wobbling.

In the years since Nathan Manly had fled to parts unknown, his son—this son, his legitimate son, his handsome, gifted, and formerly wealthy son—had assumed the status of the protagonist in a Greek tragedy.

"I'm still interested in the job." Hannah felt less guilty about keeping her own piddling little investigation quiet.

"Really?" He smiled at her, his tan perfect, his straight teeth dazzling and white.

Decision made, she said, "Perhaps we can make it work. Why don't we sit down and you can give me the details of your mother's situation?"

FOUR

"There it is." Carrick pulled into a viewpoint on the rugged Maine coast highway and stopped the car. He gripped the steering wheel with one hand, and pointed across the rocky inlet. "Balfour House."

Hannah stared at the classic nineteenth-century mansion perched on the cliff. It was massive, two stories of white stone and fanciful turrets, broad balconies, and wide windows defiantly facing off with the Atlantic. "Balfour House?" she repeated. "Shouldn't it be Manly House?"

"My mother was Melinda Balfour. She is the last of the Balfours. Since New Englanders do not lightly change their ways, it always will be Balfour House." Savagely, he opened the door, got out, and leaned one arm against the roof of the Porsche Carrera.

Hannah got out, too, and looked at the mansion, and looked at him.

The breeze frisked with the perfect fall of his brown hair, while the sun kissed the blond highlights, giving him a golden aura. But his expression, as he stared at the house, was pensive, still, almost . . . sour. She would have thought he would at least show the enthusiasm he'd shown about the car—and the car wasn't even his. He told her he was repairing the family fortunes. He told her he couldn't afford a car like this. He told her one of his friends had insisted he borrow it for the drive up here, and he'd waxed enthusiastic about its handling and speed. Maybe if the house could do zero to sixty in less than thirty seconds . . .

"Do you not *like* the house?" she asked.

"Of course I like it. If it weren't for Balfour House and its history, I would be a nobody."

A nobody. Is that what he thought of people without an exalted ancestry?

No. He must not realize how condescending that sounded. On the drive up from New Hampshire, he'd been amiable and not at all snobbish, showing off his knowledge of the towns along I-95, then, as they turned southeast toward Ellsworth, regaling her with tales of his mother's family and how their destiny had been so intimately entwined with the state of Maine. She'd been content to listen, and laugh, and marvel at the luck that placed her in this luxurious car with this wondrous man.

Now he trained those green eyes at her and said, "You have to understand what a love-hate relationship I have with Balfour House. Mother has quite a decent income in trust from *her* mother—not a large fortune, but it's adequate—and every dime of it goes to pay the taxes and do the minimum of upkeep on that pile of sacred stone. Mother could live well in Bangor or Ellsworth, in an apartment with people her own age, but she won't leave. Balfour House holds her prisoner as surely as any jail. My God, it even boasts a basement with rooms cut so deep into the rock they could be used as dungeons, and there are rumors of secret passages, although when I was a boy I searched and never found a single sign of them." Ruefulness tinged his smile.

Gently Hannah told him, "Most elderly patients don't want to leave their own homes, no matter what the advantage to them."

"Mother is not like most elderly patients. She is a difficult woman. I feel almost guilty thrusting you into this situation."

"Don't feel guilty. I always win over my patients in the end."

"I can see that it would help," he said, "if your patient was male."

She whipped around to face him. "What do you mean by that?"

"Nothing." He looked startled at the blaze of her temper.

Slowly, she relaxed. He'd made an innocuous comment, and she'd flashed back to the Dresser family's accusations. Carrick didn't deserve to be associated with them, not even in her mind. "I will do everything in my power to work with Mrs. Manly."

"I know you will." He came around and held her door.

She stood for one more moment, letting the breeze cool her hot cheeks, staring at Balfour House, and wishing Carrick hadn't described it as a prison. Sometimes it seemed her whole life had been a prison of poverty and desperation, and she didn't relish walking into another. But desperation had brought her here, and it would be a better place than the one she'd left, she knew.

Getting into the car, she settled back as Carrick shut her inside, and returned to the driver's seat. He steered the narrow winding road, turned off through the electronic gates, and drove to the front door of Balfour House.

As they walked up the steps, the door opened, and a stocky young gentleman clad in an impeccable black suit stepped out. "Welcome home, Mr. Manly."

"Thank you, Nelson. Miss Hannah Grey, Nelson is the able replacement for our old butler, Torres. Emphasis on *old*. Torres passed on four months ago."

"Good to meet you, Nelson." Hannah smiled and nodded.

Nelson performed a half bow.

Carrick tossed his keys to Nelson. "Our bags are in the trunk."

Nelson signaled into the house, and another guy dressed in exactly the same pristine dark suit took the keys and hurried to the car.

"Miss Grey's bag should be put in a bedroom close to my mother's suite," Carrick said.

"Sir?" In that one word, Nelson managed to convey doubt and amazement.

"Miss Grey is an RN, a home-care nurse from New Hampshire. Isn't that right, Miss Grey?"

"Yes, that's right," Hannah said.

"I hired her to care for Mrs. Manly." Carrick smiled approvingly at her.

Swept away by his blistering charisma, she smiled back.

"Yes, sir." Nelson's gaze flashed over Hannah.

She saw some emotion—sympathy? Skepticism?

"How is Mrs. Manly today?" Carrick took Hannah's arm and led her up the stairs and into the house.

Nelson followed. "It's difficult for me to say, sir. She has not left her bedroom in over a month."

"Damn it!" Carrick turned on him. "The doctor said she was supposed to exercise."

"According to Mrs. Manly's personal maid, she constantly uses her wheelchair, refusing even to try her walker."

Hannah listened . . . but not really. It wasn't as if she expected anything different from her patient, and besides, she was too busy gaping like a peasant at the old-fashioned glory that was Balfour House.

The foyer was round, its floor was black-and-white marble, cut into slabs to form a compass with a wide *N* at the longest point. The broad mahogany stairway swept up to the second floor in a stately curve, and an old-fashioned elevator, complete with ironwork grille, was tucked into the nearby corner. To the right and through an arch, a long dining room table stood in splendor under a series of crystal chandeliers. To the left, gilded double doors stood open, revealing a spacious grand ballroom. Her gaze rose two stories to the golden-painted cove molding and pale blue ceiling, and in her mind, she was transported to the sheer opulence of the French châteaus in Provence.

"Hannah, you are going to have your work cut out for you," Carrick said.

Hannah snapped her attention back to him. "I can rise to the challenge."

"That's the attitude." Carrick clapped her on the shoulder. "We'll go up to see her now. Then, Nelson, dinner and a nice bottle of wine to celebrate Miss Grey's stay with us. She's going to be just what the doctor ordered, I'm sure."

"Yes, sir. I'll convey your wishes to the cook." Nelson disappeared into a side door.

As Carrick and Hannah climbed the stairs and followed a long corridor, Hannah said, "I'll bet your mother despises *him*."

"Why would you say that?"

Surprised that he didn't comprehend, she said, "Nelson is a rat."

Carrick paused, his hand raised to rap on a door. "He's doing what I hired him to do."

The first tendrils of squeamishness touched her. "The role of butler does not include being a tattletale."

"You say that now. Wait until you meet Mother." Carrick swung the door open.

The air was stale. The curtains were closed. Mrs. Manly's deep voice was sarcastic as she said, "The wandering son returns."

"Hello, Mother." He turned on the overhead light, and walked toward the figure in the wheelchair. He leaned down toward her to kiss her cheek. "How are—"

She interrupted. "Who's that?"

Everything Carrick had said about his mother was true. She had a heavy face, with jowls that drooped over a sagging neck. Her mouth was small, her nose large, and she needed to wax her upper lip. Her hair was long and dark, with streaks of gray, and she wore it pulled back and tied at the base of her neck. Thick black-rimmed glasses rested on the end of her nose. She was overweight, diabetic, and arthritic, but she was also an aristocrat to the tips of her twisted and beringed fingers.

Without touching her, he straightened. "This is Hannah Grey. She's your new nurse."

Melinda Manly did not look at Hannah. She did not deign to notice Hannah. She spoke only to Carrick. "What makes you think I need a nurse?"

Carrick shot Hannah a conspiratorial smile, the kind that made Hannah wonder if all men were so insensitive. Did Carrick truly believed his mother was too dimwitted to notice or too kindhearted to care? In a patronizing tone, he said, "Dr. Thalmann says you're not taking care of yourself."

"If I'm not, that's my business. Not yours, and definitely not *hers*." Melinda Manly's voice grew deeper in its disdain.

"It is my business. You're my mother." Carrick leaned over again, this time putting his arm around her shoulders. "And I love you."

For all the affection he got in return, he might as well have hugged an oak board.

Hannah compared this woman to her own irrepressible mother, and felt sorry for Carrick. Before he could make things worse, she interposed herself into the conversation. "Mrs. Manly, I'm trained in home nursing and physical therapy, and I'm an arthritis specialist. Give me a chance, and I could ease your discomfort."

"I don't like people," Mrs. Manly said precisely.

"Think of me as a servant," Hannah invited.

"Are you mocking me?" Mrs. Manly snapped.

"Not at all." *Maybe a little.* "I met the butler. I saw the man who got our luggage out of the car. You have servants. You have someone who comes in here to clean and make your bed. You may not like them, but you're used to them. I would simply take over the care of you, and you would treat me as you would any servant."

"You'd try and make me do what I have no intention of doing."

"You're in pain. Right now. Your hip is killing you." Hannah held Mrs. Manly's dark gaze. "And you have an unpleasant tingling in your toes."

"Is that why she won't use her walker?" Carrick asked.

Hannah had made some good guesses based on the way Mrs. Manly sat and her own knowledge of arthritis and diabetes. She had captured Mrs. Manly's attention. And Carrick had fouled up by talking about Mrs. Manly as if she weren't in the room.

Hannah subdued a sigh, and waded back into the fray. "I *am* a specialist in the care of arthritis sufferers. Your son is not going to stop trying to bring someone in, so why not have the best?"

"The best, heh?" Mrs. Manly pinned Hannah with her contempt. "Who are your people?"

Hannah stiffened. She should have seen this coming. "My mother grew up in Teignmouth, New Hampshire, and so did I."

"That didn't answer the question. What was her family's name? What was your father's name?"

"Mother, you're being rude." Beside his mother's determination, Carrick sounded feeble.

"It doesn't matter, Carrick. I'll answer her question," Hannah said. "My mother's family name was Grey. My father . . . didn't stick around."

"My God. Another bastard. Like the bastards my husband fathered." Melinda Manly gave a hard crack of laughter. "Carrick, you fool, you brought me a *bastard*?"

Before Carrick could answer, Hannah stepped between them, blocking Melinda Manly's view of her son. "My parents weren't married, but I don't put up with that kind of insult, and if you had the slightest iota of courtesy, you'd know better than to spew forth venom like some twisted old snake."

"Do you imagine you can teach me manners?" Melinda Manly asked.

"No. I doubt if anyone could." Hannah turned on her heel and walked out of the room.

FIVE

"And don't bother me again," Melinda Manly said as Carrick slammed the door on his way out. She rubbed her eyes and blew her nose; then wearily, she wheeled herself over to her desk.

God, she was tired. Tired of being in pain, of being afraid, of seeing her world change and knowing she could do nothing to stop it. Tired of the intrigue . . . She retrieved the intercom speaker from the drawer, set it in her lap, and turned it on.

And there it was. The tap of footsteps, the shuffling of paper, and a low muttered curse.

Since Torres's death, when Carrick visited, he always riffled through the butler's office in the basement, looking for whatever secrets Torres had held in trust for Melinda.

So far, Carrick had found nothing.

At the same time, she wondered why her son, an obviously intelligent lad, never thought to wonder how his mother had communicated with Torres about the thousand and one details involved in running a household of this size.

This intercom, of course.

Perhaps Carrick didn't have as much intelligence as she gave him credit for. Or perhaps he gave her credit for none.

As she expected, she heard a knock on the door of Torres's office. Carrick called, "Come in." And, "Hannah! It's you."

Hannah Grey. She was infatuated with Carrick. Stupid girl. She would be better off away from him, away from this place. Melinda ran her gaze around her room. They would all be better when Balfour House washed into the sea.

Through the speaker, Carrick sounded cheerful, confident. "What do you think about my mother's condition? Can you help her?"

That girl answered, "Not unless she cooperates. She's overweight, which exacerbates her arthritis. Her color is not good. She's obviously not monitoring her blood sugar, and a stroke is imminent."

That was exactly what Dr. Thalmann said. Melinda's respect for the girl's competence took a big leap. Maybe she wasn't merely a spy. Maybe she really was a nurse.

Melinda pulled her laptop close, tapped in a search for Hannah Grey.

That girl continued. "She's intent on killing herself, so I'm doomed to failure." That girl's brisk voice sounded nurselike and practical. Yet beneath that matter-of-fact tone, Melinda heard an undercurrent of worry.

What was she worried about?

Even as the question formed in her mind, the computer gave her the information: the case before the New Hampshire commission . . . and an unusually long delay in coming to a decision. As Melinda read the details of Hannah's dilemma, she listened to Carrick's voice, so much like his father's—smooth, deep, oh so interested in the woman before him.

"With you here, at least I'll have the security of knowing that if something happens to her, there's a trained person on-site."

There were times when Melinda hated her son. Hated him, and loved him, and wished . . . but no. No wishes. Once she'd had a wish come true. Her wish had brought nothing but guilt and anguish, death and destruction. Ever since, she had feared the power of her wishes.

"You . . . still want me to stay?" Hannah sounded both flabbergasted and relieved.

"Absolutely. The important thing is that you'll listen in on Mother's conversations and watch her for any surreptitious movements."

Melinda leaned back in her chair. *Ah. Here we go.*

"What?" Hannah asked.

The rustling stopped, and Melinda could imagine Carrick looking earnestly across at Hannah, seducing her with his handsome green eyes, bending her to his will. "If she doesn't tell the federal government where my father's money is, they're going to drive her out of this house. Maybe put her in prison."

"I don't understand why they think she knows where the money is," Hannah said, biting off the words. "Your father took it with him. Isn't it fair to assume he still has it? That he's spending it?"

Good point. If only the government was as reasonable.

She continued. "By the condition of this house, I'd have to say your mother is broke."

Melinda flinched. *The girl was right. Balfour House deserved so much better. If only the fall of the Balfours had not occurred on Melinda's watch!*

"The details are difficult and complicated, and there's more to this than meets the eye." Carrick was glib, assured. "But I assure you, if my mother won't voluntarily tell the government what they want to know, then I, as her only living relative, need to find out and tell them for her. That's where you come in."

"You know what I said about Nelson spying on her." The girl sounded stiff and offended. *What had she said?*

"It's for her own good," Carrick intoned.

"I don't think I'm making myself clear. I do not spy on my patients."

"You really don't have a lot of choice, now, do you?"

Ah, now he pulled the steel blade from beneath the silken cushion.

"What do you mean?" Hannah asked cautiously.

"In New Hampshire, your nursing certification has been pulled for immoral behavior. Now here you are in Maine, trying to work without any certification at all."

"I didn't know that you . . . ," Hannah stammered to a halt. "I'm sorry that I didn't tell you the truth. I admit, I was desperate." Her voice wobbled in weak feminine appeal.

Good luck with that. Carrick cared about one thing . . .

well, two things: getting his way, and getting his hands on whatever might remain of the vanished fortune.

Hannah's voice strengthened. "But it doesn't matter whether I have current certification or not. I work for my patient."

"I'll have you arrested for impersonating a nursing professional."

"You can't do that." Hannah sounded incredulous.

Melinda could almost hear her infatuation with Carrick crumble.

"Don't be ridiculous. Of course I can. I have witnesses who will testify that you lied about your credentials. I introduced you to Nelson as a registered nurse, and you agreed you were. And of course your friend at the coffeehouse apparently doesn't know about the case against you in New Hampshire, or she wouldn't have been so eager to help you get a job." He paused delicately. "I mean . . . that young woman wouldn't have deliberately lied to me, would she? Because then she would be an accessory to this crime."

"So you want me to spy on your mother, to find out where your father hid his fortune so you can give the information to the federal government?" Melinda could hear Hannah's incredulity, and her dawning suspicion that Carrick's motives were not perhaps as pure as he had painted them. "You described this house as a prison, but this seems more like an asylum, with madness around every corner."

"So you'll do it," Carrick said with satisfaction.

"No. No!" But Hannah sounded frantic, on the verge of tears.

He had neatly and completely trapped the girl in an impasse of her own making.

Yet for Melinda, her appearance here, now, was a sign. A sign Melinda *must* do what she had only wished she *could* do.

Turning off the speaker, she stashed it in the desk, then pushed her wheelchair through the door, down the corridor, and into the old-fashioned elevator. She punched the button for the basement, and waited patiently through the slow descent, planning each word, each tone, each expression.

She got to the long corridor just as Hannah walked out of the butler's office, white-faced and shaking.

She stopped cold, looking as guilty as a child caught with her fingers in the cookie jar. "Mrs. Manly, I . . . I . . ."

"Oh, dear." Melinda pasted on her rueful face. "Please, can we talk?" She glanced past Hannah. "Is Carrick in there? Let's include him." She started forward.

Hannah moved back, and her expression was openly distressed. "I understand why you don't want me here, and I don't want to force myself on you."

"Stop fretting and follow me. We'll get this cleared right up." Melinda wheeled herself through the door and found Carrick pulling books from the bookcase, fluttering through the pages, then shoving them back in place. Cocking her head to the side, she watched until Hannah cleared her throat.

"What do you want?" Carrick snapped. "I told you the conditions to which I'm holding you."

"Are you looking for something, son?" Melinda asked.

Carrick contained his start very well. "Mother! You left your room!"

"I had to. I couldn't drive this poor child away because of my bad mood. More important, I know you're right, Carrick. I do need a nurse, and I appreciate you finding someone of such upstanding character." Melinda lavished a closemouthed smile at him.

Before Carrick could speak, Hannah said, "Actually, I have a blot on my record."

Carrick cast her a lethal glance.

But all her attention was on Melinda. "My last patient was Donald Dresser, and the Dresser family has accused me of seducing him for an inheritance."

"Who made the accusation?" Melinda knew very well. Only a minute ago, she'd read the file on the Internet.

"Jeff Dresser," Hannah answered.

Melinda snorted. "Jeff Dresser. As if anyone in his right mind would believe him. His son was so awful to Carrick after Nathan left. . . . Remember, dear?"

Carrick looked down at the book in his hand as if he'd forgotten that he held it. "I remember."

"I'd like to put a spoke in his wheel," Melinda said with relish. "So the problem's in New Hampshire?"

"Yes, Mrs. Manly." Hannah watched her, hope kindling on her face.

"I've known the governor of New Hampshire since he was born. Don't worry, Hannah. Little Scottie MacDonald will do what I tell him. You'll be reinstated in no time." Melinda gestured her toward the door. "If you took care of that old coot Donald Dresser and managed to wheedle a few dollars out of him, then I know that you're a good, patient nurse, and the right one for me. But I wonder, do you know anything about giving a party?"

"Giving a party?" Carrick leaped across the room. "What do you mean, giving a party?"

Yes, that got his attention, didn't it? He didn't want her to take control of her life. He liked her better isolated and brooding, afraid of the world and all its perils.

"The government has given me a deadline—tell them what I know about your father's fortune by November third, or go on trial for collusion in the defrauding of the Manly Corporation's stockholders." Melinda Balfour Manly, of the Balfours of Maine, would be held up to the scorn of the world, on charges that would rekindle the scandal and the gossip and the pain. "I will have to leave my home to attend this mockery. I am old. I am ugly. I am ill. And as I look back, I wonder how this came to pass." Melinda lifted her chin. "But then I remember how this house used to be when I was a child, so full of lights and gaiety. So I've decided to make myself happy, turn back the clock, and throw the annual Balfour Halloween party one last time, and when I am done, society will gossip about me, but not in pity." She took Hannah's hand and squeezed it hard, determined to seize this one last opportunity to lift herself out of this brew of misery Nathan had cooked up. "My dear, when we get done, the world will stand in awe of Melinda Balfour Manly."

SIX

I'm your brother.

Gabriel Prescott watched Carrick Manly wend his way through the clustered tables at B'wiched, the latest and best of the sandwich shops in New York City, and wished for a better way to break the news.

I'm your half brother.

But while Gabriel was very good at manipulating situations to suit his needs, when it came to tact, he could sometimes be found . . . lacking.

It wasn't that he didn't understand the need for tact. His family, the family who had given him a last name and treated him as if he really was their brother . . . they had demonstrated over and over how important the use of tact could be in relationships. His sisters always told him he could catch more flies with honey than with vinegar. But in times of stress, he sometimes said things a little too bluntly.

I'm one of your father's bastards.

Or a lot too bluntly.

The new senator from South Carolina and her husband stopped Carrick to hug him with the assurance of old friends.

Gabriel wasn't sweating this encounter with Carrick. They'd met before, many times. In fact, the first time they'd met, it had been a carefully orchestrated encounter, not long after Gabriel had first begun to suspect his father's identity.

That contact and the possibility that Carrick was his blood relative had left Gabriel feeling as if he was looking into a mirror distorted by old money and a long distinguished lineage. They had nothing in common. Nothing.

Carrick was designer suits, Ivy League schools, East Coast founding families, and country clubs.

Gabriel was foster homes, long days of loneliness, gang fights, and half-remembered nightmares that woke him in a cold sweat. He had started with nothing. He had made a million, twice, and lost it, twice, by the time he was twenty-one. He was thirty-eight now. He owned the largest security firm in the United States, had interests in a dozen different start-up enterprises and a nose for business. He knew his way around a boardroom. He knew how to fit into the Prescott family, loving his foster sisters and their husbands, and adoring their children.

But he was more at home with his fists. With a gun. With facing adversity. With winning.

Which was not to say Carrick didn't project power. He did. But it was a different kind of power. At the age of twenty-six, Carrick owned an apartment in Manhattan and Balfour House on the coast of Maine. He spoke to all the right people, knew how to sail a yacht, and he played polo—polo, for God's sake. Yet Carrick discussed money with sharp intelligence, and displayed a shrewd aptitude when summing up people's weaknesses.

Gabriel wasn't blind to Carrick's failings; since employing Gabriel, Carrick had occasionally treated him as an English aristocrat would treat a servant. Once, when Gabriel had failed to act on Carrick's concerns with what Carrick considered enough respect, he'd thrown a full-blown, petulant outburst. Neither the attitude nor the tantrum had sat well with Gabriel. But Gabriel assumed he would gain maturity and be the kind of man the other Manly brothers had become— powerful, astute, and dominant.

After all, Carrick was family.

Gabriel needed to handle this matter delicately. Because there was a pretty good chance Carrick wasn't going to like being related to someone with Gabriel's background.

"Good to see you, Gabriel. How's it going?" Carrick extended his hand.

Gabriel shook it and gestured Carrick into the chair opposite.

Delicately. Tactfully.

Before Gabriel could speak, the waitress, with flame red hair, ivory skin, and a butterfly tattoo on each wrist, stepped up to the table and placed the menus before them. "I'm Jasmine, your server. What can I bring you to drink?"

Irritated as hell, Gabriel turned on her.

She took a step back.

And he realized he must have his warrior face on. It frightened women, especially young women, and Jasmine was only doing her job. "How's your iced tea?" He tried a smile.

She wasn't buying it. She stayed well back from him as she answered, "We make it fresh every day."

"Flavored?" He smiled wider.

She stepped back again. "Plain black tea and ginger peach green tea."

He gave up on conciliation and ordered briefly. "Black tea, nonsweetened, and keep it coming."

"You bet." She wrote on the tablet.

Carrick took the menu from the waitress, and ordered a cappuccino with such charm one of her knees buckled. She wove her way toward the kitchens.

Turning on Gabriel, Carrick demanded, "What's with you? What's with the iced-tea interrogation?"

"I want it made today, I want it made in a clean pot, and I don't want any of that chai shit." Damn the waitress. Now Gabriel didn't know the right time to break the news to Carrick. Before the drinks arrived? After the sandwiches were half eaten?

"You Texans are crazy. Chai tea is all the fashion."

"Fashion?" Gabriel said, irritated. "I don't care about fashion."

"I can see that." Carrick eyed Gabriel's jeans, black tee, and running shoes.

God, New Yorkers were snobs. "*Chai* is the Chinese word meaning *We swept the tea leaves off the floor.*"

"Right." Carrick didn't laugh.

In fact, Gabriel suspected he allotted a set number of minutes to chitchat, spent them not listening, and when those minutes were up, he ruthlessly turned the conversation to himself.

Those minutes were up. "I need to hire you again."

Shit. No. Gabriel didn't want to work for Carrick.

But before Gabriel could get a word in edgewise, Carrick waved him to silence. "I hired this girl to take care of my mother. Hannah Grey. Hannah told me she was a home-care nurse and she had experience with arthritic patients. I admit, I didn't do the research." Carrick smiled like a guy who hated to admit his fault. "She had such an innocent face!"

"Is she not a nurse?"

"Oh, she's a nurse, all right, with the diploma and registration to prove it." Carrick hitched his chair forward and lowered his voice. "But she's like Rasputin. She hypnotizes the patient, makes them love her. She's had her nursing certificate suspended in the state of New Hampshire for immoral behavior. Apparently while she cared for Mr. Donald Dresser, she was slipping it to him—and he was *old*—and he was grateful to the tune of fifty grand. Worse, he wasn't the first patient to include her in his will."

Carrick now had Gabriel's full attention. "Any sign of foul play?"

"No, but they don't do autopsies on the elderly unless there's good cause."

"Do you think this nurse and your mother are . . ." Gabriel thumped his fists together.

"God, no!" Carrick's horror was almost laughable. "It's not that. But Mother won't hear a bad word about Hannah Grey."

Jasmine put the drinks on the table and whipped out her PDA. "Can I take your orders?"

Carrick gave his with a smile that melted her into a puddle.

"I'll have what he's having," Gabriel said, and waved her away. He wanted to get this problem of Carrick's solved so he could tell Carrick about their relationship. That *was* why he'd come today.

"Hannah has convinced Mother to resurrect the old Balfour Halloween party," Carrick said with an intensity that baffled Gabriel.

Gabriel shrugged. "I don't know what that means."

"The Balfours are famous in New England, and they threw their Halloween party for a hundred years. When I was a kid, I remember meeting the president of the United States at our party. Meeting the CEO of Toyota. Meeting the king of Morocco." Carrick's face softened. "Father was always home for the party. It was . . ." Reality caught up with Carrick's memories, and he snapped back to the present. "You have no idea what having the party entails!"

"I thought your mother was agoraphobic."

"She is, plus her health is precarious, plus she hasn't got two nickels to rub together." Carrick leaned forward. "Do you know what that party will cost to put on properly? And Mother insists on doing everything properly!"

"Have you talked to your mother?"

"I tried." Carrick sighed heavily. "Mother should be

preparing for the government inquest. Instead, all I hear is, *Hannah says*."

"But what is Hannah Grey going to get out of it?" That was the important question.

"What I'm afraid of . . . I am so desperately afraid that she . . ."

Gabriel said it for him. "You're afraid that your mother is going to tell Hannah what she knows about your father's fortune."

"Exactly." Carrick grasped Gabriel's arm and squeezed gratefully.

"You think if there's any money left, Hannah will remove it and leave your mother to face the consequences."

"Yes!"

Gabriel asked the question that hovered between them. "*Does* your mother know where Nathan Manly put the money?"

Carrick exploded in muffled exasperation. "I have no idea! She has never in any way indicated that she knows, but you don't know Mother. She's angry about Father's betrayal, and she never forgets or forgives. Added to that, she's secretive and distrustful of everyone, even me. The older she gets, the worse she gets. That's why this relationship with Hannah Grey is out of character."

Jasmine appeared. "Here you go, gentlemen." She placed the plates before them.

Carrick ate a few bites without visible interest, and zoomed right back to his problem. "I know Mother's odd and probably not the best mother in the world, but she's the only parent I've got. I can't let her go to prison."

Gabriel surrendered to the inevitable. "Okay. Consider me hired. What do you want me to do?"

"Do you think you could bug the house?" Carrick asked eagerly. "Fix it so we could hear what Mother tells Hannah and give that information to the government? I know it stinks, but I don't think my mother could survive the inquest, much less a trial, and certainly not prison. I've got to do what I can to save my mother's life."

"I can bug the house."

"Mother's smart, and she's observant. She's got a bad heart, too, and I don't want her disturbed."

It must be nice to feel that way about a mother, even when she didn't seem like much of a parent at all. "I've got cameras that are wireless and the size of a pencil. Will that do?"

Carrick leaned back in relief. "Yes. That will do very well."

Truth to tell, this job appealed to Gabriel. To go to his father's house, to see where he'd lived and walked . . . He had researched Nathan Manly, trying to get a picture of the guy who would build up a multibillion-dollar business and demolish it, wed a woman and destroy the marriage, romance four girls, and leave them pregnant, steal a fortune, and abandon everything and everyone he knew.

But if Gabriel was going to do this, he couldn't tell Carrick that they were brothers. Not here. Not now. That would have to wait for another day.

"I almost forgot. Here." Carrick thrust something toward Gabriel. "Here's Hannah Grey."

It was a photo, and not a good photo, either. Grainy and unflattering—her driver's license, or maybe her nursing license. It showed a blond woman, very pale, with minimal makeup, a solemn face, and huge blue eyes.

But Gabriel felt like he'd been punched in the gut.

He was looking at the woman of his dreams.

SEVEN

The house was watching her.

Hannah returned the breakfast tray to the kitchen and walked toward Mrs. Manly's suite ... and stopped in the middle of the wide sweep of stairs. She looked around, peering at the shadows, half expecting to see eyes peering back.

The house was watching her.

She examined the high ceiling, the cove moldings, the pictures that lined the walls. She saw nothing. She heard nothing.

Yet the hair on the back of her neck stirred, and her heartbeat quickened.

The house was watching her.

For the first two months of her tenure, she had not been aware of the house as a living entity. She'd been absorbed by her patient, discovering that Mrs. Manly was easily irritated by sunlight, arthritis drugs, insulin shots, healthy food, discipline, and exercise. But summer drifted into autumn, and as September turned the leaves to gold and scarlet, Mrs. Manly became a fanatic about the plans for her Halloween party. She had stated her goal: to create an image of herself as a woman who had survived Nathan Manly's defection and thrived.

Hannah's goal was a little different. She wanted Mrs. Manly to live a long life. So she had cajoled, teased, begged, and ordered her to eat better, to take her medicines, to treat her poor, racked body with respect.

They'd come to an understanding.

Mrs. Manly would cooperate with Hannah—to a point. And beyond that point, Hannah would not push.

Then, in the last week, an edgy conviction had emerged and grown.

The house was watching Hannah, and Hannah . . . was spooked.

She hurried down the long corridor toward Mrs. Manly's door, turned the handle, and leaped into Mrs. Manly's room. She shut the door behind her and stood, panting, her back against the wall.

"What's the matter, Miss Grey?" Mrs. Manly asked crisply.

"It's stupid," Hannah said.

"I'll tell you if it's stupid." Mrs. Manly stirred in her bed like a great winged bat. "What has gotten into the very sensible Miss Grey?"

"I feel like"—*The house is watching me*—"someone is watching me." Somehow that didn't sound as ridiculous as accusing a house of malevolent intentions.

"Maybe someone is." Mrs. Manly waved her closer. "Hurry up. I have to visit the powder room."

Dealing with a lady was vastly different from dealing with Mr. Dresser. Mrs. Manly used euphemisms about her body functions; Mr. Dresser had said he wanted to piss. But in a way they were so similar; they both sought death, welcomed death, rather than a long descent into old age and suffering.

Hannah hurried to her side.

Mrs. Manly grunted as she fought to sit up.

Morning was not her best time. Morning was no arthritis sufferer's best time. With sleep, the joints stiffened and movement was slow and painful.

Quickly, competently, Hannah massaged Mrs. Manly's knees and hips, then pushed the wheelchair into position beside the bed and helped her into it.

Mrs. Manly wheeled herself to the powder room and shut the door behind her, leaving Hannah to start the coffeemaker. As soon as the door opened, Hannah hurried to help Mrs. Manly get dressed. "What do you mean, maybe someone is watching me?"

"Didn't you know?" Mrs. Manly half smiled. "The house is haunted."

"Oh, come on."

"My dear girl, as old as this house is, do you think it hasn't seen violence? Anguish? Pain? The whole range of human emotions has played across this stage, and the house has absorbed them all." As she spoke, Mrs. Manly's voice dropped lower and lower. "Why do you think our Halloween parties are so successful?"

"Good treats?" Hannah ventured.

"There are ghosts here, my dear, and they do watch." Mrs. Manly looked up at Hannah's horror-stricken face and laughed. Cackled, really. "Are you susceptible?"

"Are you kidding? When I was a kid, I saw *Ghostbusters* and I didn't sleep for weeks." Hannah spoke lightly—but she wasn't joking.

"Oh. Dear." Mrs. Manly tried to quash her amusement. "I was merely kidding about the ghosts."

"Good." Because Hannah didn't know which was worse, that the house was watching her or ghosts were. Hannah poured Mrs. Manly a cup of coffee.

As she handed it to her, Mrs. Manly said softly, "Yet there are other secrets, more deadly than mere ghosts."

"Do I want to know?"

"I fear you must. It is your punishment for the unfailing integrity you've shown." But Mrs. Manly appeared to abandon that train of thought, and waved at the three-foot-wide bookshelf nestled into one corner. "This morning, I'd like you to dust my books."

The deep, rich mahogany shelves had been placed at a forty-five-degree angle to the walls. They rose from the floor to the twelve-foot-high ceiling, and had been carved into a series of Celtic knots, making the whole piece a beautiful, intricate piece of nineteenth-century art.

Hannah frowned as she approached. A very grimy piece of art. "I'll speak to the housekeeper. This hasn't been cleaned for months."

"It hasn't been cleaned since Torres died. I don't allow just anyone to dust my books."

Hannah had worked with eccentrics before, and for all that Melinda Manly was agoraphobic, she operated in a remarkably normal range. But to be fussy about who dusted her books?

"I trust you to do it." Melinda Manly smiled into her mug.

Hannah found one of the cheap towels she kept on hand for cleanup, dragged the library ladder into place, climbed up to the top shelf, and set to work. The Celtic decorations had been twisted by the woodcarver into faces with eyes that stared, and gargoyles with knowing grins. She had thought the house watched her; this bookcase really did keep watch.

Hannah pulled out each title, wiped it off, and set it aside. Variety and age varied, hardcovers and well-read paperbacks mixed, and chaos reigned. She dusted the shelves. Then as she replaced the books, she asked, "Are these your favorites?"

"Yes. Old friends, most of them."

Hannah flipped through *The Iliad*. "Do you read Greek?"

"And Latin. I attended Wellesley and my father insisted on a traditional curriculum, without merit in the job market. He was old-fashioned. He thought I would marry as soon as I graduated. Instead I waited for my prince charming . . . and we all know how *that* turned out."

It was the first time Mrs. Manly had referred to the scandal that had driven her to hide, to never step foot outside for fifteen years.

"I do know." Hannah paused delicately, then ventured a question. "But I don't understand. How could you . . . ?"

"How could a woman like Melinda Balfour, a woman who can trace her ancestry back to the *Mayflower*, and her family fortune back to the original land barons, stay married to a man who had humiliated her over and over again, with one woman after another? Is that what you're asking?"

"Yes. Yes, that's what I'm asking."

"It's easy enough. Nathan could charm the birds out of the trees. He certainly charmed me." As if the aches and pains of her age and arthritis overwhelmed her, Mrs. Manly slowly adjusted herself in her chair. "When I met him, he was twenty-three, brash, absolutely gorgeous, a prodigy on the stock market. I thought he was a genius. I thought I was the luckiest girl in the world to catch him. I didn't realize that I hadn't caught him—he'd caught me. My father tried to tell me . . ." Her breath rasped in her throat. "Father said I had never been attractive, and that I was old. Ten years older than Nathan. He said Nathan only wanted me for my money."

Every word painted a picture of impending disaster.

"Of course, he was right." Mrs. Manly's mouth puckered, and the dark hairs in her mustache bristled. "Right about all of it. Nathan knew money. He loved money. But I thought he loved me, too, so I trusted him with my fortune, my virtue, and my family's reputation. He destroyed them all."

"I am so sorry."

"And my pride. I trusted him with my pride, too, and that fell first and hardest. But it didn't matter, because Nathan took my money and built a company with it, a successful company that impressed even my father. Then . . . I couldn't conceive, and there was never a doubt whose fault it was."

Hannah could almost feel the pain rolling off Mrs. Manly in waves. "*Fault* isn't the word for it. Saying a woman can help it if she's not fertile is as ridiculous as saying a woman gets pregnant only when she enjoys it."

Hot with fury, Mrs. Manly turned on her. "Even my father said it was my fault. Because obviously Nathan had what it takes to create a baby. He screwed all those girls, fathered all those bastards—" As if she remembered Hannah's objection to the word, she stopped herself.

But Hannah heard her heavy breathing, saw the way she gritted her teeth and held herself so stiffly. Hannah slid down a step, started on the next shelf, and said gently, "At least he acknowledged and supported the children. At least he was honorable enough to do that."

"Nathan wasn't being *honorable*." Mrs. Manly wheeled herself to her night table, slammed open a drawer, pulled out a snowy-white handkerchief, and blotted the sweat from her upper lip. "He didn't know the meaning of the word. He was strutting like a bantam cock, crowing and smug. He had *sons*. Lots of *sons*."

"But you did conceive." Hannah slid down another step. She wasn't done with the second shelf from the top, but Mrs. Manly's appearance alarmed her.

The woman was red-faced, almost apoplectic. "After years of hell, of taking hormones to stimulate my ovaries to produce eggs. Do you know what happens when they do that to you? Weight gain, abdominal pain, nausea . . . not to mention I miscarried twice. I spent the pregnancy on complete bed rest. And do you know what I got for my pains? Carrick." She spat the name. "My son, Carrick."

Well. That answered any questions Hannah had about the relationship between mother and son. "Did . . . did Carrick's birth make your husband happy?"

"Yes. But then, he always was jubilant when one of his children was born. Another son to prove his manhood . . ." The bright red color receded from Mrs. Manly's face, and she smiled, a superior lift of her lips. "After Carrick, there were no more sons for him."

"What?" Hannah stood perched on the ladder, and stared at her employer.

"Not long after Carrick was born, Nathan was walking through Central Park, returning from his girlfriend's house. Right there in broad daylight, he was mugged and beaten. One testicle was crushed beyond repair; they had to amputate. The other . . ." Mrs. Manly *tsk*ed in mock sorrow. "When he recovered, he discovered he was no longer the man he had once been."

Had Hannah imagined it, or had Mrs. Manly just obliquely confessed to arranging the beating of her own husband?

"He changed then. He didn't have the affairs, but he

didn't stay home, either. He visited his sons. He spent time at the business he'd built in Pennsylvania. And he started looking beyond . . ." Mrs. Manly was looking beyond, too, staring into space as if she could see her absent husband. She whispered, "I should have seen it coming." She switched her attention to Hannah so swiftly Hannah's head spun. "Bring me *Ulysses* by James Joyce."

Hannah gaped at her.

"Hurry, girl. We haven't got all day. It's on the fourth shelf, the middle shelf, a leather-bound hard-cover, tan with black lettering."

Hannah searched. "You like *Ulysses*?" She found it jutting out from among the paperbacks, put her finger on the spine, and tugged.

Nothing happened.

"I read it in college lit." Hannah tugged again. "Personally, I found it one of the most obvious attempts of an English teacher to get his students to commit suicide from sheer boredom."

"Grip it and *pull*," Mrs. Manly directed.

Hannah wrapped her hand around *Ulysses* and *pulled*. The book popped loose with an audible *spro-ing* . . . and the wall moved.

No, not the wall, the bookcase. Hannah jumped back. She stared as, slowly, the polished wood, the heavy tomes, the gargoyles swung on a pivot to reveal a black hole behind the wall. Hand over her heart, she said, "My God. There *is* a secret passage."

"Yes. There is. How did you hear about it?" Mrs. Manly asked.

"Carrick said there was rumored to be one, but that he'd never found it." Hannah slid a foot inside, then her head, then her body and looked around.

She stood on a narrow landing, with stairs going up one way and down the other. Light slipped in from some unknown source—an unseen window, or a skylight—and illuminated dust and cobwebs. Across the way, another part of the wall was cut at a forty-five-degree angle.

"I never told Carrick about it. By the time he was old enough, I didn't trust him." Mrs. Manly's voice sounded nearer, much nearer.

Hannah turned to face her. "There's another entrance across the way?"

Mrs. Manly sat in her wheelchair. "Bright girl. In the bedroom next to mine, there's another bookcase. Every bookcase that leads to the passage is set at an angle, and somewhere on the shelves, there's a copy of *Ulysses* by James Joyce. Remove that, and it opens."

Diabolical. Mrs. Manly was diabolical. "Where does the passage go?"

"It leads from the attic to the basement, and from there, into a cave and onto the beach. Pull *Ulysses* loose, and you can step inside, shut yourself in, and escape."

Hannah pushed the bookcase shut and replaced the book in exactly the right spot. "Escape what?"

"Whatever monster is chasing you."

Hannah remembered all the things Carrick had done and said, all of the trials Mrs. Manly had suffered, and she felt dread creep up her spine on tiny spiderlike feet. "So there actually are secrets?"

"Some I know. Others I only suspect." Mrs. Manly pushed herself toward the door. "But I know we've got trouble, girl. Big trouble."

"What kind of trouble?"

"The house is watching us."

Gabriel caught a glimpse of movement on the monitor. In the corridor outside Mrs. Manly's room, two figures, the young woman and the wheelchair-bound elderly lady, maneuvered their way into the elevator and disappeared.

He turned to the next monitor. The elevator door opened on the ground floor, and they exited. Hannah Grey grasped the handles of the wheelchair and pushed Mrs. Manly into the dining room. Another monitor picked them up as she settled Mrs. Manly into her place and went down the stairs toward the kitchen.

He'd placed cameras well. He had a complete view of the corridor, a solid view of the foyer, the elevator and dining room.

While Mrs. Manly and Hannah Grey were occupied, he needed to organize one more very important camera setup.

Gathering his equipment, he sprinted out of the bedroom he occupied in the north wing, and headed for Mrs. Manly's suite. Before they returned from breakfast, he would have everything in place.

He intended to watch Hannah Grey every minute: while she worked, while she slept, while she was at leisure, and while she plotted. He intended to listen in on every conversation, monitor every phone call, learn what she liked and what she hated, who her friends were and why she had collected so many enemies. When he was through with Miss Hannah Grey, he would know everything about her—and she wouldn't know he even existed.

EIGHT

Hannah ate breakfast and worried.

Should she leave Balfour House? As Mrs. Manly
had promised, she made her call to the New Hampshire governor. Hannah had been cleared of all wrong-
doing and her accreditation had been reinstated. If she
could quit this job now, she could walk away from
Mrs. Manly and never look back. And she should.

But she *owed* Mrs. Manly. More important than that,
she would leave the old woman alone, with the Balfour Halloween party half planned and a son who
grew increasingly troublesome. Mrs. Manly never
backed down from a fight, but their arguments left her
weary and sad.

Had there been a brief time when Hannah had admired Carrick Manly? She barely remembered that
now; now she wondered why he thought his mother
knew anything about his father's fortune, what he expected to gain from the knowledge . . . and what he
would do to get his hands on the information.

If Hannah were smart, she would run. She would save herself from this house of secret passageways, with eyes that watched and judged and criticized. She'd already learned the hard way what happened when she stayed with a patient in a dysfunctional family situation. The reward of knowing she was doing the right thing wasn't worth the trouble afterward. Not even Mr. Dresser's inheritance had eased the anxiety and heartache of losing her reputation as a nurse and a woman, and the worst part was—it was her own fault. She should have kept her mouth shut about being *friends* with old Mr. Dresser.

She looked up at Mrs. Manly.

The old woman's broad jowls sagged, her small mouth turned down, and she ate with an intensity that made the silver fork clatter against the thin china.

Mrs. Manly wasn't lovable. She wasn't kind. Right now, Hannah was probably the only person in the world who even liked her. Yet Hannah couldn't abandon her to a government inquest, a humiliatingly public rehash of a lousy marriage, and a bevy of accusations that could, all too easily, result in prison time.

Hannah put her elbows on the table and her head in her hands.

My God, will I ever learn?

"So." Mrs. Manly didn't stop eating as she shot the question at Hannah. "Are you going to stay?"

Hannah lifted her head and looked at her. "Yes."

"I figured. You're not the kind who runs from trouble."

"I could learn."

"In my experience, the ones with the morals can't permanently shake them, no matter how hard they try." Mrs. Manly peered up over her black-rimmed glasses. "Are you done eating?"

Hannah looked down at her cold toast. "Yes."

"Let's go."

As she did every morning after breakfast, Hannah moved Mrs. Manly from the table into the foyer, and stopped. "Before we work on the party, shall we go for a walk?"

"No. No! My God, don't you ever give up?" Mrs. Manly's voice rose. "I am not going for a walk and you cannot bully me into exercising. Just leave me alone. I am so sick of you and your constant pushing and prodding!"

Hannah comprehended the strain on Mrs. Manly, the fears that drove her to confide in Hannah, the bigger fear that she'd made a mistake. She knew what changes loneliness and pain had wrought in a woman already wounded by life. She'd seen her snap before.

But Hannah had been raised by a mother who had taught her to hold her head high and never, ever allow anyone to denigrate her. Moreover Hannah knew better than to allow Mrs. Manly to bully her. Mrs. Manly took unfair advantage of perceived weakness.

Taking her hands away from the wheelchair, Hannah stepped away. "As you wish."

She walked toward the stairway, had her foot on the first step, when Mrs. Manly called, "Girl! You! Hannah! Don't leave me here."

Hannah continued up the stairs.

"Hannah. Don't you dare leave me here!"

Hannah kept climbing.

"Oh, all right. Hannah, I'm sorry."

Hannah paused. Turned. Looked down at her patient.

Mrs. Manly looked mulishly rebellious. "I apologized. Hurry up! I need to use the facilities!"

Hannah didn't move.

"Please. *Please* come and get me and take me upstairs. I don't want to sit here." She shrugged her shoulders apprehensively. "I feel exposed."

Hannah glanced around as if uneasy, then hurried down the stairs. Gripping the handles on the wheelchair, she pushed her patient toward the elevator. "Do you really have to go?"

"No, I just knew you wouldn't leave me to sit there if I was in need," Mrs. Manly muttered.

Wow. Gabriel sat back in his chair. That little scene had shown all too clearly the influence Hannah had over Mrs. Manly. The old lady had cracked under the strain of dealing with Hannah's mistreatment, and with nothing more than a turned back, Hannah had whipped her into shape.

"Next time you need a whipping boy, let me put through a call to Jeff Dresser, hmm?" Hannah sounded exasperated.

Mrs. Manly brayed with laughter. "Yes, or I'll call that little worm Nelson."

Interesting. Mrs. Manly didn't like the butler. Gabriel hadn't been impressed either, but Carrick had assured Gabriel that Nelson was his best ally. Certainly Nelson had put himself out to make sure

Gabriel was comfortable in his little makeshift office, and he knew everything about Mrs. Manly—her habits, her mannerisms, and the changes that had occurred since Hannah Grey came into the household. He did not like Hannah Grey, and he made no bones about her bad influence on Mrs. Manly. In that, he and Carrick agreed.

Gabriel watched the bank of monitors as Hannah pushed Mrs. Manly directly to her bedroom suite.

Good. Mrs. Manly looked tired, she would want to rest, and the ensuing activity would be an effective test of Gabriel's placement of the cameras and microphones. He could watch Hannah bully and coerce her, get the evidence Carrick needed to fire her with just cause, and maybe, just maybe, get the information about the missing Manly fortune.

Personally, Gabriel thought Carrick was kidding himself there. If Melinda Manly knew anything about the fortune, she would have accessed it somehow, if only to pay for the upkeep on this museum of a house. Gabriel glanced around at the bedroom where he had set up his equipment, and noted the tired drapes, the faded rug, the moth-eaten bedspread. The dresser where he'd placed his laptop was a massive piece of nineteenth-century walnut art, but the maids had run the vacuum cleaner into the legs so many times they were chipped, and some long-grown kid had carved his name into the trim. The whole place smelled musty, as if it hadn't been opened in years—and this was only a single room among dozens like it. He didn't know Mrs. Manly, not yet, anyway, but what he'd seen on the monitor had shown a woman proud of her heritage.

Yeah, she would have used the money for Balfour House.

Hannah was of average height, slender to the point of looking fragile. She lifted Mrs. Manly out of the wheelchair and helped her into bed, and Gabriel realized the frailty was deceptive. She adjusted Mrs. Manly's pillows and covers, tested her blood sugar, then prepared an injection and handed the needle to Mrs. Manly.

Mrs. Manly glared at it tiredly.

"All right. I'll do it." Hannah's voice held a hint of an East Coast accent, and she sounded so gentle, Gabriel blinked in surprise.

But in his business, he'd learned never to trust a kind voice or a sweet face. In his business, he'd learned never to trust at all.

She gave the injection, then strode around the room, closing the curtains, lowering the lights. She moved like a nurse, long-legged and fit, with that characteristic steady, silent tread.

He couldn't see her face, but her hair was blond, almost platinum, and cut around her chin in a bob that swung to the side when she turned her head.

Her ears stuck straight out, and he grinned about that.

"Two weeks until Halloween," Mrs. Manly said. "How many RSVPs have we received?"

"Over two hundred. Everyone is coming."

"Of course they are. No one would miss the chance

to see Balfour House and the crazy old hermit woman who lives there." Mrs. Manly closed her eyes.

Carrick was right. Hannah had no business urging her to have this party.

Hannah walked to the desk, pulled out a clipboard, and consulted it. "We've got politicians, singers, actors, ministers—"

"Respectable people?"

Hannah laughed. "A few."

"Have you arranged for security?"

Oh, hell. Another problem to deal with.

"That never occurred to me."

Of course not. You might be playing in the league with the big girls, but you don't know the drill.

"If we're going to have all those politicians, actors and other disreputables, we'll have to have security." Mrs. Manly gestured restlessly. "Call my man, Eric Sansoucy. Sansoucy Security, in town. I haven't talked to him in fifteen years, but he knows me."

Going to Mrs. Manly, Hannah took her pulse. "You should rest."

In a tired voice, Mrs. Manly said, "Get me a copy of *The Ivy Tree*. Second shelf up, on the right."

"Not *Ulysses*?" Hannah sounded as if she were joking.

"No. I'm not interested in reading the self-indulgent ramblings of a drunken Irishman."

"So why keep the book?" Gabriel wondered aloud.

"Is that why you chose that title?" Hannah asked. "Because it's so awful?"

"No one who has ever read it would pick it up again," Mrs. Manly said. "At least, not on purpose."

It had happened before. Gabriel had stepped into the middle of a conversation, and he had no idea what they were talking about.

Hannah walked toward the bookshelf. She reached up, looked up, and he whispered, "Wow."

No wonder she managed to seduce fifty thousand dollars out of her last patient. She looked like a china doll with huge blue eyes and dark lashes that fluttered like a fan. Dark lashes . . . Gabriel knew that meant she dyed her hair or used mascara with the skill of a wizard. But looking at her, he didn't care.

She had the kind of eyes for which a man would willingly sacrifice his life, his honor . . . and his fortune.

She had great lips, too, full and soft, and her cheeks were full and soft, and he was looking down her blouse, and her breasts looked full and soft.

As an illusion, it worked for him. Big-time. With any luck at all, she'd do something deplorable, he'd have to interrogate her, and she'd offer herself as a bribe to save her long, pretty neck.

He supposed he'd have to refuse. But damn, he could enjoy the fantasy while it lasted.

She chose the book and took it to Mrs. Manly, who opened it, placed it on her chest and closed her eyes. "Don't forget to call Eric."

"I'll do it right now." Hannah walked to the computer and opened the browser to the yellow pages.

Without opening her eyes, Mrs. Manly said, "The number's in my address book."

Hannah shut the laptop, reached into a pigeonhole

in the desk and brought out a badly worn binder with flowers on the front and pages thrust catawampus between other pages, and slowly leafed through. "I can't find it in the S's. What's it under?" she called.

"E, for Eric."

"Right," Hannah muttered. "Silly of me."

At the computer, Gabriel typed in the code to take control of the phone system. He brought up his software program to change his voice, viewed the choices, and selected *New England*. By the time Hannah had dialed out, he had everything in place.

His cell phone rang.

He answered, "Sansoucy Security. Trent Sansoucy speaking." As he spoke, he typed in a search for Sansoucy Security, and frowned. The damn place was out of business. In fact . . . another quick search proved he had a bigger problem.

"Is Eric in?" Hannah sounded brisk and businesslike.

Eric Sansoucy was dead. Had been for six years.

"Eric's on a much-needed vacation"—Gabriel figured if Mrs. Manly didn't know Eric was dead, she sure wouldn't know whether he was in the sunny Bahamas—"and he won't be back for another three weeks. Can I help you?"

"You're Eric's . . . ?" She let the question hang in the air.

He watched her as she spoke, a little frown puckering her forehead. She knew Mrs. Manly wouldn't like this development; he had to make this good. "I'm Eric's son."

"What's wrong?" Mrs. Manly was sitting up, alerted by the tone of Hannah's voice.

Hannah put him on hold, but of course Gabriel heard her through the microphones. "Eric is on vacation. This is his son."

"His son? Eric is gay!"

Oops.

Mrs. Manly continued. "Anyway, any son of Eric's is too young to be running the office. Ask him how old he is. Ask him!"

Hannah came back. "I'm Hannah Grey, Mrs. Melinda Manly's companion at Balfour House. She is in doubt about your—"

"Age and my father's sexual preferences? Yes, I got a lot of that when I first moved here, but when he was in college, Dad experimented and here I am." Gabriel watched as Hannah transmitted the information, as Mrs. Manly digested it, nodded, and reclined once more.

Relieved, Gabriel leaned back in his chair. One hurdle down.

Hannah came back on the line. "Thank you for reassuring us, Mr. Sansoucy. Now—Mrs. Manly is reviving the Balfour Halloween party, and we are in need of security. Would you be able to handle it?"

"Halloween is a busy time for us, but I'm sure Dad would insist we do everything we can for Mrs. Manly and Balfour House. I assume you'll want the full party security treatment?" Gabriel had arranged security for many a party, and as he talked about the arrangements, he watched Hannah relax. He had reassured her that this part of the planning would go without a hitch.

Mrs. Manly sat up again. "Ask him if he can come early to look the house over."

Hannah interrupted him and in a firm voice, said, "If you could transmit a copy of your plans for Mrs. Manly to look over, that would be appreciated. In the meantime, can you come to see what arrangements you'll need to make?"

Mrs. Manly continued. "Because when he finds cameras and microphones, I'm going to grab Carrick and shake him until his teeth rattle."

Damn. She was a smart woman. She'd figured Carrick might have commissioned surveillance. A good thing he could hear their conversation. That would be the only thing to save his ass.

Smoothly, Hannah said into the mouthpiece, "Since it's been so long since Sansoucy Security has been to Balfour House, we'd like you to do a thorough examination of the house and gardens and see what needs to be done to bring security here up-to-date."

"We'd be glad to do that," Gabriel said with the right mix of eagerness and professionalism. "Dad's technical specialist is Susan Stevens. Can I make an appointment for her to visit?"

Hannah put him on hold again, and said, "He's sending someone named Susan Stevens."

"I want the boss," Mrs. Manly said fretfully. "Have him come instead."

Hannah came back. "Mrs. Manly would like to have you personally handle her security."

"I intend to, and that means giving it my best. And my best is Susan Stevens. Believe me, Miss Grey, you don't want me to do anything technical." He put humor in his tone. "I'm a disaster with a camera or a computer."

She responded to his humor with a smile of her own. "What is *your* specialty, Mr. Sansoucy?"

"I tell people what to do."

"So you don't do anything."

"That's right. I'm an administrator."

She laughed, a low, warm, soft chuckle that made him break a sweat. "I've worked with men like you. Hospitals are full of them."

"You understand I'm not really good at being an administrator yet. Sometimes I forget I'm in charge and actually *do* something, like file a paper or make a decision."

"If you keep that up, you'll never get promoted to . . . whatever it is that's above administrator."

"Dictator."

"So you'll be conquering a small country soon?"

He was looking straight at her—not that she knew it—when he replied, "I already have one in mind."

But she seemed to know what he meant, because she caught her breath and sat up straight. "All right, Trent. You've convinced me about Susan Stevens." She nodded reassuringly at Mrs. Manly, who reluctantly nodded back. "Let's set up that appointment."

"Right." Gabriel responded to her efficient tone with one of his own, and they concluded their business and hung up.

But although she didn't know it, he was still there.

NINE

Gabriel leaned back in his chair and smiled. He had done that well. Very well.

For Hannah hung up and sat with her hands in her lap, a bewildered smile on her face.

"You were flirting with that man." Mrs. Manly rolled onto her side and stared at Hannah.

"No, I wasn't." Startled, Hannah surged to her feet. "Why do you say that? We were talking about security."

"What you said and the way you sounded were two different things." With something to occupy her mind, Mrs. Manly didn't seem as tired.

Hannah stopped and thought. "Maybe. But . . . oh, well." She laughed. "He's got a nice, deep voice, but it's like listening to a deejay on the radio, and then seeing him in person. The man with the great personality and great voice turns out to be sixty, bald, and three hundred pounds."

"Are you so shallow about appearance?" Mrs. Manly had a sharp voice and a way of poking at people that made Gabriel wonder why someone hadn't done away with her years ago.

But Hannah gave right back to her. "You bet. If ever I'm going to find a man, he's got to be about my age. Nursing is my profession. I don't have any wish to care for my husband's infirmities. Not unless I know he'll be around to care for me in return. He must care about his health. He's got to eat right and work out."

Gabriel poked at his belly. He'd been so busy installing cameras and microphones, he'd neglected his exercise. If he weren't careful, he'd sit in front of the monitors for hours, fascinated by Hannah Grey. And as he told the people he hired when he hired them, a strong body was one of the requirements for being in security. He wouldn't allow them to be in less than top condition—and he expected the same from himself.

He dropped to the floor and started a set of push-ups.

"What about the bald?" he asked the monitor. Not that he cared. He had a full head of straight black hair, but a man inherited the gene for baldness from his mother's side of the family . . . and he knew nothing about his mother's side of the family.

"As for the hair," Hannah said, "I suppose I don't care."

"Why would you? It's not his mane you look at when you buy a stallion."

Gabriel came off the floor with a bound, and gaped at the monitor.

"True." Hannah stood beside the bed, and she looked completely serious. "Although I'm not convinced it's the size of the package that matters. It always seems to me that a man can ride with any equipment if he's smart enough to spend the time warming up his filly."

Gabriel hadn't done surveillance for a long time—he didn't have to. He was the boss. And back in the days when he *had* done surveillance, it had been drug busts or cheating husbands. He hadn't ever watched women talk about men. And he'd certainly never imagined that a conversation about men and their sexual activities would be discussed so . . . so calmly.

He was horrified. And embarrassed. And riveted.

"Don't forget. He's got to dismount with finesse." Mrs. Manly sounded as if she were teaching a riding class.

"Yes, there's nothing worse than a guy who tumbles out of the saddle before he's back at the stable." Didn't Hannah know she shouldn't talk about sex with a woman more than twice her age?

"Do you know," she said, "since my mother died, I haven't had anyone who was interested in me enough to ask me what I wanted in a man?"

"You're an intriguing case, Hannah Grey. You're beautiful. You should have the world on a string." Mrs. Manly tapped her fingertips on her book. "Instead you're so cautious you hide in sickrooms caring for old people."

Obviously stung, Hannah said, "I don't hide! The sick people need me."

"I'm not arguing that I don't need you. You've convinced me that I do."

Aha. She had, had she? Exactly as Carrick had told him.

"But you do hide. I wonder why." Mrs. Manly rested on the pillows, observing Hannah from eyes heavy with thought. "It can't be Jeff Dresser who drove you underground."

"No." Hannah spoke emphatically.

"No, what?" Mrs. Manly raised her brows.

"No, I'm not playing that game. I'm not going to show you my scars because you're bored."

Mrs. Manly almost smiled. "How about because I showed you mine?"

"You wouldn't have done it if necessity hadn't driven you to it."

What scars? What necessity?

Mrs. Manly continued to rag on Hannah. "You wanted me to be interested in you."

"Not that kind of interested. I have found that showing my tender underbelly invariably leads to my guts being ripped out."

"You are a frighteningly private person. I wonder what secrets you hide."

Yeah, Mrs. Manly, you aren't the only one.

But the invalid seemed to know she'd pushed Hannah as far as she could. "So about your ideal man. You want a young man who cares for his health, hair optional. What else?" Before Hannah could answer, Mrs. Manly held up a finger. "Don't give me that *sense of humor* stuff. What do you really want?"

Hannah answered so promptly, Gabriel knew she'd given it a lot of consideration. "I want a man who doesn't want to use me for anything—I don't want to be a vehicle for revenge or be the pretty thing that gives a man prestige. I liked old Mr. Dresser, and I appreciate the inheritance, but I didn't appreciate being the one who helped him teach his family a lesson, and I think he knew people were going to say I slept with him. I won't be used like that again."

"What else?"

"I want a man who doesn't lie to me. I want to know the truth about him, and when I think I know it, then I'll tell him the truth about me." Hannah ran her fingers through her blond hair. "I am so sick of men and their lies. Jeff Dresser telling the nursing commission that I took the family silver and screwed his dad, while the silver's rattling around in his car from the *one* time he came to visit his dad."

"What *else*?" Mrs. Manly was insistent, curious, and Gabriel wanted to cheer her on.

"I want a man who sticks around. Not one like my father who was there for a good time and gone when it was time to show some responsibility. Oh, and did I mention I expect him not to have a wife?" Hannah glanced at Mrs. Manly. "I'm sorry. I didn't mean to . . ."

Mrs. Manly waved her explanation away. "We both have our battle scars." She stretched out her hand to Hannah.

Hannah took it.

Mrs. Manly said, "I have to believe that somewhere, sometime, a woman will marry a man who's honest and brave and loyal, and they'll live happily ever after. If I didn't believe that, if I didn't believe in love, I would have ended it long ago."

Hannah stood looking at Mrs. Manly, obviously surprised and touched. "I suppose if you, of all people,
can believe, I can believe."

Mrs. Manly held on to her. "You're a good girl. Genuine. Strong. Moral in a way I don't see anymore. I'm
sorry for what's going to happen, but it has to be you."
Mrs. Manly's mind seemed to be wandering as she
said, "There's no one else."

Hannah thought so, too, for she leaned closer. "Mrs.
Manly, are you all right?"

Mrs. Manly still stared intently.

"I don't like these moods swings." Hannah freed
herself. "Let me check your blood sugar again."

Mrs. Manly seemed to snap back to the present. "For
God's sake, it's not my blood sugar. I'm old and tired,
and if everything goes as planned, I'm going to die
soon. Don't I get to brood occasionally?"

"Yes, and I get to check your blood sugar when I
wish."

Gabriel watched Hannah perform the task again,
and thought how very well she had acted the whole
farce. If he didn't know better, he would have believed
she really was disillusioned about love. If he hadn't
seen that scene downstairs, he might have believed
she cared about Mrs. Manly. If Carrick hadn't told him
about her scams, and both Nelson and the state of
New Hampshire hadn't supported Carrick's tale, he
might have believed she was a bedrock of honesty and
integrity.

He would have believed . . . but he didn't. He was a
man of logic. All the evidence pointed to Hannah's

perfidy. And Gabriel had spent too long looking for his family, for his blood kin, and he had them at last. Four brothers, good men, all of them.

So he believed his brother Carrick.

TEN

The next day, after breakfast, as if the previous day's tantrum hadn't even occurred, Hannah moved Mrs. Manly into the foyer, and asked the question she always asked. "Before we work on the party, shall we go for a walk?"

"Yes."

Hannah almost tripped on her own feet. Although she always hung the walker on the back of the chair, it had never been used, for Mrs. Manly *never* wanted to go out. Tentatively, she said, "Shall we go outside?"

"Where else would we take a walk? In the corridor? Of course we have to go outside." Mrs. Manly sat like a lump, waiting, while Hannah tried to figure out what had changed. Because Mrs. Manly hadn't been outside the entire time Hannah had been here, and if Carrick was to be believed, Mrs. Manly hadn't been outside for fifteen years.

"What's the matter, girl?" Mrs. Manly gestured with her ring-covered hands. "Push me."

Hannah grasped the handles of the wheelchair and headed toward the entrance.

"Open the door," she said to the butler.

"Miss Grey?" Nelson hovered indecisively.

Hannah's voice sharpened. "Open the door and bring two hearty men to help me get Mrs. Manly down to the walk."

"I can't do that. Mrs. Manly doesn't go outside," he said.

Mrs. Manly lunged forward in the chair. With slow, precise words, she said, "Mrs. Manly does as she pleases. Mrs. Manly is the owner of this house, and if, within the next two minutes, you don't get someone here to help Miss Grey, Mrs. Manly will fire you, and by the time my son hears of it, do not mistake me, you will be long gone, never to return."

As her voice rose and the steel of her personality made itself clear, a slow red heat climbed up the butler's face. He stiffened and bowed. "Yes, Mrs. Manly." He strode out.

"Insolent pup," Mrs. Manly muttered. "Carrick hired him, but I pay him. He has lessons to learn."

In seconds, Nelson returned with two young men dressed in denim overalls, with smudges on their hands. "My apologies for their appearance," Nelson said. "They're gardeners."

Mrs. Manly waved his explanation away. "Just get me outside."

"I'll push her through the door. You boys help her down the ramp and . . . where would you like to go, Mrs. Manly?" Hannah asked.

"Take me to the top of the cliff," she said.

Nelson looked at Hannah so alarmed that Hannah wondered what Carrick had told him. As Hannah pushed her out the door, she said, "You heard Mrs. Manly. The top of the cliff."

It wasn't really as wild a place as it sounded; every day, Hannah ran along the top of the cliff. A paved path looped up in a long, slow curve to a tumble of huge, smooth granite boulders, and then down toward a sliver of beach, and then up again to the boundary of Balfour land. In the summer, tourists and locals strolled along the walk, trespassing with the Balfours' tacit permission. Yet the climb was steep, and the two young men were sweating heavily by the time they reached the top.

Hannah set the brake on the wheelchair.

Mrs. Manly raised her hand imperiously. "That will do. Return for us in an hour."

The two young men stood there, uncertain. Then one of them bobbed his head, and they hurried back down the path.

Mrs. Manly shook her head. "No one knows the rudiments of courtesy nowadays."

Hannah stifled her grin. "You have to give them points for trying."

"Points for trying." Mrs. Manly snorted. "Give me a hand."

Hannah hurried forward and took her arm. "What are you doing?"

"I'm walking."

"But . . . you . . ." Now, up here, where there was no one to help in case she fell, Mrs. Manly wanted to *walk*?

"For God's sake, girl. If I fall, we've got my cell phone. Now give me your arm!"

Hannah did, hefting her out of the chair and pushing the walker under her hands.

Mrs. Manly leaned against it, and not until she said, "All right. I've got it," did Hannah step away.

The path was flat here, and Mrs. Manly headed for the pile of boulders twenty feet away. Once there, she carefully leaned against the broadest one and shut her eyes as if the exertion had exhausted her. But when Hannah hurried toward her in concern, she opened them again and said, irritably, "Stop looking so worried. This is what you wanted, isn't it?"

"Yes. But I thought we'd take it in smaller steps."

Mrs. Manly smiled, a painful grimace that faded as she looked out over the ocean. "I don't think we can. Push the wheelchair away. Then come back here."

Hannah did as she was instructed, returning to sit beside Mrs. Manly on the warm granite.

"This really is the prettiest spot in the world," Mrs. Manly said. "I'd forgotten how beautiful it would be, so I suppose for that, I should be grateful. But . . . the burden of the house has dragged me down for so long. Too long."

The breeze whistled around them, blowing the scents of sea and salt and adventure.

"You don't have to stay here." Hannah gestured across the sea, across the land, and over the thin strip of beach. "You can sell it, give it to the state as a park, run away—"

Mrs. Manly laughed, a long maniacal cackle. "I

can't. I'm stuck here until the day I die." She leaned forward in the chair. "Because I know where Nathan deposited his fortune."

"Oh, no." Hannah slid back until she rested flat on her back on the rock, staring up at the blue sky, trying not to hear, trying not to comprehend. "Don't tell me this."

"Who else can I tell?" Mrs. Manly's face inserted itself into Hannah's view of scattered and swiftly moving clouds. "You're the only one I can trust."

Hannah stared into the old woman's insistent eyes. "Who did you trust before?"

"Torres."

"Damn." Hannah covered her eyes with her hand, trying to shut herself off from the terrible truth.

Mrs. Manly yanked Hannah's hand away. "Torres was supposed to outlive me. Instead he keeled over from a heart attack at sixty."

"That son of a bitch."

"You just can't find dependable help these days." Mrs. Manly's mouth crooked cynically.

"You sure can't." Hannah lifted her head. "How *did* you know where . . . where he put the money?"

"I observed. I analyzed. I pried into the records. I found Nathan's offshore account. I was never as dumb as he believed."

No. No, Mrs. Manly was not dumb.

Mrs. Manly looked down at the mansion, crumbling into decay. "From the day Nathan left me, it was always my intention to funnel the money out of the account and back to the people who had worked for and invested in the company. After I died, I mean. I have no intention of being around for that ruckus."

"Of course not," Hannah said ironically.

"So first I fixed it so no one could tap that account. I'm a Balfour. I understand finance."

Hannah was in awe. "How did you find out who should receive the money? There must have been thousands of people he cheated."

"I am his wife. I had access to the financials. And yes, there were thousands, and yes, the computer program to return the money took two years to write." Mrs. Manly smirked. "That's why I hired Torres. Carrick always thought he was a lousy butler. Actually, he was a hacker from Argentina, in the country illegally. He acted as my butler, and kept the program current. I paid him very well for his services, and kept him away from the border patrol."

"Did you trust him that much?"

"I don't trust anybody with that kind of money, so I learned enough about computer programming to keep him honest."

"So you are giving the money back to the people Nathan robbed, because they were the ones who were hurt most by his defection."

"Look. Don't give me credit for a warm and giving heart. I don't give a damn about them and their puny little lives. But I *am* a Balfour. We live lives of honor. We take care of our people." Mrs. Manly's chest heaved, as if being two hundred feet above sea level was too much for her, as if she couldn't get enough oxygen. "Nathan walked away without a backward glance, leaving me to clean up his mess. And I will."

"*Noblesse oblige*, huh?" Hannah smiled at her, not believing a word of it.

Mrs. Manly grunted, unwilling to admit to any finer feelings except the ones she'd been trained to feel. "I'd tell Carrick, leave the whole matter to him, but Carrick . . . it's my fault. By the time I got pregnant, I knew what Nathan was. I knew his son could be charismatic, talented, and absolutely without morals or worth. But I thought . . . I let myself hope for a real child, a legitimate son who would stop Nathan from wandering. I was a fool."

"The other children were real, too," Hannah said gently.

"Not to me. I didn't care about the first one. Or the second one. I'd been raised to think every great man had the right to take a mistress or two. Even though everyone knew about the infidelities, even though Nathan bragged about his sons, I could hold my head up, because now I had a son, too." Mrs. Manly looked down toward the wheelchair. "I realized almost at once Carrick was like his father—a charmer who was rotten to the core. I tell myself that if I'd had Carrick to myself, I could have fixed him. Injected him with some character, some morals. Instead, I had to watch while his father swooped in every month or so, teaching him by example how successful a man could be if he didn't give a damn about doing the right thing."

"That is a difficult role model to overcome," Hannah said gently.

"Do you know, I've followed the other sons' careers. They're men. Real men, with ambitions and work ethics and now every one of them is married and loyal to his wife, and happy. They started out with so much less than Carrick, and now they have everything, because they built their lives on good foundations." Mrs. Manly's hands shook. "I hate Carrick because he's a worm willing to betray me for a dollar. He's a failure. My failure."

"My mother used to tell me that she could teach me the right thing to do, but in the end, I was responsible for the person I became. It's true of me, and it's true of Carrick. He's not your failure. He's a failure of his own making."

Mrs. Manly lifted her head. "You are a nice girl, but you're not a mother. There isn't a mother in the world who believes she couldn't have done better with her child. Certainly not me."

"Certainly not you," Hannah agreed. Certainly not this woman who carried responsibility to such extremes.

"I don't trust him. The house *is* watching us, because somehow he's fixed it so it does. Anything I do, he's recording it. Anything I say, he's recording it."

Hannah glanced down the hill. "You think your *wheelchair* is bugged?"

"I don't know. Why don't you check and make sure?"

"I will." Hannah started to climb off the rock.

Mrs. Manly stopped her with a gesture. "In a minute. Right now I don't want anyone to know we know."

"Correct." Because whoever would put video cameras in an old woman's house and microphones in an old woman's wheelchair was truly a scum bucket of epic proportions.

"Why didn't you come forward when Nathan disappeared?" Hannah asked.

"The government considered me right from the beginning. If I had admitted knowing where the money was, they wouldn't have said, *Thank you*. They'd have said, *We knew it all along*, and put me in prison."

Hannah squared her shoulders. "All right. Tell me what I need to know."

Mrs. Manly didn't even have the decency to act surprised by Hannah's decision, and she certainly wasn't grateful. "You can't tell anyone before I'm dead. Any sooner, and I'll go to jail when the government realizes that I knew the location of the fortune and whisked it away from their greedy, grubby hands."

"Right." Hannah nodded.

"All you have to do is get down to the butler's office in the basement. You were there the day you arrived."

"I remember." How could Hannah forget? It was there she'd first discovered Carrick's perfidy.

"The computer on the desk has a program called Household Accounts."

"Household Accounts," Hannah repeated.

"Open it, and go to Silverware, Inventory."

"Silverware, Inventory."

"The password is capital B, as in Balfour, capital H, as in House, small N, as in Nathan, capital M, as in Melinda, small C, as in Carrick, asterisk, 1898, as in the year Balfour House was completed. Not started, completed."

Hannah repeated every word, visualizing them, using her finger to trace them on the stone. Yet as she did, fear built in her. She didn't dare forget the password. She didn't dare leave Balfour House. She was all too aware of the precariousness of her position. She was trapped here, waiting for Melinda to die, or for Carrick to do something desperate. After Mr. Dresser's death, and after living her whole life on the brink of disaster, she had glimpsed financial security. A brief flash, and then it was gone, lost in an often-regretted moment of defiance that had branded her as a tramp and Mr. Dresser as an old fool.

Now she was back on her feet, with money in the bank, working in a job she did well. If she lost all that again, and through a series of circumstances that had nothing to do with her . . . she couldn't bear it. She didn't want to bear this burden of integrity for Melinda, and she was afraid, afraid she'd end up in prison—or worse.

Yet . . . Mrs. Manly was surrounded by isolation, pain, and betrayal. She had nothing. She had no one.

"Once you enter the password, a blank screen appears. Then there's a request for a code. My husband set up that code." Bitterness dripped from Mrs. Manly's voice. "What do you suppose it is?"

Slowly, Hannah shook her head.

"Mysons. No spaces. Cap M. Type it in." The bitterness spread to Mrs. Manly's smile. "The code was supposed to release the money to Nathan's account in

Switzerland. But Torres went to work, and changed the program. Once you type in the code, the funds will be dispersed to the families who invested their savings in the firm and employees who were loyal to the end." She patted Hannah's arm. "There's nothing for you, I'm afraid. I can't change the program. I don't know how. Your only reward is knowing you're doing the right thing."

"I don't want a reward. I want peace."

"What about justice?"

"I do want justice—as long as someone else does the heavy lifting." Hannah was only half joking.

Mrs. Manly's cackle made her sound like the Wicked Witch of the West. "We all make our decisions. Would you really want to live with yourself if you let thousands of people be robbed by one deceitful man?"

"No, I suppose not." But Hannah didn't want to die for them, either. "Is all the money there? Did he use none of it?"

"He got away with nothing," Mrs. Manly said with satisfaction.

"So the bulk of the fortune is there, and has been collecting interest for fifteen years." The idea boggled Hannah's mind—but not as much as another revelation that occurred, took root, and grew. "Nathan Manly . . . where *is* he?"

Mrs. Manly no longer cackled or smirked. She sneered with all the contempt of an American aristocrat for a plebeian. "He's dead somewhere, a ghost planning his vengeance—on whoever was fool enough to kill him."

ELEVEN

Carrick strolled through the crowd outside Mango, the hottest club in New York City, and as he moved toward the bouncer, he heard the comments sweep through the people behind the ropes.

A voice, hard and impatient. "Who is he?"

Breathless. "He looks like Brad Pitt."

Disdainful. "No, Brad Pitt is too old. He looks like that guy who made a million dollars in one day on the stock market."

A restless snort. "No, it's German Maddox, the actor who's going to play the new Batman villain."

Carrick deliberately didn't look at the female; he didn't want to know if she was young or old, fat or thin, pretty or a dog. But he was pleased.

"That's Carrick Manly." Carrick always planted someone to put out his real name.

"Who's *he*?" It was the same female who'd mistaken him for an actor.

Carrick frowned.

"He's that rich playboy whose father ran away with the family fortune," his plant said.

"So where's *this* guy get his money?" The strange female was considerably less impressed.

"Nobody knows," his plant informed her, "but he's always welcome in places like this."

Right on cue, the bouncer waved Carrick inside.

Music screamed. Lights flashed. Metal palm trees stood in clumps around the tables. It was supposed to be decorated like a desert island. Instead it looked like a beach on acid. He recognized half a dozen young actresses, celebrating their youth and sex and fame with as much energy as their diets and their drugs would allow them. The actors were here, too, and the politicians' kids, and people who were famous for having a family fortune or creating scandal.

And he was one of them. His family fortune was gone, and the scandal was his father's, but when most men would have given up and started from scratch, he'd set his goal on remaining one of the elite, and nothing proved his success like being welcomed to Mango.

Today had been a bitch of a day. Tonight, he needed to be at Mango.

He started to work his way toward a table, one where three girls watched him with interest. They were probably nineteen. They were undoubtedly high. And if he didn't get to them, someone else would.

He was almost there when someone caught his shoulder.

He turned in annoyance.

The man had his head shaved, wore dark glasses,

and was dressed in a business suit. He was nothing special, yet some preservative instinct told Carrick he was a force to be reckoned with. "Who are you?"

Shaved-Head Guy spoke in his ear. "Osgood would like to see you."

Shit. Nobody knew who Osgood was. Nobody knew what he looked like. No one ever saw him, or if they did, they didn't admit to it. Until this minute, Carrick hadn't known whether to believe the rumors that Osgood existed, much less owned the club. Osgood had a fearsome reputation—one that kept the police quiet about the "irregularities" of the bar.

And now . . . Osgood wanted to see Carrick. A crappy end to a shit-ass day. "What does he want?" Carrick asked.

"I'm not privy to Osgood's business." The guy turned and walked away without glancing back to see if Carrick followed.

He did.

They walked toward the restrooms, then veered suddenly toward the blank dark wall. The guy did something, Carrick didn't see what, and a door opened. They entered a dim corridor, one that looked like something out of a prison movie, and walked toward the end, toward a narrow metal door with no handle. Again the guy performed his magic, and the door creaked open.

The guy gestured Carrick inside.

Carrick didn't want to go. He had the ugly feeling he knew why he'd been summoned, and this could not be good.

"Don't linger in the hall, Mr. Manly. Come in," a warm, plumy male voice called.

The guard slammed his knee in the middle of Carrick's back. Slammed it so hard Carrick stumbled forward into the room, fell onto his hands and knees, and collapsed with a wheeze. A rib had cracked, and his left kidney was bruised.

Shaved-Head Guy stepped in behind him and shut the door.

The walls were painted gray. There wasn't a picture or a window in sight. It smelled funny, like sweat socks. And Osgood sat behind a desk, a reading lamp pointed outward. It was an arrangement that left him in the dark, but Carrick had the impression of a slight build and middle age, sort of like the guy who made rye bread for the New York City delis. Not impressive at all.

Then Carrick tried to stand.

Shaved-Head Guy kicked him behind the knee and he went down again.

Osgood didn't have to be impressive. He had his hired muscle to be impressive for him.

"Now, Mr. Manly, there is the problem of your unpaid bar bill." Osgood rustled some papers.

"I can pay the bar tab." Carrick suspected he'd sprained his wrist. He also suspected unless he got this bill taken care of, his wrist would be the least of his problems.

"It's over twenty thousand dollars."

"What?" Carrick got one foot under him and started to stand. "There's no way I've downed twenty thousand dollars' worth of booze."

Osgood flicked his finger, and Shaved-Head Guy kicked Carrick sideways into the wall.

As Carrick crumpled to the floor, Osgood said, "There are the rentals for the personal performance room over the bar, and for the performers. There are the cigars and the smack."

"Still not twenty thousand," Carrick gasped and flinched, but Shaved-Head Guy didn't move.

"Did I forget to mention I also own Rachard's in Soho, and Bitter's in Greenwich?"

God. Carrick had been spreading his business around, figuring if he didn't owe too much any one place, he'd be okay. It had always worked before. How was he supposed to know Osgood owned them all? "I can pay."

"Really?" Osgood asked.

"I have my ways." Carrick sure as hell wasn't going to tell Osgood how thin his finances were running.

"Your bank account is empty. Your apartment isn't your own. Your friends won't lend you another dime." Osgood laughed as if indulgently amused. "You're in such bad financial shape, you don't dare walk into Saks for fear they'll repossess your shoes."

"How do you know what's in my bank account?" Pure rage brought Carrick onto his feet in a flash. "You damn well better not be snooping around—"

Shaved-Head Guy racked Carrick so bad, lights exploded behind his eyes. He screamed like a girl and collapsed, writhing and holding himself.

Through the thrum of blood in his ears, he heard Osgood say, "You don't learn very quickly, do you, Mr.

Manly? You don't stand in my presence. Not when you owe me money with no way to repay me. You crawl."

When Carrick got his breath back, he said, "I don't crawl."

"We'll see," Osgood sounded amused.

Silence fell, broken only by Carrick's own harsh gasping.

First he debated trying to stand again. Then he wondered if he should show more defiance.

Then, as the silence lengthened, as Osgood sat without a sound, as Shaved-Head stood motionless, Carrick's imagination began to brew.

First he remembered how easily Shaved-Head had brought him down.

Then he considered the gossip about Osgood—that he was a pedophile, a rapist, a sadist, that he was responsible for a cemetery's worth of the mutilated bodies found in New York Harbor.

Finally Carrick recalled that no one knew where he was . . . and no one really cared. He was afraid to ask, but he was afraid not to ask. At last, he painfully cleared his throat and whispered, "What do you want?"

In a warm, encouraging, satisfied voice, Osgood said, "It seems you believe that your mother knows where your father's fortune is hidden. . . ."

TWELVE

Hannah ran away from the house, up the cliff walk, down the cliff walk, her shoes hitting the concrete at a steady rate. The cold wind blew in gusts off the ocean, the waves crashed against the cliffs, the salt air lured her onward. She kept an eye on the swiftly moving clouds, knowing only too well that she didn't want to be caught two miles from the house when the projected autumn storm blew in.

But she didn't want to go back, either. The last-minute arrangements for the Halloween party, the pressure of knowing Mrs. Manly's secret, the scrutiny of Balfour House itself made each run more important than the last. She'd begun to slim down; her jogging pants were loose around the waist, and not merely because the elastic was old. Warmed by the exercise, she stopped at the first-mile marker, slipped off her hoodie, and tied it around her waist. She scanned the landscape; she was alone, except for one tourist sitting on the highest point on the property, a pair of binoculars in his hands. The Maine coastline was rich in wildlife, attracting birders from all over the world. This guy was hardy, sitting out here with a knit hat pulled low over his ears and a huge down coat wrapped around his body, watching the seagulls wheel and dip on the breeze. She waved, never thinking he'd notice anything so insignificant as a human being.

He startled her by waving back.

Maybe he wasn't as big a geek as she had imagined.

She started off again, fixing her sights on the top of the next hill—when her earpiece beeped. No one ever called her while she was on her run, so this couldn't be good.

She slowed her pace, pulled her cell out of her pocket and looked at the ID, expecting to see Balfour House. But no, although the number tripped a vague memory in her brain. She touched her earpiece. "Hello?"

"Hannah? Is this a good time?" The deep voice sounded vaguely familiar, too, warm and soft, like a tender hand sliding down her spine.

Then she pegged it. "Trent. Trent Sansoucy."

"You remembered. I'm flattered."

He must have called the house and gotten her cell number. But why?

His voice changed, became concerned. "Are you sick? You sound like you're having a heart attack."

She laughed and sped up again. "I'm exercising."

"You're gasping."

"I'm on a run. Gasping is a good thing. What can I do for you?"

"Susan Stevens is available now, and I'd like to make an appointment for her to come in and do her magic." He was all business, his East Coast–accented voice sounding a little more Boston than before. "I'd like to get her in there before the party."

"Me, too. How soon can we have her?"

"Tomorrow, if you like."

"Tomorrow is perfect. Both Mrs. Manly and I are uneasy with the situation as it is."

He went on the alert—she could tell by his voice. "Why? Have you seen anything? Heard anything?"

"Um . . . no." She was not going to tell him she thought the house was watching her. He'd probably decide she was crazy, because, well . . . it was crazy. But despite her lectures to herself, that itchy, creeping feeling of being watched had never faded.

He must have heard her hesitation, and said sternly, "You should inform me of whatever you suspect."

So she told him the easy part, the factual part. "I suspect that with the government accusing Mrs. Manly of hiding information about Nathan Manly and his fortune, there is the possibility that someone might want to pressure Mrs. Manly into revealing what she knows, and they might do it violently." She didn't add that Carrick Manly was her top suspect. Most people hadn't glimpsed that slimy side of Carrick, and even she didn't think he would actually resort to bloodshed.

The trouble was, when she'd met him, she had never suspected he would want Hannah to spy on his mother, either, and be willing to blackmail her to get his way.

"I'm concerned about that, too. I had hoped that hadn't occurred to you."

"I'm glad that you didn't dismiss my fears." She labored up another hill. "Sometimes I wonder if I'm being paranoid."

"Just because you're paranoid, doesn't mean they're not after you."

She chuckled, as he meant her to.

"Truthfully, when it comes to danger, women tend to ignore their instincts when they shouldn't." Trent sounded so warmly concerned, she got that hand-down-her-spine feeling again. "Is there anything specific that bothers you?"

What the hell? She might as well tell him. He'd probably heard dumber things. "The house is old and it creaks in the wind, so I hear footsteps that aren't there. It's more than the money. It's the whole *Nathan Manly hasn't been seen since he disappeared* thing." No matter how hard Hannah tried, she hadn't been able to forget Mrs. Manly's conviction that someone had killed Nathan, and that he was planning his vengeance. "I guess you could say I'm afraid of ghosts."

"You're afraid of Nathan Manly's ghost? I thought he was still alive somewhere."

"That's what they say, but nobody knows for sure, do they?" Hannah had said too much, and she reined herself in, going back to the facts. "I'm more afraid of intruders, especially since I'd be the one defending Mrs. Manly."

"Surely the servants would step in. The butler?"

"Nelson? No."

Trent was silent for a long moment. "Then you're right to feel uneasy. So I'll send Susan at ten tomorrow?"

"Ten would be good." She could make sure Mrs. Manly got dressed, ate her breakfast and took her meds, before Susan showed up.

"We'll get the security set up as soon as possible."

"Thank you." Hannah liked that he didn't make her feel stupid.

"So . . . how far do you run?"

How far do I run? She repeated the question silently to herself. Trent wasn't getting off the phone. He was making conversation.

She relaxed and smiled. Was Mrs. Manly right? Their last conversation had been flirtatious. Had he enjoyed it? "I run two to four miles a day, depending on the weather and how much time I have."

"The weather doesn't look too good today." She heard the breeze whistle across his mouthpiece; apparently he was outside, too.

"Good point." She looked out at the clouds, tall, purple, and menacing on the horizon. She turned and headed back. Three miles, up and down slopes, through the grove, and along the cliff, to the house. In her distress about Mrs. Manly's account, she hadn't been paying attention. She'd come too far. She was going to get drenched.

"Why did you run so far?"

"Sometimes I need to get away."

"She's a difficult woman. Mrs. Manly, I mean. My father always said so."

Hannah bristled at his assumption that Mrs. Manly

was the one who drove her from Balfour House. "She's had far too many disappointments in her life"—her husband, her son—"and far too much responsibility on her shoulders. It's given her a hard shell, but on the inside, she's a good woman."

"It's good of you to defend her." He flailed around like a guy who knew he'd put his foot wrong, but didn't know why or how. "Does she remind you of your mother?"

"God, no. My mother was . . ." Hannah laughed aloud. "If you looked up *joie de vivre* in the dictionary, there was a picture of my mother. Life wasn't good to her, either, but she never let it get her down."

"She sounds great." He still sounded cautious.

Hannah supposed she had stomped on him a little too firmly, so she kept chatting. "She insisted we travel, have fun, enjoy ourselves when we could. We went to the Renaissance festival every year, and she always bought me a present—a scarf, or a ring, or a face carved into a knot of wood. Mom spoke French fluently, loved the French culture, worshipped French cooking. So we ate out once a week at a little café that specialized in French country cooking. We always split a dessert afterward—*mousse au chocolat*, or an éclair, or *crèpes à la Normande*. Vacations were usually a car trip to a bed-and-breakfast in Pennsylvania or somewhere close, but one year, when I was fourteen, one of her doctors won a trip to Provence, and he said he didn't have time to go, so he gave it to her."

"Just like that, he gave it to her."

There was an edge to his voice. Cynicism, she

guessed. But she assured him, "He was a good guy. I think Dr. McAllister did it because he knew how much Mom wanted to go. I think it was the best time of her life. I know it was the best time of mine." Without warning, Hannah choked up.

The memory of that time flashed so brightly in her mind: sitting in a small bistro, smelling the blooming lavender, watching her mother turn her face up to the warm sun and smile. . . .

Hannah stopped running, turned and faced the oncoming storm, hoped the ragged edge of her breathing sounded like panting.

Trent waited just long enough for the constriction in her chest to ease. "What happened to her?" He didn't sound curious; he sounded kind and as if he really wanted to know.

That hand again, caressing her back, easing her pain.

Directly below her, the thin slip of sandy beach stood exposed by low tide. The dark turmoil of the waves called to Hannah, and a narrow path twisted its way through the rocks and the bearberry. Defying nature, she stepped off the paved path and into the wild. "She suffered from rheumatoid arthritis." Hannah slipped a little in the gravel, caught herself, kept going.

"Hannah?" Trent sounded worried. "Are you still running?"

"I am really, really running." The beach got closer. The wind picked up. The ocean got wilder. And Hannah kept talking. "Mom's last hip replacement was difficult. She'd had so many, you know, and we always existed on the edge of disaster. Her boss was not under-standing—in fact, Mr. Washington would have fit well as a character in a Dickens novel—and Mom went back to work too soon." The path ended three feet above the sand. Hannah jumped. Landed. Let the brief triumph sweep away the bitterness of her words. "She was run-ning his errands, fell down his stairs, and died."

"Good God, that's horrible." Trent sounded blankly astonished. "How old were you?"

Hannah walked up the beach, the damp sand hard-packed beneath her shoes. "Sixteen, but believe it or not, I was quite capable and survived very well." She was proud of that.

"How? How does a sixteen-year-old with no parents manage to get herself a bachelor's degree in nursing?"

"Scholarships, mostly. Mr. Washington was per-suaded to settle a small sum on me, also, but that barely covered my living expenses. He was a respected lawyer, you know." The spray splashed on her face. The clouds grew taller.

"You have to be resentful. You must want revenge, if not on him, then on other men who are indifferent bastards."

She didn't like that. Trent sounded like some radio personality with a pop-psychology degree. "It's hard to avoid hoping that someday Karma catches up with Mr. Washington, but I don't dwell on it. My mother had her reasons to be bitter, too, but she refused. She said, 'We have to *live* a little, make ourselves happy, or what's the use of all the suffering?' And she was right. I know she was." Ahead of her, the rock cliff, dimpled with shallow caves, swung far out into the waves. Hannah didn't want to take the short, steep path that led to the top, back to civilization, to Balfour House, to Mrs. Manly, her illnesses, her challenging request and Hannah's unbearable responsibilities.

But what else could Hannah do? She was running out of room on the beach. The storm surge was driving the tide higher and higher. If she stayed here, she'd be swept away.

So she climbed.

"I hear the ocean. Are you still on the path?"

"Why wouldn't I be?" She glanced up when she stepped onto the pavement, and caught sight of the birdwatcher, standing on the rocks on the highest spot on the estate, his binoculars sweeping the area. The binoculars found her and stopped, almost as if he'd been looking for her. Then they moved on.

She wanted to tell the fool that with this storm, even the seabirds were going to ground. But he was too far away, and as she watched, he seated himself again and scanned the horizon.

The first drops of cold rain splattered her forehead. She untied her hoodie, stuck her arms in it, and started running even before she had pulled up the hood.

To Trent, she said, "Thank you for asking about my mother. I don't get to talk about her very often. When she died, my friends were afraid to say much for fear I'd cry, and then everyone forgot her, except me. So this has been pleasant, if a little one-sided."

"It's been interesting. I feel like I have insight into why you became a nurse."

"Yes, there's no mystery about me."

"That's not true. A lot of women would have figured they'd done their stint and swear never to care for another patient."

"Instead, I want to save the world." A gust of wind pushed her sideways. She stumbled, righted herself, and kept running. "Dr. McAllister told me I'd have to get over that or I'd burn out, and he's right. I'm twenty-four, my last three patients were elderly and passed on in my care, and I can't take much more. My next patient will be younger, one I can teach to live, not help to die."

"Yes, it can't be good . . . to have to help them die." His voice sounded muffled, like he was talking through a cloth. "Will Mrs. Manly die soon?"

"She's in better shape than when I came here," Hannah answered tartly. Then she sighed. "But no, she's not going to live forever. She doesn't even want to."

It was raining harder, and she wasn't sure what he said, but it sounded like, "Is that what you tell yourself?"

With a roar, the heavens opened. Rain sluiced down in buckets, pummeling her, filling her shoes with water, saturating her clothes. "I gotta go," she shouted.

"Talk to you next time," he shouted back.

She shut her phone and ran as hard as she could toward Balfour House.

He might be bald. He might be short. He might be overweight. But she hadn't enjoyed a conversation so much in years.

Of course, she'd been the one doing the talking.

Despite the rain that dripped off her nose and chin, she smiled. Next time they talked, it would be more balanced. She'd ask a few questions herself.

Next time.

In an excess of good spirits, she leaped up the stairs onto the porch, and hugged herself in delight. He had said he would talk to her *next time*.

Turning, she looked out over the Balfour estate and saw the birder leaping off the rocks and running toward the paved path.

She hoped he got inside before lightning struck.

To get back into Balfour House unseen, Gabriel had to take the long way around, staying out of sight of the windows until his last dash into the back door and up the stairs. In his room, he shook like a dog, then headed for the bathroom. He put the binoculars on the vanity and dropped his sopping-wet clothes on the cracked linoleum floor.

My God, the North was miserable in the winter. Worse, Northerners would look you in the eye and tell you this wasn't winter—this was autumn.

He flipped the shower on hot, and when the steam was rising in the tub, he climbed in. He was so cold his toes hurt, he shivered so hard his bones rattled, but he had to say he'd learned a lot today.

He'd learned why Hannah was a natural with arthritis patients. He'd learned how she'd learned the craft of extortion, and why she thought it was such an easy way to make money. He'd even learned why she figured she was justified. If she was telling the truth—and from the research he'd done, she was—that deal with her mother's death had been a bitch for a sixteen-year-old to handle.

But he'd also learned she sincerely missed her mother. Hannah had liked her mother. She had admired her mother. Her mother, who gave birth to her without benefit of matrimony. Her mother, who accepted a trip given to her by her doctor. But still . . . didn't her affection for her mother mean that she had more than a shriveled soul, bereft of emotion?

Yeah. It did.

He'd learned something else, too.

He'd learned that he liked the way she moved. Even viewed from a distance through binocular lenses, she showed an athlete's prowess and endurance.

But also . . . she admitted Mrs. Manly would die soon.

Okay. She looked like the woman of his dreams.

Yet he couldn't trust her. And he didn't dare love her.

But he couldn't wait to talk to her again.

THIRTEEN

Hannah had come to detest Balfour House.

The autumn wind tossed dried leaves against the windows of the study and moaned around the eaves. A steady cold rain dripped off the roof, and far below, the ocean roared with the passing of the first storm of the season. The clouds dimmed any light from the afternoon sun, and Hannah shivered as the cold crept through the gray stone walls and into the study, where she and Mrs. Manly studied the checklist one more time.

And someone was watching her.

A knock sounded on the door to the study.

"Come in," Mrs. Manly called.

Susan Stevens stuck her head inside. "Mrs. Manly, I've done my check of the house, and I have my report."

"Good." Mrs. Manly glanced at Hannah, pleased and expectant. Surely now they would hear the truth—that Carrick was having their every move electronically scrutinized, hoping to hear the truth about his father's fortune. "Come in."

Susan Stevens didn't look anything like Hannah's idea of a security expert. She was probably thirty-five, tall and willowy, with brown eyes and wavy brown hair she pulled into a careless twist at the back of her neck. She applied makeup so flawlessly Hannah wasn't surprised to discover she had been a former beauty contestant, and although she wore jeans and T-shirts and, when working outside in the nippy air, sweatshirts, she made each piece of clothing look as if she'd bought it from a top designer.

Mrs. Manly turned her wheelchair to face Susan. "Have a seat. Would you like some coffee?"

"That would be fabulous." Susan's nose was attractively rosy. "It gets cold early up here."

"Hannah, ring for a fresh pot," Mrs. Manly ordered. As Hannah spoke to the hovering servant, Mrs. Manly told Susan, "It's the end of October. Of course it's cold."

"I'm from Houston. It won't get cold in Texas until Thanksgiving. Maybe." Susan smiled fondly. "Sometimes it doesn't freeze all winter."

"I myself like the four seasons," Mrs. Manly intoned.

"Winter is overrated," Susan said pleasantly.

Hannah laughed. "I've thought that myself." Especially in February when the snow turned to ice on the streets and the wind ripped at her flesh.

A discreet knock sounded at the door, and Hannah retrieved the freshly brewed coffee. As Hannah poured, Susan opened the folder she held and handed Mrs. Manly a piece of paper.

Mrs. Manly accepted it. "What brought you up here to work for Sansoucy Security?"

"I go where I'm needed." Susan accepted the cup from Hannah and added sugar and so much cream the brew turned a swirling tan.

"But Maine seems like quite a change for you." Mrs. Manly watched Susan so closely, Hannah wondered what she saw.

"The advantage of being single again is that I can see the country as I wish," Susan said firmly. "But I promise you, I will be here for your party."

"As a guard?" Hannah was surprised. "I thought you were the technical expert."

"I am. I work every angle I can. In this business, it's best to be indispensible. Now." Susan leaned forward. "Here's my report, with three different plans to increase security here at Balfour House."

Susan spoke enthusiastically about placing cameras and microphones outside, at all the entrances, and in the corridors and public rooms, but Mrs. Manly wasn't listening. Hannah could tell she wasn't listening. Hannah had the feeling the same variety of expressions crossed her face as crossed Mrs. Manly's: first expectant, then puzzled, and finally, when Susan persistently said nothing about finding cameras and microphones hidden in the corridors and the rooms, disappointed.

When Susan finished, she leaned back and sipped her coffee. "Of course, I know our clients are always interested in options, but in this case, where the home is historical and filled with valuable antiques, I would recommend the full security package. Frankly, I'm amazed that you haven't had any break-ins."

"I just . . . I thought we did have some security cameras. During your evaluation, did you not find any?" Mrs. Manly asked.

"No." Susan sounded politely uncertain. "You have an outmoded alarm system, but it hasn't functioned for years."

"I see." Mrs. Manly placed the bids on her desk. "I'll take your suggestions under advisement. Thank you so much, Susan, and I'll see you in three days, if not sooner."

Susan turned a blank face to her.

"On Halloween," Mrs. Manly reminded her.

"Yes. The party." Susan put down her cup and stood. "I'll be the one dressed as a security guard—in a dark suit." She laughed.

"Make sure you wear a mask," Mrs. Manly warned. "The guests won't be allowed in without costumes, and I expect the security guards to respect my wishes as far as they are able."

Susan looked dismayed.

"Don't worry," Mrs. Manly said. "I'll have extra masks."

As Susan left, Mrs. Manly turned to Hannah. "Some people hate to join in the spirit of Halloween."

"Some people do."

Mrs. Manly watched the door Susan had closed behind her. "What do you think, Hannah? Is she incompetent? Did she not notice the cameras and microphones?"

"She certainly gives the air of knowing what she's doing." Hannah picked up the paper with the bids on it, and scanned the list. "This seems complete. I don't know what else she could add."

"Does she have any reason to conceal the fact we're being watched?"

"I don't know what it would be. Carrick could have bribed her, but he would have had to bribe Sansoucy Security, too, and that seems so . . . far-fetched."

"Farsighted," Mrs. Manly corrected. "Furthermore, I know Carrick. He would never hire a small local firm. He always wants the best, and obviously the best could never be *here*."

"And the truth of the matter is . . . *we* think she's telling the truth." When Mrs. Manly looked inquiringly at her, Hannah said, "We're talking freely as we haven't since we first spoke up on the cliff above the sea."

Mrs. Manly sighed. "You're right. But . . ."

"But why was the hair standing up on the back of my neck right now? Why do I constantly feel as if someone was watching me? If it's not some flunky of Carrick's spying on us . . . then who is it? The ghost of some Balfour ancestor?" Hannah thought she was making a joke.

But she shivered. No wonder Halloween took place at the onset of winter. It didn't make sense, but something about the failing sun made a person hark back to the ancestors' memories of ghoulies and ghosties and long-legged beasties. No matter what Susan said, Hannah was convinced some dark *thing*—some memory locked away in the attic—held sway in this house.

"Nonsense." Mrs. Manly chuckled. "You really are susceptible to atmosphere, aren't you?"

Outside in the foyer, the door opened and shut, then opened and shut again. They heard a murmur of voices; then Nelson stepped in and announced, "Mr. Manly has arrived."

"Mr. Manly?" Color washed out of Mrs. Manly's face. She placed her hand over her heart, and Hannah realized she wasn't as unaffected as she pretended.

Then Carrick stepped over the threshold.

Mrs. Manly collapsed back into her chair. "Oh. It's just you, Carrick." Turning on Nelson like a ferocious guard dog, she said, "Mr. Nathan Manly is gone, disappeared God knows where. My son is Carrick. Just Carrick. Remember that. Call him that."

Nelson lost a little color, too. "Yes, Mrs. Manly."

"Take a chill pill, Mom." Carrick strolled into the room with such an air of authority, he might have been a commander going into battle. "It's not like Father is coming back here. He's drinking champagne on a beach somewhere, surrounded by babes."

How had Hannah ever thought this callous jerk was attractive?

Her feelings must have shown on her face, because he said, "What? In a week, Mother has to appear in federal court to testify that she had nothing to do with stealing the fortune. She might as well get used to having the whole scandal dragged out into the public eye again."

But no one got the best of Mrs. Manly. As he leaned down to kiss her, she pinched his chin and turned his face toward the light.

His left eye, left cheek, and nose were swollen and yellow, purple, and green with a fading bruise.

"Who did you anger?" Mrs. Manly asked.

"I was in a fight." He was favoring his left side.

And Hannah noted he didn't seem as well put together as he had—he hadn't shaved in two days, and his pants looked as if he'd slept in them. Going to the window, she looked out at the auto court. A Camry sat there, its small trunk gaping as one of the footmen removed two suitcases and an overnight bag.

So this time, Carrick hadn't driven a borrowed Porsche.

Mrs. Manly turned his knuckles to the light, but they were pristine. "Too bad you didn't land any blows."

An angry flush climbed in his face, and he folded his hands away from her. He took two steps away, and looked around the study, strewn with well-organized piles of papers, contracts for the caterer, the decorator, the extra staff, the food supplier. "Wow, Mother. You're out of your room. I had no idea Miss Grey would be such a little miracle worker."

"She has been the best present you ever brought me." Mrs. Manly pretended to think. "Wait. I believe she's the only present you ever brought me. And of course, I have to pay her salary."

He gave Hannah a shrug and such a friendly smile she wanted to edge closer to Mrs. Manly and safety.

"You're early for the party. It's not for three days." Mrs. Manly sat perfectly still, watching her son as he paced around the room, examining the contracts.

"I thought I could help," he said.

"We've got everything under control," Mrs. Manly answered. "Don't we, Hannah dear?"

"We do." Hannah wished Mrs. Manly didn't use her to poke at her son. "But I'm sure as the time gets closer, emergencies will occur, and we'll be grateful for Carrick's help."

"I wouldn't count on it," Mrs. Manly said. "He's not fond of work. But he is fond of luxury. As a matter of fact, I would venture to guess that's why he's here today. He ran out of money. Didn't you, Carrick, my boy?"

He whirled toward his mother. "It's nothing I can't recover. It's not like I'm going to ask you for capital. Not when you're spending"—he picked up the decorating contract—"twenty-five thousand dollars on transforming this old rock pile into Sleeping Beauty's castle."

"It's my money," Mrs. Manly said.

"You don't have any money, at least not enough to throw this party *and* support Balfour House over the next year." He attacked like a man about to lose everything he valued. "*What* are you thinking?"

"I'm thinking I'm going to be living in prison next year," Mrs. Manly said flatly, "and the fate of Balfour House will not be in my hands."

"It doesn't have to be that way." He paced forward and knelt at her feet. "If you would just tell me where Father's fortune is—"

"I don't know," Mrs. Manly said.

"Why don't I believe you?" His voice rose.

"I don't know." Mrs. Manly watched him without pity.

"I don't believe you. You *do* know something." He stood, abandoning his pleading, and towered over his mother, his hands clenching over and over.

Hannah couldn't stand that. Enough was enough. She pushed him with a firm hand.

He swung on her, his fists half rising, the bruises on his face bright against the pale fury of his complexion.

He was a bully, and he scared her. She wanted to back off, run away. But she couldn't. She couldn't leave Mrs. Manly to him. So she lifted her chin and stepped between them.

For a long moment, Carrick stared at her, his face ugly, and she thought . . . she wondered if he would hit her. And if he did, if he would stop.

Then his face cleared, and he acted wounded. Wounded and impressively incredulous. "For God's sake, Hannah, I have her best interests at heart. She's my mother."

Hannah took Mrs. Manly's wrist. As she expected, her patient's pulse was racing. "Carrick, excuse us. I need to take her to her room."

"I would never hurt her," he protested again.

As Hannah pushed her from the room, Mrs. Manly said over her shoulder, "Not until you have that information out of me."

FOURTEEN

Gabriel stared at the monitor.

Not until you have that information out of me. What the hell did that mean?

Carrick stepped into the foyer and yelled after the two departing women, "What the hell does that mean, Mother?"

Mrs. Manly laughed. Cackled, really.

Carrick muttered a curse, went back into the study, and slammed the door.

He was younger than Gabriel, and he'd been spoiled by wealth, then given a hard knock with his father's defection, but . . . *grow up.*

Hannah pushed Mrs. Manly to the elevator. As the doors shut, she asked, "Why do you do that?"

"Do what?"

"Practically tell him you have what he wants."

Mrs. Manly laughed briefly. "He's going to believe what he wants, and this way, he's always on his toes."

"Or on mine." The elevator doors opened onto the second floor, and Hannah pushed Mrs. Manly down the corridor toward her room.

Gabriel had been listening in on their conversations for twelve days now, and except for the two calls to Hannah, he'd been bored out of his mind. Party planning was not his thing, and the two-hour discussion of which shade of pink to use on the climbing roses almost put him in a coma.

Now Susan had reassured them, told them no one was spying on them, and in ten minutes he'd been more entertained—and given more information—than in all of the preceding twelve days.

They entered the bedroom and went through the ritual to which Gabriel had become so accustomed. Mrs. Manly used the bathroom. Hannah took her blood sugar and gave her her medications. Mrs. Manly climbed wearily onto the bed. As Hannah straightened her covers, Mrs. Manly said, "Hannah, don't falter now. There's too much at stake here. A billion dollars. A thousand lives."

Gabriel hitched his chair closer.

Did she say what he thought she'd said? Was Mrs. Manly insinuating she'd told Hannah Grey where the money was and how to access it? When? How? Before he'd arrived?

No. No, because if she had, Hannah would be gone. Wouldn't she?

That was the assumption he'd been working with, because once she had the information she'd come for, what reason would she have had to stay?

"If you don't stop letting Carrick upset you so much, you're going to have heart failure."

"As long as it's fatal, I don't care." Mrs. Manly took a deep breath. "Then I wouldn't have to go to court."

"Yes, but then Carrick has won," Hannah teased. "And all this party planning will be for naught."

"You, young lady, are too smart for your own good." Grasping Hannah's shoulders, Mrs. Manly pulled her close. She looked into her eyes so earnestly Gabriel was riveted. "Do you remember?"

"Every word." Hannah was just as earnest. "I won't forget."

"Then I can rest." Mrs. Manly released her.

The two women leaned back, took breaths as if they'd been riveted by an over-the-top movie spectacular—*Titanic* or the newest *Batman*.

Gabriel thought hard about what Mrs. Manly had actually said. She obviously despised poor Carrick, and from what Gabriel knew about her personality, she would taunt her son merely for the pleasure it would give her. As for what she'd said to Hannah . . . in a few days, Mrs. Manly faced the feds. She might be talking about the fortune without knowing anything about it.

Or . . . she might know, and be planning to confess all to the government.

If that was the case, the federal prosecutors would cut a deal, and that would take a load off Carrick's mind. And apparently Carrick was starting to crack under the pressure, because he had been a thorough ass to his mother.

On the other hand, if she did know how to access the fortune, and she had given Hannah the details, and Hannah was still here . . . did that mean Hannah had been the victim of bad press from the Dresser family and from Carrick?

"Hannah, I want you to be careful. Very careful."

"I will, Mrs. Manly," Hannah said in a soothing voice.

"I know you think I'm a foolish old woman, but the rage in Carrick goes all the way to the bone." Mrs. Manly closed her eyes as if tired and ashamed. "That's a trait that runs in the family. If he thinks you have betrayed him . . ."

"I'll be careful. I promise."

Gabriel waited to see if they said any more, but Mrs. Manly relaxed, and in a minute a rattling snore shook the room.

Hannah smiled fondly, as if that noise comforted her.

Maybe it did. She waited for the moments when Mrs. Manly was asleep and she was free to sit and read, or watch TV, or do as she was doing right now, and stare, troubled, into space.

In Gabriel's business, if something walked like a duck and quacked like a duck, it almost always was a duck. Worse, he knew very well how much his desire for Hannah made him want her to be as clean and pretty and honorable as she appeared.

It was possible. That was the other thing he'd learned in this business. *Anything* was possible.

There was movement on the monitor that scanned the corridor outside his bedroom.

Carrick limped toward the door, irritation radiating from him.

Little brother really looked like his ass had been kicked. What had he done to deserve that?

Gabriel thought he knew. He'd seen the expensive suits, known about the Manhattan apartment, suspected the wild lifestyle. The kid was learning the hard way that a man had to work for what he got.

Turning down the sound, Gabriel faced the door.

Carrick slammed the door wide, stepped in, and slammed the door shut. "Have you found anything yet? Have you?"

"Nothing definitive." Because he *didn't* know anything definitive, and there was no point in raising Carrick's hopes when he had a chance, with Susan's intervention, to discover the truth.

"What is taking so damn long? Have you missed something?"

"It's all being recorded."

Carrick kept attacking. "Nelson says you're the one who sits and listens. You never allow someone else to take over—"

"This is a delicate situation, and in this case, I don't trust anyone else."

"There's been no progress." Carrick paced up and down in front of Gabriel. "How long do you think I'm going to pay you for no progress?"

Gabriel had only so much patience, and Carrick had just reached the end of it. "You haven't paid me at all," he said precisely.

Carrick stopped and stood still, staring into space, his fists spasming. "Is that *all* anyone cares about?"

So Gabriel was right. The boy was living beyond his means, and someone had taken exception. Reining in his irritation, he said, "I am monitoring the situation. I can't *make* them talk—"

Carrick leaped on that. "If I provoke Mother some more—"

"—although now I think we've got a chance." Briefly, Gabriel filled him in on the changes Susan had wrought.

"Good." Carrick limped to a chair and sat.

"Yes." Mindful of Hannah's worry, Gabriel continued. "But if you cause your mother a heart attack, we're lost. Dr. Thalmann gave Miss Grey digoxin to administer in case of heart failure, and a tranquilizer to calm her in case of distress."

"Really?" Carrick hitched his chair closer and stared. "A tranquilizer."

Something about the way Carrick watched the monitor made Gabriel say, "You have to face the fact this might not turn out the way you want."

Carrick glanced at Gabriel. "You don't know what you're saying."

"I'm saying that there's nothing you can do, or I can do, if your mother doesn't know where the fortune or your father is, and there's *really* nothing we can do if she does know, and refuses to reveal the information." Gabriel had never given older brother–type advice, but he was compelled to now. "Think, Carrick. You'll never forgive yourself if you pressure your mother and something fatal occurs."

From the cold stare Carrick turned on him, Gabriel realized the advice was not appreciated. "I'm not accountable to you. You're simply the hired help."

But Gabriel didn't put up with that shit from anyone. "This hired help doesn't have to work here, and if you're planning violence—"

"Violence? Me?" Carrick's head snapped back, and his eyes gleamed with fury. "You've been listening to her. You've been listening to Hannah. Has she seduced you, too? Have you lost your mind?"

Okay. It was time to calm things down. "Are you sure of your facts? I haven't seen any evidence of Hannah's guilt."

"Facts?" Carrick scrambled to his feet. "Let me remind you that she lost her nursing certificate for sleeping with and possibly killing one of her patients. Now she's working on my mother, trying to weasel information out of her so she can take the fortune and run, leaving my mother to take the fall. Have you even been listening in on their conversations? Should I hire someone else to take over?"

"No." No, Gabriel would not allow another man to observe Hannah at work, while she slept . . . and while she bathed.

Had she seduced him? Yes, without even knowing he was there. And he . . . he had become the worst sort of pervert, watching and wanting her. Wanting a woman who didn't know he existed.

Gabriel stared into Carrick's eyes, enforcing his will

on his despairing, desperate younger brother, calming him, bringing him back to normal. "I assure you, I've been listening and watching, and I'll continue to listen and watch. If you'd like to review the video, I'd be glad to transmit it to your computer." He paused and let Carrick digest how much time was involved in all these days of video. "In the meantime, consider this fact. The closer we get to the party, the closer we are to the court date, the more pressure your mother feels, and the more likely that she'll break. You have to be patient."

Gabriel's efforts must have worked, for Carrick took a long breath. "You're right. I know you're right." He placed his hand on Gabriel's arm, and his fingers convulsed. "I just . . . if Mother goes to prison, I don't know what will become of her."

With a conviction formed from watching Melinda Manly day and night, Gabriel said, "She's a sharp old bird. If she can help it, she won't let it go that far."

"She's a stubborn old bird. She'll push it as far as she can. To her death, if necessary."

"No one ever takes it that far."

"You don't know my mother."

FIFTEEN

The phone rang in Hannah's bedroom, and she turned from her book and stared at the old-fashioned black corded princess phone.

It never rang. Who would call her?

Then she rushed to pick it up. Mrs. Manly must need something.

"Hannah. Hi, it's Trent."

"Trent?" She took the phone away from her ear and looked at it.

"Is this a bad time?" His rich voice with that distinctive accent stirred the hair at the base of her neck.

"No. Is there something wrong? With the security, I mean." Because she was already in bed for the night, but that didn't mean she couldn't leap up and get dressed in a hurry. Nurses were like cops. They rose to the occasion.

"Everything's fine." He sounded soothing, gentle. "My job is not the only reason I call a beautiful woman."

That stopped her headlong rush toward the closet.

"This is a bad time," he said.

"No. No!" She sank back on the bed and thought . . . a beautiful woman. To the best of her knowledge, no one had ever described her as a beautiful woman. It made sense that the man who did had never seen her. "You don't know what I look like."

"I'm in security. I know your deepest secrets." Now he sounded droll and self-deprecating.

"Right. I forgot about that." She looked in the mirror over the old-fashioned chest of drawers and grimaced. She had washed her face clean of makeup, she wore her oldest, thinnest nightgown, and her hair looked like a bird had nested in it. Yet the call had put a warm glow in her cheeks.

"Besides, I can imagine what you look like, can't I?" he asked.

Since she'd been imagining what he looked like every time they'd talked, she had to agree. "I suppose you can, but if you've come up with beautiful, you're going to be sadly disappointed when you see me at the party."

"I doubt that." His voice deepened. "Do you know the fantasies I've had about nurses?"

"I can imagine, and they're not true," she said with severe finality.

"No. Please. Don't crush my dreams."

She laughed.

He seemed fine with that, waiting until she finished before asking, "What are you up to now?"

"I was . . ." She looked around. She sat in the canopy bed, surrounded by travel guides, while the TV rumbled along on the Weather Channel. She grabbed the remote and muted the sound. "I was trying to get a forecast for the party tomorrow night."

"The local station is calling for cold and crisp on Halloween. That'll make my life easier, I can tell you. No umbrellas to fool with, and there's nothing more miserable than standing outside, watching the cars arrive, while a cold rain drips down your neck."

As he meant her to, she grinned. "Not exactly the glamorous life I'd imagined for a security agent."

"Glamorous?" He snorted. "Would you call babysitting some rich girl as she rocks from one nightclub to another glamorous?"

"No, that sounds difficult."

"Horrendous. Glamorous? Like spending hours tailing a cheating husband to get photos of his newest affair, knowing all the while he's going to buy off his disgruntled wife with a jewel?"

Was that how it had been with her father? "Never did they make a jewel big enough to let me forgive that."

"I don't get it, either." He seemed to remember something else. "Oh, and let's not forget the glamorous times spent trying to break into a sealed account on a computer."

She stiffened. Was that a random comment, or was he fishing for information? "Why would you do that?"

"You'd be surprised at the criminals who keep all their records on their computers. I've helped convict several embezzlers that way." He sounded amused and not at all personal.

Sp this was her chance to discover his trade secrets. "How *do* you break into a sealed account?"

"First we try the usual passwords people use. You know, stuff like their names done in numbers or their birthdays typed in backward."

Mrs. Manley's code was much more complex, but still Hannah needed more details. "So I shouldn't use my birthday typed in backward?"

"Definitely not. If it's not a birthday typed backward, we have to use the descrambler on the computer." He sounded smug. "That always gets us in."

"But then you have to find the right files, right?" She chewed on her thumbnail as she waited for the answer.

"Half the time the files are right there on the desktop, cleverly named something like Accounts or Figures." She could almost see him shaking his head in disbelief. Then he recalled himself. "Listen, you don't want to hear about my boring job."

She did. She really did. But how much information could Trent give her? There was no real help to be had here. In this situation, with so much money waiting to be released, she could depend only on herself.

"So I'll tell you a secret."

She leaned forward, crossed her arms over her uplifted knees. "Yes?"

"This job is a cover for my real profession."

"Which is?"

"I'm actually a British secret agent. You may have heard of me." He paused dramatically. "Bond. James Bond."

She found herself sitting, book forgotten in her hand, smiling foolishly. "The name doesn't ring a bell."

"Damn. I was afraid of that." He audibly brightened. "I suppose I'll have to take you on one of my thrilling adventures before you'll know me."

"I love thrilling adventures."

"I'll arrange for one. But don't tell anyone the truth about me, or I'll have to kill you."

"My lips are sealed." She picked up the *Eyewitness Book of Great Britain*. "But only if our thrilling adventure is in Cornwall."

"Cornwall? Maine?"

"No, Cornwall, England. Isn't England where James Bond is from?"

His voice suddenly changed, became crisp and upper-crust British. "Right you are. From England, that's me. Dashing, debonair—"

"Dapper?"

"There's no need to call names."

She giggled.

"What's your interest in Cornwall?" He really did a *great* British accent. If she hadn't know better, she would have sworn he really was English.

"I've always wanted to go there: Land's End, grand storms, and King Arthur. The Maine coast seems as if it's *similar* to Cornwall."

"I would love to see you in Cornwall, standing on the rocks, looking out to sea, with the wind blowing through your hair."

She lifted her head as if she could feel the storm's

rampage. She ran her fingers through her hair, and imagined what it would be like to be there as the waves dashed themselves on the rocks . . . and be there with him.

"Of course"—he dropped the British accent and sounded like himself again, very Northeastern—"I'd love to see you anywhere."

She dropped her chin and rubbed her hands over her bare arms, her brief fantasy over. She had to remember, no matter how great this guy's voice was and how well he flirted, he was old and bald and overweight and wore paisley-print socks.

And married. He was probably married.

"I suppose the best part of all that standing around at parties is the food. I mean, the hosts do let you eat, don't they?" *Subtle. That was subtle, Hannah.*

His voice turned very serious. "*I* don't let me eat. When it comes to fat content, the food these caterers serve at parties is as bad as fast food, and while part of this job is making sure the bad guys don't get in, the other part is being able to chase them down if they do show up. Fitness is a big deal for me and everyone in my company."

"Your dad's company," she reminded him.

"Yeah. My dad's company."

And there she had it. Trent was buff.

But probably still old, married and bald.

Although not too old, or how would he chase down those bad guys?

As if she'd asked the question, he said, "I'm thirty-eight. I figure I've got another fifteen years of knowing

I can handle the field work—as long as I don't get hurt, I mean. Then I'll reevaluate." His voice turned humorous. "Of course, if I get married, my wife might have something to say about my hours."

"Oh. You're not married?" She thought she sounded light and airy.

In contrast, he sounded very serious. "No, Hannah, I'm not married."

She pumped her fist in the air.

"Nor am I bald."

She jumped so hard she dropped the phone. She scrabbled around in the covers, retrieved it, and put it to her ear. "B-bald?"

"Isn't that what women always worry about? Whether a guy is bald?"

"Don't forget the paisley-print socks," she muttered.

"What?"

"So you have a lot of hair?"

"It's black and thick. No gray hair yet." He paused while she worked on her mental picture of him. "How about you?"

"I'm twenty-four. I'm blond. I don't think I have gray hair, but if I do, it doesn't show."

"I *like* blondes."

"I like guys with black hair."

"I wear it short—"

"So when you wrestle the bad guys to the ground, they can't grab it and incapacitate you?" she guessed.

"That, and the fact the British Secret Service manual says I have to keep it short."

"I forgot about that." She gave up on subtlety and simply interrogated him. "What color are your eyes?"

"What color do you think they are?"

"Black hair, so . . . brown eyes."

"That's right."

"You wear dark suits and white shirts, and good shoes because while you have to be comfortable when you stand, you also have to be able to run in them, and your job requires that you look elegant." She had built the picture of him in her mind.

"I like this. You are going to recognize me as soon as you see me." His deep voice became almost smoky.

His image shimmered so close she could almost see him.

"Tell me about yourself. What do you look like?" When she hesitated, he said, "Blond, I know, so . . . blue eyes?"

"Yes. Blue eyes, fair skin."

"Freckles?"

"Oh, yeah." The bane of her life.

"I like freckles."

She took a deep breath. The guy wasn't saying anything extraordinary, but at the same time . . . he was saying the right things. "Everything else is pretty normal."

"Best feature? Quick, don't think about it."

"I've got nice lips."

"Ah. Kissable." He approved.

She smiled.

"Worst feature?" he asked.

She sighed.

"Come on. Tell me," he coaxed.

"My ears stick out."

"A lot?"

"They're not big, and my hair is very thick and I keep it cut right, so you can't see them most of the time."

"Hannah, do they stick out a lot?"

"Yes! Fine. They do!"

Her reward for honesty was a soft, warm chuckle in her ear.

"When I was a teenager and going to my first dance, I tried to glue them back." Why she was confessing this, she did not know.

"How did that work out?"

"I used gum. It got stuck in my hair, and—" She waited until he stopped laughing, and said primly, "I had long hair, and I had to get it all cut off. It was very traumatic."

"I'm sure it was, at the time. But you don't care anymore. You're smiling."

She put her fingers over her lips as if to hide them from . . . the telephone. "How do *you* know I'm smiling?"

"I can hear it in your voice."

He was smiling, too. She could hear it in *his* voice. "The guy who was taking me to the dance was a jerk about it."

"Teenage boys are always jerks," he assured her. "I know. I was one."

Now he was about as far from jerkdom as it was possible for a man to be. Now he was . . . sweet and hot as cocoa. "Okay. Now it's your turn. What's your biggest secret?"

"I was more than a jerk when I was a teenager. I was a hoodlum." It sounded like a joke.

So she joked back at him. "Really? Leather coat and all?"

"Yes. I stole a leather coat." Except he was serious.

Her mouth dropped open.

"Hannah?"

"I'm here."

"And shocked."

"I guess I am. You just seem so—"

"Law-abiding? I assure you I am . . . now."

She imagined a young black-haired punk in a leather jacket, slouching down a rough city street, his gaze flickering toward the shadows in the alley, always vigilant for attack, yet safe . . . because he was the best with a knife, the best with his fists, the toughest. . . .

She caught her breath with a gasp.

The silence had gone on far too long.

"Trent?"

"I thought maybe now that you knew what I'd been, you didn't want to speak to me anymore." He was still serious. So serious.

"No, it's not that. I was picturing you as a—"

"Gang member. I was part of a gang. It's not glamorous. It's mean and it's ugly. I got sent to juvy for a year, and I was lucky. Lucky to get caught. Lucky to get out alive."

It didn't matter what he said. The image of the slouching dark-haired boy grew stronger in her mind.

Wryly, he asked, "You're picturing *West Side Story*, aren't you?"

The image vanished with a small pop, and she giggled. He was right. She saw him snapping his fingers, ready to dance to the music in her head. And when she finished laughing, she yawned.

At once he said, "I should let you sleep. I know Mrs. Manly and her party have you hopping."

"I enjoy it." She didn't want him to hang up.

"I'm looking forward to tomorrow night."

"I am, too."

"Trent," he added.

"What?" Why did he say that?

"I am, too, *Trent*," he insisted. "I like it when you say my name. I like the sound of it on your lips."

She bit her lower lip, and even though he was nowhere in sight, she didn't know where to look.

"You know"—his voice had that deep timbre again—"when we see each other, it'll be the first time. But we'll recognize each other."

She was increasingly breathless. "You can look for the woman with the ears that stick out."

"I'll look for the shy blonde with the dusting of freckles across her nose."

He made her thrill with every word. She lightly rubbed the skin between her breasts, over her heart.

"Don't expect too much," she warned faintly.

"We would recognize each other even if we'd never had this conversation. Our eyes will meet and we'll know . . . just know."

She pressed her legs together, shifted uncomfortably

as arousal hummed through her veins. "Are you trying to seduce me?"

"Am I succeeding?"

She laughed, and she was proud of the carefree sound. "No, but it's fun to listen."

He hesitated as if he wanted to challenge her. Then he said, "You can't say I didn't try."

"Good night . . . Trent."

"And there we have it." He sounded faintly humorous. "I couldn't seduce you with all the words in the dictionary, and you seduce me with a single syllable."

"Trent," she repeated that single syllable. "Good night, Trent." She listened to Trent groan again, and hung up the phone smiling.

Had he seduced her with his conversation? She'd told him no.

She was the world's biggest liar.

Thank God. If he knew how easily she responded to him . . .

She thought about him, how she would see him tomorrow night, and how he couldn't be as handsome and as wonderful as she imagined. Yet she *was* going to see him, so he couldn't have lied too much.

Maybe he was short—her height. Less.

But she couldn't convince herself it mattered, because she kept hearing his groan as she said his name.

He'd sounded like a man in the throes of climax.

And she . . . she was a woman who had been aroused by every word he'd uttered.

She wiggled down, off the pillows, until she was flat on her back and staring at the ceiling. She imagined him, not the young, tough thug, but the older man, scarred by experience, with the body of a fighter and the face of a dark angel. She imagined him above her, pressing her into the mattress, kissing with all the passion of his wild nature, opening her to him. . . .

As Hannah twisted on the bed, wrapped in her fantasies, Gabriel stood hunched over the monitor, breathing hard. Each time she touched herself, he groaned again, imagining himself there above her, coaxing a response from her and giving of himself in return.

She was everything he had wanted in a dream woman. Everything he had ever wanted in his soul mate.

Hannah Grey was everything to him.

SIXTEEN

"You look happy." Mrs. Manly rested on the bed, dressed in her costume, and watched Hannah prepare the tray of sterile syringes and medications Mrs. Manly *might* need when she returned to her room.

"I am." Hannah ran through the list of possibilities in her mind. Mrs. Manly's blood sugar would be off, she'd be exhausted, her blood pressure might be high, she might have angina, she might need a tranquilizer.

"Because the party is finally here?"

"Yes. That's it." Hannah smiled at the sterile syringes she carefully placed beside each vial, checked the labels once again, and made sure they were organized just so.

She *was* happy. That conversation last night had made her remember how good life could be when one had friends and . . . a lover.

Not that he knew he was her lover. For that very reason, fantasies were remarkably safe.

"It's been a lot of work for you," Mrs. Manly said.

Satisfied with the arrangement on her tray, Hannah

turned to Mrs. Manly and started a last-minute check of her pulse, her blood pressure, and her blood sugar. "I've enjoyed it. It's been completely different from any of my other assignments. If the whole world suddenly gets healthy and the nursing gig fails, I'll go into party planning."

"You'd be good at it. You're very efficient." Mrs. Manly's color was good; her eyes were bright.

"You're looking forward to the party, too," Hannah observed. Mrs. Manly's vital signs were perfect; she was in good shape for an overweight, aging diabetic with heart problems.

"It's my last hoorah before going to court about Nathan's fortune. I might as well enjoy it." Her voice sounded as displeased as always, but she looked less bitter.

Hannah placed her hand on Mrs. Manly's shoulder. "When you go to court, I'll be there at your side."

Mrs. Manly covered Hannah's hand with her palm. "That is a relief. You've helped me, and I appreciate every moment that we've spent together."

"Even when I made you eat right?"

"Even then." Mrs. Manly lifted herself on one elbow. "In fact, as a reward, I had a costume made especially for you."

Hannah was hanging up the blood pressure cuff, and she paused. "What is it?"

"It's in that garment bag on the hook." Mrs. Manly looked as if she were bursting with mischief. "Go look at it."

Hannah walked over and pulled down the zipper to reveal the costume in its full glory.

It was a white uniform, the kind nurses wore in the fifties, with white stockings, white granny shoes, and a starched nurse's cap with wings and a black stripe across the brim.

"Mrs. Manly!" Hannah was aghast.

What had Trent had said the night before? *Do you know the fantasies I've had about nurses?*

"It's just right," Mrs. Manly said. "You can comfortably dance in those shoes. The stockings have seams up the back—"

Hannah lifted the ruffled garter belt and the sheer white nylons, and looked at Mrs. Manly with shock and inquiry.

Mrs. Manly smirked. "You're going to be very popular. Men have dreams about nurses."

"So I've heard." Hannah fitted the narrow white winged mask over her eyes. She looked in the mirror, and thought about how much she and Trent had said last night, and how much they'd left unsaid. She thought about seeing him tonight, and that he was going to think she'd worn this . . . for him.

And she wondered if at last her luck had changed for the better. "Thank you, Mrs. Manly. I know I'll enjoy the costume and the party in equal measure."

"Good." Mrs. Manly waved her toward the bathroom. "Go and change. I want to be in place when the first of the guests arrive."

*   *   *

Gabriel stood outside on the steps of Balfour House, dressed in a black business suit and a black velvet Phantom of the Opera mask, and watched the guests arrive at the Balfour Halloween party.

There were considerably more than two hundred of them, people of all ages and backgrounds. Everyone who had received an invitation had brought along a friend, and since many of those friends were prominent politicians, Broadway stars, famous doctors and authors who made their names writing tell-all biographies or scandalous romances, they could not officially be called "party crashers." They were instead "lending prestige to an already-glittering event."

One of the young ladies, dressed in a skimpy Cleopatra costume, stopped and looked him over. "What are you supposed to be?" She had a sultry voice that went well with the sheer gold outfit, so thin he could see right through it to her.

"A security guard, ma'am," he answered without a hint of humor.

Behind her mask, her eyes grew round and wide, and her bosom heaved with such excitement her nipples strained to escape. "That's a wonderful costume."

Was she really that dumb? "Thank you."

"When you're done playing at security, come in and dance with me."

Her father—no, her boyfriend, for he wrapped his arm around her waist in a way that said *Mine*—said impatiently, "Stop flirting with the help."

His rebuke to her and Gabriel would have been

more effective if he hadn't been wearing hose, silk knickers, and a white wig. He knew it, too, because he planted his feet and squared his shoulders at Gabriel.

Gabriel stared back impassively.

When the guy didn't get a rise out of him, he yanked at the girl hard enough to jerk her off her feet. She tumbled into him, then continued obediently toward the door. But she cast Gabriel a lingering smile that let Gabriel know she didn't care if he was the help or not—she'd still dance with him.

Susan Stevens walked over from her position on the other side of the steps.

Gabriel braced himself.

In a fake, squeaky voice that went badly with her willowy frame, she said, "Oh, Mr. Security Man, you're so tall and strong, won't you make my dreams come true?"

"You're jealous that she didn't come on to you."

"No." She dropped back into her usual low, sexy voice. "Glory alternates between dumb and crazy, and I can't handle that."

"Glory?"

"That girl."

He glanced toward the open door. "You know her?"

"You don't?"

"I'm supposed to?"

Susan sighed deeply. "She's the hot singer du jour, a sex symbol since she was thirteen—"

"Ick."

"—And currently living with her record producer who is wayyy too old for her."

Gabriel jerked his head toward the house. "Is that him?"

"That's him. Steve Chapman."

"Must be why she's shopping, and why he's worried." He glanced toward the line of cars snaking their way up the drive; he could finally see the end. For two hours they'd been arriving, and he was ready to go inside and . . . see Hannah.

As soon as he allowed himself to think of her, the memory of her self-induced pleasure flooded his mind. He had watched her imagine a lover and, at the peak of her climax, heard her groan his name. He had observed her long after she'd turned off the light and gone to sleep, and even now, the remembrance made his body tighten in anticipation.

After last night, he definitely wanted to see Hannah.

"It looks like the worst is over," Susan said. "Why don't you go in and check out the party, boss?"

Gabriel turned his head and looked at Susan. "Why?"

"For one thing, you're not slated to be on duty. Good thing. You seem distracted. Maybe there's someone inside who's caught your interest." She smiled in a way that told him that, in her estimation, there was no maybe about it.

He had been concentrating on his job . . . but Susan had a way of observing people, a gift that he respected, because she didn't just observe—she interpreted their actions and speculated, usually correctly, on their motivations, their plans, their intentions.

Tonight, she had seen something different about him. Something more.

She had seen his obsession with Hannah Grey.

But he wasn't going to admit to anything. If she found out he had taken all the shifts on this job so he could watch their prime suspect brush her teeth, Susan would never let him hear the end of it.

"Fine. I'm going to make my rounds. Inside. Call Mark if you need him."

"Right." Susan placed her black Stuart Weitzman flats firmly on the step, put her hands behind her, and observed as another beautiful young thing, accompanied by another old codger, got out of a car. "It's a parade," she muttered.

With a nod to the ever-vigilant Nelson, costumed like an eighteenth-century footman, Gabriel walked through the large double doors.

He couldn't believe how the place had been transformed. Every crystal chandelier, every marble floor, every swirl on the antique furniture had been cleaned, polished, waxed. The decorations had been created with a professional hand. Draperies of black and purple silk, billowing beneath the slow breath of well-placed fans, created a cavelike entrance, which funneled the guests toward the ballroom, where the band played big-band tunes from the forties, music that lured the guests to the dance floor, and waiters circulated with champagne and appetizers.

There the draperies changed, became velvet painted to resemble castle walls that mounted all the way to the second-story ceiling. Real roses with real thorns climbed the velvet panels, and here and there, red and purple silk swayed like dancing skirts.

Yep. This was Sleeping Beauty's castle, all right. Even if Gabriel hadn't recognized it, Mrs. Manly's costume would have provided the final clue.

She sat smack in the middle of the longest wall, on an ornate throne on a raised dais, wearing a black cape with a purple silk lining and a headdress with two pointed black horns, and she held a staff with a glass ball at the top and a stuffed raven atop that.

The costume was a genius of camouflage. Mrs. Manly had aged since her last public appearance—there was no concealing that—but the throne gave her a seat as she greeted her guests, the faint green tinge of her makeup hid the pallor of her skin, and her stooped shoulders seemed like part of her evil character.

Come to think of it, it wasn't so much a disguise as a revelation.

Gabriel glanced at Carrick, standing at his mother's right hand, and approved his costume—a long black cape with a stand-up collar worn over dark trousers and a white ruffled shirt. Except for the ruffles, he didn't look like an ass, and no matter how you cut it, most of the men in here did.

Gabriel watched some guy dressed as a condom walk past. Okay, he didn't look like an ass. He looked like a prick.

At last, Gabriel allowed himself to look at Hannah.

She stood behind and to the left of Mrs. Manly's throne, and even though it was obvious she was Mrs. Manly's companion, she attracted almost as much interest as the elusive Mrs. Manly herself. Maybe it was because word of her notoriety had preceded her.

Maybe it was because Mrs. Manly introduced everyone to her as they came through. Personally, Gabriel thought it was because she was so sexy, he broke a sweat just looking at her.

She wore a nurse's costume, a white dress belted at the waist, with a knee-length skirt, long bloused sleeves, and a tongue depressor and a small flashlight in her breast pocket. Her cap sat perkily atop her blond hair. Her stockings were white, with a seam up the back, and how she kept them up, he couldn't imagine . . . here. If he stood here and imagined what she wore under that dress, he would be unfit for duty, because she wore a nurse's costume . . . just for him.

She made him want to fake an illness so she would put him to bed.

He stared long and hard, secure in the knowledge that his eyes were hidden behind his mask, but then . . . she must have felt his stare, because she looked around. He couldn't see her eyes, and she couldn't see his, but for the first time, they were looking directly at each other.

Just as he had predicted, she recognized him.

Was this what he had hoped for? That music would swell and birds would sing? That they'd see each other across a crowded room and know that they'd found true love? That he'd know without a doubt that she was innocent of all the sins with which she'd been charged?

It was goddamn romantic. It was also goddamn stupid, lusting after a black widow that caught her victims, sucked the life out of them, and tossed their lifeless husks aside.

Still . . . he was not a victim, and he was forewarned. He could handle this. He could handle her.

Mrs. Manly looked between the two of them, then spoke to Hannah, who started and turned her attention to Mrs. Manly.

The connection between Gabriel and Hannah was broken.

Good. Good, damn it. He had work to do, and it would be better to let Hannah wait.

He slipped away to the back of the ballroom to check on his men, make sure there was no trouble, that they were following orders.

They were. The guests were confined to the ballroom, the corridors, and the restrooms that had been set aside for their use, and while a few had grumbled when turned away from self-guided tours of Balfour House, they were easily distracted when steered to the dining room, with its heaping buffet table.

Pleased, Gabriel paused to watch the company, and as he stood there, over and over he heard the recurring theme.

"What do you suppose is going to happen with Nathan Manly's widow?"

"What do you suppose she's going to tell the feds?"

"Do you really think all the money is still around?"

"Nathan spent it."

"The government wouldn't waste their time. They know something."

"Then why didn't they call her in sooner?"

"They've got new information, of course."

Gabriel thought that the senator who said that probably had a valid point, one worth investigating.

From his point of view, the party was a success. There were no incidents of violence, no obvious drug use, and no one who needed to be ejected. He thought Mrs. Manly also would consider the party a success: power players from all over the world were here, they were having a good time, and wine and gossip were flowing freely.

Which was why he was surprised when Nelson touched his arm. "Mr. Sansoucy?"

Not Gabriel Prescott, but Trent Sansoucy. "Yes."

"Mrs. Manly wants to speak to you."

Gabriel looked across the turbulent ballroom toward the elevated throne. Carrick had disappeared into the crowd, but Mrs. Manly still sat there, with Hannah on a stool beside her. "Thank you," he told Nelson, and walked through the dancers toward them.

When he got close, Mrs. Manly gestured him over. "Are you Eric's boy?" she asked.

"Yes, Mrs. Manly."

Hannah took an audible breath, and slid her stool back an inch.

Yeah, honey, I'm a guy who's not sick and not easy to kill, not bald, not fat, and not short. I'm your worst nightmare.

Carrick wandered over, a drink in his hand. "Can I get you anything, Mother?"

"Don't be irritating, Carrick. When I want something, I'll send Hannah," Mrs. Manly said with crushing finality.

"Right." Without visible sign of hurt, he turned to Gabriel. "How about you?"

"He's in charge of security." Mrs. Manly thoroughly looked Gabriel over. "Although I would have never guessed you were Eric's son. You don't look at all like him."

"I think he does," Carrick said.

Yeah, you'd better step in here, bro.

"Maybe . . ." Mrs. Manly still stared. "He does remind me of . . . someone. I suppose it must be Eric."

"Genetics are a funny thing," Gabriel said in a low, hoarse voice. He had listened to a recording of his own voice as it came through the changer. It was higher than normal, with that nasal East Coast accent, and he had practiced it until he was satisfied he could fool Hannah—if he didn't say too much.

Mrs. Manly drew back. "You have a cold?"

"Laryngitis," he answered.

"That's not contagious, is it?"

"Not this kind." As long as he concentrated, he sounded pretty good. Like he belonged in the Northeast.

"Fine then. Enough of that. This is Hannah." Mrs. Manly waved her hand at her nurse. "You've been talking to her on the phone. Stop drooling at her and take her out and dance."

"Mrs. Manly!" Hannah looked everywhere except at him.

"Thank you, Mrs. Manly. I'll do that," Gabriel said at the same time. Reaching out, he presented Hannah with his outstretched palm.

She looked at it, then looked at him, refusing his silent demand.

He smiled, a slow curl of the lips that mocked her hesitation. "Mrs. Manly commands. We both obey."

"Put like that . . ." She placed her hand in his.

His fingers closed around hers.

And the air around them sizzled.

SEVENTEEN

Hannah watched his smile fade. He looked down at their linked hands, then up toward her face.

She couldn't see his eyes. His mask covered his forehead and cheeks, and slithered over his nose and down one side to his chin. Yet she knew he saw her better and more completely than any person had ever seen her before.

She waited, breathless, for him to speak, to flirt, to say the things he'd been saying all week on the phone—the things he had said last night.

"Dance?" he asked.

That was brief.

"Only because Mrs. Manly ordered me to," she answered.

He chuckled, a slow rumble of amusement that mocked her hesitation, and tugged her, hard and fast, into his arms. "You like that."

"What?"

"That you don't have to make the decision, that she

made it for you." His voice sounded muffled. Muffled, and a little . . . off.

Laryngitis, she told herself.

"Do you flatter yourself I would dance with you without her command?" she asked.

"I don't know." He pulled her onto the dance floor and into a slow fox trot. "How big a coward are you?"

She took a quick breath at his clever, rapier-fast thrust, then thrust back. "It's only a dance." She waited, pleased with her clever reply.

"And a nuclear explosion is just a big display of fireworks."

That was flattery . . . but it felt like the truth. "Okay. You won that round."

"That's better," he murmured somewhere north of her head.

"What's better?"

"You just relaxed."

"How would you know?"

"You've been tense for days."

"How would you know?"

He swung her in a half-circle, keeping her close, leading so firmly she followed intuitively. "Your voice."

"My voice was tense?"

"Umm." His breath warmed the top of her head.

"And now it's not?"

"Not tense. Aware." Slowly he swung her in a half circle. "Of me."

Funny. She felt very tense as she asked, "And you?"

"Very aware. Last night . . ."

She tried to pull back.

He controlled her, kept her close. "Last night, after we spoke . . . did you think of me?"

"Speaking to you was very pleasant." That sounded dry and cool. "I've enjoyed all our conversations."

She felt his shoulders shake as if he suppressed laughter.

She leaned back and looked up at him. "What?"

"My reaction to our talk last night was more than pleasant. I was . . ."

"You were . . . ?"

"I desired to meet my mystery woman more than anything I've desired in my life."

The way he said *desire* made her shiver.

He smiled at her, a half smile that told her he'd felt her shiver, and he knew why.

"Are you . . . ?" She paused. *Are you pleased with what you see?* But no, that wasn't the question she wanted to ask. "Did I describe myself well enough?"

"I knew who you were as soon as I saw you."

"Because I was standing next to Mrs. Manly."

"No." He hugged her close again, pressed her head against his chest, and said exactly the right thing. "I would know you anywhere."

"And I would know you." She listened to his heartbeat, to the rush of breath in his lungs. "Anywhere."

Beneath the veneer of talk and motion, something was happening . . . to them.

The sounds of the music, the talk and the laughter died away, leaving them alone together in a place where warmth shimmered between them and light made her close her eyes. She leaned her head against his chest. The cool, wild scent of him made her dizzy, and the exercise made her breathless.

Surely it was the exercise.

But how to explain that she seemed to be melting into him? All the parts that touched him grew warm and pliable, and all the parts that touched those parts were losing tension, like steel heated by flame.

She looked off to the side, afraid of what he'd see if she gazed into his masked face. Afraid he'd somehow know what she'd done last night after she'd hung up the phone, that he'd know what she'd imagined . . .

That dance ended, and another began, a swift-moving blare of a fifties tune. She stepped away from him and smoothed her hair, almost relieved to be away from the intensity of dancing with the man who was both stranger and lover. He'd held her close, far closer than was necessary, and she could now testify that her speculation about him was completely off. He wasn't old or bald or plump. He didn't wear a corset; that was all him under that suit.

Yet at the same time, she still hadn't *seen* him. The dim light of the faux castle concealed far too many details, while his mask hid his upper face and distorted even his jawline.

He placed his hand against the small of her back to lead her from the dance floor, and that was too intimate, too commanding, and yet she welcomed his guidance. To have someone of her own, someone to lean against, and to know that someone would walk with her through the loneliness and the danger to a place of safety . . . that had been more than she could ever hope.

They had barely met, and already she trusted him. Already they had been lovers . . . not really, but the sound of his voice had brought her to orgasm.

And he didn't know.

Thank God.

"I feel like I know you." He had a quirk in his cheek, like a guy who had already heard the joke—a joke that she didn't get.

"We have been talking for a while," she said.

"Am *I* what *you* expected?" The quirk deepened.

"Exactly what I expected." In her best and wildest dreams.

He stopped her at the far end of the dance floor close to the dining room. "I'm going to fill a plate for us to share. All right?"

"Yes. I'd like that."

He brushed her cheek with his fingertips, turning her face up to his. "You'll wait here?"

"I'll be here."

He left, and she turned toward the queen's throne, wanting to make visual contact with Mrs. Manly, to make sure she was as well as she claimed to be.

Mrs. Manly wasn't there.

Hannah jumped as if someone had stuck her with a pin. She walked toward the dais, threading her way through the dancers, using her elbows when necessary to clear the way. The crowd parted, and Hannah spotted Mrs. Manly, standing on the edge of the dance floor, gripping the back of a chair, talking to her son.

No, not talking to her son. Their body language made that clear. She was reading her son the riot act.

Hannah sped up. What had he said to get her up off that throne and standing by herself? And smiling? Mrs. Manly was smiling at her son in a most unpleasant manner. What had he said to make her look at him and *smile*?

By the time Hannah made it to Mrs. Manly's side, she was breathing hard from exertion and worry. "Mrs. Manly, how can I assist you?"

Carrick cast her one loathing glance and walked away, striding like a man caught in a passion of fury.

Mrs. Manly sagged against the chair.

Hannah caught her under the arm. Mrs. Manly was drenched in sweat and trembling from the effort of remaining upright. Hannah whispered, "Let me call Nelson. He'll bring your wheelchair. It's behind your private exit—"

"I am not leaving this ballroom in a wheelchair. I'll walk, thank you." Mrs. Manly's voice was scathing.

At least she had agreed to leave, even if she insisted on doing it with her pride intact. Hannah estimated the distance to the black velvet drapery that hid the door. "Twelve steps. You have to hang on for twelve steps."

Mrs. Manly nodded genially at the guests milling nearby. "I will not fail."

She made it, of course, and if Hannah hadn't been holding her arm, she wouldn't have known the effort

Mrs. Manly exerted. Mrs. Manly even stopped to gossip with one of the preeminent Washington, D.C., columnists about the latest vice presidential scandal.

But once behind the door, her knees collapsed.

As Hannah maneuvered her into the chair, she cursed Mrs. Manly's pride, her insistence that no weakness be shown, and most of all, the empty corridor. Hannah took her pulse. It was racing. "Chest pain?"

"Yes."

"Hang on." Hannah pushed Mrs. Manly into the elevator and pressed the button for the second floor. "We'll get you to your room and I'll give you an injection." And call an ambulance, although Hannah didn't tell her that.

"That . . . little . . . twit," Mrs. Manly gasped. "He dared—"

Hannah wanted to wring Carrick's aristocratic neck.

"What did he say?" Hannah should have never left Mrs. Manly alone. What was she thinking, going off to dance and flirt with some guy she'd never met?

"Carrick said I knew where . . . the . . . money . . . is."

Come on. Come on. The elevator had never been so slow. "Never mind. You can tell me later. Save your breath."

Mrs. Manly paid no heed. "He said the . . . government knew . . . I knew." The doors opened, and Hannah hurriedly pushed the raging Mrs. Manly out and down the corridor. "I asked how they had found out, and he . . . that little brat!"

It wasn't a stretch for Hannah to guess. "He told the government that you knew about the fortune?"

They entered Mrs. Manly's bedroom.

Hannah glanced at the bed. Someone had placed a red rose on Mrs. Manly's pillow. Great gesture. Bad timing.

"He did it to . . . smoke me out." Mrs. Manly tried to get a long breath.

Hannah hurried toward the medications tray. "But you didn't admit it was true." When Mrs. Manly didn't answer right away, she stopped and slowly turned. "Mrs. Manly, you didn't tell him you knew? Did you?"

"Yes. I told him. And told him . . . he was *never* getting . . . it. Never getting a . . . dime!"

"Oh, no. Mrs. Manly." Hannah collapsed against the desk and stared in horror at the defiant Melinda Manly. "How could you?"

"It's too late . . . for reproaches. It's . . . done." Mrs. Manly was still angry enough to lift herself out of her chair and stagger to the bed.

Hannah leaped to help her. Together, they rolled her onto the mattress.

Mrs. Manly's head crushed the delicate rose. She sprawled there in her wicked queen costume, and her hands shook as she ripped off the headdress. "He made me so . . . angry. Just . . . like his father. *Just* like his father. Betraying . . . me at every . . . turn. *What the hell is poking me?*" She pulled the flower out from under her head, stared at crushed petals, then flung it to the floor and sucked at the wound on her hand.

Hannah pushed up her sleeve and took her blood pressure. It was one seventy over one ten. She checked her blood sugar. Mrs. Manly was headed for a stroke or heart attack. Now.

Picking up the phone, Hannah called nine-one-one for an ambulance.

It was a measure of how badly Mrs. Manly felt that she didn't object.

Hannah brought the tray with the neatly arranged medications and their syringes. She gave Mrs. Manly a nitroglycerine tablet to stabilize her heart. "You need to calm down. Take big breaths."

Mrs. Manly paid no heed. In a rush, she said, "Hannah, I want you to go down there right now and send the money off."

"The government will put you in jail." Hannah prepared the injection of insulin and another of the tranquilizer diazepam.

"The government's going to send me to jail anyway, thanks to my Judas of a son. And besides . . . you have to do it tonight." For a flash of a moment, Mrs. Manly looked defiant and ashamed . . . and sorry. "I told him you knew."

Hannah froze, syringe in hand.

"I know. I know. That was stupid. I was in a rage. I said too much. But he's just like his father, and I couldn't . . . By God, that kind of betrayal twice in one lifetime is too much for any one person to stand."

Hannah couldn't feel sorry for Mrs. Manly. She was too busy feeling sorry for herself. And frightened. When she remembered how much money was involved, and the way Carrick had looked at her, she was scared to death.

But a glance at Mrs. Manly convinced her to tend to the business at hand. "I'll go down and send the money, but first, let's deal with keeping you alive another day. First the insulin." Hannah gave the injection efficiently, quickly.

As she always did, Mrs. Manly groaned and rubbed the site. "I put money behind the photo on my desk. Two thousand dollars. You may need it."

Hannah glanced at the photo, a picture of Nathan and Melinda Manly on their wedding day. "Okay."

"You can go down via the secret passage behind the bookcase. Remember, any bookcase that's at a forty-five-degree angle will contain a copy of *Ulysses*, and that's the book that will open the latch." Mrs. Manly was talking fast.

"Got it."

"Do you remember the codes to activate the account?"

"Don't worry. I do." Hannah wished she could forget. "Now let's give you the diazepam to take the edge off and calm you enough to go to the hospital, and maybe sometime tonight you can sleep." She swabbed Mrs. Manly's arm, gave her another quick injection to calm her nerves and perhaps her heart.

Satisfied she'd done everything she could to stabilize Mrs. Manly until the paramedics got here, she turned away to place the syringes in a sterile container.

"Can't breathe." Mrs. Manly clawed at her collar.

Hannah turned back to help her. "You're hyperventilating." She shoved a pillow under Mrs. Manly's head. "Just breathe—"

"No. Can't . . . breathe." A faint blue color crept in around Mrs. Manly's lips. "Dear girl . . . I think you've . . . killed . . . me."

"What?" Hannah grabbed her stethoscope, shoved Mrs. Manly's costume aside, placed it on her chest, and listened.

Mrs. Manly's heartbeat, her lungs, were inexorably slowing.

"No!" Hannah grabbed for the EpiPen filled with adrenaline. She plunged it into Mrs. Manly's chest.

"No . . . use," Mrs. Manly gasped. "Carrick . . ."

"This is impossible!"

"Betrayed . . . ," Mrs. Manly said with her last breath.

"No! This isn't happening!" Hannah leaped on the bed, put her fists together, and slammed them on Mrs. Manly's breastbone. Five pushes over her heart, then a breath into her lungs, then five pushes over her heart—

Behind her, she heard someone open the door. "Get help!" she shouted.

"What have you done?" Carrick said in a loud, deliberate voice. "Hannah Grey, what have you done?"

And suddenly, it all made sense.

She stopped doing CPR. She slipped off the bed and picked up the medications. They were labeled correctly. Nitroglycerin, insulin, diazepam . . . Her eyes narrowed at the vial of diazepam.

It wasn't the same vial she'd placed on the tray earlier.

She'd prepared an injection for Mrs. Manly. She'd

done it secure in the knowledge that she'd checked and rechecked the arrangement of the medications on the tray in case she faced the kind of emergency she had just faced.

And someone had changed the medications.

Carrick had changed the medications.

She took Mrs. Manly's pulse. She felt the old lady's heart give its last, feeble beats. And she knew . . . she had killed Mrs. Manly.

EIGHTEEN

Someone shouted at Hannah.

Carrick.

Someone grabbed her and pulled her off the bed.

Susan Stevens.

In a daze of horror and disbelief, Hannah looked around the room. Guests and security guards, servants, Nelson, filled the room, staring at her, staring at Mrs. Manly's still figure.

"She gave Mother an injection, and Mother died," Carrick was saying loudly.

Hannah wrestled her way free of Susan's grip, leaned over the bed, and shut Mrs. Manly's eyes.

Her patient was dead. Her friend was dead. Mrs. Manly . . . was dead.

"Hannah Grey is known in New Hampshire as the angel of death. Her nursing certificate was pulled for immoral behavior. An investigation would prove she killed her patients there, too." Carrick was on a roll.

But what was he trying to accomplish? She'd never

killed another patient. . . . She glanced at Mrs. Manly's still face.

But it took only one.

One man dressed as a zombie pushed his way forward, clicking photos with his cell phone. A woman in a cat costume took photos with a small digital while she shouted questions at Carrick and Hannah. This was a freak show.

Dear God, help me.

"I'll call the police," Nelson said. "Miss Grey needs to be removed from this house immediately."

Hannah was innocent, and not one person in here would believe her. Because she had done it. She'd killed Mrs. Manly . . . with Carrick's eager assistance.

"I'll call Mr. Sansoucy," Susan Stevens said.

Hannah took a quick, pained breath. Oh, yes. Call Trent Sansoucy. Because she wanted to find herself condemned in his eyes, too.

Hannah scrubbed a quick hand over her face.

What did Carrick think he was going to accomplish?

He thought he was going to keep her from accessing the fortune, of course. She remembered how quickly he'd disappeared after Mrs. Manly had told him the truth, and cursed the conversation Mrs. Manly had held with the Washington columnist. Because that had given him time to come up here and . . . She glanced at the tray.

If Mrs. Manly hadn't been in such distress, if Hannah hadn't been in a hurry to get her her medication, maybe she would have seen that one of the vials had been switched. Maybe not. If only she had been paying attention . . . if only Carrick hadn't deliberately made his mother so angry she needed to be tranquilized . . . if only . . .

Carrick stepped between her and the tray. Leaning down, he stuck his face in hers. Softly, he said, "If you tell me now, I'll get you the best lawyers. I'll get you cleared of all charges. If you tell me."

It never occurred to her to play dumb, or to agree to the deal. Instead, just as softly, she said, "You can rot in hell."

"And you can rot in jail." He raised his voice. "Do you have anything to say for yourself?" He sprayed spittle on her face.

Deliberately, she wiped it off. Looking him right in the eyes, she answered, "I'm innocent, and you know it."

He straightened. "Get her out of here. Get her away from my poor dead mother. Get her out of my sight!"

Susan Stevens tried to hustle her out into the corridor.

Hannah resisted long enough to snatch the photo off the desk.

Susan reached for it.

Hannah clutched it to her chest and glared. "I asked for a picture of her, and she promised I could have it."

Susan hesitated, then withdrew her hand and pushed Hannah into the corridor.

Hannah looked at her. "I didn't do it."

"It looks like you did." But Susan didn't look convinced. Gripping Hannah's arm, she glanced around. "I have to stash you somewhere." The phone on her belt buzzed. She checked it and grimaced. "A text from . . . from Trent wanting to know what the hell is going on. Apparently the word's already spread."

Hannah needed to escape. Now. Before the cops came. Before Trent arrived. Before law enforcement got organized.

She said, "I'm going to throw up." It didn't take a lot of acting to appear pale and desperate. "I'm going to throw up. Just let me . . ." She staggered, making sure she appeared weak and dizzy, into the empty, dusty bedroom next to Mrs. Manly's, the one with a bookcase that stood at a forty-five-degree angle. The bookcase with its copy of *Ulysses*.

There was a bed, a desk, a chair, an old large Persian rug laid on top of old faded gold shag carpet.

Susan stood in the doorway, clearly unsure what to do. "You're sick? Are you poisoned, too? Do you want me to call someone?"

"Carrick." Hannah leaned against the wall in front of a monstrosity of a sixties-style floor lamp. "I need to talk to Carrick."

Susan didn't budge, but shouted down the corridor, "Hey! You! Nelson! Get Carrick over here!"

Hannah slid down the wall and carefully placed the picture frame on the floor. With a wretched groan, she leaned sideways and unplugged the lamp. With another groan, she put her head between her legs. Not because she was really ill, but because she needed to hide her flushed, furious cheeks.

Carrick arrived. "What is it?"

A quick peek proved he stood in the doorway, Susan at his shoulder.

"I want . . . I want to . . ." Hannah moaned piteously. "I want to confess. Carrick, I'll do whatever you want."

He took a few eager steps inside. "You're ready to talk?"

"Yes. Whatever you say." She staggered to her feet, grabbed the lamp and leaned on it, her face turned away from his.

"You! What's-yer-name!" He spoke to Susan. "Leave us alone!"

In a tone of disgust, Susan said, "Sir, that is really a bad idea."

You don't know the half of it. Hannah gripped the lamp with both hands.

"Go. On." Carrick sounded fierce with excitement. "Get. Out."

Susan's phone rang. She cursed, answered, said, "Hurry up, boss. We need you." Her voice faded as she walked down the corridor.

She was gone.

Trent was coming.

Hannah was out of time.

In one smooth motion, she lifted the lamp, turned, and charged. She experienced one moment of satisfaction as Carrick's eyes widened in terror.

She slammed the base into his chest.

He flew out the open door into the corridor.

She dropped the lamp, and with her foot, slammed the door shut. She locked it just in time.

Someone threw his body against it.

But this was an old house, with solid wood doors and casements. It would take an ax to get through.

Or the key.

Hannah dragged the dainty wooden desk chair over and stuck it under the knob. Dimly, through the heavy oak door, she could hear shouts in the hallway, and from outside, the wail of sirens. The desk wasn't so easy; it was heavy, and when she got behind it and shoved, it turned on its side with a thump that shook the floor. It took all her strength to shove it against the casement, and even then, she couldn't maneuver it so it was tight.

Two good-sized men could push this aside.

Sweating and swearing, she tugged the Persian carpet across the floor and tangled it in the legs of the chair.

That would slow them down.

She ran to the bookcase and searched for *Ulysses*'s distinctive tan leather binding. She missed it the first time, took a long breath, and assured herself Mrs. Manly had promised it would be there.

It was on the second shelf on the left next to the wall. She yanked hard, staggered backward. The bookcase opened with a squeal. Caught in a fever of fear and excitement, she hurried forward inside the dark cavernous hole—and skidded to a halt.

The picture frame. She couldn't leave it behind. She needed that money.

She wanted that photo.

Out in the corridor, they were hammering at the

door with something big. With each blow, the wall plaster crumbled around the casement.

Hannah snatched up the photo and returned to the secret passage. The passage was as dark and quiet as a tomb—which was exactly where she would be if they caught up with her. She tried to shut the bookcase behind her, but the creaky old mechanism resisted her attempts.

The lock on the bedroom door made a metallic sound as it was unlocked. The door opened a fraction of an inch and slammed into the chair and the table.

"Hannah!" It sounded like Trent . . . but not quite. This voice was harsher, deeper, with an accent she couldn't place. Whoever he was, he battered himself against the door. "Hannah, open this door!"

They'd be in the room soon.

She dropped the picture frame. The glass shattered. She gritted her teeth, and pulled with all her might.

The latch clicked into place.

She breathed in small panicked gasps that hurt her lungs.

She was alone, desperate, friendless. She had Mrs. Manly's word that this secret passage would take her, undetected, to the beach.

But Hannah had never set more than a foot inside, and for years, Mrs. Manly had barely left her room.

It was possible Carrick had found the secret ways through Balfour House, and if he had, this flight was nothing more than a trap—a trap that would lead her to prison . . . or death.

Pulling the little flashlight out of her breast pocket, she switched it on.

It worked.

She picked the picture frame up off the floor, shot the narrow beam around and found the edge of the stairway.

Thank God for double A batteries.

She started down into the darkness.

NINETEEN

Gabriel raced up the stairs, pushing past guests and servants, his feet thumping on the wood, listening to the shouting through his speaker phone and wishing he had never allowed Hannah out of his sight. Because something had happened—he couldn't quite understand what Susan was saying—but he heard words like *murder* and *Carrick* and *Hannah*.

He hit the corridor outside Mrs. Manly's bedroom and saw Susan running toward him. "What?" he asked. "What?"

She grabbed him by the arm. "Hannah killed Mrs. Manly. Carrick caught her. She convinced me she was sick, to allow her into the bedroom next to Mrs. Manly's, and once she was there, she knocked Carrick out the door."

Gabriel saw his brother writhing on the floor, clutching his chest and gasping.

Susan kept talking. "She barricaded herself inside. I don't know what she's thinking. She's trapped."

"She killed Mrs. Manly?" Gabriel hadn't even processed the first sentence.

Susan comprehended far too much. "I never saw it coming, either. I thought she was . . . Man, Gabriel, I am so sorry."

She put her hand on his arm, and nothing she could have done made this as real as her disbelief, her sympathy.

Gabriel looked in Mrs. Manly's bedroom, saw a motley assortment of guests and servants milling around. He heard them gasp words like *murdered* and *poisoned*. A reporter took photo after photo of the motionless pale body on the bed. Some guy dressed like a zombie used his cell phone to capture every aspect of the scene. Some woman dressed like a cat hovered over the tray of medications, snapping photos, and as Gabriel watched, she moved a syringe into a more photogenic position.

With a volume that got the attention of every person in the room, Gabriel shouted, "Unless you have official business in here, get out!" Directly to the female, he said, "And don't touch anything."

The servants looked startled, the guests indignant. The female said, "I am a reporter for the *Bangor Free Press* and I have the right—"

"Out!" He pointed to the exit.

She jumped, and something about him must have convinced her he meant business. She started backing toward the door and babbling, "The people have the right to *know*!"

"And you have the right to go to jail for contaminating a crime scene," he said coldly. The cops were going to have a fit.

She knew it, too, because she left in a hurry, probably to send off her photos.

Nelson took over, shoving people out. In the corridor, one of Gabriel's men arrived and briskly directed them down the stairs.

Turning back to Susan, Gabriel asked in a low voice, "Are you sure Hannah did it?"

"Carrick witnessed the act." Susan indicated the still-moaning Carrick. "We've got the video. Do you want to go watch—"

"Later. But first . . ." He walked to the bedroom where Hannah cowered within. He turned the knob.

It was locked.

He hit the door with his shoulder.

It was solid oak.

He didn't care. Over and over he smacked the door, putting the strength of his shattered illusions behind him.

"Stop it." Susan grabbed his arm and threw him off-balance. "Let me open the lock."

He stepped back, breathing hard, and watched her kneel at the door and pull a long thin, sharp knife from the pocket of her jacket. A weapon and, in this instance, a lock pick.

"Gabriel. Gabriel, call . . . ambulance," Carrick said faintly.

Nelson rushed out of Mrs. Manly's bedroom. "Sir!" He hurried to Carrick's side. "What happened?"

"She hit me . . . with a lamp." Nelson helped Carrick

push himself up against the wall. "Broken ribs. Again. Worse."

Gabriel switched his attention to Carrick, examined him visually, decided he was right. He had a broken rib or two. He'd live. "I'd say your ribs are the least of our problems."

"And she killed my mother." Carrick's voice caught, and a tear squeezed from the corner of his eye.

"An ambulance is already on the way." Gabriel could hear the sirens, screaming madly.

Susan turned the knob. "It's open." She pushed on the door. It smacked something. Something big.

Gabriel returned to the assault, smacking the door with his shoulder. "Hannah! Hannah, open this door!"

Nothing. Hannah said nothing.

And treacherously, his sense of rage and betrayal turned to worry. "Susan! Get somebody under the window in case she decides to jump."

Susan started to say something, probably to point out that a jump from the second story wouldn't kill Hannah.

He challenged her with a stare. "Or in case there's a tree she can climb down."

"Right." Susan called for backup outside and up here.

"She wouldn't dare jump," Carrick said. "She'd better not."

Gabriel noted Carrick spoke well enough when he was angry. "Nelson, get a couple of your burliest men. One woman barricaded this door. We can damn well push it open."

They did, but it took four of them.

Gabriel squeezed through first, prepared for a blow to the head, a gunshot, prepared for an ambush, any-thing . . . except an empty room. He looked around, noting that the window was locked from the inside. "Hannah. Come out," he called.

No answer.

With increasing disbelief, he looked in the bath-room, the closet.

She wasn't here.

Susan got in next, shoving the furniture and the area rug away from the door.

Carrick came through, supported by Nelson on one side and one of the footmen on the other. "Where is that bitch? I want to see her face when I . . . Where is she?"

"Don't move," Gabriel said.

Carrick kept walking.

"I said, *don't move.*"

Carrick froze.

Gabriel stood in the middle of the room, looking at the patterns in the carpet. Before the party, some maid had vacuumed it, and since that moment, no one ex-cept Hannah had been in here. He saw her footprints from the door to the wall, the mark she'd made while she sat on the floor. He saw the lamp she'd used on Carrick as a battering ram, and then . . . then there were marks by the bookcase. Something had been swung open there. He walked over and yanked on a shelf. Nothing moved. The thing was solid. Turning, he drilled Carrick with his gaze. "Are there hiding places in the walls?"

"No. Not that I found. Supposedly there are secret passages, but I never found those, either." Carrick's voice rose. "Gabriel, are you trying to tell me that you lost her? You lost the woman who murdered my mother? She escaped somehow through some mythical secret passage and I'll never see her brought to justice?"

With a cool gaze, Gabriel considered Carrick. "Since I'm not the one who let her hit me with a lamp, I'm going to have to say that, no, I didn't lose her. You did. Now—Nelson, get someone to break open that bookcase. Call me as soon as you do." He turned to Susan. "Come on. We're going to look at the video."

They walked past his sputtering brother and into a corridor now guarded by Gabriel's men, and bustling with EMTs and emergency personnel.

"Is there video for that bedroom? The one with the bookcase?" Susan asked.

"No. I didn't set up in the empty rooms. The more fool me." Gabriel strode toward his office lined with monitors and digital surveillance equipment. It took only a second to cue up the video for the last hour of Mrs. Manly's life. He ran the ballroom, the corridors, the elevator, and her bedroom simultaneously, and almost at once they saw Carrick in Mrs. Manly's bedroom.

At once, Susan asked, "What the hell is he doing in there?"

The bed was turned back, and Carrick smoothed the pillow, then placed a red rose in the center.

Susan sighed and relaxed. "Poor guy."

At the same time, they caught the image of Mrs. Manly and Hannah entering the elevator.

Mrs. Manly raged, "That little twit. He dared—"

Gabriel turned up the sound.

Susan pointed at Mrs. Manly's flushed face. "She already looks ill there."

"Yes," Gabriel agreed. The woman had been in poor health, and only the slightest push would send her into the great beyond. And who knew that better than Hannah?

Mrs. Manly continued, "Carrick said I knew where the money is. He said the government knew I knew." The two women exited the elevator. Hannah made some comforting noises. "I asked how they had found out, and he . . . that little brat!"

"He told the government that you knew about the fortune?" Hannah asked.

"Whoa. Do you suppose that's true?" Susan asked.

"No. I don't know." Gabriel didn't want to think of that. He needed to listen, to see.

In Mrs. Manly's bedroom . . . "He did it to smoke me out," Mrs. Manly said.

Hannah walked to the medications and the syringes, laid neatly on a tray. "But you didn't admit it was true."

"Did she just say what I think she said?" Susan asked.

"Mrs. Manly knew where the fortune is, and she told Hannah." Gabriel comprehended, but he could scarcely believe. All the watching, the listening, and to find out now that these two women had always—

Hannah's voice rose. "Mrs. Manly, you didn't tell him you knew? Did you?"

"Yes. I told him. And told him he was never getting it. Never getting a dime!"

"Look at her face." Susan pointed at Hannah. "She's horrified. She must have been afraid Carrick was going to make her testify about the fortune and she would lose it."

"It's too late for reproaches. It's done." Mrs. Manly climbed on the bed, ripped off the headdress. "He made me so angry. Just like his father. Just like his father. Betraying me at every turn. What the hell is poking me?" She pulled a flower out from under her head, flung it to the floor.

"Listen to her talk. She's wheezing," Susan said.

"I know." Gabriel wished he didn't.

Hannah took Mrs. Manly's blood pressure and her blood sugar. She called nine-one-one.

Susan noted, "That was a tactical error. The jury is going to note that she called for the ambulance before she needed it."

Hannah brought the tray with the medications and syringes. She gave Mrs. Manly a tablet and told her to calm down. Mrs. Manly told her to go and send the money off.

"The government will put you in jail." Hannah prepared two injections.

"The government's going to send me to jail anyway, thanks to my Judas of a son. Besides, you have to do it tonight." Mrs. Manly looked sorry. "I told him you knew."

Syringe in hand, Hannah stared at Mrs. Manly, and the expression on her face . . .

"She looks like she's ready to shriek at Mrs. Manly," Susan said. "Mrs. Manly knows it, too. Do you suppose Hannah abused that old woman?"

"I never saw evidence of it." But had Gabriel seen only what he wanted to see? Had he deliberately overlooked mistreatment of some kind, all because he'd grown too fond of Hannah Grey?

Mrs. Manly kept talking. "I know. That was stupid. I was in a rage. I said too much. But he's just like his father, and I couldn't . . . By God, that kind of betrayal twice in one lifetime is too much for any one person to stand."

"She really doesn't think much of Carrick, does she?" Susan asked reflectively. "Neither of them does."

"Carrick said Hannah was influencing his mother adversely." Gabriel was listening to the video and responding to Susan's comments. He knew he was making sense. Yet he had never felt like this in his life, as if a great stone sat on his chest and crushed the air out of him. No, not the air—the hope. Because he knew what was coming. He had to watch, but he couldn't stand it. He couldn't stand it if Hannah had really killed Mrs. Manly. And he knew that she had. Every word of this conversation condemned her.

"I'll send the money, but first, let's keep you alive another day. First the insulin." Hannah gave the injection efficiently, quickly.

Susan pointed as Mrs. Manly groaned and rubbed the site. "Clearly, she was in pain already."

Mrs. Manly said, "I put money behind the photo on my desk. Two thousand dollars. You may need it."

"No wonder she grabbed that picture frame!" Susan said.

When Mrs. Manly gave specific instructions on how to get into the secret passage, Susan promptly called the information down to Mark.

Mrs. Manly asked if Hannah remembered the codes to activate the account, and Hannah coolly agreed she did.

Then the horror started. Hannah gave Mrs. Manly another injection.

"Can't breathe." Mrs. Manly clawed at her throat.

"You're hyperventilating." Hannah placed a pillow under Mrs. Manly's head. *"Just breathe slowly."*

"Dear girl, I think you've killed me." Then, *"No use,"* Mrs. Manly gasped, and she called for her son. *"Carrick . . ."*

As Hannah listened to her heart, gave her another injection, did frantic CPR, Susan watched intently. "Hannah's doing everything right, going through the motions."

"She even looks upset. Maybe she didn't know it would take effect before she could escape." Gabriel was proud of how calm he sounded, how analytical.

With her last breath, Mrs. Manly whispered, "Betrayed . . ." And she was dead.

Gabriel stood stiffly, propelled to his feet by anguish and fury. "I've seen enough. I'm going down to join the search. I will find her."

Susan watched him stride away, and whispered, "Then God help Hannah Grey, because she hasn't got a chance."

TWENTY

Hannah hurried down the steps in the secret passage, her heart pounding in her ears. She hated the silence, so profound, so alone. She hated that darkness, so thick and old. At the same time, she feared sound, she feared light, she feared the moment her pursuers ripped open the walls looking for her, found the book-case and the secret passage, and set off in hot pursuit, baying like a pack of bloodhounds.

The stairs kept turning, zigzagging through the hidden parts of Balfour House. The stairs leveled off on the main floor, and as she walked along the long wall, she could dimly hear music and voices. The ballroom. A few steps more, and it was quiet again. She passed an entrance, the back of a bookcase. Then down she plunged again, the steps winding, then leveling off, winding, then leveling off. She knew she was in the basement when once again she saw the outline of a bookcase.

There she hesitated, her hand on the latch.

If she were a good person, she would do as she had promised Mrs. Manly. She would come out of hiding, go to the computer in the butler's office, bring up the program, punch in the code, and return Nathan Manly's fortune to the people.

But Hannah wasn't a good person. She wanted to live, to be free, and if she was captured, she knew without a doubt she'd be convicted of murder and sentenced to prison—or even executed. Judges and juries were notoriously harsh on nurses who betrayed their patients' trust.

She wasn't going to do the right thing. She was a coward.

But guilt prodded at her. Taking the thin pen out of her breast pocket, she wrote in tiny letters on the wood on the back of the bookcase.

Household Accounts. Silverware, Inventory. Capital B. Capital H. Small N. Capital M. Small C. Asterisk. 1898.

In case she forgot. In case she died and someone someday found the code. Not Carrick, but . . . someone.

Then she hurried on.

The stairs plunged down again, leveled off, and abruptly the walls and floor turned from boards to stone. She stopped and shone her light around. She was in a cave. It was dry but cool. The floor sloped down. The ceiling got lower. And at the far end, she could see a wall.

Mrs. Manly hadn't sent her into a trap. Had she?

Hannah walked forward, grateful for her flat rubber-soled shoes. They gave her the traction she needed to cross the rough stone . . . to the wall at the end of the tunnel. The wall with a thick metal door.

The hinges and the lock showed spots of rust, and the lever shrieked as she pressed it down.

It didn't open.

She pushed it up.

It didn't open.

She licked her dry lips, and frantically shot the flashlight around the cave.

There. There on the floor. A dull glint of metal. A key on a ring.

She grabbed it, fit it in the lock, and turned. Inside the lock mechanism, she felt a grinding as years of rust were dislodged. The tumblers and pins rasped past one another, moving slowly when she needed to hurry. Hurry.

She pushed against the key. The shaft began to twist, to warp. Just as she feared it would break off in the lock, the mechanism clicked into place.

She pressed her hand against the door. It was cold. Freezing against her palm. What was on the other side? The police? A furious, murderous Carrick? Or a cold-eyed, accusing Trent?

Yet she had to go forward.

She knelt on the rough stone floor, set the picture frame down, and opened the back. Just as Mrs. Manly promised, there was money. Hundreds, fifties and twenties. It would save her life—if her life could be saved. If she could escape Balfour House and the estate without being detected.

She stuffed the cash into the capacious pockets in

her skirt, then lifted the photograph away from the glass. It showed a glowing Melinda, dressed in her wedding gown, clinging to handsome Nathan's arm.

Hannah had no time, but she couldn't leave the picture here to be found by the searchers or, worse, never to be found at all. Carefully she folded it down the middle, then ripped it in half and tucked Mrs. Manly's image into her breast pocket. With a violence that spoke volumes, she crumpled Nathan and tossed him aside.

Standing, she pulled the key from the lock. She turned off her flashlight and placed it in her pocket. Pressing the lever down, she leaned against the door. Something fought against her, something more powerful than rusty old hinges. She cracked the door an inch.

The wind gusted through the opening with all the vigor of an incoming winter storm. She held on to the handle, desperate that the door not slam back and alert any searchers of her whereabouts. Taking a breath, she stepped out of the cool cave and into the blasting wind. Carefully, she shut the door. She locked it.

The searchers inside wouldn't easily follow her.

She stood in the extension of the cave. In the distance, she could see a faint lightening of the night. *The entrance.* And beyond that entrance, she could hear the roar of the ocean.

No wonder the metal hardware on the door was rusting. Day and night, night and day, the wind blew salt spray up the fifty-foot-long passage toward the door.

Briefly, she turned on her flashlight and shone it around. The walls were narrowing. Here and there the

rock ceiling had collapsed. She turned off the light—
and walked. The scent of the sea grew greater, the
rocks slippery with spray. The closer she got, the
stronger the wind, the more she was sure she was in
deep trouble. Mrs. Manly had promised her the beach.

She was walking into the waves.

She placed her hand against one wall, and she didn't
stop. She didn't stop when the icy water filled her
shoes. She didn't stop when the brutally cold waves
rose to her thighs. She caught her breath in agony as a
wave broke against her stomach. Her teeth chattered,
and tears of frozen pain trickled down her cheeks. She
plowed steadily forward, hoping the water didn't lift
the cash out of her pockets, realizing it didn't matter
because she wasn't going to live through this.

Just as she was ready to die of hypothermia, the wall
beneath her hand took an abrupt left turn. The cave
opened and she walked along the base of the cliff,
where the waves had undercut the granite. With a sigh
of relief, she realized she was hidden from searchers
above. Slowly, slowly, the ground beneath her feet
sloped up out of the ocean.

Clouds covered the full moon, muting its pure light,
but she could see enough to know she was on a path,
a narrow path that wound and turned ever upward,
taking her to the top. Still the wind blasted her, and
she shuddered in frozen agony as the sand and water
squished in her shoes.

She was afraid. So afraid. Afraid her numb feet
would slip and she'd drop onto the rocks and into the

waves below. Afraid that somewhere above, the mob waited. . . .

Carrick waited. . . .

Trent waited. . . .

But although light glowed from the still not visible house, she saw no trace of any human figure on the top of the cliff.

Did they think she was still inside Balfour House?

Probably. They probably didn't believe she would do what she'd done to escape. By God, *she* didn't believe she'd done what she'd done to escape.

She reached the top of the cliff and crouched there, assessing her location. The house was far to the left and down. She'd managed to come out near the spot where Mrs. Manly had first told her about the fortune and charged her to distribute it on her death.

With gritty hands, Hannah wiped tears off her cheeks. Yeah, like that was going to ever happen.

Through the increasing howl of the wind, she could hear sirens shrieking. At the house, emergency vehicles and police cars, blue and red lights flashing, lined up at the front door. A throng of people milled out on the lawn and trampled the flower beds. With a savage smile, Hannah realized that Mrs. Manly had got her wish—her party had become the most talked-about event of the year.

Standing, she cut across the rise and looked over the other side—and realized she'd found the promised land.

Cars. A hundred cars were parked on the flat below. Limos. Mercedes. BMWs. A couple of luxury SUVs.

Somewhere, somehow, surely one of them had the keys still in the ignition.

She stumbled down the slope, shivering in the cold, telling herself if she just hurried, she'd warm up, and knowing that was crap, with the temperature dropping and the wind chill at freezing or below.

Still she walked. She couldn't give up now, not when she could see lines and lines of cars, unguarded by anything but their isolation in a field on the rocky edge of the Atlantic Ocean. Unguarded because . . . because the drivers and the valets had raced to the house to be part of the excitement?

Yes. Probably.

Undoubtedly.

She reached the first car and looked inside. Keys glinted in the seat.

Her heart leaped at this first turn of good luck.

But that car was blocked. She couldn't get it out. She had to find a car on the outer edge. Encouraged, she stumbled forward, occasionally glancing inside a vehicle, and always seeing keys. Keys in the seats, keys in the ignitions. With the security on the estate, no one was supposed to steal these cars.

She got to the outer ring of cars and stood, undecided.

What should she steal? A limo would be too obvious, but this Mercedes SL 600 Roadster seemed out of her class. . . . The door opened under her hand, and a heady, new-car, expensive-leather smell filled her head. Drawn by the warmth in the car, she slipped into the driver's seat and looked around for the keys.

They weren't visible.

But a fur coat was.

A fur coat tossed carelessly across the passenger seat.

Hannah grabbed it and pulled it around her shoulders. The cool silk lining quickly warmed around her body. She wriggled her arms into the sleeves. She pulled the luxurious fur under her rear and around her thighs.

She shut the door and untied her shoes. She threw them into the back, wiggled her frozen toes and thought about how remorseful she should feel, ruining some woman's mink with her wet, salty body.

A laugh sputtered out of her.

The coat was the least of it. She was about to steal a car.

This car, if she could just figure out where the keys were hidden. She checked the glove compartment and the console, scanned the back. She sat, discouraged and desperate, and stuck her frozen hands into the coat's pockets.

And there were the keys. She pulled them out and stared at them. Stared at them and realized this was a keyless ignition. They were here, and she could have started the car at any time.

So she did.

She pulled out of the line of cars, holding her breath, fearing a shout of discovery. But the engine was expensive and quiet. No one realized the car was leaving, and if they did, they thought the owner, or the owner's chauffeur, or a valet was driving.

With the lights off, she painstakingly steered around the ruins of the old carriage house and down the narrow winding road. . . .

Eventually, the car warmed up and she turned on the heater. Eventually, the tiny road met the main highway, and she turned north, away from Balfour House. Eventually, she drove west. And eventually, she intended to leave Maine altogether.

She hoped never to return.

Although . . . She smiled a smile that looked more like a snarl. She would never, as long as she lived, forget the sound Carrick made when she slammed him with the lamp and knocked the breath out of him. It was the best thing that had happened that day.

She refused to think of Trent.

He was best forgotten.

TWENTY-ONE

Gabriel walked into B'wiched in New York City and headed right for the table where, almost a year ago, Carrick had first shown him Hannah's photo. Gabriel didn't sit there because he had any sentimental attachment to Hannah. Quite the opposite. He sat there because he preferred to sit with his back against the wall. That way, no one could sneak up behind him and blindside him.

Once was enough.

The waitress hustled over. "I'm Asta." She was new, young, with hair dyed black-hole black, and she was looking him over.

He didn't care. He'd been burned. He wasn't about to step back into that fire. "I want iced tea—black, not sweet, not flavored. Please." He added the *please* because when he'd lived with the Prescotts, he'd learned good manners, although lately, even the starkest civility had seemed too much trouble.

"Right away." Asta leaned over to put a menu on the

table, giving him a clear shot right down the front of her black blouse to a pair of smooth, perky boobs. "If you need anything else, anything at all . . ."

"There'll be two of us for lunch." He took another menu, and waved her away.

That was what civility got him. A waitress who wanted to chat when Gabriel wanted to get this business with Carrick over with at last.

Carrick stepped through the door. It was the first time Gabriel had seen him since that god-awful night last year. Carrick hadn't changed; his appearance was as polished as ever . . . although perhaps he was a little thinner. Certainly, a haunted expression had etched a few lines around his mouth.

But then, his mother had been killed last year in circumstances that had sent Gabriel into a fury of anguish and pain. Gabriel had spent four months tracking Hannah Grey through twelve states. In Becket, Massachusetts, he'd located the fat head who, based on his belief that anyone who wore a fur coat and drove a Mercedes couldn't lie, had reissued her a money card for her account, even though she had no ID. In Philadelphia, Gabriel had located that very fur coat on a homeless woman. In Chicago, he'd located the stripped remnants of the Mercedes. Then, in Minneapolis, he'd lost Hannah's scent. All trace of her had disappeared.

He hadn't given up. He would never give up. He would find her and bring her to justice for what she'd done to Mrs. Manly, to Carrick . . . and to him.

Because for a few brief, glorious moments, he'd forgotten she was a suspect, and trusted her. Loved her. Loved the illusion of who she was. She'd made him a failure, she'd made him a fool, and she'd broken his heart.

No, not his heart—his dreams.

He would never forgive her.

Now he sat in this chair, in this restaurant, again, to say what he could no longer put off.

I'm your brother.

I'm your half brother.

I'm one of your father's bastards.

"Hello, Gabriel." Carrick offered his hand, and in a somber voice, said, "I'm glad you called. I hope this means you've finally gotten over what happened last autumn. No one could have suspected the depths of Hannah Grey's infamy, and no one blames you for—"

Gabriel couldn't stand the sympathy and the earnestness anymore. He came to his feet. "Carrick, I'm your half brother, one of your father's bastards."

Carrick's hand jerked back against his side. For a split second, his face was blank with shock and an ugly dismay. Then a smile split his face. "By God, you played me!"

"I did." Gabriel sat. Better to give Carrick the dominant position here. It cost Gabriel nothing, and it would put Carrick at ease.

"So it wasn't an accident that you showed up when I needed someone to find my brothers." Carrick looked as if he had control of himself, but his voice shook a little.

Gabriel spread his hands in deprecating dismissal.

"At first I had nothing more than suspicion, so when the case against your mother hit and you needed help—"

"You moved into position. Very clever." Carrick pulled up a chair, and his eyes gleamed with honest admiration. "I never saw that one coming."

Gabriel leaned back, relieved.

He had to admit, he'd been worried. No man liked being set up, no matter how good the reason. But maybe it was the blood connection, maybe it was Carrick's "Life is a game" attitude, but the guy seemed to honestly admire Gabriel's deception.

The waitress popped up again. "Hi, I'm Asta, and I'm here to wait on *you*. What can I get for you two gentlemen?"

Gabriel shoved a menu toward Carrick, ordered a pork sandwich with sweet potato chips, and by the time he was done, Carrick was ready to order his caprese salad and chardonnay.

"I'll bring that food right out," Asta trilled.

As she bounced away, Carrick said, "Whoa."

"Yeah. It's not just her boobs that are perky." No matter what had happened in his life, Gabriel had never been such a cynic. Now his sister Pepper told him he had passed *cynic* and had gone right into *bitter asshole*.

Gabriel looked up from the menu to find Carrick examining him. Carrick's gaze lingered on the harsh lines of Gabriel's bone structure, the tanned skin, the straight black hair, the blade of a nose. "I should have recognized the eyes. Your mother had to be . . . what? Hispanic? Native American? Aztec? Mayan?"

Gabriel shut the menu. "All of those, maybe. When I was four, she abandoned me, so I don't have the details." The details were lost in the screams of a terrified child and the rusty stain of old dried blood.

"Didn't Father support you? I mean, until he left? He was always good about that, I thought."

"I apparently slipped through the cracks. So to speak." Gabriel could joke about it. He simply didn't think it was funny. "It took DNA to turn my suspicion into certainty, and all the results are in. We're one big happy family. Five brothers. Five women Nathan Manly seduced and impregnated." Whoops. Gabriel had forgotten about that tact thing again. "Except for your mother. We can't say he seduced her. He married her."

"He married her for her money, so I'm going to guess that, yes, there was a seduction involved."

Gabriel wondered at Carrick's lack of concern. Most guys were a little sensitive when they talked about their mothers' sex lives.

But Carrick was talking about his in-wedlock father, so maybe that made a difference.

Or maybe he had spent so many years being knocked around about his father's corruption, he'd lost the ability to be sensitive.

Or maybe he just hid his feelings well.

All interesting theories, and important when it came to understanding this complex man who was his brother.

"Did he father more sons?" Carrick asked. "Am I going to have more . . . surprises popping up every damn time I turn around?"

So Gabriel wasn't the only one whose tact failed him. "There's a mystery we'll never completely solve. I've done the research. I've examined your father's—*our* father's—travel logs, and his personal financial records. Perhaps there are other sons like me—sons he conceived in his travels, sons he lost track of—but I don't think so. He seemed very conscientious about his little habit."

"You have to wonder what he was thinking."

"I've seen it before. Guys who spread their sperm throughout the land."

"He wasn't a salmon," Carrick said with irritation.

"I guess not. I never met him."

Asta put their plates in front of them, giving them another good flash of the boobies, and when they paid no attention, she flounced off to a more appreciative table.

"My father was a good father. Generous, kind, lots of fun when he was around." Carrick's mouth turned down. "But there was never a time when I didn't know he had other sons."

"Your mother told you?" Seemed out of character.

"No. Until he was gone and the scandal broke, she never admitted she knew. The servants told me about my father and his . . . predilections. And my class-mates jeered about it. When Father was gone away on 'business' "—Carrick used air quotes—"I used to imagine him talking to the other boys, playing ball with them, helping with their homework, the way he did when he was home, with me. I felt cheated. In some ways, my childhood was as difficult as yours."

Gabriel snorted. "No."

With a lofty disregard for the facts, Carrick said, "Father taught me one thing for sure. When you're headed into the brush, always put on a raincoat."

"Oh, me, too." Although since the moment Carrick had shown him Hannah's picture, Gabriel hadn't cared about other women. Hannah . . . well, he wanted Hannah, simply Hannah, and she was a whore, a thief, and a murderer. One dance, and she'd done a pretty good job of ruining sex for him.

He sure as hell hoped it wasn't forever. But he wasn't taking any bets.

"So. You're my brother." Carrick tapped his fork on the table. "Do you still work for me?"

"No. I'm working this case for myself now."

"You're pretty intense about this one." That seemed to make Carrick uneasy.

"Yeah." Gabriel tried to joke. "Besides, I don't offer a family discount."

"Such business acumen. *Daddy* would be impressed." Carrick's mouth quirked, slamming his dimple into position.

From a table nearby, Gabriel heard a woman softly moan. Yeah, Carrick still had the lady-killer effect.

"I don't appreciate being compared to Daddy." Now Gabriel was *not* joking.

"It's inevitable, man. There's no escaping heredity. Heredity is the bitch queen of fate."

But Gabriel had spent time with his other half brothers, Roberto Bertolini, Devlin FitzWilliam, and Mac MacNaught. The brothers were more than merely their father's children. Their mothers had left their marks on their sons, and the men, each one, had used their own minds, their own hearts, their own spirits to fashion their lives. Gabriel admired them. They were good men, and Carrick, if he would drop the tendency toward melodrama, would be a good man, too. "Heredity is not a trap, and to believe otherwise is an excuse for weakness."

As if the whole subject gave him a headache, Carrick put his fist to his forehead. "It's a trap for me," he muttered.

Carrick was feeling sorry for himself. Poor little rich boy.

Although he had few funds now. Right?

Without warning, Gabriel pounced. "Has Hannah accessed your father's fortune?"

"No. The account is still intact."

"So you know where the account is now."

Carrick hesitated. "It's so much money, and people have begun to take an interest."

"People." Gabriel didn't like the sound of that. "As in people besides the government?"

Carrick looked from side to side and said softly, "Just . . . keep it down, huh?"

Gabriel leaned forward. "Are you in trouble?"

"Nothing you can help with."

"Do you need money?" Gabriel had always wondered how Carrick had maintained such a lavish lifestyle. Maybe by living beyond his means?

"No." Carrick lifted his chin. "I made a bundle selling interviews about Mother's death."

"I saw." Gabriel hadn't approved. In his experience, talking to the sensationalist media was always trouble, and in this case, sleazy and heartless.

"I suppose I shouldn't have profited by that whole gruesome mess," Carrick said defiantly, "but the news shows were going to get their information from somebody, and I figured it might as well be me."

Okay, fine. They had different philosophies about the press. "So what's the problem?"

"Nothing." Carrick's voice rose. "Jesus, what makes you think there has to be a problem?"

Gabriel kept his voice level. Quiet. "Because Hannah Grey *does* know how to access the fortune. I've watched the playback a hundred times. The things your mother said to her, the things she said back, make that clear."

"So?"

"So why hasn't she done it yet?"

"There's some special time of the year when it can be accessed? Or . . . or she needs some kind of sophisticated software she can't get to while she's on the run?" Carrick made the same guesses Gabriel had made.

"Something like that. What's for sure is that at some point, she will clear out the account. Finding Hannah is my priority." For more reasons than he wanted to say.

"You're sure you'll find her?"

"I have surveillance in place to watch her bank account. If she tries to access her money, we'll have her." She hadn't done it yet, nor had she contributed to her social security account. So what was she doing for

income? "I have good sources all over the country"—
Gabriel hoped to hell she hadn't made it across the
border to Canada or Mexico—"and I pay well. In cases
like this, all it takes is one greedy, observant person to
turn her in."

"Maybe she's dead."

"No." No. Hannah couldn't be dead. Gabriel
wouldn't allow that to be true. "We're investigating a
lead right now."

"A lead?" Carrick seemed torn between excitement
and dismay.

"A slim lead. In Houston. From a homeless lady.
Who is crazy. Literally." Gabriel had spent far too
much time following up false leads, yet his gut told
him this time they'd hit the jackpot. "Sometimes, the
offer of a reward is all it takes to clarify the mind."

"You'll keep me apprised of all progress."

"You're the first person I'll tell. But there's more."
Gabriel hated to tell him this. "I've developed connec-
tions in the government, and I know why the investigation was opened in the first place."

"You do?" Carrick shuddered as if someone had just
walked over his grave.

Gabriel pushed the sandwich away. The conversation had made him lose his appetite. "Three and a half
years ago, an informant filed a report."

"Who?"

"Someone close to your mother."

"Hannah," Carrick said immediately.

"No, this happened long before Hannah came on
the scene."

"Right. Right. Of course. I forgot. The government opened the investigation a while back." Carrick wiped his palms on his napkin. "Then . . . Torres. The old butler. He died almost two year ago, but Mother told him everything."

"It's possible, but not likely."

"Why not?"

"Torres died too soon, and whoever did it was hoping to put pressure on Mrs. Manly, catch her in the act of retrieving the money, and get his cut."

"Or take it all," Carrick said.

"Exactly." The boy showed he had a grip on the logistics of the situation, too. He made Gabriel proud. "I don't believe in coincidence. Whoever told the government that your mother knew about the fortune probably also put Hannah in place to try and pry the information out of her before the government hearing."

"Right. That makes sense." Carrick nodded as if only now did he realize that Gabriel *would* crack the case. "So you're looking for two people. One unknown, and Hannah Grey."

"By the time I finish my investigation, we'll know who our mystery thief is, and we'll make him sorry."

"Is he Hannah's lover, do you suppose?"

"It's possible," Gabriel said harshly.

"More than possible, I would say. Maybe they need to meet up before they can access the account!" Carrick sounded excited, as if he'd discovered the key to the puzzle.

"Maybe. All I know is, I am going to find Hannah Grey, and I will get every last scrap of information out of her." Gabriel smiled with some pleasure as he considered the torments he would use on her.

He hoped she resisted for a long, long time.

Carrick stood on the sidewalk, smiled like a fool, and waved Gabriel into a cab and off to the airport to return to the wilds of Texas. Then he pulled his cell phone out of his pocket and searched for the one number he'd input, but never called.

A familiar, hateful voice answered after one ring. "Mr. Manly, it's good to hear from you at last. I hope you have news about the fortune for me."

"I think you'll want to take care of something before it gets to be a problem. It seems my security man is sure Hannah Grey knows how to access the offshore account. He's going after her now, thinks she's in Houston, and once he gets that information—"

"I don't think he would go far with that amount of money before he was, shall we say, deprived of it?" The voice sounded almost amused.

"You don't understand." Carrick really needed this handled. He'd had enough of brothers hanging around, talking about business and wondering what he did for a living. They would want their own cuts when they broke the code to access Father's fortune—he knew it. Everyone would want a cut, especially . . ."Gabriel Prescott will turn it over to the government. He is that kind of guy."

The voice on the other end of the line sharpened. "You're sure?"

"Very sure."

"Well, then, Gabriel Prescott has officially become a pest to be removed, and Hannah Grey has become a resource to be discovered."

"Whatever you think best, Osgood." Carrick hung up and said to no one in particular, "I was hoping you would say that."

TWENTY-TWO

Hannah stepped out of the air-conditioned comfort of the Wal-Mart in Houston, Texas, and the September heat hit her like a fever. It was autumn at home in New Hampshire, but here the pavement was so hot it burned through the thin soles of her shoes, and the heat rose in waves that smelled of motor oil, an ice-cream cone melting on the concrete, and the Dumpster behind the store. Not far away, the cars roared along the 610 loop.

She walked down the row of cars toward the quiet neighborhood behind the store, toward the Metro bus stop, and hated Texas. She hated the humidity, she hated the giant cockroaches that populated the bathroom at night, she hated her job checking at Wal-Mart, she hated the variety of accents—smooth Eastern Indian, rapid Spanish, the tonality of Vietnamese, and most of all, that twangy Texas accent she heard everywhere.

She adjusted the backpack she carried with her

everywhere, the one with all her worldly possessions, and felt the familiar trickle of sweat start down her spine.

But it wasn't really Texas she hated.

She was homesick.

She wanted to live in New Hampshire, in a town where she knew people. She wanted to shuffle her feet through the falling leaves, feel the first bite of winter in the air. She wanted to work as a nurse, in a hospital, not as a checker. . . . She wanted to know she would not have to move on again soon.

If she could save enough, she'd go to California.

But who was she kidding? She didn't dare access her own account. The cash Mrs. Manly had left her ran out four months ago, in San Antonio, and she would never be able save money working for minimum wage. She could hardly feed herself. She lived in the misery of a dorm in a hostel in the museum district. The people who ran the place had taken pity on her and let her stay on as one of their permanent residents, but the other permanent residents were odd, to say the least, and one old woman was watching her with a glint in her eye that made Hannah very uncomfortable.

But the old lady was half senile. Surely she didn't remember last winter's newscasts . . . and Hannah had changed her appearance, dyed her hair a mousy brown and let it grow, and pierced her ears multiple times. She dressed like a teenager, made sure she looked younger than her twenty-five years.

She felt older. A lot older.

That was the trouble. Mrs. Manly's murder had

struck a chord with the press. The story had been covered on every television station, on the Internet, in the papers.

Melinda Manly, Wife of Notorious Industrialist, Womanizer and Thief Nathan Manly, Murdered by Nurse She Trusted!

Carrick had been interviewed time and again, his expression tragic as he related the story of how he had hired Hannah to help his mother . . . and instead she had killed her. At that last sentence, his voice always trembled theatrically. The guests at the party had told their stories, each one more fantastic than the one before. Even Jeff Dresser had had his moment of glory as he related how she'd screwed his poor old father to death and, in the same sentence, threatened to have the body exhumed and examined for foul play.

Worst of all, the video of Hannah injecting Mrs. Manly with the fatal dose of curare had played on screens and monitors time and again. They never showed how desperately she tried to save her with CPR. No, never that. But they went over and over how curare was an ancient South American paralyzing poison known as arrow poison, and described how it cruelly killed Mrs. Manly by slowing and then stopping her heart and lungs.

Who had taken the video? How? Susan Stevens had told them there were no videos or microphones. Yet the video existed, so Susan had lied, and Hannah had failed. Failed in a long line of failures.

Now she lived her life in fear and poverty, looking over her shoulder, always afraid the police would catch up with her and arrest her, or worse, Carrick Manly would locate her and . . . Well, she didn't know what he would do, but she would never make the mistake of underestimating him again. She'd given the injection, but he'd replaced the medication, knowing full well what would happen.

He had killed his own mother.

She turned onto the street lined with cars and houses, old bungalows guarded by high, dense hedges, mixed with a few brand-new McMansions looking dominant and out of place. The neighborhood was in transition, run-down and yet in demand because of its proximity to downtown. She stopped under a huge old live oak, taking a moment to savor the shade and the peace of being away from demanding customers and her prick of a supervisor.

But almost as soon as she stopped, she caught a glimpse of a man walking along the sidewalk toward her.

In an instant, and with the expertise gained from eleven months on the lamb, she sized him up: midthirties, tall, fit, Hispanic, dressed in well-fitting jeans and an expensive golf shirt.

Her heart started the low, steady thump she had come to associate with danger. She wanted to run. Instead, she started toward him—better to pass him than to have him follow her. She kept her gaze away from his, yet observed him out of her peripheral vision. He had striking green eyes, and he was watching her, smiling pleasantly like a man who liked what he saw.

That wasn't the problem. She was attractive. Men

still looked at her. And this guy appeared to be decent enough—but what was he doing here? By Wal-Mart, by the bus stop? He was out of place.

He was about two car lengths away from her, still watching her, still smiling, when twenty feet behind him, another man opened the door of a parked car, leaned out and took aim with a small, lethal-looking pistol.

Hannah reacted purely on instinct. She screamed, "Down!" and dove for the pedestrian.

At the same time, he leaped for her. The gunshot sounded, a blast in the quiet afternoon.

He crumpled facedown on the concrete.

Something hit her left wrist—a ricochet, a rock, twirling her sideways, making her stagger into the hedge. Furious and frightened, she recovered and flung herself on top of the stranger. Her hands skidded across the blistering hot pavement, and knew she was going to feel it later.

But not now. Now all she could feel was the guy beneath her. He was still warm but motionless. Unconscious. Dead? Maybe dead.

Please, God, not dead.

The man in the car slammed the door, gunned the engine, and peeled away from the curb.

He'd be back. When he realized she was still alive, he'd be back.

TWENTY-THREE

Grabbing the wounded man—*not dead, please don't be dead*—beneath the armpits, Hannah pulled. Hard. It hurt. Hurt her wrist so badly, tears trickled down her cheeks. She dragged him into someone's yard, behind a high, dense hedge. She looked around, expecting to hear someone scream or shout, to come to her aid.

The house was lifeless. If anyone was on this street, he was hunkered down, terrified of the gunfire, just like her.

Fine. She would do this on her own.

She slid her hand around the man's neck and pressed her fingers to his carotid artery.

His heart beat strongly.

He honest to God wasn't dead. It was the best thing that had happened to her in almost a year. "And to you, too, I suppose," she muttered.

She wanted to collapse in relief, but he was face-down in the grass with blood leaking from beneath his hip. She pulled off her backpack and rummaged through it, grabbing the first piece of cloth that came to her hand.

Man, he was bleeding all over the place. "Can you hear me?" she asked. "I'm going to press on your wound."

She jumped when the guy answered her. "Is the shooter gone?"

"Yes."

He lifted his head. "Do you see any more suspicious-looking characters?"

"Only you."

He pushed himself over with arms and his good leg, and looked up at her. "Can you stop the bleeding?" He spoke quickly, tersely, like a guy who was familiar with situations like this. With shootings and violence. Maybe the nice jeans and name-brand golf shirt were merely a cover. Or maybe he could afford to dress well because he was a drug dealer. Maybe he'd been shot in some turf war.

And maybe it didn't matter. As long as it was possible that he had been shot in her place, she would care for him.

Hell, she was a nurse clear down to her bones. She'd care for him no matter what the circumstances.

"Have you got a phone?" she asked.

He grimaced in pain as he dug into his jeans pocket and pulled out a cell.

"You call nine-one-one. I'll bandage you, slow the bleeding." She pressed the cloth—damn, it was her Usher T-shirt—under his hip, and realized the blood that covered his thighs came from the exit wound at the front.

She fumbled in her backpack again, grabbed another piece of cloth, and pressed it on the front wound, then pulled out her ball of twine. "Can you lift yourself?"

"Yeah." He did, and while she wound the twine around his hips, he asked, "You carry twine in your backpack?"

"You never know when you're going to need it." When you're on the run, she meant. She had a first-aid kit, too, but nothing in it would take care of a gunshot wound. "Nine-one-one," she reminded him. "You're going to be fine, but not if you bleed out here in the grass."

While she tied the two shirts—the other was her plain white tee; this incident had put a serious dent in her wardrobe—he made the call.

"I've been shot," she heard him say. "Pick me up at"—he glanced toward the house—"323 Wisteria. Green house, cracked paint. We're behind the hedge of ligustrum."

Ligustrum. She glanced at the dense green leaves. She hadn't known what it was. So he must be from Houston.

But he hadn't called emergency . . . had he? Was he a cop assigned to find her, bring her in?

He must have read her mind, because he cut off the call, took her good wrist in a firm grasp. "An ambulance would take too long. I called my chauffeur. He'll be here in less than a minute."

His chauffeur? She stared into his green eyes. She didn't know what to say. *So you are a drug dealer? So you're rich? So you're a rich drug dealer?*

"I haven't thanked you," he said. "You saved my life."

"No. Really, no, I'm sorry. I . . ." *I'm sorry. That guy was aiming for me and hit you.* Not the thing to say. "I know it hurts, but you'll be fine." Her wrist really burned, but she couldn't look away from his hypnotic eyes. He held her with his gaze as surely as he held her with his grasp.

"If you hadn't yelled, he could have killed me."

"No, really, because—" *Don't say it. Don't tell him who he was aiming for.*

"Then you shielded me with your body." His other hand grasped her fingers, thoroughly keeping her in place. "You're the bravest person I've ever met."

"No. No, I'm not. I had a responsibility because—"

Out on the street, a car pulled up. A door opened.

She tensed.

"It's my car." He smiled tightly, a man in pain, yet intent on reassuring her. "I recognize the sound of the engine."

Footsteps sounded on the broken concrete sidewalk. A broad-shouldered black man dressed in a dark business suit stepped into the yard. He looked down at the wounded man, and in a tone of disgust, he said, "Hey, boss, I leave you alone for ten minutes, and you get shot?"

"Daniel, don't nag," her patient said.

"I'm not nagging. I'm stating the facts." Yet as

Daniel talked, he leaned over Hannah's patient, running his hands over his bones, observing the blood-stained jeans. In a gentle voice, he told her, "I'm going to pick him up now. Won't hurt him more than I have to, but he needs to go to the hospital." She caught her breath as he hefted her patient into his arms.

The patient groaned, in obvious agony, then called, "Come on, girl. We've got to get out of here before they come back!"

All right. Good point. She didn't want to be shot. She didn't want to die. She didn't know who this guy was, but if he could hide her away from Carrick and his lies and his assassins, she didn't care. She didn't have any scruples anymore. She couldn't afford them.

"Thank God, miss, you were in the right place at the right time," the chauffeur said. The back door of the car was open. Leaning in, he gently placed her patient on the leather seat. "Thank God you could care for him." He helped her in beside . . . the guy.

She had to find out his name.

He must have been thinking the same thing, because he said, "Who are you?"

The chauffeur shut the door behind them. He slid into the front seat and started the car so smoothly she didn't even notice they were moving.

She sat on the floor beside her guy. "I'm Grace." She'd been using that pseudonym for the past year, because in Hebrew, *Hannah* meant *Grace*, and every time she said that name, it was like a prayer of thanksgiving. Thanksgiving because, by the grace of God, Hannah was still alive and free.

"I'm Gabriel." Her guy offered his hand.

She placed her fingers in his broad palm and shook, then gasped and winced.

He held her firmly, gently, and turned her hand up to the light. "You're hurt, too." He sounded like he cared.

"I didn't realize." She scowled at the scrapes the pavement had made. They weren't serious, but her other wrist . . . my God. The *pain*. In these circumstances, with Carrick onto her . . . this was unmitigated disaster.

"Hey," Gabriel said, "it's okay. We'll take care of it."

She tucked her wrist under her arm, and looked around wildly. There was just so much blood. She hadn't expected that much blood. She hadn't expected to feel woozy from pain and shock.

Maybe he was going to die? From blood loss? She should reassure him, and urge the chauffeur to hurry because—she focused on the blood that blotted her clothes—because there was so much blood. "I just have some scratches. No biggie." Her voice was fainter than it should have been. "It's you we have got to get to a hospital."

"We're going to a hospital." He was the one who was shot, and he was the one making the soothing noises. "It's a private hospital where my friend works. He's a doctor, and he'll contact the police because it's the law, and everything will be on the up-and-up."

"Oh." She hadn't even thought about that. A gunshot wound had to be reported to the cops. And that meant . . . she couldn't stay with him. She couldn't rely on him to keep her safe from Carrick. She had to get away as soon as she could.

"I think maybe you'd better lie down." Gabriel watched her from narrowed green eyes. "You look ill."

"I'm fine. Really. I'm fine. I just . . ." Now that the trauma was over, she felt faint and sick to her stomach, and she wanted to put her head down on Gabriel's broad chest and sob her heart out.

That would go over well.

But as she had so often over the past eleven months, she blinked back the tears. "It will be a relief to get you checked into the hospital and know you're going to be taken care of."

"Checked in? No, they're not going to check me in."

"Yes, they will." This guy was obviously unclear on the concept. "You've been shot, and it's not a minor wound, either. It's a through and through."

"I don't care. They're not keeping me. So I'm going to need a nurse."

"Look—" Her first ride in a limo, and all she could think was that she hoped she didn't throw up on the leather seats.

He overrode her objection. "I'm going to need a nurse. Someone who'll go to my home and stay with me, and administer painkillers—"

She flinched.

"And make sure my fever doesn't spike." As he watched her, he already looked fevered. "You're a nurse."

"No, I'm not," she said automatically.

"You did a hell of an imitation of one back there."

"First-aid course."

"Then you, the expert with the first-aid course . . . you could go home with me and take care of me."

She would never work as a home-care nurse again. Never. It had taken her long enough, but she'd learned her lesson. "No."

"If you won't do it, then I'll go home by myself."

"Fine."

The limousine slowed and stopped. Daniel hopped out, came around, and leaned in to lift Gabriel out of the seat.

Gabriel groaned piteously and went limp.

"Damn, boss, this is bad." Daniel hurried toward the emergency entrance.

Without a second thought, Hannah grabbed her backpack, scrambled out of the car, and followed.

TWENTY-FOUR

As Hannah trailed Gabriel inside, the small hospital jumped to attention. The ER nurses produced a gurney, placed Gabriel on it, and pushed him into a private examining room.

Hannah hovered in the doorway. "Dr. Bellota has been called," one of the nurses informed her as if she had the right to know, and steered her toward a metal straight-backed chair.

Hannah placed her backpack on it and stood there, wanting to go, needing to get out before she was trapped, but desperate to see that Gabriel would be all right, that someone else hadn't been caught in this tangled Manly web . . . and killed.

With an easy stride, the doctor walked in. He was short, overweight, about sixty, with a shock of wavy white hair and sharp brown eyes, and an imposing presence that proclaimed he was in charge. "What did you do now, Gabriel?" he asked heartily.

"Stepped in front of a bullet." For a man who'd been

shot a half hour before, and hanging limply in his chauffeur's arms five minutes ago, Gabriel sounded strong and rational. "If Grace hadn't yelled a warning, the bullet would have been a lot higher and slightly more fatal."

"Only slightly, huh?" As Dr. Bellota washed his hands, he cast a sharp glance at her bloody hands and clothes. "Grace, were you hit?"

Hannah had trained in a hospital like this, and the familiar sounds, scents, and sights took her back and made her give her report with brisk efficiency. "No, Doctor, he took the bullet. It's a through and through, a loss of blood but no bones or vital organs hit."

As he dried his hands and donned gloves, Dr. Bellota considered her thoughtfully, then watched the nurses cut away the twine and bloodstained T-shirts, and peel back Gabriel's pants. "Good job," he said to Hannah. "Medical training?"

"Yes." *Wrong answer.* "No. First-aid course."

"Good first-aid course. I wish they all were this comprehensive." He bent over Gabriel's wound. "Clean shot. That makes my job easier."

"Any permanent damage?" Gabriel asked.

"Doesn't look like it, but only time will tell."

Hannah relaxed against the wall, woozy with relief. "There was a lot of blood."

"There always is." Again Dr. Bellota leaned over Gabriel. "We've got someone from HPD on her way over."

Hannah shrank into a corner.

The doctor continued. "If you can stand it, I'd like to

hold off on the pain meds until you've spoken to the officer."

Gabriel watched Hannah as he said, "I'll hold off on the pain meds until I'm at home."

Dr. Bellota snorted. "You can't go home. Judging by her clothes and the dressings we removed, you're down a pint of blood. I'm keeping you for observation."

"No, you're not." Gabriel was definite.

"Damn it, Gabriel—"

"Stow it, Dean. I'm not staying here."

"You'll need a nurse."

"Grace can do it."

Dr. Bellota glanced at her again. "She *says* she's not a nurse."

Gabriel spoke quietly to him.

They held a quick consultation, the kind that made Hannah edge toward the door.

Dr. Bellota called one of the nurses over.

She came to Hannah, and with the polished smile of a professional healer, she said, "Grace, I'm Zoe, and I'm a physician's assistant. Dr. Bellota wanted me to take you down to have your arm checked out."

Hannah tucked it tighter into her pit. "It's fine."

Gently Zoe pulled it free. One glance, and she spoke sharply. "This is *not* fine. Doctor, come and look at this."

Hannah focused on her wrist. She expected to see a scrape. Instead something had torn her skin back, baring muscle and bone . . . and blood. Lots of blood.

It wasn't merely Gabriel who had been shot. The bullet had ripped through his leg and across her wrist, and the blood she wore . . . wasn't all his.

The lights dimmed. A buzzing started in her ears. And with a faint moan of humiliation, she collapsed.

Gabriel leaned on one elbow and watched Dr. Bellota examine the unconscious woman on the floor.

Examine Hannah Grey.

Her complexion was parchment white, her lips and eyelids almost blue. Blood streaked her cheap clothes and pooled beneath her hand. She was thin, way too thin, almost dead from the ordeal of killing Mrs. Manly and running . . . from him.

Zoe wound gauze around the frail wrist.

Bellota lifted Hannah's eyelid. "How long's it been since she ate?"

"I don't know. I just met her on the street when she flung herself on top of me." A point that was bothering Gabriel quite a lot. He would have preferred if she'd screamed and run. It would be more in character for a murderess.

On the other hand, he already knew she was a complex creature, a study in contradictions.

"She's shot, but a bigger problem is, she's malnourished. Can you sign a form for treatment for her?" Bellota viewed Gabriel sternly. "You are her brother or husband, aren't you?"

"I sure am. I'm also the guy who's paying for her treatment." Hannah Grey wasn't going to die on him now. Not when he had her firmly in his grasp.

"Right." Bellota stood as Zoe trundled in a gurney. "Get her hooked up to a saline drip."

"D5W?" Zoe asked.

"Right, let's get her blood sugar up. Then run an MRI on that wrist. Don't let the lab tell you they don't have time." Bellota frowned at Zoe. "I want it now."

"Then, Doctor, you call it in." Zoe assembled the bag and the drip chamber, then inserted the needle in Hannah's arm.

Hannah twitched. Her eyelids quivered.

Gabriel released a slow sigh of relief. She was responding. Not a lot, but she was still here.

Bellota grunted, but did as Zoe instructed. When he got off the phone, he said, "The lab'll take her now. Whatever you do, *don't* let her get up."

"*Don't* let her walk out," Gabriel added. When Zoe raised her eyebrows, he said, "Keep an eye on her. And keep the police away."

"Right," Zoe said.

Gabriel had dealt with her before; Bellota respected her, and she was one smart woman, who understood far too much without a word being said.

She nodded at him, then pushed the gurney into the corridor.

Gabriel collapsed back on the damn uncomfortable bed.

"Now you've got to stay in the hospital," Bellota said with satisfaction, "because she'll need to stay."

"She'll run if she can, and I've played hell finding her. So get me ready to go, because we're leaving."

Of all the ways he had imagined this capture would go, this scenario had never crossed his mind. He'd considered talking her into giving herself up. Considered lulling her into trusting him, then announcing who he was and slapping the cuffs on her. Considered seducing her and then . . . Well, he'd never got beyond seducing her.

He certainly hadn't thought he would feel both grateful to her, and sorry for her. "Get Daniel in here, please. I need to talk to him."

Bellota jerked his head toward one of the nurses, then went back to work on Gabriel, poking and prodding and making him groan. "What in the hell have you gotten yourself into this time?"

"I'm not exactly sure. That's what I want to talk to Daniel about." Because Gabriel didn't believe in coincidences, so—why had someone shot him?

Hannah woke up on a gurney being trundled through hospital corridors. She stared up at the passing fluorescent lights on the ceiling and wished she didn't feel so wretched. She'd been shot, too. The police would want her statement. She needed to leave—and if she stood up, she'd throw up. And collapse.

This was her nightmare. She was living her nightmare.

Nothing escaped Zoe's sharp gaze, and from behind Hannah's head, she said, "Doctor ordered an MRI on your wrist."

"I can't pay." Although Zoe had probably figured that out.

"Mr. Prescott will take care of it," Zoe said, and when Hannah would have objected, she added, "You saved his life. It's the least he can do."

"Fine." Hannah had to resign herself to that. She didn't have a choice. Carrick had found her, so she had to go on the run again, and if she was going to make it, she needed to be healthy.

She needed money, too, but she'd figure that out later.

The way the doctor and the nurses treated Gabriel told Hannah one thing. "He's not a drug dealer, I take it."

Zoe threw back her head and laughed. "No. No, he's quite a respectable businessman."

So what was he doing in that neighborhood? Shopping at Wal-Mart?

But it wasn't like he was looking for hookers—wrong location for that—and Hannah supposed he could have been visiting in one of the McMansions.

Which meant he *had* been shot in her place, and if he knew that, he wouldn't be so grateful.

The medical team was brisk and efficient, performing the MRI and letting her look at the results without committing to an opinion.

But Hannah had an opinion. The wound needed stitches, some clever sewing to correct the damage to muscles and tendons, but all in all, it looked pretty good. And right now, she felt pretty good. She knew it was an illusion fostered by the saline drip, but if she could figure out a way out of here . . .

"The films will go down to Dr. Bellota to be read, and he may send you on to a specialist," Zoe said.

"To check for nerve damage."

Zoe watched Hannah carefully flex her left hand, then touch each of her fingers to her thumb. "Are you sure you're not in the medical profession?"

Of course Zoe recognized another nurse, and that was another piece of the identity puzzle Hannah couldn't afford to have slip into place. So Hannah ignored Zoe's oblique accusation, saying only, "The good news is, my hand does what I want it to do. The bad news is, I imagine I'll need stitches. Do you do that?"

"The bullet did damage. Dr. Bellota will want you to see a plastic surgeon."

Hannah placed her good hand over Zoe's, looked into her eyes, and took advantage of the sisterhood of nursing. "Help me out here."

Zoe chewed her lip, then made her decision. "I can't do the stitches, but . . ." She wheeled Hannah back down to the ER and into an examining room. Quickly, efficiently, she bandaged the wrist. "I'm taking the films to Dr. Bellota now. I'll get right back to you." She whipped out of the examining room and headed down the corridor.

Hannah wasn't going to get a better chance. She unplugged herself from the drip, cursed the fact she'd lost her backpack, and headed for the exit.

She had almost made it out when Daniel stepped in front of her, smoothly blocking her way. "Miss Grace, Mr. Prescott is on his way out, and he asked me to escort you to the limo."

She stood in the waiting room, looked up at the big black man, and said, "I am not going to the limo."

In a calm, coaxing voice, he said, "Now, Miss Grace,

if you don't go home with Mr. Prescott, Dr. Bellota will have kittens right here in the emergency room. If you need to go somewhere first, I'll be glad to drive wherever you need, wait for you to pick up your things—" He held up her backpack.

She caught her breath. All her things were in her backpack, and he held it just out of reach. "Can I have that?"

"Of course, miss. I'll put it in the car for you." He smiled in a way that might have been comforting in a smaller, less-toned, less-determined man. "Mr. Prescott has a nice private penthouse apartment located in the Galleria, where the two of you can recuperate in peace and quiet."

"If *I* have to recuperate, what good will I do Mr. Prescott?"

"I'll be there to help haul his lazy ass around to the bathroom and whatnot. Don't you worry. You won't hurt your wrist having to deal with him."

She tried to step around Daniel.

He moved to thwart her. "Don't you worry about Mr. Prescott getting fresh with you, either. He would never hurt a woman, and anyway, I suspect that gunshot's going to slow him down some."

She wished Daniel would let her go. Let her walk into the early-evening sunshine and disappear into the city, and figure out how to hide from Carrick's men. Because they wouldn't miss twice.

Oh, God, what was she going to do? Racket about from place to place like a pinball while innocent pedestrians got shot by Carrick's cut-rate assassins?

"Wait until you see that penthouse, Miss Grace. It's gorgeous and plenty big enough for the two of you, and of course I'll be there to take care of you, so you'll have a chaperon." Daniel glanced over her shoulder. "Here he comes now, looking all riled about whether I did my job and caught up with you."

She turned to see Gabriel, sitting up in a wheelchair pushed by Dr. Bellota himself.

Gabriel looked pale and sweaty.

Dr. Bellota looked grim.

He pushed Gabriel up to her. "Against my better judgment, I'm going to let Gabriel go home."

"You haven't got a choice," Gabriel said.

"That's why I'm doing it." Dr. Bellota took Hannah's wrist and checked her pulse. "How you managed to convince Zoe, the finest doctor's assistant I've ever worked with, to let you go—"

"She didn't let me go. I tricked her!"

"Right." Dr. Bellota obviously didn't believe that, but at least Zoe was off the hook. "Daniel, I depend on you to keep them both in bed—*in bed*—for seven days. If they'd stay in the hospital, it would only be five days, but no"—he laid on the sarcasm—"Gabriel has to go home."

"Nag," Gabriel muttered.

"And Grace has an important appointment with the Grim Reaper." Dr. Bellota put a hand on her forehead. "Daniel, help her out to the car."

Daniel wrapped his arm around her waist and, her brief surge of energy gone, she leaned into him.

Dr. Bellota pushed Gabriel out into the still, damp

heat and toward the long black limo parked in the patient loading zone.

"I'll be by in the morning to check on them," Dr. Bellota said.

A doctor who did house calls. Gabriel Prescott must *really* have a lot of money.

"I've had prescriptions called in to the pharmacy. They'll be delivered within the hour. Daniel, follow the dosage instructions exactly."

"Yes, Doctor." Daniel slid Hannah into the car and onto the smooth leather seat, then placed her backpack at her feet.

"Don't worry, Grace. That penthouse is a great place to recuperate," Dr. Bellota assured her.

"Yeah, that's what *I* said." Gabriel winced as Daniel picked him up and placed him on the seat beside her.

"Don't give me any trouble or I'll have you committed to the psych ward, which is what I should do to keep you here." Dr. Bellota ran his hands through his thick white hair. "Call for any reason, and otherwise, we'll see you both in the morning."

Daniel shut the door and left them in the quiet, cool, expensive and oh so comfortable interior, then got in and drove with quiet competence through the fading light toward the penthouse everyone said would be so perfectly safe and comfortable.

"Put your head on my shoulder before you pass out." Gabriel had a way about him. He didn't so much suggest as order.

"You're in worse shape than I am."

"Yeah, I feel like shit, but having a pretty girl against

my chest will cure me faster than Bellota's prescriptions." He wrapped his arm around her. "Come on."

She did. Like a fool, she did.

For almost a year, she'd been alone, not touching, not trusting, never telling the truth, watching, always watching, always in fear. Now she had her nose pressed into a man's broad chest, and she felt . . . safe. He smelled good, like laundry soap and clean male, and beneath her cheek, his chest felt firm, muscled. He exuded the illusion of shelter, and right now, that was exactly what she needed. Because she hadn't experienced anything like this since—

She gasped and sat up. Since Trent Sansoucy.

Gabriel held his hands up. "What did I do?"

"It's not you. I can't believe what happened. I can't believe . . ." She couldn't believe they'd caught up with her. She passed her hand over her suddenly moist eyes.

"I know. I know."

Hannah watched as they passed into the Galleria, the high-end mall with four anchor stores, an ice-skating rink and so many expensive shops people came from Mexico and across the U.S. to shop there. She had never been inside.

At the south edge of the Galleria, a tall building loomed above the mall. There the limo turned into a shady parking garage and ascended a ramp. A gate opened into the private lot, and shut behind them. They parked in a place designated for the penthouse, and Daniel said, "You two stay put for a second while

I get the wheelchair out of the trunk and bring it around."

She leaned forward to touch Gabriel's forehead. It was warm, but not feverish.

He caught her good wrist. "Listen. We didn't discuss salary."

She pulled back. "What?"

"I'll find out what the going rate for private care is, and I'll pay you half again as much."

She wanted to slap him. "I'm sick, too, and imposing on you. So what are you paying for?"

He released a gust of laughter. "I don't pay for my pleasures, if that's what you're thinking. But I know it's going to take me longer to recover than it'll take you, and by the time you feel better, I'll be the crankiest patient you've ever had. I hate being wounded."

"Yes." She could buy that. Most patients, especially men, had only so much tolerance before they started flinging themselves at the restrictions given for their care.

"Plus, I'm grateful that you yelled about the gunman, impressed that you threw yourself over me to protect me, and indebted for your care. Paying you a good salary is the only way I can settle my debt."

She thought about that. "Okay." Okay, that made sense. And she needed the cash. If this guy was on the up-and-up, and both his doctor and his chauffeur had gone to pains to assure her he was, then staying at his penthouse would get her off the streets for a while and give Carrick's pursuit time to calm down, and it certainly looked like he wouldn't get in here any too easily. "Okay."

Daniel opened the door and reached in for Gabriel, helping him out of the car and into the wheelchair.

Hannah followed, and when Daniel saw her backpack, he took it from her. "I won't drop it, miss, and you can have it back as soon as we get upstairs."

"All right," she muttered and handed it over. Not that it mattered. The only thing she had that was worth anything was Mrs. Manly's access code, and she carried that in her head, not her backpack. But when you could carry everything you own in one backpack, you got attached to it.

Daniel inserted a pass key into the elevator control panel, sending the elevator to the top of the high rise in such a swift, silent ascent, Hannah had to pop her ears. The doors opened into Gabriel Prescott's penthouse, and she stepped into another world.

TWENTY-FIVE

The gunshot had obviously left Gabriel half crazed with pain, because he watched his woman step into his penthouse and experienced a bone-deep contentment.

It didn't matter that Hannah wasn't truly his woman, or that she had murdered for profit, or that he wanted to kill her himself for destroying his last, small, vital spark of faith in humanity.

Somewhere, that primitive part of him that did not respond to logic or good sense told him it was right to have Hannah in his home where she belonged.

If he could take comfort in anything, it was in her obvious anxiety as she looked around. "This is, um, really nice."

"Thank you." It *was* really nice. As soon as one of Gabriel's people called to report that some crazy woman living in a hospice in Houston had contacted them about the reward, and the photo she submitted was a positive identification on their computer program, Gabriel had sent Daniel out to find someplace nice, furnished, with good security. "I've taken the whole top floor." Because that way, the elevator was the only way in, and he had total control of who came and went.

He had total control of *her*.

She groped for her backpack, taking it out of Daniel's hand as if it was a security blanket. Yet she was too exhausted to lift it, for she dragged it across the burnished tile and the Oriental rugs to the floor-to-ceiling windows with the view looking south. She looked out as the sun set, and lights popped out all along Highway 59 toward Sugar Land. "Spectacular."

Daniel hadn't asked him why he wasn't immediately turning her over to the police or to Carrick. Gabriel had been in such a foul mood for the past eleven months, he didn't have to ask. He knew.

The boss had developed an obsession with a cold-blooded killer.

"The master bedroom is to the left," Gabriel said. "That's mine."

She wandered over and looked in. He knew what she saw. A huge room with a California king bed in the center, a lounge chair and end table by the window, a working desk with laptop and desk chair near the bathroom. Bedroom and home office combined.

"The guest bedrooms are to the right. Pick whichever one you want."

She looked back at the doors that led to the guest bedrooms, then at him.

She didn't recognize him. Not at all. Not his real voice, not his unmasked face. The voice-changing software, the Phantom mask, and the dim light at the Balfour Halloween party had done their jobs.

Yet she was still uneasy, probably because of the situation, but maybe because she sensed his interest. His interest . . . Yeah, on the ride here, it had been all he could do to keep his interest to himself. The only thing that had kept him in check was the sure knowledge that he needed to get her up here to keep her—and if she tried to escape, he couldn't stop her.

That irritated him, too.

"Daniel will take care of me." His voice was compulsively harsh.

She read his tone correctly, and jerked back as if he'd rejected her.

His irritation ratcheted up a notch. How *dared* she pretend to be sensitive?

Luckily, before he spoke, Daniel stepped in. "Don't pay him any mind. Mr. Prescott's cantankerous when he's hurt." He spoke gently, apparently as seduced by Hannah's surface innocence as Gabriel had been . . . once.

And he was right. Gabriel wanted her here, not calling for help, not trying to steal away. "Go to bed, Grace. Daniel will bring you something to eat and your pain meds."

"If you're sure . . ." She staggered as if her knees could no longer support her.

"I'm sure. Good night, Grace."

Gabriel and Daniel waited until they knew she had found a bedroom and shut the door behind her.

"The camera in there works, right?" Gabriel said.

"Sure does. I checked it myself." Daniel smiled without humor. "What's the matter, boss? You didn't want her near you when you're helpless? You a coward?"

"That's not cowardice. That's intelligence."

"I guess." Daniel, as cynical as any person who worked for Gabriel could be, stared after her. "She seems so genuinely nice."

Turning to Daniel, his chauffeur, bodyguard and friend, Gabriel asked, "Do you want to view the video again? The one where the nurse who showed Mrs. Manly such care deliberately shot her full of a poison that stopped her breathing and her heart . . . while she was fully aware?"

"No. And neither do you. There for a while, you watched it so often I thought you'd lost your mind."

"I was finding it." She looked different than he remembered, different than she had in the video. Any hint of softness had disappeared; she was too thin, with gaunt cheeks and narrow lips she kept pressed tightly together. Her cheap clothes hung on her, her jeans were so thin he could see air through them, and her tennis shoes were duct-taped together. Her large blue eyes seemed smaller, narrowed, and watched everything and everybody with suspicion.

Life had not been easy for Hannah Grey.

Good.

"But she did holler when someone was going to shoot you," Daniel said.

"Or shoot her." Yet for all Gabriel recalled the litany of her crimes, he still remembered how she had pressed herself over his bleeding body, shielding him from the possibility of flying bullets, and the way she'd dragged him behind the hedge when she'd been shot in the wrist—that was the dichotomy of Hannah Grey. At Balfour House, for the weeks that he'd monitored her every move, she'd been a kind, caring nurse—except for that one defining moment of murder.

So tonight he would sleep and heal, and in the morning, they would talk. Soon he would know everything about Hannah Grey that it was possible to know. Soon he would understand it all.

"She doesn't know you," Daniel said.

"She barely heard my real voice. She never saw my face." Bitterly, Gabriel reminded Daniel—and himself. "But she is the best actress I've ever seen. She could get an Academy Award for breathless innocence in the category of wholesome."

"I know. You're right."

"Find out who fired that shot today and why." Because Gabriel had thought he was simply going to make first contact with Hannah. He sure as hell hadn't expected to be shot.

"I'm already on it."

"And find out which one of us he was trying to hit."

"Right."

"Daniel?"

"Yes, boss?"

"Most important—don't let her get away. One way or another, I'm getting a full confession, and then—I'm bringing her in."

TWENTY-SIX

When Hannah awoke, the bedside clock said two thirty a.m. Her mouth was dry; her wrist throbbed and burned.

More interestingly, she wasn't boiling hot. She wasn't freezing cold. The mattress was not lumpy, not hard, firm in the right places, soft in the right places. She smelled good, like the soap she'd used in the shower she'd taken before she went to bed. She wore a clean pair of men's striped pajamas. And she had food in her belly. She was, for the first time in eleven months, comfortable.

Gradually she pulled herself into a sitting position. She flipped on the lamp, swung her feet over the edge of the bed, and waited. She didn't feel too bad. Her wrist burned, and it was getting worse, but she wasn't sick or faint. She slipped to her feet and waited again. Not bad at all. She walked to her bathroom—each bedroom in this fancy penthouse had its own bathroom—got a drink of water and used the facilities.

When she came out, she caught her breath in surprise.

There in the chair by her bed, Gabriel sat, wrapped in a robe, a crutch leaning against the wall behind him.

Aghast, she asked, "What are *you* doing up?"

"Daniel's asleep, and I thought you'd want your pain medication."

Before she'd gone to sleep at eight, after a meal of minestrone soup and whole-wheat bread sent up by the Italian restaurant downstairs, Daniel had given her her antibiotics and a single pain pill. With the assurance he'd be there for her if she needed him, he'd gone off to take care of Gabriel. Now . . . "Daniel's *asleep*?"

"He hasn't got a gunshot wound to keep him awake," Gabriel said.

Maybe it was the wee hours of the morning, maybe it was being on Gabriel's home turf, but he made her uneasy, as if he could touch her with his gaze . . . and had.

He was looking now. She was totally covered—the pajamas were too big, the sleeves dangled over her wrists, the legs bunched around her feet, and the drawstring knotted around her waist kept the pants up. Maybe he wasn't, but *she* was totally respectable. Yet she had contracted to act as his nurse, and she might pretend to be untrained, but for her own peace of mind, she needed to see if he was all right. And to do that, *she* had to touch *him*. The last eleven months had been hard on her; she actually had to work up her nerve before she walked over and placed a hand on his forehead. "You don't seem to have a fever. How do the dressings feel? Tight? Does the wound feel hot?"

"My leg hurts like a son of a bitch, but it's a normal hurt—not infected. I think I dodged that bullet, if you'll pardon the term." He grinned, a sharp, white-toothed slash of amusement he asked her to share.

Startled, she smiled back and realized—this guy was good-looking. She'd recognized it before, of course, that first time she'd seen him, but her reaction then had been dominated by the wariness of a woman who had lived on the streets. Now she knew he was respectable, and wealthy, and felt an obligation to her. And it was the middle of the night, the lights were low, and he appeared—she didn't know—almost Valentino-like in his looks and intensity. His eyes were deep-set, raw, wild. The skin on his face was stretched too thin across high-set cheeks and a proud, dominant nose.

She smoothed her hand across his forehead.

His lips . . . Well, his lips were perfect for kissing.

That was a dangerous thought.

She stepped back.

"Grace."

She turned back to him, expecting a request for something to eat or drink.

"How is your wound?" he asked.

She looked down at the bandage Zoe had put in place. The white edges were already dirty and damp; she'd tried to wash her fingers and splashed up too far. "It's okay."

"Let me see." Reaching out, he gripped her good wrist and brought her close.

The warmth of his grip, the sense of being shackled, made her breathless. Yet he wasn't doing anything, really. Invading her personal boundaries a bit, but probably he didn't look at it that way. Some people had different definitions of what was acceptable and how soon. He made her wildly uncomfortable, and she didn't understand, would never understand, how a man who was in such lousy shape could exude such a still, smoky danger.

Without an ounce of respect for Zoe's work, he unwrapped the gauze, loosening it carefully from the wound. "Damn it!"

"I thought it looked pretty good." She didn't think any such thing, but the sight of her injury, inflamed, muddy with dried blood, seemed to anger him.

"I shouldn't have taken you out of the hospital. But you wouldn't have stayed, would you?" He assessed her silence correctly. "All right. Tomorrow we'll get someone in to clean this up." He lifted her other hand and lightly touched the scrapes on her palms. "You must have skidded across the sidewalk."

"Honestly, I don't remember. All I remember is being so scared that he'd keep shooting." At the memory, her heartbeat accelerated.

He held each of her hands in each of his, and examined the damage as if he saw something more than scraped palms and swollen knuckles.

Prudently, she removed herself from his grip. "I was lucky. We were lucky. We're alive and not seriously injured. That's cool, right?"

"Right." He picked the prescription bottle up off her

table and read, " 'One tablet every four hours.' Has it been four hours since your last one?"

She rolled the gauze back over her wrist. "It's been at least six."

He shook one out into his palm and offered it. "Then you'd better take this and climb back in bed."

She picked it up carefully, without touching his skin.

He pointed to the water bottle—one she hadn't noticed before—on the bedside table.

She put the pill to her mouth, then hesitated.

"What's wrong? Do you think I will poison you?" He sounded smoothly dangerous, the purr of a lion before it pounced.

She blinked at him, startled. "No. No, I was wondering when you're due for a pill, and if you want me to get it for you. I am supposed to be—"

"Caring for me. I know. But I've got about another hour to go before I can hit the drugs again." The sharp lines around his mouth told too clearly how difficult that hour would be.

She swallowed the pill. She climbed into bed, lay down, and pulled up the covers.

"You don't think I would poison you, then?" he insisted.

"I don't know what you'd get out of it if you did." She yawned, and turned on her side to face him. He was more than merely intense. He was weird. "Besides, isn't that the bottle the pharmacist sent over? Sure looks like it."

"It is."

"That's not poison—that's pain relief."

"Is that how you look at it?"

She lifted her head off the pillow and stared at him. "Huh?"

His expression twisted as if he were in anguish. As if he *were* in pain.

Okay. She knew what to do. "Where are you from?"

"Why?" He shot the question at her.

"I thought we'd chat for a while, distract ourselves from how lousy we feel." It was a tactic she'd used before on her patients many times.

"Ah. Well." He seemed to need to think about his answer. "I'm originally from South Texas."

She didn't think he was lying, but he was not being any too detailed. "You do have the slightest bit of an accent. Is your family still there?"

"I was in the foster system until I was about eleven. Then I got adopted. The parents were killed and I was alone again." His recitation was dry.

"I'm so sorry!" That explained the harsh cast to his face; the body that was both solid and whipcord thin. This man was a fighter. "But look at you! Look at this place! You grew up and made something of yourself."

"I suppose. How about you? Are you from Texas?"

"No, I'm from the East Coast, and like you, I have no family." She meant to stop there, but he shifted uncomfortably, and the nursing directive *Distract the patient* kept her babbling on. "My mother raised me alone. She didn't tell me much about my father, just that he was in the service when he met my mom, and that once she was pregnant with me, he took off."

Gabriel had been composed as he told his story.

Now his green eyes kindled with anger. "What an ass."

"Yeah. We lived in a small town and the other kids made fun of me."

"I can relate."

She was starting to think her earlier alarm was simply the middle-of-the-night jitters, because Gabriel was really nice. Of course, as the pill kicked in, she was growing more gregarious and the world looked like a rosier place. . . . "So I used to imagine he was an international spy who'd had to go on a mission and was trapped behind enemy lines. I used to sit in social studies and dream that he would walk through the door, and all the mean kids would be in awe, and Mom and he and I would be a family."

"Kids do have their imaginations." Although he obviously didn't know what to make of hers.

"I grew up and graduated from high school, and he never showed up. My mother died about that time. . . ." Hannah's voice faltered. She cleared her throat and wished she hadn't started this story, because she was embarrassing herself with memories she'd thought long forgotten and sentiments Gabriel didn't want to share. But the drugs must have kicked in, because words kept burbling out of her like water out of a fountain. "I went to nursing school across the state. As far as I knew, my father was in a different universe. Then one day, I was training at the hospital, I walked into a Navy veteran's room to talk to him about his physical therapy, and his wife and daughter both saw what I couldn't. The guy in the bed, recovering from shoulder surgery—he was my father. Then I recognized the face. And the ears." She laughed with almost no wobble. "It was my face, and my ears."

"They couldn't have been as pretty on him." Gabriel leaned across and dimmed the bedside lamp.

That made it easier to keep talking. "His wife kept saying things like *How dare you?*, like I'd come in on purpose, and she pushed me out the room, while the patient—my *father*—looked embarrassed. Annoyed." Hannah clamped her mouth shut. There. She was resolved. Not another word.

"Did you see him again?"

So much for her resolution. "After his wife went home, I hung around, expecting he'd call for me. He didn't. He was born and raised two towns over, his parents still lived there, and he'd gone back to retire. He didn't want to know me. My existence was nothing more than an inconvenience and all the bright imaginings of my childhood died that day." Oh, my God, that sounded so poetic and pathetic, and worse, tears were trickling onto the pillow. "Could I be any stupider? Crying over a father who was never there and never wanted to be there."

"You're crying because it's a tragedy."

"Not a new tragedy by any means."

"But it's your tragedy." He plucked a tissue out of the box on the nightstand and handed it to her.

"Thanks." She blotted at her face and closed her eyes so she didn't have to look at him.

Gabriel Prescott was an interesting guy. His voice

sounded familiar, but she couldn't quite place him. . . . If she only concentrated hard enough . . .

And she slid right into sleep.

Gabriel painfully came to his feet and looked at her. He supposed the story was true. That was the interesting thing about her—she didn't lie or cheat. She didn't have any faults except for a tendency to collect money unfairly. Oh, and to murder her patients.

Leaning closer, he listened to her breathing. He put his hand on her shoulder and rolled her over. The pain meds had put her under. Tucking his crutch under his arm, he limped to the backpack she guarded so jealously. Taking it into the living room, he dumped it out on the coffee table.

From the master bedroom doorway, Daniel asked, "Find anything interesting?"

"Not yet." Gabriel cast him a sharp glance. "Did you catch forty winks?"

"My alarm just went off. You're due for your meds in fifteen minutes." Daniel walked over and examined the hodgepodge of stuff Hannah carried. "She should be a Boy Scout. She's always prepared."

A second pair of thread-bare jeans, three pairs of panties, five pairs of socks, twine, duct tape, a small pair of scissors, a canteen.

"What's in it?" Daniel asked.

Gabriel unscrewed the cap and sniffed cautiously. "Water."

Bandages, a tube of generic antibiotic ointment, a long, sharp knife—Gabriel handed that to Daniel. "Let's keep that out of her hands."

One worn, limp tennis shoe.

Gabriel held it and looked at Daniel, then stuck his hand inside. The cloth on the inner sole was pilled and worn, and when he pressed on it, he felt the outline of something underneath. He pulled out the liner—and found Hannah's money card, the one she'd weaseled out of that idiot banker in Becket, Massachusetts. Gabriel weighed it in his hand. "What do you think?"

"Let her keep it," Daniel said immediately. "If she gets away—"

"We can track her. Right." Gabriel put it back, tucked the sole back in, and they finished the search.

A small, cheap notebook and a pen were stuck in an outside pocket.

Gabriel flipped through it. It was blank. All it held was a wedding photo, torn to remove the groom, leaving only a young Mrs. Manly, her face shining with hope and happiness.

Gabriel closed his eyes in pain.

"I'd say she was collecting souvenirs of her kills, except she doesn't have anything from anyone else."

In knee-jerk defensiveness, Gabriel said, "The Dresser family exhumed old Mr. Dresser's body, and he died of nothing except old age."

"I know. Except for that video, Miss Hannah Grey is clean as a whistle." Daniel turned the backpack inside out and examined the canvas.

There was nothing here that gave information on where and how to access Manly's lost fortune.

Daniel put the backpack back together. "Are you

going to call your brother Carrick and tell him that you've got her?"

"No. He'd ask whether I had the code, and why not, and when I told him I'd been shot, he'd be blank, like he didn't understand what that had to do with the situation."

"You're getting sort of skeptical about your brother." Daniel's voice was totally neutral, which in its way, said everything Gabriel needed to know.

"He's just a boy." Gabriel handed over the twine and the tape.

"He's twenty-seven. What were you like at twenty-seven? How many jobs had you held? How many millions had you made?" As if he couldn't be silent anymore, Daniel shot the questions at Gabriel.

"He's had special challenges."

"Your other brothers have all had to face the challenges of being illegitimate, and losing their father, and learning to become men in a world that would just as soon crush them under its heel. They're all the kind of guys who make me proud to be a guy. They've got morals and self-respect and wives who adore them and who they adore."

This kind of honesty was what came of having a chauffeur and bodyguard who was also a friend. So Gabriel ignored the implied criticism of Carrick, and concentrated on Daniel's praise for Nathan Manly's other sons. "They are great, aren't they?"

"Yes, and to see you come together this summer, and bring all your families—Mr. Roberto from Italy, Mr. Mac from back east and Mr. Dev from South

Carolina—well, that did my heart good. That's what you've wanted ever since I've known you, to find your blood kin and be folks with them."

Recalling their Fourth of July picnic at Gabriel's ranch, and how much fun they'd had, Gabriel relaxed. "It was like one huge, rambunctious, extended family."

"It wasn't *like* that. That's what it *was*." Daniel got right in Gabriel's face. "And where was Mr. Carrick?"

"He was . . . busy." Which Gabriel knew was code for *not interested*.

"Huh."

Daniel was right. Carrick was no kid, yet Gabriel thought of him that way. He went to clubs, he hung out with celebrities, his only income seemed to come from interviews about his mother's death, and that showed a ghoulish lack of heart.

Gabriel knew all that, but . . . Carrick was his *brother*. In his most assured tone, he said, "I'll let Carrick know what's going on when I've got all the answers."

TWENTY-SEVEN

Gabriel woke to bright daylight, a thermometer stuck in his ear, and Dr. Bellota's voice booming, "Prescott, you are the luckiest son of a bitch I've ever met."

Gabriel opened his eyes a slit. "I was, until you showed up."

Dean Bellota boomed with laughter. "I'd say you were surly because you're convalescing, but these days, you're always surly."

Daniel laughed, too.

Gabriel was not amused.

From the head of the bed and off to the side, Hannah said, "Gentlemen, you're upsetting the patient."

Under the cool rebuke, the guys changed their laughs to coughs.

Hannah. Hannah was here.

Gabriel pulled himself up into a sitting position and turned to look at her.

She stood clad in his pajamas and robe, holding an

armful of pillows, looking like hell. She was pale, her mouth taut, her eyes shadowed.

Yet with a reassuring smile, she leaned across the mattress and stacked the pillows behind him. "Dr. Bellota is here to do your exam, but your temp is normal and your color is good. I'm sure this is merely a formality."

"For God's sake, Grace," Gabriel growled, "sit down before you fall down."

At his words, she went from pale to pasty. Leaning against the headboard, she said, "I'm fine."

Dr. Bellota put his hand under her arm. "This is what happens when you don't listen to your doctor. I told you to get off your feet."

Gabriel grimaced with pain, but he moved to the side. "Lay her down here."

"I'm fine," Hannah repeated.

No one paid any attention.

Daniel placed a pillow.

Dr. Bellota manhandled her onto the mattress.

Everyone viewed her prone figure with concern.

"I'm *fine*!" she snapped with finality.

"Let me decide that." Dr. Bellota checked her pulse, blood pressure, and temperature. He checked her pupils and listened to her lungs. Finally he unwrapped her wrist and looked it over, his brow knit. He cast a meaningful glance at Gabriel.

Gabriel nodded.

"You're right, Grace," Dr. Bellota said. "You are fine."

"I told you so." She started to sit up.

Dr. Bellota pressed her back down. "Except that

you're suffering from exhaustion and malnutrition, and I'm sending over a plastic surgeon to look at this wrist. You'll need stitches, antibiotics, pain relief, not to mention complete bed rest and three meals a day."

She tried to object.

Dr. Bellota spoke right over the top of her. "Plus a few snacks."

Daniel slipped out of the room, and came right back with a tray with two steaming bowls. "I was going to serve this to you when the doctor left, but let's have it now."

She watched him organize the meal. "I am making extra work for Daniel."

"It's chicken and dumplings." Daniel placed the tray across her lap.

She took a long breath of the rich, meaty, thyme-scented broth, and her complexion flushed.

Gabriel wanted to swear. She had been on the run. She had been starving. And while he knew she deserved every last misery she'd visited upon herself, he couldn't stand to think of her suffering.

"Don't you worry, Miss Grace." Daniel put a spoon in her fist. "As long as you stay right here, caring for two cranky invalids shouldn't be much different than caring for one."

"Right here?" She laughed weakly and took the first spoonful. Her eyes half closed in pleasure. "You mean in this apartment."

With good humor and an almost-imperceptible twinkle of mischief, Daniel said, "If you were across that big living room, that would be an inconvenience, but as long as you're sharing this king-sized bed with Mr. Prescott, I can keep an eye on you both."

Gabriel shot him an admiring look. Daniel was a diabolical genius. Now she was confined to his bed. With Daniel to stand guard against any murderous "incidents," the forced intimacy of two people in a king-sized bed, and a little artfully applied flattery on his part, she would soon tell him what he wanted to know.

She flung a horrified glance at Gabriel. "No, I . . . I can't sleep with Mr. Prescott!"

"Now, Miss Grace." Daniel's voice rumbled with reassurance. "As badly as you two are banged up, no one's going to think there's a horizontal tango going on. Heck, Mr. Prescott's too weak to even hum the tune."

"Daniel," Gabriel said threateningly.

Hannah's pale face blushed a rosy red. "Daniel, you do not want to fix twenty meals a day for me."

"Three meals and two snacks," Dr. Bellota said.

"Daniel *doesn't* cook. He *does* takeout," Gabriel said.

"Since this is going to go on for a while, I'm going to call one of those services that delivers meals to the house." Daniel headed out the door. "That way, we can control the nutrition."

"Good plan, Daniel," Gabriel approved. Among the three of them, they were closing the door on Hannah's prison.

She scowled and tried very hard to sound authoritative—difficult while eating. "I should go back to my job at Wal-Mart."

"You can care for Gabriel after you're feeling better," Dr. Bellota said.

"He'll be feeling better then, too." She looked down, surprised, as her spoon clattered in the empty bowl.

Dr. Bellota took the tray away, then shook out her pills and handed them to her with a glass of water.

"It's a gunshot wound. I won't be one hundred percent for another six months," Gabriel assured her.

As if that settled everything, Dr. Bellota whipped out his scissors and said, "Gabriel, let's see that leg and make sure this foolishness of coming home didn't cause a setback that will knock you off your feet for a lot longer than six months." He set to work cutting off the bandage, and by the time he had cleaned the wound, rewrapped it, and scolded Gabriel again for leaving the hospital . . . Hannah was asleep. Not just slightly asleep—profoundly asleep, with her hand tucked under her cheek and her mouth slightly opened like a child's.

Dr. Bellota took her pulse again and, with the familiarity of long acquaintance, said, "I hope you know what you're doing, Gabriel Prescott, holding that woman hostage."

"Before she came here, she lived in a hospice. Surely this is better than that."

Dr. Bellota plowed on as if Gabriel hadn't spoken. "She's been a nurse, no doubt about it. Why she would lie, I don't know, but it can't be good."

"I sleep lightly. She won't turn over without me knowing."

"You sleep lightly? You were out like a light when

I . . . oh." Dr. Bellota sighed. "You're swearing off your pain meds."

"Yes."

"You're a fool, but as long as you keep taking your antibiotics, you'll be okay," Dr. Bellota said. "I'm sending Dr. Holloway over this afternoon to work on her wrist, and I'll be back tomorrow to check you both."

"We'll look forward to that. There's nothing I like as much as having some ham-fingered guy poke around in an open wound."

"Could be worse. Could be a prostate exam." Dr. Bellota sounded cheerful enough, but he frowned as he packed his travel bag.

"Dean, I do know what I'm doing." Gabriel relaxed back on the pillows. "Do you know the saying 'Keep your friends close, and your enemies closer'? I'm keeping her close."

"Which is she, a friend or an enemy?"

Gabriel smiled bitterly. "She's worse than an enemy. She's an old lover—and I'm not done with her yet."

TWENTY-EIGHT

Hannah stretched as she woke, feeling lazy, thinking she would spend the whole day reading the funnies and watching baseball.

It was Sunday, wasn't it?

Unhurriedly, she opened her eyes—and Gabriel was watching her.

She was instantly wide-awake, stiff and still as a rabbit beneath a mountain lion's scrutiny. "Hello." *Great conversation starter.*

"You look better." He leaned on his elbow, in her personal space again.

"Thanks, I guess." She dragged the covers up to her chin and sat up.

"No use being modest. You've been sleeping next to me for three days." A half smile played on his lips. "If there's anything to see, I've seen it."

She glared down at him, offended, while he lounged around on her half of the bed.

"There *is* nothing to see," he reminded her. "You're wearing my pajamas. They're boring."

"Right." He wasn't looking at her like they were boring.

"Besides, if I'd had any thoughts of frolicking, the snoring would have put me off."

Her teeth snapped together. "So you're a sensitive soul."

"I don't think so, but women don't usually sleep while they're in my bed, so I don't know for sure." He laughed.

But it was probably true. "You really are a jerk. And get over to your own side of the bed!" With her good hand, she shoved at his chest.

He tumbled over, still laughing, and when she went to give him a smack for good measure, he caught her wrist.

Her irritation faded.

His amusement died.

As they looked at each other, her breath caught in her throat, and she felt something she hadn't felt since . . . well, since a year ago Halloween. The memory of Trent, and the party, and that one brief, magical dance, had the effect of making her snatch her hand away. "I . . . need . . . to . . . use . . . the facilities." She inched off the bed, never taking her eyes off Gabriel.

Because he never took his eyes off *her*, not even when she turned her back and hurried toward the bathroom. She knew, because she felt his gaze.

She shut the door behind her. She locked it, although why, she didn't know. He probably had a key. But he also gave off vibes like, on the briefest pretext, he'd join her in the shower. She believed in sending a message, and that message was *no*.

She took care of the most pressing matters, then saw a new pair of women's gray cotton lounge pants and a cornflower blue racer-back shirt laid out on the counter. A plastic bag, the perfect size for wrapping her wrist, and a rubber band had been placed on top of the clothes.

Was Gabriel trying to send *her* a message?

She looked in the mirror.

Probably he was. She'd been sleeping for days, waking only to eat, a lot, and brush her teeth, and now she looked like Rip Van Winkle without the beard.

She flipped on the shower, covered her cast, and headed into the huge shower stall.

It was great. It was beyond great, with showerheads that squirted her in all the right places and some of the wrong ones, an overhead rainstorm that sprayed at random times, and a dozen different shampoos and soaps.

She was in love . . . with a shower.

She also, for the first time in a year, felt like herself. She wasn't exhausted. She wasn't hungry. She wasn't scared. She was Hannah Grey, and standing here in Gabriel Prescott's shower, she realized she had to make plans to do something besides run. She stilled, and thought hard.

She could not scuttle across the face of America forever. Even if Carrick hadn't found her, she was slowly wearing down, becoming someone driven by fear and sorrow, always running and going nowhere. She had to make a plan. She had to do something that would stop this madness.

She had to go to the cops or the feds or . . . someone.

She took a long breath of steamy air.

And she would. But first, she was going to enjoy her shower—she sniffed all the shampoos and decided on bitter orange—and take a moment to luxuriate in this time of safety. Not even the bothersome bandage could lessen her pleasure as she soaped and scrubbed and finally stood there in bliss.

One thought disturbed her peace.

What was she going to do about the unwelcome sense of closeness she experienced with Gabriel? For three days, she'd slept with the guy. On the rare occasions she woke up, he was always stirring, and he personally poked food down her throat as if he was an eagle and she his chick. She didn't *know* him, but at the same time . . . last night, some instinct brought her to consciousness. She lay on her side, facing away from him, tucked into his body, his arms around her. He had been breathing deeply, as if he was asleep, but at the same time, a hard-on pressed against her rear.

She knew guys got involuntary erections at night. More important, she was wearing his pajamas and he was wearing underwear and a T-shirt, so they were well clothed. And he had never touched her intimately; he'd never twitched a finger toward sexual harassment. But that erection made her realize a couple of things she'd been steadfastly ignoring.

He was a strong, healthy, normal guy with strong, healthy, normal appetites that no gunshot wound was going to hinder.

She was a strong, healthy, normal woman with

strong, healthy, normal appetites that had, frankly, never in her life been appeased. Not that she'd tried too hard, since in high school and college guys were a disappointment, and while batteries could satisfy the basic urges, they left a lot to be desired when it came to affection afterward.

And for all she and Gabriel had nothing in common except getting shot at, still they shared that smoky sexual awareness that tugged like a burnished chain between them.

It was something that would have to be dealt with. She simply didn't know how.

When finally she stepped out of the shower, she could hear Gabriel talking to somebody. Nobody answered him, so she figured he was on the phone.

She dried and dressed, then cracked the door and stood listening to him, not the words, because that would be eavesdropping, but the affectionate, bantering tone that made her heart ache a little with envy. When he hung up the phone, she stepped into the room. "You have a family."

He looked startled; then he withdrew, and she realized she hadn't meant to, but as far as he was concerned, she had invaded his privacy.

Then he relaxed against the pile of pillows under his back. "I have three foster sisters. That was Pepper, and somehow she heard I'd been shot." His mouth quirked ruefully.

Hannah took another step toward him. "She wasn't happy."

"She ripped a strip off my hide."

When he said stuff like that, she could hear the echo of his Texas upbringing in his voice.

"I told her not to tell the other two, but I guess it's way too late for that. I'll be getting more phone calls." Now he grimaced. "I hate when they yell at me."

"You could have called them." Hannah wandered closer. "You know, while I was snoring."

"I didn't want to interrupt you. Besides, they'd tell me I need a safer job."

Hannah opened her mouth to ask what his job really was.

He didn't give her a chance. "The thing is, they've got a thing about not losing me again."

"Again?" Now this was interesting. Hannah perched on the side of the bed.

"Remember I told you the Prescotts took me in when I was eleven? Mr. Prescott was a minister."

"You were raised by a minister?" Hannah thought about all her suspicions about him, and wondered whether that meant she should discard her suspicions or consider them confirmed.

"In a small Texas town. Yeah. His wife brought me home like a stray cat and announced they were keeping me. And they did, which was a big scandal in that town. Half Mexican, half God knows what, all trouble was the way the big ol' gossips described me." Gabriel didn't like the ol' gossips. She could tell by the way his lips, usually full and inviting, got thin and turned down at the corners.

"What kind of trouble?"

"I had no background. I spent the first part of my

life being knocked around the foster-care system, knowing no one wanted me and knowing why—because I screamed in temper all day and screamed with nightmares all night."

Nightmares. She would ask . . . but not yet. Not while he was talking.

"Then the Prescotts took me in, and I was home. If I screamed in temper, they took me aside until I could control myself. If I screamed at night, they were there to hold me. They told me . . . Mr. and Mrs. Prescott told me that God was always there for me, and when the nightmares came, I could pray and God would comfort me. They told me that God valued me as much as the white kids who lived in their big houses with their parents, who were married, and they told me to look around. They asked me if I thought those kids who had parents who pushed them to be the best in baseball or gymnastics were happy. If the kids whose parents divorced were happy. If those kids who made fun of me for being a nobody really thought they were better than me, or if they were compensating for something." Gabriel laughed. "Mr. Prescott said that, straight-faced, and Mrs. Prescott scolded him, and he said I didn't understand what he meant, and I assured him I did."

"Oops." Hannah struggled to contain her amusement.

"Right. He gave me a *look*, and later, he told me that sometimes telling the truth doesn't mean you have to say everything you know." Gabriel laughed again. "I realized then he liked having me around. He had three daughters and a wife. I was the other guy in his life.

He took me hunting, taught me to shoot. He took me when he had to buy a present for his wife. He dragged me along to the men's group at church. Some of it sucked, but in the end, I knew it was cool. I belonged."

"That *is* cool."

"Until I was thirteen." A sudden onset of pain made him pale, and Hannah didn't think it was his wound that was bothering him. "Mr. and Mrs. Prescott were murdered."

"Murdered?" She hadn't been shocked to hear he'd been in foster care. He had the self-sufficient air of a man who'd been on his own his whole life. But this . . . "Why?"

His eyes half closed as if he were weary, and she felt suddenly guilty. His wounds were so much worse than hers, and she felt so strong now. Selfishly, she'd kept him awake and talking.

"I'll tell you what," he said. "If you'll have dinner with me tonight, I'll tell you the whole story."

"Who else would I have dinner with? I mean, we're stuck here in the condo together. . . ."

He watched her from beneath those heavy lids, and she realized—he didn't mean dinner. He meant *dinner*.

She sat very still. He was dangling an attractive piece of bait, but in her experience, bait always concealed a hook. In this case, she knew very well what that hook was . . . yet the bait was so very, very attractive. She took a slow, careful breath, intending to say the right thing, say no, keep this relationship on a safe footing. Yet instead she blurted, "I would love to have dinner with you."

TWENTY-NINE

Hannah had a date.

She had moved into the bedroom where she had first slept, and now she leaned her hands on the cool granite countertop in the bathroom. She looked into the mirror at her own shining eyes, and told herself to calm down. It was just a date, and she was stupid to be so thrilled, especially when she'd slept with the guy she was dating.

Okay, technically she had *only* slept with him, nothing more.

But she wanted him and he wanted her, and right now she was balanced on that razor's edge between excitement and fear, between hoping they would make love and knowing if they did, she would pay a price.

Picking up a brush, she ran it through her hair, wished it was blond again, wished she could have it styled, wished her wrist didn't hurt. . . . She dropped the brush on the counter.

The gunshot wound ached all the time, and when

she twisted her wrist, pain shot up her arm. Nevertheless she refused to take anything more potent than aspirin. Not now. Not tonight. Tonight, she needed her wits about her.

Gabriel Prescott was a powerful man, with powerful appetites and a personality and presence that impressed even when he was silent. If she yielded to the urge to have sex, she knew in her bones the experience would shake everything she believed and desired—and not necessarily in a good way. Compound the physical and emotional mess with her legal problems, and she foresaw trouble.

She splashed on a quick light coat of makeup.

But she wanted him.

At the very least, she wanted to hear the rest of his story.

She dressed herself in Gabriel's simply fabulous pair of pajamas, slipped into the terry-cloth robe Daniel had brought her, twirled in front of the mirror, and sighed. The pajamas were too big. Light green color, baggy, and calf-length, the robe wasn't a good style. But she had nothing else to wear, so . . .

She headed into the bedroom—and stopped.

The door to the living room was closed. But someone had been in here, probably a large African-American fairy godfather, for laid out on the bed was a dress, and not just any dress. This was the kind of dress models wore to movie premieres.

With reverent hands, she lifted it and held it before her. It fell to her ankles—a long, simple drape of red silk with twisted silk shoulder straps and a low swag back. One side of the narrow skirt was slit all the way up to her thigh. She'd never owned anything like it in her life, and she wanted so badly for it to fit.

In a sudden hurry, she dropped it on the bed and tore off the pajamas and robe. Picking up the gown, she stepped into it and pulled it up. The silk slithered up her thighs, over her hips and breasts. She slid her arms into the straps.

It fit. It fit like someone had measured her.

Remembering the way Gabriel looked at her, she thought perhaps he had. He had measured her with his gaze and in his arms as they'd slept together. He was a man who knew almost too much about women.

Hannah walked to the dresser. Strolled, really, because in this gown, she moved differently, all fluid grace and ease, and when she did, her leg slid through the daring slash in the silk, a sexy invitation to any man who saw her.

To Gabriel.

The figure in the dresser mirror looked long and lean. The thin silk molded her breasts and hips, and when she turned and looked, she saw that it swathed her rear as lovingly as a man's hands. The back swung in a low, sexy drape to the base of her spine, and the straps clung on her shoulders. The dress was absolutely magnificent—and it absolutely required some underwear.

She glanced back toward the bed.

A minuscule pair of matching panties had fallen to the floor. There was no matching bra.

She picked up the panties and scrutinized them,

front and back. She would have to categorize this as a daring thong. "How could I have missed these?" she asked sarcastically.

The empty room didn't answer, so she pulled on the panties.

She looked again in the mirror, then looked for a bra. No, no bra. Her nipples were just . . . out there.

Using the hairpins she found in a box in the dresser, she gathered her hair into a careless upsweep.

On the floor beside the bed, there were shoes, a red pair of low heels. They fit, but she took perverse pleasure in knowing they were too narrow.

So Mr. Gabriel Prescott didn't get everything right.

A light tap on the door made her jump. "Yes?"

Daniel said, "Miss Grace, I'll be leaving for the evening, but if you'd like to come to dinner with Mr. Gabriel, I've served it on a table by the window."

"All right. Thank you."

A pause, and then he asked, "Did everything fit? Do you like it?"

"It did, and I do. Did you pick it out?"

"No." Daniel chuckled. "Not me. Mr. Gabriel knew exactly what he wanted. I simply had to find it."

Of course. She had known that before she inquired.

She waited, self-conscious, a few more minutes, then walked—no, strolled—toward the door. She swung it open and stepped into the living room.

The lighting was low. The music was jazzy and slow. The white-clothed table was by the window. Gabriel stood lighting the candles on that table.

He was silhouetted against the night, a solid, strong

form of a man in a dark suit and tie, and for one moment, he reminded her so strongly of Trent Sansoucy, tears stung her eyes. Then he glanced around and straightened, and he was Gabriel Prescott again. "My God," he whispered. "My God. You're a walking, talking dream come true."

She blushed at the way he looked at her. "It's the dress."

"It is most certainly not the dress." His husky voice was a seduction of appreciation.

"Well, it's not the underwear," she muttered.

"What?"

"Nothing." She walked—no, strolled—to stand beside him. "It really is the dress. It makes me taller and thinner and more . . ." She waved her hands. "Just more."

"No. It's you." Leaning down, he put his lips on her forehead. "It's definitely you."

That was all, but he made her feel giddy and flirty. Thank God for the uncomfortable shoes keeping her sane, or she'd throw herself at him right now. "You look good, too."

"Thank you. This isn't as comfortable as my pj's, but it's a little more formal." He pulled one of the chairs out from the table. "The doctor won't let us have wine, but he'll let us have iced tea." He made a face.

She laughed.

"And Daniel brought us a fabulous dinner from Café Annie. We should enjoy it while it's warm."

Hannah sank into the chair, and under the cover of the table, she discarded her shoes.

Gabriel seated himself opposite. He lifted the first two covers off the food and referred to the list at his elbow, telling her, "For appetizers, we have black bean terrine with goat cheese and a salad of seared rare tuna with roasted beets and frisée."

The savory odors hit her nose, and her appetite brightened for the first time in a year.

He lifted more covers. "For the main course, we have wood-grilled Gulf shrimp with potato-and-cheese enchiladas, wood-grilled lamb chops with black olives and mint, and wood-grilled filet mignon with smoked cheddar and green chili grits."

Each plate presented an enticing masterpiece of color and texture, and her stomach growled.

He gestured toward the last three covers placed on the coffee table. "And for dessert—"

She interrupted with a laugh. "Who's going to eat all this?"

"We didn't know what you would prefer." He looked bemused and solemn. "We didn't want you to go hungry."

The low light painted shadows in the hallows of his cheeks and just below his brows. The candlelight danced on the individual strands of his shiny black hair. His lips looked soft, his eyes were compelling, but what really held her attention were his hands: large, capable, with long, broad, dexterous fingers that spread butter on a roll and offered it to her.

"I don't think I will go hungry," she said softly.

His smile promised a meal, and so much more.

They ate slowly, lingering over the rich mix of flavors,

their conversation desultory, centering on the Houston traffic, the shopping in the Galleria, and the excellent restaurants in the area. Yet they said one thing and meant another, talking trivia while feeding each other in a primal ritual of feasting and satisfaction.

He spoke of the unique flavors of filet mignon and green chili grits, and insisted she try a bite off his fork.

She exclaimed over the shrimp and the enchiladas, put some on his plate, and watched as he chewed, his strong white teeth flashing.

All the while they spoke, they were waiting. Waiting as the tension between them built.

As their appetites wound down, Gabriel reached across the table and caught her hand, his touch warm and insistent. He ran his knuckles across hers. "Let's adjourn to the couch."

She looked into his eyes. They beckoned like emeralds, rich with mystery and with promise. Did he realize he could seduce her with a smile, a glance?

Of course he did. He was the kind of man she should fear: rich, powerful, ruthless. Like Carrick Manly.

At the thought, she flinched and pulled her hand back.

"What's wrong?" Gabriel said.

Yet Gabriel was completely different. He wasn't movie star handsome. He didn't flash his wealth and his charm to impress. His features were severe, like the impervious stone heads carved by the long-ago Mayans. He seldom smiled. He seldom frowned. His emotions, when he showed them, shone in his eyes and his words. He was a man with depths she couldn't wait to plumb.

He had nothing to do with Carrick Manly.

"Shall we see what Daniel brought us for dessert?" She discarded her napkin and stood, aware once more of Gabriel's gaze as it caressed the slim line of her body. He made her feel like she belonged in this dress.

She strolled to the couch and curled into the corner, very aware that her thigh was exposed by the slash in the skirt. Aware, and pleased, because Gabriel couldn't look away. She caressed the soft brown leather sofa and watched as he casually discarded his jacket and tie, dropping them on the back of his chair.

The white shirt turned his skin to toast, and the row of buttons drew her gaze down to his belt. "I'll get the coffee," he said.

She watched him walk to the kitchen. She liked his build—powerful shoulders, broad chest, and a taut rear that looked good in suit pants.

He returned with a tray loaded with a stainless-steel thermos, sweetener, and cream. He placed the tray on the table, and when she would have sat forward, he gestured her back. "I'll pour. You look *right* there."

Right? His expression didn't say *right*. His lips pressed together, and his eyes flashed with possessiveness; he was fiercely, possessively glad to have her in his clutches.

And if she were smart, she would be feeling wary.

Instead, she felt as if, after a long, horrible trip, she'd come home.

He served the desserts on the coffee table—Texas

pecan pie with vanilla ice cream and caramelized orange sauce, sweet plantain tamale with caramelized pineapple and coconut ice cream, and a cheese plate—and after she tried a nibble of each, she couldn't eat another bite.

Because she wanted to kiss him, to hold him, but first, there were things that needed to be said.

So reluctantly, she faced him and reminded him, "You promised you would tell me about your family."

"Yes." He looked like he regretted that promise, but he didn't default on their agreement. "It's an ugly story. My adoptive parents were murdered by one of the town's leading citizens. He made it look like they'd stolen the church funds, abandoned their family, run for the border, and wrecked their car. The cops went along with it, either because it was easy and titillating or because the son of a bitch who killed them paid them off." Gabriel bit off each word.

She wanted to do something for him, something that would bring him a little comfort. So she put her hand in his.

He clasped his fingers around hers, held them on his knee. "The family was torn apart, all of us sent to foster care in various parts of the country. Only I didn't stay. I was mad. Just like before."

"And scared, just like before?"

He looked at her, startled.

"The nightmares, remember?"

"You understand me almost too well."

She was flattered, yet at the same time, she knew she had barely scratched the surface of this complex, multidimensional man.

"The nightmares . . . I would dream I was standing in the middle of the busy freeway, up against the concrete barrier, screaming with fear as the cars sped past." His eyes were a dark, dark green that gazed at a place she couldn't see.

Taking care not to make a sudden move, she eased her hip closer to him. "Why would you dream that?"

His attention snapped back to her, and he said fiercely, "Because it wasn't a dream. When I was four, my mother abandoned me in the middle of the freeway, and when the police came to pick me up, I wouldn't go. I said my mama told me to stay there." The man he was echoed the boy's anguish. "I had to be forcibly removed."

Tears filled Hannah's eyes and rolled down her face. "Sorry." Maybe she still wasn't quite one hundrd percent healthy, because normally she didn't cry about a long-ago tragedy.

He handed her his handkerchief.

She tried to keep her makeup from running, tried to get herself together. "Sorry. I'm being silly, I know, but when I think about that terrified little kid, I just . . . My heart aches." Her voice broke on the last word.

Her tears didn't seem to make him uncomfortable. Instead he watched her closely, as if gauging her sincerity.

And that well-developed cynicism made her heart ache more. "Sorry. Silly," she repeated.

"Everything came out all right." He waved his hand around as if to distract her with his splendid view and his leather furniture and his personal elevator. "As you can see."

"Your mother . . . she never came for you?" Her voice was husky with strain.

"The news stations publicized the incident, but . . . no. It's not like a woman who dumps her kid on the freeway is interested in his welfare." He smiled with a hard hint of scorn. "I've never told anyone about my mother and my nightmares. I don't know why I told you."

She smiled back, mocking his derision. "Because I told you about my father, and I never told anyone that before. Because we've got a lot in common—we both overcame having loser parents and made something of ourselves."

"So we won't tattle on each other, because we've got enough embarrassing information that we can blackmail each other."

Her amusement died; sometimes his cynicism went too far. "No," she said definitely. "We won't tell anyone, because we trust each other."

"Do we?"

"It would appear we do."

"Then . . ." His voice dipped to a warm, deep, seductive tone. "I hope you would trust me to make love to you."

As he had so many times before, he took her good wrist in his hand . . . but this time, everything was different. His bronzed skin was flushed, his green eyes heated, and he rubbed his thumb across her knuckles, a warm, soft brush of desire. Lifting her hand to his lips, he kissed it, his breath warm and scented with coffee.

The desire between them grew taut.

Her heart began a low pounding, and she flushed and leaned toward him.

He caught the back of her head and kissed her, a slow melding of their lips and tongues . . . and souls. His other hand stroked her bare arm, her shoulder, and then, as if it were naturally the next step, he found the sway of her breast and pressed the soft mound in his palm, then captured her nipple between this thumb and forefinger. He explored the shape, then rubbed the material over it, tantalizing her with the pull and the rub of silk.

Her breath came faster, her blood surged in her veins, and deep inside, the desire she felt for him grew into an ache and a need.

Kissing her all the while, supporting her head in his palm, he rose over the top of her, sliding her back on the couch until her head rested on a pillow. Her rear skated across the silk, the hemline rose to her knees.

One of his legs was on the floor. His other knee rested beside her hip. His free hand grazed her exposed thigh, and he murmured against her lips, "You've been driving me crazy all night. You know that, don't you?"

"You picked the dress," she reminded him.

He drew back and stared into her face. His palm caressed her leg. "It's not the dress," he said fiercely. "It's you. You're so strong, so resilient . . . such an enigma. I want to know you, to delve out all your truths."

She took a quick indrawn breath. "My truths are too—"

"Dangerous? Like you?"

"Why would you think that?" He frightened her. He excited her. When he looked at her, he saw too much. She was afraid he saw the truth.

He made her want to run . . . and he made her need to stay.

"Because you are dangerous to me." His fingers flexed at the back of her neck, massaging and yet holding her in place.

His body imprisoned her, yet . . . this prison was right. This prison held nothing to fear. Reaching up, she pulled his shirttails out from beneath his belt and opened his shirt, one button at a time. He waited, the only sign of his impatience his chest as it rose and fell. When his shirt hung loose from his shoulders, she ran her flattened palm across his chest, bare of hair and rippling with strength. "You're so beautiful," she said throatily.

His gaze grew harder, hotter, more intense, a magnet that demanded her attention. He pressed her knee up against the back of the couch, opening her.

His fingers cupped her thigh, then slid toward her panties. Her tiny, barely there panties. He pushed them aside. His thumb slid along her crease.

She gasped, her lips slightly apart. She wished he'd stop, wished he'd hurry, wished . . .

His touch struck her like lightning, hot, fast, finding her, entering her.

In shock, she arched off the couch.

"You're already damp." His voice was warm and low, a soft arousal to accompany all the rest. "All evening I've been watching your breasts as they swayed, your nipples as they hardened and relaxed, and wondered what you felt like inside." His finger plunged into her again. "I've wondered if you would respond to me like I respond to you, with every fiber of my being, or if it was all a sham to draw me into your flame."

She wanted to object. Why would he think her a sham? How could he even imagine such a thing?

Was he seeing too much of the truth?

Then his thumb found her clitoris.

Unable to hold back, she groaned.

"Yes," he whispered. He rubbed her in a slow, soft circle. His finger drew out and went deep again.

Orgasm struck, blinding her to her surroundings, to her memories, to everything . . . but him. As he rubbed her and fed her sensation after sensation, she was always aware of Gabriel's body over her, Gabriel's eyes observing her, Gabriel's scent enveloping her, Gabriel's hand inside her. Compelling, convincing, irresistible, Gabriel was everything she'd ever wanted.

Gabriel was hers.

When she finished and lay panting beneath him, she realized a few things. He had slipped down on the couch beside her, put his arm under her shoulders, and held her close against his body. His fingers still cupped her inside and out. And he watched her as if her orgasm had been his. "That wasn't a sham," he said. "I felt every pulse and every tremor."

She could barely breathe, but she managed to ask, "How do I know . . . you're not a sham?"

In a leisurely movement, he drew his hand away. He

pulled off his belt, unzipped his pants. Once again he rose above her. Taking her hand, he placed it on his belly and slid it down into his shorts.

Her fingers closed around his erection. It was hot. It was hard. It was large and glorious, and inside, she clenched with renewed desire.

Above her, his face was taut with strain. "When I look at you, when I touch you, when I'm with you, I can't think of anything else but what it would be like to be in your arms and show you . . ."

"What?"

"The color of pleasure."

THIRTY

Gabriel held his breath as Hannah made her decision.

Standing, she walked away from him toward the bedroom door—and he realized she had no intention of becoming his lover.

That was fine. For no reason he could figure out, he'd shared too much about his past.

Except that perhaps she was right—she'd told him her secrets, and he felt safe in telling her his. But for all her talk about common experiences and having loser parents and making something of themselves, what really made him feel secure was knowing she would be going to prison, and she wouldn't have the time or inclination to gossip about his nightmares. She'd be too busy living her own nightmare.

Too bad that fact made him feel like shit, like a lousy, betraying son of a bitch who tried to seduce a woman he didn't want to want. Too bad the idea of her in prison made him want to take her to Mexico, give her some money, and set her free, his principles and his brother be damned. Too bad the mere thought of all that sweet-smelling purity behind bars made him hurt in his body and his brain. Too bad that the very first day he'd seen her photo was the day he'd lost his mind.

Then . . . Hannah stepped through the bedroom door. And beckoned. And he realized—she stood in the *master* bedroom.

His breath caught in his throat. He forgot his scruples, pathetic though they were. All he could see, all he could think, was *Hannah. My dream. My love.*

He limped toward her, his gaze clinging to the smooth sheen of the gown, to the glow of her shoulders, to the dangerous sparkle of her eyes.

She stepped back to let him inside, and shut the door behind him. And locked it. "With that wound, you shouldn't be doing this at all," she said throatily. "So—get on the bed."

He hesitated, caught between the desire to dominate and the desire to be loved. Love triumphed, and he backed toward the end table, leaned against it, discarded his shoes and socks. . . .

She leaned against the door, her palms flat against the polished wood. "You might as well take it all off." She held up her bandaged arm. "I'd do it for you but, you know, my wrist . . ."

His shirt slipped easily from his shoulders. He felt foolish when he fumbled with his zipper, wondering where his usual smooth moves had gone. Evaporated, apparently, under the heated gaze of the wide-eyed siren of a nurse.

When he peeled off his underwear, those eyes got wider. "That's . . . impressive."

He chuckled, flattered against his will. "The bandage on my thigh or the erection?"

"I've seen bandages a lot bigger than that one," she assured him.

"What about you? You've been wounded, too. You should be in bed with me." He threw back the covers and indicated the smooth, clean expanse of sheets.

For the first time since the evening had begun, she was uncertain. Her lids fluttered down over her blue eyes, and she smoothed her tongue across her lips. "Yes. I suppose I should." Reaching up, she fiddled with the twisted straps on the gown.

When she dropped one off her shoulder, his knees gave out, and he had to sit down on the bed.

When she dropped the other, he bit back a groan.

Carefully she inched her arms out. For one precarious moment, the silky material clung to her breasts, then slithered down to her waist. The gown caught on her hips. She did a shimmy that sent his blood pressure through the roof.

And the dress fell to the floor.

She was naked. Almost naked. Except for the scrap of red silk some designer was foolish enough to call panties.

He'd been looking at the shape of her nipples underneath that glorious red dress. Being the kind of guy who could multitask, he'd been spilling his guts about his nightmares and, at the same time, speculating about the exact shape and color of her nipples. Now he could see them, round, peach colored, flawless, those very nipples perched on the crests of two of the nicest boobies he'd ever seen.

For the first time since that bullet had torn through his thigh, he was pain-free.

True. He'd seen Hannah naked before. While they were in Balfour House, he had seen her showering, putting on makeup, plucking her eyebrows. Which should have turned him off, because in his experience, there was nothing like that slice of real life to take the blush off the rose.

But no. It hadn't worked that way with Hannah. He'd seen it all, wanted it all, and been frustrated as hell that he couldn't touch, feel, smell, love. . . .

Now he realized the truth. The difference between seeing her on a computer monitor and seeing her in person was breathtaking, like seeing a photo of mountains, then seeing the actual Rockies.

And that tiny silk thong gave the whole viewing experience a special zest, like he was getting a tour in a limo.

He took a long breath to calm himself.

But before he had even managed to give her tits his full appreciation, she dropped the panties and stepped out. And walked toward him.

The shape of the body surpassed the beauty of the dress. Mountains became the whole national park.

The woman was blond all the way.

And he was almost dizzy from lack of oxygen.

She leaned over him.

He leaned back.

She smiled, a slow, inviting smile that made him wonder who was seducing whom. In slow motion, he lifted his hand and slid it along her collarbone. The contrast of his tanned copper fingers against her silky pale skin made him frantic to grab, to take.

But he had promised her all the colors of pleasure.

He always kept his promises.

Taking her by the waist, he guided her over the top of him and urged her down, to lie flat on her back on the snowy-white sheets. He looked into those big blue apprehensive eyes. "Let's see if we can make your dreams come true."

"What about your dreams?" Her voice quavered a little.

She was afraid. She was taking a chance on him, and he kissed her warmly, deeply, tasting her mouth and finding it as voluptuously sensitive as he had imagined. When he lifted his head, she caught her breath, and slowly, her blue eyes blinked opened. He waited until she had focused, then said, "As long as I'm holding you, all of my dreams have already come true."

Hannah lay with her head on Gabriel's heaving chest, hearing the thunder of his heart and exulting in the knowledge that, even while he had plied her body with all the skills known to man, she had driven him into a sweet and equal madness.

Even now, when the frenzy was over, he held both arms around her, as if she were a treasure he feared would escape.

She couldn't fool herself. They didn't know each other.

But he fulfilled her requirements for a man.

He had never used her. Quite the opposite. When she performed what was nothing more than the right thing to do—yell when someone shot at them—he insisted on repaying her with his hospitality and his care.

He hadn't lied to her. She knew who he was, and she knew he kept his promises.

She didn't know if he would stick around, but . . . she stroked his chest.

He kept his promises very well. During their long, leisurely loving, he had touched her with hands filled with magic. He had smiled as he kissed her belly, and he didn't stop at her belly. He kissed her intimately, his tongue caressing her clitoris, until orgasm lifted her on an ocean swell and carried her to shore. Then . . . then he'd entered her, slowly, carefully, filling her with himself until she was frantic with need. Only when she urged him onward with desperate moaning and clutching hands had he allowed himself the ultimate bliss.

More important, he hadn't despised her for being illegitimate or for sharing her silly father fantasies or talking about that humiliating, awful meeting with the man who had slept with her mother. Instead, Gabriel had done what he could to put her at ease. In return, he had shared something very special, very real, very personal.

Today, in the shower, she had faced the facts. She had

to do something about Carrick Manly and his greedy quest for the fortune. She had to seek help, or she would die and Mrs. Manly would never be avenged.

She knew only one man she could trust.

Gabriel Prescott.

Taking a big breath, she slid out of his arms. She leaned her elbows against the mattress and looked into his troubled face. And she said, "I have something to tell you."

The next morning Hannah was still asleep when Gabriel unlocked the door and limped into the living room.

Daniel sat at the coffee table, eating and watching CNN on his laptop. At the sight of Gabriel, his dark handsome face lit up in a grin. "Been getting any?"

"Shut up."

"Because it's been a long drought around here, and you've been grumpy enough to have a dwarf named after you."

Gabriel sat down, helped himself to a slice of the double-meat, double-cheese, all-the-vegetables, thin-crust pizza and repeated, "Shut up."

"Better eat up. You'll need your energy for when you go back in there."

"Shut . . . up."

"Tell me why I should."

"Because I need you to fucking find out who shot at us."

Daniel straightened, offended. "I've got the organization working on it, but whoever it is, he isn't letting out any information."

"Look. She told me some stuff that . . ." That Gabriel didn't know whether to believe. That he didn't want to believe, but that explained so much.

"What did she tell you, boss?" Daniel sounded more than curious. He sounded as forlorn as Gabriel felt.

Gabriel felt as if his soul had been ripped in half.

Was Carrick the villain Hannah painted him to be? A man who would kill his own mother for a fortune?

Or was Hannah the grand manipulator, telling the story to stake claim to her innocence?

Either way, Gabriel lost something very precious to him.

"She's good, isn't she? I knew she wasn't guilty." Daniel sounded satisfied.

Gabriel wanted Carrick to be a good man. He needed Carrick to be part of his family.

And he wanted Hannah to be the woman of his dreams.

He couldn't have both.

Did he believe his brother Carrick, or did he believe his lover, Hannah?

One of them was a liar and a murderer. The other was much wronged.

Finishing his slice, he wiped his face and hands and stood up. "If you want to be sure about Hannah, we need to know who did the shooting and why. Now."

Daniel pulled up his e-mail program. "I'll make it a code one."

"You do that." Gabriel headed back into the bedroom.

THIRTY-ONE

Hannah was running, running for her life, but she couldn't run fast enough because she was pushing Mrs. Manly. Someone was chasing her, pointing a gun and shooting. But it wasn't Mrs. Manly in the wheelchair. It was Gabriel. She did CPR, but the blood poured out of him, and he died there in her arms. She looked up into the black eye of the pistol, then back down at the body in her arms. But it wasn't Gabriel anymore. It was Carrick, and he was staring at her. Pointing the gun and staring at her . . . Carrick's green eyes . . . green eyes . . . She was on the verge of knowing something, something very important. . . .

The click of the door brought her out of the nightmare. She sat up, covered with sweat, her heart hammering.

Gabriel stood there, his back against the door, dressed in a pair of jeans and, as far as she could tell, nothing else. He ran his gaze over her and smiled as if he liked her naked and disheveled. "I'm going to take a shower. Want to help me?"

"I think I'd better wake a little bit more." She rubbed her head fretfully. She wanted to sit here and *think* about what the dream was trying to tell her. *Something important . . . something so dreadful . . .*

"Did I wear you out?"

"I'm fine."

He sauntered over and sat beside her, a smug beast of a man. His fingers drifted down her breastbone, and he watched as if fascinated by the contrast of colors and textures. "You always say that when actually . . ." He took a long breath and shifted his gaze to her face. "Dr. Bellota was right. You were exhausted, and I spent all night making love to you. I really did wear you out."

She tugged the covers up. "You're the one who was shot through the thigh. I was just . . . barely shot."

"Bellota says I'm a disgustingly healthy animal, and he wishes all his patients recovered as quickly as I do." Leaning forward, he kissed her forehead. "Go back to sleep."

"I'm *fine*." Man, he was irritating.

"I'll be out in five minutes," he promised.

"Don't get your leg wet." She ought to help him wrap it, but her dream . . . something about Carrick's eyes . . .

Gabriel made a face. "Ten minutes. I'll be out in ten minutes. Then we can nap together."

She didn't want to nap. She wanted to remember that dream—the dream that even now was drifting away from her. . . .

He headed toward the bathroom, and she watched

him, the man she had trusted with the truth. He looked strong, healthy. He walked with almost no limp. His recovery had been nothing short of miraculous, and still, she had dreamed he had died, that he had turned into Carrick. Then . . . then . . . "Damn it!" she muttered.

The whole thing was muddled in her mind, the message lost in Gabriel's arrival.

But maybe it was a warning. Certainly she should find where Carrick was, to discover what he was doing. She should make sure he couldn't find her and hurt Gabriel, because . . . because her subconscious abruptly hummed with anxiety.

Flinging back the covers, she leaped to the desk. She opened Gabriel's laptop and typed *Carrick Manly* into the search engine.

She got a hit right away, a new interview in *Oui-Gee* magazine, a periodical that catered to the people interested in the occult. She clicked on the article and found herself staring back at an artfully posed photo of Carrick with his dimples in full bloom.

He was handsome—she had to give him that. That was why he'd managed to extend his fifteen minutes of fame into an hour. And in a way, she was glad, because while he was in the public eye, she could follow his movements. She could be safe.

She scanned the interview. He talked about losing his mother, of course, and how all the signs had pointed to the danger of having a celebration in that particular house on that particular Halloween. As always, he was a figure of tragedy and high drama, recounting the tale of Nathan Manly and the lost fortune. But this time, down at the bottom, the interviewer asked him about the good luck of finding his half brothers. He assured the interviewer that family was so important to him, he had hired a security firm to locate them. Not surprisingly, precognition had made him hire a very special man, Gabriel Prescott, and Gabriel had turned out to be his brother, too!

Stunned, breathless, Hannah read the interview again. And again.

And in case she didn't believe the printed word, there was a small photo of Carrick and Gabriel, sitting at a table in a restaurant, sandwiches before them, talking intently.

The image imprinted itself on Hannah's retina.

She slammed the laptop closed.

It wasn't possible. *It could not be possible.*

But it was. That was what she'd been dreaming. Gabriel had turned into Carrick—because Gabriel had the same green eyes.

As he washed, Gabriel cursed the plastic wrap and the duct tape that kept his bandage dry. The whole thing took too long to put on, and it took too long to take off, and all the while, Hannah was lying in bed alone and worried about her confession to him. That was the real reason she hadn't come in the shower with him. She was afraid he didn't believe her.

The hand that held the soapy washcloth slowed.

She was afraid for good reason. He didn't believe her. Did he?

Was he willing to condemn Carrick without asking for the truth? If he did ask for the truth, would Carrick tell him?

Did Carrick even know what the truth was?

Would Carrick admit to killing his own mother?

No, never.

But he'd done it. Damn it.

Gabriel slammed his fist on the wall of the shower.

He'd done it all.

Because Carrick would do anything for money, and once Gabriel had suggested that Hannah probably knew the code to access the fortune, Carrick had needed only one thing: confirmation. Knowing Mrs. Manly, knowing how easily irritated she was . . . she'd given it to him.

Gabriel played the video in his mind.

Carrick had been in the party. He'd gone to his mother's room, dressed in the long vampire cape, and placed a red rose on her pillow. Afterward, he had stopped by the tray where the medications and syringes had been laid out, and for a vital few seconds, his cape had covered the tray.

That was when he'd made the switch.

He hadn't needed his mother anymore, except as a means to an end. Except as a means to pressure Hannah into giving him the code.

It hadn't worked, because Hannah got away. Even if she hadn't, she would never have betrayed Mrs. Manly's trust.

No wonder Carrick had looked a little worried in New York City. He needed that money.

Had Gabriel known all this before? He'd seen that video a hundred times, yet never had he allowed himself to think Carrick had done the deed. Gabriel could have enhanced the video to see details—he would now, and look to see if Carrick was wearing gloves, or if there was a chance he'd left a fingerprint on the medicine bottle. But Gabriel hadn't wanted to admit his brother's possible guilt to himself.

What had changed?

Hannah. Hannah had changed everything.

Mrs. Manly hadn't been a fool. She had trusted Hannah, because Hannah was as genuine as she seemed.

Gabriel was the fool.

In a hurry now, he rinsed and got out of the shower. He needed to talk to Daniel about Carrick, consider how best to go about trapping him without harming anyone else. He needed to talk to Hannah about remaining indoors and out of sight.

He needed to tell her . . . who he really was.

THIRTY-TWO

Gabriel walked into the bedroom, hoping Hannah wasn't already asleep. He needed to tell her the truth as soon as possible. He needed to hold her, convince her he truly believed her story, discuss the strategy for catching Carrick in the act, and what kind of deal they would cut with the feds before she gave them access to Nathan Manly's fortune.

He needed to tell her he loved her.

But she was gone.

He hit the living room at a dead run and skidded to a stop.

She was circling the perimeter of the huge room, dressed in his lounge pants and racer-back shirt, walking as fast as she could.

He gaped at her. "What are you doing?"

She grimaced and waved a hand at Daniel.

"She says she needs exercise. Nordstrom is sending up some workout clothes, and I was telling her there's a gym on the fifth floor."

Gabriel shot him a glare.

Daniel shrugged his shoulders like, *What's the harm?*

"Are you well enough to exercise?" When she didn't answer, Gabriel said, "Grace?"

"Oh! Sure. I got enough sleep. And you warmed me up." She shot him a glittering smile. "I'm actually getting a little twitchy being in bed. I'm not used to being idle."

Idle. Well. That put him and his lovemaking in their places.

"I'll get into my workout clothes." Daniel headed for his room. Daniel loved to exercise, and apparently Hannah wasn't the only one getting twitchy.

"I'll change, too." Gabriel tried to catch her eye. "Want to come and help?"

She shot him another one of those million-volt smiles. "If I did that, we'd never make it to the gym, and I'm getting a little stir-crazy, being up here. Not that it's not a gorgeous place. Big living room!" She kept walking. "But are you sure you should exercise at all? Dr. Bellota said you were to stay in bed for seven days."

"Dr. Bellota is a conservative old poop."

She laughed. "Go and change. I'll wait for the workout clothes."

He didn't want to leave her alone to accept the package, but he reminded himself—he trusted her.

He retreated to the bedroom.

It was that right now she seemed to be acting . . . oddly.

He got into a pair of shorts and a T-shirt, and was

tying his shoes when he heard the buzzer. He paused and listened, poised and ready in case. In case of what, he didn't know, but for no reason he could put his finger on, that impression of wrongness nagged at him.

He heard her speak, heard someone answer, heard the elevator door close. He made himself finish tying his shoe, stood, and walked into the living room.

She sat on the couch, transferring her new shoes and clothes into a gym bag. He would have sworn she heard him come in, but she didn't look up.

"I need to tell you something." Maybe this wasn't the best time to confess the truth, but a sense of urgency was driving him.

"Hmm?" She looked up as if surprised.

"It's complicated, but I'm not who—"

Daniel bounded into the room. "Are we ready?"

"Yes!" Bag in hand, Hannah stood. "Not quite. If you both will give me a private minute . . . I won't be long." She headed toward the bedroom and shut the door after her.

"Sorry, boss." Daniel hung his head and looked sorrowful. "I didn't realize you were having a moment."

"I was going to tell her I believed her."

"All the way?"

"All the way."

"About time." Daniel was intelligent, intuitive, and a friend, and his blessing meant a lot.

"It probably wasn't the right moment, anyway." Gabriel rubbed the stubble on his chin and wished he'd taken a moment to shave. "When I tell her who I really am and what I've done, she's going to—"

"Blow a gasket."

"Hannah's not like that."

"You are kidding yourself. You spied on her. You slept with her, and she doesn't even know who you really are." Daniel counted off the list of Gabriel's sins on his fingers. "You'd better roll on your back like a puppy, because she is going to beat you with a slipper."

The door handle turned.

"*Shh,*" Gabriel said.

She walked out, still in the lounge pants, and said, "Are we ready, gentlemen?"

Daniel pulled his pass card out of his wallet, stuck it into the elevator panel, and pressed the DOWN button. "Let's go."

Hannah walked into the elevator ahead of them, faced front, and leaned against the wall. She smacked her bag into the rail, and it made a clinking sound.

She stiffened with guilt and worry, but they didn't say anything. They didn't notice.

Okay. Just act cool.

Gabriel stood next to her and wrapped his arm around her.

She had to act natural; she couldn't screw this up now. So she tilted her head onto his shoulder, and tried to pretend he was some other man. A guy who was honest and true, although in her experience men like that didn't exist. She was out of the penthouse, and if she played her cards right, she'd be so gone Gabriel Prescott would never find her again.

The slick, deceitful bastard.

The elevator made a fast descent.

He kissed the top of her head.

She tried not to gag.

He tried to turn her face up to kiss her mouth.

She pulled away and whispered, "Not in front of Daniel!"

The doors opened, and she bounded out. She glanced both ways, then back at the guys and asked, "Which way?"

"To the left," Daniel said.

"Come on!" She walked with the excess of energy that only the pure flame of absolute rage could give her.

The gym was marked with a discreet little sign, and Daniel used his pass card to let them in.

She surveyed the field of battle. This was a great gym. It was a perfect gym. It was clean. Mirrors covered one wall and a huge window covered the other. A machine dispensed bottles of water and energy drinks. There were four treadmills, four elliptical machines, four exercise bikes. There was an area to lift weights and do ab work, and eight professional gym-weight, massive black heavy machines.

Two women were on the treadmills, chatting, and they were sweaty and red-faced, so hopefully they'd be done soon.

Life was good.

"You guys go ahead. I'm going to change." Hannah headed for the ladies' room, and before the door shut behind her, she heard their low, worried buzz.

She wasn't quite pulling off the carefree act, but they weren't alarmed. Yet.

Going into one of the small dressing rooms, she placed the bag on the bench, careful to make no sound. She unzipped it and pulled out the workout clothes.

Perfect. A pair of black capri pants, a black hoodie, and a pink patterned tank. Not too flashy, just right. The shoes were good, too. In fact, the shoes were . . . She sighed in delight. She hadn't been able to afford shoes like this for almost a year. Cross-trainers, white and pink, with good support. She was in heaven.

She didn't waste time—didn't want the guys to get nervous—but changed, cursing the bandage on her wrist as it caught on the sleeves coming off and going on. Her arm still hurt. But she'd had bigger challenges in her life, and this one wasn't going to stop her now.

She tossed the lounge pants and top in the garbage. She was either going to make it out of here, or she wasn't, but no matter what, she would never wear those damn clothes again.

They were tainted with memories.

Folding the hoodie, she placed it in the bottom of the bag, arranged everything to her satisfaction, and zipped the bag *most* of the way closed. She walked out in time to see the two women getting ready to walk out. She watched carefully, and all they did was push, and the door opened right up.

Great. No pass card needed.

She looked at the guys. "We're alone."

They grinned at her, grunted, and went on working the weights.

She'd suggested the right thing. They were both blissed out, doing man stuff, showing off.

Daniel stopped to strip off his T-shirt. The guy was a black-skinned god, his chest and arms corded with muscle and glistening with sweat, his legs shaped like an Olympic runner's.

Gabriel kept his tee on, but she knew what he looked like, and the memory of his body made her perspire without lifting an ounce.

For a moment, her heart quailed. This was going to take timing and luck, and lately her luck had been nonexistent.

She raised her chin.

So it was time for her luck to change.

She put her bag beside an exercise bike, sat down, and set the resistance to nothing. She might have told the guys she wanted to work out, but in truth, for what she had planned, she would need all her strength. She started pedaling, scrutinized the room, and finalized her strategy.

In a chatty tone, she said, "So. When do you guys celebrate your birthdays?"

"A man as old as the boss never celebrates his," Daniel said, and ducked and laughed when Gabriel flung a towel at him.

"I was abandoned, so I'm not sure when my birthday is." Gabriel spoke matter-of-factly, without self-pity—a man simply stating the facts. "The Prescotts decided I was born on July Fourth, Independence Day, and my sisters always make sure there's a cake along with the fireworks."

"Neat." His sisters sounded nice. Too bad the niceness hadn't rubbed off. Zeroing in on her real target, she asked, "How about you, Daniel? When's your birthday?"

"You going to buy me a present?" He grinned at her.

"Yes, something to prop up your poor, shriveled ego," she snapped.

Now Gabriel laughed.

"She must be getting better," Daniel spoke to no one in particular. "She's grumpy."

"I am not. I just want to know. . . ." She took a breath and calmed herself. "Oh, well, if you don't want to tell me, I can't bake my special pie for you."

"I do love me a pie," Daniel said. "What kind?"

"Boston cream pie. A yellow cake filled with vanilla custard and topped with chocolate glaze." She dangled her tastiest bait.

Daniel frowned as if he thought she was pulling his leg. "Doesn't sound like pie to me."

"I've had it. That custard is rich and the chocolate drizzles down the side and pools on the plate. . . ." Gabriel smacked his lips.

"But, Daniel, if you don't want it . . ." *Come on*, she thought. *Come on, come on!*

"Okay! My birthday's April twenty-second."

"What year?"

"Nineteen eighty-eight."

With that, she had everything she needed.

Daniel put down his weight and frowned at her. "But April's a long ways away. How am I going to wait?"

"When I go upstairs"—which if everything worked out as she intended, that would never happen—"you might be able to persuade me to do a little prebirthday baking."

"Do I get a Boston cream pie, too?" Gabriel asked.

She smiled gaily, and joked, "You had better believe that you are both going to get your just deserts."

Except, of course, she wasn't joking.

After that, it was about a half hour—thirty long, agonizing minutes of waiting and watching—before she was able to say to Gabriel, "You need to stop."

"Why?" It was a knee-jerk, tough-guy reaction.

"Because you got shot four days ago, and you look like you're going to pass out." It was a fact. He looked worn-out. Of course, she'd egged him on, but her first and greatest hope had been that he would stay in the penthouse and rest. After all, she didn't really want the guy to die from overdoing it.

Instead, she wanted to kill him.

Daniel put down his weight and examined Gabriel. "She's right. You look bad."

"I'm fine," Gabriel said irritably.

She chuckled. "That's what I say when I feel like hell, too."

Gabriel was annoyed for one more minute. Then, with a sigh, he surrendered to the inevitable. "I suppose I am tired. One lousy gunshot wound, and I'm down for the count."

"We'd all better go up." But Daniel glanced wistfully toward the treadmills. He was obviously into his training.

"You stay here. I can make it upstairs on my own. I'm not that out of it." Gabriel used a towel to wipe his sweaty face. "Are you coming, Grace?"

Obviously, he was expecting her answer to be *yes.*

As if.

"Oh. I was hoping . . ." She put on her disappointed face. "Just a few minutes on the elliptical—twenty minutes, I swear—and I'll be up."

"I'd be happy with another twenty minutes, too," Daniel said. "Don't worry. I won't let her go up on her own. On account of her arm, you know."

"I do know," she said.

The guys stared at her.

She must have sounded a little sarcastic, so she smiled with all her might.

"All right. I'll, um, see you up there." Gabriel pulled his pass card out of his pocket. "We can shower to-gether."

His voice got deep and warm and vibrant.

My God. No wonder she thought he sounded familiar.

He was Trent Sansoucy.

He was Gabriel Prescott.

He was the biggest liar in the world.

"Yes, we can shower together." *Never as long as I live.*

She waved as he walked out the door, then hopped off the bike. "Daniel, do you have money on you? I'd like a water."

"Sure thing." The guy was good natured for a jailer, and trusting, too, because he walked into the men's dressing room, leaving her alone.

Grabbing her bag, she carried it to the line of weight machines. She needed a tall one with a wide, heavy base and solid metal uprights. She needed one that looked complex. And she needed one close to the door. The second from the door looked ideal. She placed her bag on the seat, and opened it wide.

"Hey!" she said when Daniel walked back out, carrying his wallet. "I don't know if I can figure out how to use this thing, and even if I can, with this wrist, I can't change the weight."

"Wait a minute. I'll help you. Don't hurt yourself. The boss will kill me." He stuck a bill in the dispenser, got her a bottle of water, got himself an energy drink, and came right over, ready to help the weak little woman.

"Here, let me hold those." She took the bottles and his wallet.

"Thanks." He leaned on the upright and bent over to change the weights.

The machine didn't even sway.

Perfect.

"The weight is way too heavy." She put everything down near the door, and reached into her bag. "Whoever was working this must have been in fabulous shape."

"The weight's not that much. Men's muscle mass is a lot greater than women's. That why when we work out—"

She stumbled against him, knocking him to his knees. "Whoops. Sorry. I tripped on the—"

" 'S all right." He tried to look up.

She slammed his head against the pole. "I'm getting faint . . ." She fastened one end of the handcuffs to the upright.

He shook his head to clear it.

She grabbed his wrist and shoved it into the other cuff. "Darn, I guess I'm not as well as I thought—"

She clicked the lock, grabbed her bag, and ran—just in time.

Fast as a snake, he lunged for her.

The metal handcuffs jerked him back. The machine rang like a bell.

The astonishment on his face did her heart good.

"Now, listen, Miss Grace, listen." Blood trickled from a cut on his forehead. "You don't want to do this." He spoke softly, gently, but all the time, he was straining against the cuff.

She grabbed the bottles and his wallet and dropped them in her bag. "I so want to do this."

"Mr. Prescott's going to be angry with me. You're a nice lady. You don't want the boss to be angry with me." Daniel twisted the cuff around and around, straining to get free, and he was still using that soft, kind, begging-for-understanding voice.

"I don't give a damn whether he's angry with you." She put one hand on the door. She needed to get out of here before someone else walked in, but she couldn't resist one last shot. "Do you really think you're going to break that handcuff? It's a good one. I got it out of the bedside drawer on Mr. Prescott's side."

Daniel stilled. "Oh, no."

Her voice swelled with fury. "What was he going

to do? Arrest and cuff me when he'd finished *screwing* me?"

"No, Miss Grace . . ." Daniel checked, then used her real name. "Miss Hannah, he believes in you. He really does, and if you'll just—"

"I don't care whether he believes in me. I am done with Gabriel Prescott." She walked out the door, down the stairs, and into the bustling Galleria mall.

THIRTY-THREE

They had been down in the gym too long.

Gabriel sat on the couch in the living room, stared at the elevator door, and tried to decide if he was being paranoid or not.

But Daniel and Hannah had been down in the gym for almost forty minutes. And they'd promised twenty.

Probably they were chatting with someone who had come in, or Daniel was into his weights and Hannah was too polite to say she wanted to come up, or . . . or the workout had been too much for Hannah, and she was unconscious, or the guy who had shot Gabriel had made it past the building security and had killed them both.

Gabriel got up and limped to the elevator, then limped back.

If he went down there and nothing was wrong, Daniel would call him an old woman. And if danger threatened, there was nobody Gabriel wanted at his side more than Daniel. The man was fast, strong, and dangerous, a fourth-degree black belt in karate and a second-degree in kung-fu.

If only Gabriel didn't feel so uneasy. His gut was telling him something. Something to do with Hannah.

She had started acting strangely . . . when?

When he was in the shower.

What had happened to give her a stiff smile and eyes that glittered as hard as sapphires?

She'd heard something. She'd talked to somebody.

He checked the phone, the outgoing and incoming history. Nothing there.

She'd seen something.

He looked around, but he'd left nothing incriminating lying around.

She'd found something on the computer.

He headed into the bedroom, to his desk. He opened the laptop. It came out of sleep.

And there it was. An interview with Carrick and a photo of— "Shit!"

Gabriel swung out of the chair. He headed for the door.

The phone rang. He grabbed it as he walked past, didn't recognize the number, almost threw it aside. But it only took a second to push TALK.

At once Daniel was yelling in his ear. "She's gone! She escaped! For God's sake, boss, send the hounds out. We've got to find her!"

In the penthouse master bedroom, Gabriel packed a clean shirt and a clean pair of jeans into his carry-on, and listened as Daniel gave his report.

"Me and the guys, we've reviewed every tape." Daniel was hoarse from all the shouting he'd done in the gym yesterday, trying to get someone's attention so he could get free of the cuffs. "First thing she did was put on her jacket and pull up the hood. Good move. We had her when she exited the stairway into the Galleria. Then she hit the elevators, and we lost her. Next time we found her, it was ten minutes later. She goes to an ATM on the first level, accesses her money card, and gets a thousand dollars."

"Her money card." Gabriel wished to hell he'd taken it when he found it. "She must have grabbed that while we were changing into our workout clothes."

"She's pretty crafty for an amateur." Daniel realized he sounded admiring, and straightened up. "Next thing, she's using *my* money card to take a thousand dollars out of *my* checking account."

"How did she get your PIN number?"

"I don't know."

Observing Daniel's pout, and remembering her pointed questions, Gabriel asked, "For God's sake, Daniel, you don't use your birthday backward, do you?"

"*No.*"

"Daniel." Gabriel bent a stern gaze at him.

Daniel threw up his hands. "All right! I do! But no one knows my birthday except—"

"Except for a pretty woman who offers to make you a Boston cream pie."

"Yeah." Daniel was as chagrined as any guy who had been suckered. "Only crooks know that backward birthday trick."

"Security people know, too." Gabriel remembered his phone conversation a year ago, the night before the fateful Halloween party. "I told her about it."

"Boss, how could you?"

"I never foresaw her stealing your wallet," Gabriel said tartly. "So she took you for a little walking-around money."

"Yeah. Great." Daniel held an ice pack to his bandaged forehead.

If Gabriel were in a laughing mood, he'd be chuckling, because Daniel was notoriously tight with the dollar. "She can go wherever she wants with two thousand dollars." He went into the bathroom.

"Where she wanted to go was the Saks day spa."

Gabriel came back out, holding his partially packed shaving kit, wondering if he'd heard right. "The day spa?"

"That was where we lost her for a long, long time." Daniel looked lousy, as if he'd been up all night. Which he had. "We were talking to the cab companies. We mobilized people on the streets, who fanned out in all directions. We talked to the cops. We didn't think to check the massage tables."

"She got a massage?" Gabriel couldn't help feeling a little proud. The spa was pure genius.

"She got a massage. She got her toes done and her fingers done. She got a facial. Somewhere in there, they brought her lunch." Daniel consulted his list. "A chicken salad sandwich with grapes and pecans on a bed of fresh salad greens, a whole-wheat roll, and a glass of champagne."

"What the *hell*?"

"I said that, too, only I used a different word." Daniel passed him a photo, taken from above, of a blonde with a spiky short haircut, dressed in dark jeans, a white silk button-up shirt, and a black duster, walking out of the spa. "Last but not least, she had makeup applied and her hair colored and cut."

"Ah." That put a whole different complexion on the spa experience. Gabriel studied the photo. "Are you sure this is her?"

"That's her. The ID software nailed her, and when we interviewed the beautician, she ID'd her, too. She must have done the clothes shopping the first time we lost her."

"She looks great." Gabriel tucked the photo in his jacket and went back to filling his shaving kit. "What next?"

Daniel came to the door. "A cab picked her up at the Nordstrom entrance and took her to the Wal-Mart where she worked."

"Now *that's* interesting." Gabriel headed back into the bedroom.

Daniel moved aside.

Flinging his shaving kit into the suitcase, Gabriel asked, "What did she do at Wal-Mart?"

"She went to the ladies' room, went into a stall, and came out about five minutes later. One of her coworkers was parked in another stall, and she reports seeing someone kneel on the floor—"

"Hannah must have been desperate to do that. Those floors are disgusting."

"And the employee heard the lady rummaging around behind the toilet. We checked for tape residue. It was positive."

"Hannah had a fake ID." Gabriel zipped his carry-on.

"Of course she did. So she could rent a car at the Sugar Land airport and drive to God knows where." Daniel popped three aspirin and scowled.

Gabriel gave a soft laugh.

"What?" Daniel snapped.

"She cuffed you to the machine. That sweet, little female knocked big, tough Daniel silly. She cuffed you to the machine."

"She tricked me!" Daniel gingerly touched the cut on his forehead.

"You needed five stitches," Gabriel reminded him.

"Do you think I don't know that? Do you think everyone in the business isn't laughing?" Like the expert tactician he was, Daniel switched topics. "What are you going to Maine for? She's not going to Maine. She's running like hell to Mexico and she is never coming back."

Gabriel knew how to switch topics, too. "Any word on who shot me?"

Daniel shifted uncomfortably. "A rumor. No, not even a rumor—a breath of a rumor. Something about New York City."

"New York City. So it is Carrick." Gabriel picked up the suitcase.

"If it's true, then . . . yeah, probably." Daniel waggled his head with uncertainty, then clutched it and winced.

"Is the plane prepped to fly?" Gabriel limped for the door.

Daniel grabbed the car keys and followed. "I still say you're making a mistake. She's not going to Maine."

Gabriel kept walking "Flight plan filed? Pilot ready?"

Daniel sighed. "We even washed the windshield. You know Dr. Bellota is going to shout when you don't show up for your one-week checkup, don't you?"

"I should be back by then."

"If you're not dead."

"My leg is fine."

"I meant from a new bullet hole."

"Good to know you have confidence in me." Gabriel knew where Daniel was heading.

In a wheedling tone, Daniel said, "Let me come with you."

"You suck at breaking and entering."

"I'm great on backup."

Gabriel stopped and considered. "You'll stay behind unless I call you?"

Daniel perked up. "Yeah, boss."

"And if I do call you in to assist me, you won't let a girl beat you up and cuff you?"

"Give me a second to pack." Daniel headed for his bedroom. "While you blow it out your ass."

Gabriel grinned. Then his grin faded.

Carrick had sent an assassin.

For Hannah? Unless Carrick had figured out the way to access his father's fortune, it didn't make sense to kill the one person who knew.

So . . . for Gabriel? But why? Did he think Gabriel knew too much?

All Gabriel wanted to do was keep Hannah safe, and to do that, he had to find her.

He'd spent the night trying to figure out what she was thinking, what she had planned.

Somehow she intended to do as she had promised Mrs. Manly and transfer the money into the accounts of the people who had lost so much when Nathan Manly destroyed his company and disappeared. To do that, she had to go back to Balfour House.

There, he feared, she would die.

And Gabriel wondered—in his quest to discover his past, had he lost his hope for a future?

THIRTY-FOUR

To the casual eye, Balfour House was deserted. The lawn was overgrown, the withered leaves lay where they'd fallen. The windows were blank and frosty, without curtains or warmth.

But as Gabriel walked around the house, he recognized the signs that someone had been here. He saw car tracks leading into the garage—more than one car—and footprints through the frosty grass—more than one pair.

Driven by a fearful urgency, he pulled the remote from his black leather jacket, and tuned it to access the surveillance system still in place. If the electricity was off, he was screwed, but if it was on . . .

"Ahhh." The handheld screen flickered.

The computer upstairs in his former office had been brought to life. Now, as he waited for the surveillance program to boot up, he pulled out his lock-pick set and prepared to open the front door.

But the first rule of breaking and entering was to

check to make sure the door was locked . . . and this one opened at a turn of the hand.

Someone was inside.

He darkened the monitor on the handheld, pulled the pistol out of the holster at his side, swung the door wide, and waited.

Nothing happened. He listened, then stepped inside.

Fresh footsteps wandered across the dust that coated the marble floor.

Yet the silence set him on edge. It was too much, too deep.

He faded into the shadows under the stairs, waiting for the computer to perform.

Some of the most valuable furniture and paintings had gone to auction, leaving blank spaces on the floor and faded squares on the wallpaper. The temperature hovered around fifty degrees, and Gabriel guessed another Maine winter would destroy anything left in here.

Did Carrick not intend to sell the house and its contents? This neglect would lower the value on a priceless nineteenth-century mansion. To lose money on a sure sale . . . that didn't seem like Carrick. So . . . what was Carrick doing?

A quiet beep alerted Gabriel that the computer had gone through its paces, and had started to run the program that activated each on-site camera for a ten-second glimpse of the every corridor and room. But the house had too many rooms, and Gabriel didn't have ten seconds to waste, so he speeded up the roll to two seconds.

Yet it took a full two minutes before he located Hannah.

Gabriel stopped the roll, and observed the scene in the butler's office in the basement.

There, Carrick sat before the desk in a straight-backed chair. He stared at the creaky old computer. Hannah sat in the ancient leather desk chair. She wore her new clothes and her new hair style with pride. Her chin was up. She was smiling scornfully. And Nelson, the butler, held a Beretta pointed at her heart.

Gabriel texted Daniel *911*, and set off at a run.

Hannah divided her attention between that lousy little weasel Nelson and that lousy big weasel, Carrick.

"Did you really think I wouldn't watch for you?" Carrick stared at the computer, his face aglow—he'd just seen the total amount in Nathan Manly's account.

"Think? No. Hope? Yes." Hannah rocked the old chair back and forth. Tithe springs creaked rhythmically. *Creak, creak. Creak, creak.*

"I knew the key to Father's fortune had to be here, or you would have got away with it long ago. You had to come back here." Carrick didn't look at her. He couldn't tear his gaze away from the screen.

"I did have to come back. To keep a promise." *Creak, creak. Creak, creak.*

"To my mother. Isn't that touching?" Carrick rubbed his hand over his chest as if to calm the beat of his heart. "I admit, I'd hoped for more."

"You'd hoped for more?" Her voice rose involuntarily. "Money? More than that?"

"How much is it?" Nelson asked in a hushed whisper.

"About a billion," Carrick said.

Hannah corrected him. "A billion five."

Carrick glared at her.

"What? Doesn't he get a percentage?" She rocked the chair back and forth. *Creak, creak. Creak, creak.* "What disappoints you about a billion five?"

"It's not the amount. This program is so primitive. The screen looks like the intro to a child's learning program." Carrick ran the mouse up and down, back and forth. "What do we have to do next?"

"It's probably pretty simple. All you're doing is transferring money from one place to another." Actually, to about a thousand other places, but she wasn't going to tell him that. "So far, it's working the way Mrs. Manly said it would." *Creak, creak. Creak, creak.*

Carrick turned on her, eyes wide and wild. *"Would you stop that?"*

"What? That?" She rocked one last time. *Creak, creak. Creak, creak.* "Sure."

He took a breath and calmed himself. "What comes next? How do I transfer the money into *my* account?"

"What makes you think I would tell you that?" She injected all the scorn she felt into her voice.

He turned and looked straight at her. "If you don't, I'll have Nelson shoot you in one foot, and then the other foot, and then—"

She held up the hand with the bandage on her wrist. "All right. I get it."

Disaster stared her in the face, and she didn't really know how to avert it. She didn't have the information he wanted. All she was capable of doing was performing the transfer into the stockholders' accounts. Which meant, when she'd done it, Carrick was probably going to shoot her anyway, out of spite and frustration.

"So how do I make the next step?" Carrick demanded.

She pushed herself across the floor in the chair, and the springs squalled and moaned. *Creak, creak. Creak, creak.* When she, and the chair, reached his side, she could see that his teeth were on edge. That gave her some satisfaction. "You're into the base program. Now go to Household Accounts."

He located the icon on the desktop, and opened it.

"Find Silverware, Inventory."

The cursor trembled on the screen. Carrick's hand trembled on the mouse.

Hannah liked knowing he was nervous. "Now—I input the password." She tried to edge him aside.

He refused to move. "What password?"

"What difference does it make?"

"I don't trust you to do this right. I might have to do it over."

She jabbed him with her elbow, using the bony end like a sword. "If that's what you think, what would keep me from lying to you?"

Nelson shot the Beretta. The blast made her ears ring. The wheel on her chair blew into little plastic shreds. She was thrown to the floor to land on her wrist, and she writhed in pain.

When the scarlet dots had stopped swimming before her eyes, she looked up to find not one, but two Berettas pointed at her.

Carrick held one of the compact pistols, and he handled it like a man who knew how to shoot. "Come and sit on your squeaky chair." He patted the seat. "And tell me what I want to know."

He was not, as she had previously thought, a bad seed. He was crazy.

She glanced at Nelson. He knew it, too, but greed held him in servitude.

Good luck on seeing any of your cut.

Moving with an excess of caution, she lifted herself off the floor and perched on the chair, tilted and wobbly from the shot. *Creak, creak. Creak, creak.* This time she tried to contain the noise; she didn't want to irritate Carrick further. Not when life was now measured in seconds.

She whispered, "The password is capital B, as in Balfour, capital H, as in House, small N, as in Nathan, capital M, as in Melinda, small C, as in Carrick—"

"That bitch of a mother of mine." Carrick typed in each letter, and as he did, he rocked back and forth on his heels.

Hannah took a breath. "You killed her. Isn't that enough?"

"She deserved it."

"Wow." Hannah couldn't believe it. "You confessed."

"What difference does that make? No one will ever know." But he was annoyed, as if he hadn't intended to tell the truth, not even to the people he planned to kill. "The password. What else?"

She repeated, word for word, Mrs. Manly's instructions. "Asterisk, 1898, as in the year Balfour House was completed. Not started, completed."

Carrick indicated the green screen. "All right. I've done it all. Is that it?"

"That's all so far. If you'll let me live and give me a share, I'll give you the final code."

Nelson gave a growl.

Carrick waved him to silence, then turned the gun on her again. "You are in no position to make a deal with me."

"Look." Her voice was shaking, but she had to stall him in the hopes that . . . that Gabriel would somehow follow her here. Because he might not love her—she guessed he didn't even like her—but he did love justice, and he wouldn't let his brother get away with this. "You have to promise me on all you hold dear— promise me on this fortune—that I can walk out of here alive. Because otherwise, you're going to shoot me anyway, and I've kept this secret for too long to die without my share of the loot."

Carrick snorted softly. "Sure. Sure, I'll let you live and give you . . . a half percent of the billion."

"A half percent of the billion five," she corrected.

"Sure."

"That's not fair. That's more than I'm getting." Nelson, the idiot, sounded honestly peeved.

Could he look into Carrick's mad eyes and really think he would live to collect?

"Okay." She pointed a trembling finger at the one empty box on the screen. "Put the cursor there, and type in *Mysons*, one word, capital M."

"You." Carrick pointed at Nelson. "Keep her covered." He placed his pistol into the holster strapped around his chest. He leaned down, placed his hands on the keyboard, and *his* fingers were trembling, too, as he typed in the letters.

Mysons.

The code hung there on the pixels. She could hear the computer working, working, transferring, changing a thousand people's lives.

If she didn't live through this, she could die knowing she had done some good in this world.

Small comfort for a woman who wanted to live.

"After this, I'll be into the account and I can transfer the money as I wish, right?" Carrick pulled a crumpled sheet of paper out of his pocket and placed it at the top of the keyboard.

It was a bank account number.

"Is that in Switzerland?" she asked.

"Don't be foolish. Nobody does Switzerland anymore."

Okay. She guessed she should remember that *The Bourne Identity* was only a movie.

At last the program showed progress. One minute the screen showed the green screen with the amount in small letters.

Then . . . the green pixels shrank away from the edges. Green became gray and gray became black. There was one last glowing speck of green, and then . . . it was gone. All gone.

"Wh-what's happening?" Carrick tapped on the screen. "Is that what it's supposed to do?"

"I think so." She leaned back. The chair wobbled and rocked, but before it fell, she caught herself and perched carefully on the edge, positioning herself just . . . so. "That code sent the money to the proper accounts for repayment to the Manly investors and employees."

"What?" Carrick came to his feet.

"What?" Nelson echoed.

"Not only that, but if the government decides to prosecute for the loss of the fortune, I'm not responsible. You're the one who typed in the code." She didn't laugh; she was too scared.

But she wanted to.

"What?" Carrick screamed.

She flipped the chair into his hip, knocking him sideways, slamming him into the wall. She scrambled away, ready to dodge, ready to run.

Nelson caught her around the waist.

And in the doorway, someone laughed.

Gabriel laughed.

Everyone froze.

Except Gabriel. He leaned against the doorframe, shaking his head in amazement. "Honestly, Carrick, did you really think Hannah Grey was going to help you steal our father's fortune? You don't know her at all."

Gabriel had come. He had followed her. Hannah experienced one bright, glorious pinnacle of pure joy. Then—

"Don't you dare laugh at me!" Carrick pulled his pistol.

Gabriel pulled his.

Carrick pointed at Gabriel.

At Gabriel.

With the scream of rage, Hannah smashed Nelson's nose with the flat of her hand, and leaped toward Carrick.

THIRTY-FIVE

Hannah jumped into the line of fire.

Gabriel twirled his pistol. His shot went wild. Sheetrock showered from the ceiling.

Carrick's pistol roared.

His bullet hit Hannah.

She flew backward, slammed against the wall, collapsed into a heap.

Carrick stood, slack-jawed in surprise.

Nelson lowered his pistol and stared. "Carrick, what did you do?"

Gabriel could hear nothing but the sound of someone's harsh breathing. His own. It was his own, as he tried to understand . . . Dead? Hannah was dead?

No. Not dead. Not dead.

Yet her eyes were closed. Her head was cocked to the side. She looked like a broken rag doll.

Most important, she'd been not three feet from Carrick. No one could survive a shot from that close distance.

Dead. Hannah *was* dead.

How could he have screwed up so badly?

He turned his gaze away from her body. He looked up at Carrick. He knew that somewhere close, an agony of grief waited to pounce. But he held it off with a shield of fury.

Like a man who had glimpsed his death, Carrick stumbled backward against the desk; then swiftly and with purpose, he raised his pistol again.

Gabriel could have shot him. He was faster. He was better. But that wasn't how he wanted to do it.

Grabbing Nelson by the arm, he swung him at Carrick.

Carrick's Beretta roared again.

As the bullet struck him, Nelson jerked. His chest blew. Blood spattered the walls, the floor, Gabriel. He dropped like a rock. Dead.

Before Nelson had even hit the floor, Gabriel lowered his head and charged like an enraged bull. He caught Carrick around the waist. He slammed his skull into his chest. The Beretta went flying, and Carrick gave a grunt as all the air left his lungs. Gabriel came up and caught him under the chin with a right uppercut, then used both his fists to rearrange his nose. Carrick crashed into the computer, smashing the monitor. Glass shattered. Gabriel picked Carrick up by the shirt and belt and tossed him into the shards.

He wanted to hurt him. He intended to kill him.

Carrick must have seen the murder in his face, for at last he fought back.

He was good. Thank God, someone had given this boy lessons in self-defense.

Because Gabriel didn't want him to go easy. He wanted Carrick to believe he had a hope of surviving, and he wanted to know that Carrick would see that hope dwindle.

Carrick slammed the edge of his hand against Gabriel's throat, making him gag and fall back.

Gabriel kicked Carrick in the kneecap, and felt the fibula crack.

Carrick fell, and the scream of his agony didn't mend Gabriel's heart, but it felt good, like revenge . . . for Hannah.

That moment of anguish for his lost love was Gabriel's downfall.

With his good leg, Carrick kicked out, catching Gabriel's thigh right over the healing gunshot wound.

For a few vital seconds, Gabriel's vision went black.

When he woke, Carrick was gone.

Carrick dragged himself through the basement corridors. He needed to get out. He needed to hide. He'd never faced death before, but he'd seen it now, in Gabriel's eyes.

The fortune was gone. His mother was dead. Nelson was dead. . . . Oh, my God, the blood! His brother Gabriel intended to kill him.

Osgood waited in the city for his cut of the fortune. He waited, and when he discovered Carrick had failed to secure the money, he would take Carrick apart, piece by piece, and smile while Carrick screamed.

Carrick couldn't run fast or far. That bastard Gabriel had kicked him hard enough to break his leg.

So he had to hide.

Hide where?

When he was little, he used to play down in the basement, but after his father left, his mother had gotten weird about where he could go in the house. The basement had been off-limits for him and the servants. Only Torres had had an office down here.

Mother had even sealed off the kitchen and built a new kitchen on the main floor . . . but Carrick remembered where the old room was. If he could find a way in, he could hide until Gabriel left, until the cops stopped searching, until Osgood . . . God. Osgood would never stop searching.

Carrick had to call a halt to his trek. He was whimpering in little gasps, and he felt his consciousness slipping away.

Then the distant sounds of running feet, of men shouting, brought him to attention.

They were coming to get him.

He started down the corridor toward the old kitchen. There in the corner in the wall . . . it looked like the outline of a door. And there was a handle inset in the Sheetrock. Hurriedly he inserted his fingers and twisted the knob. The door swung open on creaking hinges. He scuttled inside, shut himself in, and groped for a light switch.

He couldn't find it. It was dark. So dark. Not a spark of light, and the only sound was the hum of an old refrigerator.

He eased himself along the wall, groping, groping. . . . He found another door, a metal door, and another handle, a lever handle. He opened it, and a gust of freezing air blasted out.

He'd found the freezer unit, a massive meat locker from the nineteen fifties. There the hunters in the family had brought their wild game—their venison, their caribou—after it was butchered. As a child, he'd been in this thing with the old cook, and he remembered . . . there was a light in there, a chain dangling from a bare bulb fixture in the middle of the eight-by-ten space.

He stepped in. The door slammed behind him.

In the freezer. He was stuck in the freezer.

In a panic, in the freezing air and pitch-black darkness, he grabbed the lever and turned it.

Nothing happened. The door didn't open.

He was breathing in gasps, the cold air burning his lungs.

But he had to calm himself. There had to be a way out. A safety latch of some kind. Right?

Okay. Okay. He had to find the light. It was here. He knew it was.

Once he got the light on, he'd figure out how to open the door. In the meantime, there was no reason for the hair on the back of his neck to prickle, and the only reason he had goose bumps was because of the bitter cold.

He stretched out his arm toward the center of the locker. He swung from side to side, trying to find the chain.

Something icy brushed his fingers, like a frozen spiderweb.

He gasped in horror, then realized—he'd found it. That was the chain. He groped again, found it, got a good hold, and tugged.

Light flooded the empty locker. Empty except for . . . his father.

Nathan Manly sat huddled in a corner, dressed in a business suit, covered in frost and frozen solid, his eyes wide-open and staring right at Carrick.

So Carrick did the only thing he could.

He screamed, and screamed, and screamed.

THIRTY-SIX

Broken in body and in spirit, Gabriel eased himself up against the wall and texted Daniel with his location.

He couldn't believe Carrick had managed to crawl away. Gabriel must have really put the fear of God into that kid. He only hoped he'd sent him right to hell . . . because Carrick had already returned the favor.

Hannah was dead.

He looked over at Hannah's still body huddled against the far wall.

He had spent his life never imagining that a woman like her would come his way, and when she did . . . he had scorned her. He had doubted her. Then, finally, when he should have been saving her, she had saved him. She'd stepped in front of a bullet meant for him. She'd done it not once, but twice.

A world without Hannah Grey . . . that *was* hell.

The gunshot that had killed Nelson had sprayed Gabriel with blood, but the mess didn't concern him. Rather, it was the blood that seeped from his gunshot wound at a steady pace, soaking his jeans and leaving a scarlet puddle on the floor beneath him. If Daniel didn't get here soon, if an ambulance didn't arrive right away, Gabriel was finally going to die.

So let him die holding Hannah in his arms.

Painfully, he dragged himself over to her. Tenderly, he lifted her off the floor.

She groaned.

He jumped so hard he bumped his head against the wall.

"Hannah." He pressed his hand to her carotid artery. "Hannah!"

Her heart pulsed against his fingertips. She was alive. Alive!

Of course. When Carrick shot her, there wasn't any blood. She should have been covered with blood, gallons of it. Where was it?

Gabriel groped for his phone with one hand. As soon as Daniel answered, he said, "Send an ambulance."

Daniel must have already consulted his own handheld monitor, for he said, "Already did. I'm on my way."

Gabriel snapped his phone closed. He clutched either side of Hannah's shirt and ripped. Buttons flew, and when all was revealed . . . he couldn't believe his eyes.

Hannah wore a bulletproof vest.

"Clever, clever girl." She was the brightest, bravest, most honorable woman in the world, and she was *alive*. Wild with joy, he wrapped her in his arms and hugged her. Hugged her tight.

At once, she came to life in his arms. She struggled wildly, gasping, slapping at him. "Stop. That hurts!"

"Right." Quickly, gently, he placed her on the floor.

She rolled to her side, hugging herself, breathing harshly.

He replayed the fatal scene in his mind—she had leaped at Carrick, Carrick had shot, and she'd flown backward, propelled by the force of the bullet. The bullet had hit with enough impact to do damage. He caressed her forehead and asked urgently, "Where did the bullet hit you? Did it break any ribs?"

"It hit me right on the breastbone." She took a long breath. "And it hurts likes hell. So yes, something is probably broken." She opened her eyes, saw Nelson's blood-soaked body, and averted her gaze. "What happened to him?"

"He got in the way." With careful hands, Gabriel helped her to turn over, away from the gruesome sight. He wanted to hug her again, to comfort her, to help her forget. But he was stuck with stroking the hair off her forehead and being happy, so happy, that she was alive. "What made you . . . ? Thank God you wore the vest."

"What made me wear the vest?" She asked the question he'd been wary of voicing. "I was dumb enough to return to Maine to keep my promise to Mrs. Manly, but I wasn't careless. I was afraid Carrick would be waiting for me." She tried to work herself into a sitting position.

Gabriel sprang to help, holding her arm, her shoulders.

She took a long, slow breath, testing the limits of her pain. "If you hadn't come, he would have killed me, vest or no vest. So . . . thank you."

"You're welcome." Gabriel tried to put his arm around her.

She shoved him away.

So she was angry. She had every right to be. Still, he could smooth this over. All he had to do was let her know what she'd done for him, how much he appreciated her . . . that he loved her. "I did no more than return the favor. In Houston, you saved me, in more ways than one. You saved my life, and you saved my soul."

"Yeah. Sure." She considered him with calculation. "So we're even?"

"We'll never be even." Didn't she understand? "You taught me what love is."

She snorted. "Pull the other leg and see what you get."

"What?" Gabriel's exaltation began to fade.

"Just because you came and rescued me, do you think I've forgotten who you are and what you did?"

It seemed this wasn't going as well as he had hoped.

"You lied to me. You lied to me in every way possible. You lied to me here at Balfour House. You lied to me in Houston. You thought I was every sin out of the Old Testament wrapped into one wicked package." She spoke quickly, then clutched her chest and grimaced. In a softer tone, she said, "So let's call it even, and go our separate ways."

"We can't do that. I might have doubted you once, but I realized you weren't as awful as I thought." Bad choice of words, but he was getting rattled. "What I mean is, I realized in the shower that I love you."

"I don't love you." She clearly articulated each short word.

How could she be so willfully blind, so exasperating? "You *do* love me."

"Don't be ridiculous." She scrambled to her feet without a sign of the pain she must be experiencing.

"Of course you love me. You threw yourself in front of a bullet for me." He tried to stand, too, but his leg wouldn't support him, and his head buzzed from lack of blood.

"What did you do?" He thought it impossible, but her voice was sharper than it had been when she was flaying him alive. "Gabriel, you fool, you've killed yourself this time."

And, as his consciousness faded, he heard Daniel's voice say, "Don't fret, Miss Hannah. I've got the first-aid kit, and the ambulance is on the way."

But when Gabriel came to in the hospital, Hannah was nowhere in sight.

THIRTY-SEVEN

The December sunshine was cold and bright as Hannah entered the federal building in Bude, Maine, for the hearing to decide whether she would be charged with obstruction of justice and aiding and abetting a criminal in pursuit of larceny. She had refused to hire a lawyer. She had only a little more than twenty thousand dollars of Mr. Dresser's bequest left, she had plans for that money, and she wasn't going to spend it paying someone to defend her for something she didn't do and of which she had wanted no part.

Besides, the hearing to clear her of murder charges had been swift and uneventful, given Carrick's babbling confession and the new evidence offered in the video. She figured this would be more of the same.

She entered the courtroom, filled with elegant polished wood lovingly created by early-twentieth-century craftsmen. The courtroom was full—she was big news—but she walked through without looking right or left, gave her name to the bailiff, and seated herself at the front. She was alone, but she preferred it that way.

A man in a business suit came to stand before her, and offered his hand.

She took it and looked up, startled, into the handsomest face she'd ever seen.

In a voice tinted with the faintest trace of an Italian accent, he said, "My name is Roberto Bartolini. I am a lawyer, and with your permission, I will serve as your defense."

She felt a little punch-drunk from looking at the face and the shoulders and, wow, the face. "Thank you, but I intend to defend myself."

"If you will permit me to explain?" He glanced over at the lawyer for the federal government. "I must tell you Mr. Moore is young, hungry to take his law degree into a political office, and this is his first high-profile case. He has declared his intention to make a mark for himself, and he cannot do that if you walk away a free woman."

She looked at Bert Moore, then back at Roberto Bartolini. "How do you know that?"

"He was talking in the local pub. Lawyers." Roberto shrugged expressively. "Someone buys us a few drinks. We get drunk, and we say things we shouldn't." He smiled with an excess of charm. "Just like real people."

She wanted to smile back, but she'd learned to be wary of men who offered to do her a favor. In the past, she had paid dearly for those favors. "While I appreciate your offer, I don't think I can afford you." Because the suit he was wearing fit him like a glove, and his

French cuffs were held together by gold cuff links with chunks of stone that looked like real diamonds. *Big* diamonds.

He still clutched her hand, and now he bent and kissed her fingers. "I seek no payment. My brothers and I—we have taken an interest in your case." He waved a hand toward the benches.

She turned to see what he meant, and there they were, two more tall, broad-shouldered men sitting behind her. The family resemblance was slight. She probably would never have guessed they were brothers. Except for the . . . "Oh." She yanked her hand out of Roberto's grip. "You're Nathan Manly's sons."

Roberto seated himself in the chair beside her. "How did you guess?"

She looked at him, then looked back at the other two men.

They smiled at her.

"The eyes." Those damn green eyes.

"Yes." Roberto's lips curled with scorn. "Our father, he gave us nothing except the distinctive green eyes."

"Look, I don't want—"

"*Shh.*" Roberto put his finger to his lips. "The judge enters."

The hearing took an hour, and it seemed Roberto was right. Bert Moore intended to use the case to bring himself into the public eye.

Thanks to Roberto, he did just that, but not in a good way. Instead, he made a fool of himself in front of a large contingent of news reporters.

And while she should have been paying attention to

the proceedings, concerned about the possibility of prison, she was instead wondering what Gabriel had told his brothers about her, why they had really come . . . whether Gabriel himself lurked somewhere close. She wanted to examine the spectators, look for the face that haunted her nights. She wanted to interrogate Roberto about Gabriel: his health, his whereabouts, and his full family history.

Most of all, she wanted not to care.

She was acquitted of all charges, and the press clamored to interview her. They never stood a chance, for she left the courtroom in the center of the triangle formed by the three brothers.

Out on the sidewalk, Roberto shoved Hannah into the front seat of a big black Cadillac Escalade.

A quick look around proved that Gabriel was nowhere inside.

The biggest brother got in the driver's seat; the other two guys hopped into the back. As they skidded away from the curb, Roberto spoke from right behind her. "Miss Grey, allow me to introduce you. Mac MacNaught is driving. He's a banker."

"Good to meet you, Hannah." Mac never took his eyes off the road.

"Good to meet *you*." She groped for her seat belt and buckled it.

Roberto continued. "Beside me, Dev Fitzwilliam. He's a hotelier."

"It's a pleasure." Dev grinned, obviously relishing the speed.

"A pleasure." These guys were insane, not at all like

their brother, who was coldly, intensely sane. In fact, when she remembered the way he had fooled her, she would have to say he was cold. Except when he . . . Well. No. He was cold and hard and she hated him.

Roberto finished, "You know me, I'm a lawyer."

"A good one." She held on as they careened around a corner.

"We were hoping you'd like to go to lunch." Mac glanced in his rearview mirror, and goosed it. "There's a tearoom across town with, you know, scones and flowered wallpaper and stuff."

"Once he loses the press, we'll drop you off," Dev said.

"Drop me off?" They had *better* lose the press soon, because she was getting carsick.

"The wives wanted to meet you." Roberto leaned forward and said, "Mac, you shouldn't drive on the sidewalk."

Hannah turned her head to stare at the men. "The wives?"

"Our wives. And Gabriel's sisters. It's all one big"— Dev waved his arms—"extended family."

"What if I don't want to meet them?" Hannah asked.

Except for the squealing tires, the car got very quiet.

"I suppose we can drop you off at your hotel, but . . ." Mac took a long breath. "Man, I do hate to upset Nessa. She's pregnant, you know."

Looking like a pack of big, sweet St. Bernard puppies, the guys all looked pleadingly at Hannah.

"I didn't know." She didn't even know who Nessa was. Mac's pregnant wife, apparently.

"The thing about the Prescott girls is that they're all so fiercely protective of Gabriel." Dev pointed. "Mac, turn here."

They went around the corner on two wheels.

"Now turn here." Dev pointed again.

Mac took that turn just as quickly.

Roberto looked behind them. "You lost them. People certainly stare in this town, don't they?"

"When you drive like maniacs, they do!" Hannah said.

"*Maniacs* is such an extreme word." Mac slowed to five miles above the speed limit.

"And there are *our* wives, too. Not pregnant, but they went to such trouble, and when they don't get their way, they're unhappy." Dev grimaced.

They were back to that.

"And when they're unhappy—" Roberto began.

"We're unhappy," Mac finished. "Not that you should feel any obligation because we got you off on the federal charges and out of the courthouse without having to deal with the news reporters."

Hannah couldn't tell whether she was exasperated or charmed. "You guys are not only pussy-whipped— you're experts at ladling on the guilt."

"We don't like to call it pussy-whipped," Dev said. "We like to call it *Trained in Compromise and Negotiation*." He laid his hand, palm up, across the seat.

Mac slapped it in congratulations. "As for being experts at ladling on the guilt—desperation will have its way. And here we are!" He pulled up in front of a charming early-twentieth-century bungalow with the shingles placed in waves across the roof and an exterior painted various shades of soft pink and light blue.

The men actually shuddered when they looked at it, as if the lace curtains in the windows threatened their manhood.

Hey, at least Hannah was now certain Gabriel was nowhere inside.

Dev got out and opened her door.

She slid out and realized Roberto and Mac were standing on the brick walk, waiting to escort her inside. But first—

Roberto hugged her and kissed each of her cheeks. "It was an honor to represent you today, *cara*."

"Thank you. I appreciate all that you—"

Mac pushed Roberto to the side. "Yeah, yeah, he's a great lawyer. I'm a great driver."

"Thank you for driving," she said.

He embraced her, too, very gently, as if he feared he might break her.

Dev waited his turn to hug her. "And I'm the great navigator. They call me the Grand Homing Pigeon."

"We could have used the GPS," Mac said from the corner of his mouth.

Dev didn't even turn around to answer. "Not at the speed you were going." He smiled kindly at her. "Good to meet you, Hannah. We've heard so much about you. Looks like it's all true."

"Well . . . thank you." She wanted to ask if that was a good thing or not, but decided against it. She looked up at the blue front door, painted with pink roses, and took a breath. She climbed the stairs and put her hand on the knob, and looked back at the guys.

They all smiled.

Mac made little shooing motions.

Fine. But she would rather have faced an entire room full of federal prosecutors than Gabriel's sisters.

She opened the door and stepped inside.

THIRTY-EIGHT

A lady in a ruffled apron and cap waited for Hannah.
"Are you here for the Prescott party?"

"I guess." She glanced out the window.

The guys were standing on the sidewalk, waiting,
like military officers ready to stop a retreat.

She was so stuck.

"This way," the hostess said.

Hannah's first thought when she stepped into the
room of chattering women was that she was glad
she'd worn a good suit. These women all looked
great—and they were all total strangers. Except for the
pregnant lady. That must be Nessa.

The chattering stopped. Every eye turned to her.

Six. There were six of them.

The following outcry made her jump.

"Hannah!"

"So glad you came!"

"So glad the guys got it right!"

"So glad that prosecutor got what he deserved!"

They lined up in a female imitation of the guy lineup outside.

A smiling lady with brown hair and big, blue eyes hugged her and said, "I'm Hope. These are my sisters, Pepper and Kate. We're the Prescott sisters."

Hannah embraced each of them, wondering what the sisters thought of her and her relationship with Gabriel, thinking she'd never felt so socially awkward in her life.

Hope continued, "This is Brandi Bartolini. Her husband was your lawyer." Brandi had to lean down to hug Hannah—the woman was tall, built, and gorgeous.

Scary.

"Meadow Fitzwilliam." A pretty woman with a merry face whose husband was the Grand Homing Pigeon.

"Nessa MacNaught." Mac's wife.

Nessa had to lean forward over her belly to hug Hannah, and her sweetly accented Southern voice murmured, "Sorry if little Mac kicks you. It's been a very active day."

"It's okay." Hannah had never felt so unprepared, so alien, in her life.

Hope hooked her hand through Hannah's arm. "We've ordered a formal tea: scones, clotted cream, cucumber-and-watercress sandwiches, and lemon curd. We can't wait to celebrate your win."

"In court, you mean," Hannah said.

"That, too." Pepper grinned.

"Mostly for lassoing Gabriel," Kate said.

Hannah stiffened. "I did not lasso Gabriel."

"You ought to be bragging." Meadow clapped Hannah on the shoulder. "We didn't think anyone could make him yearn and ponder, but you did it."

Hannah let them place her at the head of a long table, and no one heard her ask, "He . . . yearned?"

At least, no one seemed to hear her.

Hope sat on one side of Hannah. Brandi sat on the other. The other women took their places with a surety that told Hannah the arrangement had been discussed in advance.

The waitress placed three-tiered plates with artfully placed pastries and sandwiches.

"First." Hope placed a photo album on the table at Hannah's elbow. "We thought you'd like some pictures of Gabriel."

Hannah slid her gaze toward the album, then back up to Hope's face.

Pepper leaned forward and fixed Hannah with her gaze. "We've got a few photos from when he was a teenager—we lost most of those when we lost our parents—but we included several shots of him in his twenties, and when he bought the ranch, and the ones where he was given an award from the Texas governor."

Hannah pulled the napkin off the table and onto her lap, deliberately not touching the album.

"There're a couple in his headquarters in Houston, with Daniel and some of his staff." Brandi smiled at Hannah. "You know, he's created the most successful security firm in the U.S., but he's got other thriving concerns."

"He's got the ranch near Hobart, Texas. That's the

town where Hope, Pepper, and I were born," Kate said.

"It's a working ranch, too. Of course he has the cattle concerns leased to a neighbor, and the oil wells are pumping." Pepper beamed with pride.

"Don't forget to mention the place he bought near us in South Carolina." Meadow poured tea into her flowered china cup and passed the pot. "It's lovely. Small but so comfortable and the kids love to go there and play on the beach."

"He bought the penthouse in Houston, too, which is convenient for his work," Nessa said.

"I've been there." Hannah bit off the words.

Nessa fixed Hannah with her gaze. "He has all these places to relax, and he knows how, but at the same time, he's a real hands-on boss. He works with his security guys. He likes the physical demands of getting out in the field. It's dangerous sometimes, so we're looking to you to rein him in."

The conversation came to a halt.

Everyone looked at Hannah and waited.

But she knew better. She was not going to let any one of his relatives, no matter how charming, bully her into speaking to Gabriel Prescott. Instead, she fixed Kate with her gaze. "So. I think I've seen you reporting on *GMA*?"

"That's right," Kate said. "I do the occasional political reporting for the network, but most of my work is in Texas."

Determinedly, Hannah led the conversation to less personal topics.

The women followed her more or less willingly. Only Meadow had to be restrained, in a low-voiced discussion with Brandi, from questioning Hannah about her intentions.

The sandwiches had been consumed, the scones exclaimed over, and all the social niceties dragged out, when at last Nessa unhurriedly got to her feet. She stood with the flat of her hand pressed to her back, and spoke to the whole group. "I hate to break up this lovely gathering, but Mac's here to pick me up. It's time for my nap." She walked to Hannah and took her hand. "It has been such a pleasure to meet you. I hope we meet again."

Hannah stood and accepted another embrace. "It has been a pleasure. Thank you for your kindness."

"That's my ride, too," Brandi said.

"I've got a plane to catch." Pepper grimaced and confided to Hannah, "I live in Idaho, and trying to get there from anywhere is more difficult than you can imagine."

A general exodus followed, with each lady telling Hannah of her pleasure in meeting her, then taking her leave. When the dust had settled, only Hope remained, sitting beside Hannah.

One look at her expression, and Hannah had the same sick feeling she'd had in third grade when she'd been told to stay behind after class. She sank down in the chair, grabbed the bull by the horns, and said, "I'm not interested in Gabriel's money. I'm not interested in his businesses. If and when I get involved with a man, I want to know a couple of things right off the bat. I want to know he's not going to lie to me, and I want to know he's not going to use me. I want to know he's going to stick around, and most of all, I want to know he's not going to sic his family on me to persuade me to marry him."

Hope fixed Hannah in her level gaze. "He didn't sic us on you. We came on our own."

"Oh, come on." Did Hope really expect Hannah to believe that?

"He doesn't know we're here."

Yes. It did appear Hope expected Hannah to believe this. Hope couldn't have looked more sincere—or more severe. "Oh," Hannah said with considerably less heat.

Hope continued. "We came because we love him, and because he's miserable."

"He's miserable?" Hannah reflected for a moment. "Good."

"We agree. He told us what he did to you, and he deserves to be miserable. Just . . . not forever." Hope leaned across the table. "I've known Gabriel since my mother brought him home, looking like a starving stray dog, and he's a good man."

"He told you what he did to me, and you still say he's a good man?"

"I didn't say he always gets it right. He is, after all, a man." Hannah could scarcely argue with that. "But he tries. If he has a failing, it is too much loyalty to his friends and family—and Carrick was his family."

"I hope he rots," Hannah muttered.

"Carrick?" Hope asked.

Resentment built in Hannah. Resentment that Hope

would imagine she meant anything else, and that she dared to question her. "Yes. Carrick."

Hope relaxed against the chair. "I suspect Carrick will rot, although in an asylum rather than in prison. His encounter with his father did not come out well."

Hannah smiled tightly. That had been the best part of watching the news, seeing the replay of Carrick's rescue from the meat locker, his wild-eyed babbling, and the realization that Mrs. Manly had become a recluse to protect her secret—she hadn't let her husband leave her, after all. When he tried, she had locked him in the freezer. His body had been in Balfour House all the time.

"Gabriel will do anything for the people he loves. When my family was separated, he used all his resources to search for Pepper and Kate, and we would never have been reunited without his expertise. He helped get Meadow and Dev together, and Ness and Mac, and his greatest happiness is when we're all together at his ranch for a barbecue." Hope viewed Hannah sternly. "He's had a rough life."

Hannah faced Hope without flinching. "Welcome to the club."

"Yes, it's true." Hope half smiled. "We've all had our rough beginnings. In Gabriel's case, it's made him both kinder than usual, to us, and more suspicious than normal . . . of you. I'm sorry for that, but like you, he's seen the worst side of life. The worst side of humanity. His strength is that he's a man who knows what he wants—a home and a family with the woman he loves."

"That is *so* touching." Hannah didn't try to temper her sarcasm. "Do you know what he said before he collapsed in the basement of Balfour House?"

"Oh, no." Hope put her hand to her forehead. "I'm not going to like this, am I?"

"He said, *Of course you love me. You threw yourself in front of a bullet for me.*"

"He actually told you you loved him *of course*?"

"That's right." Hannah leaned back, sure that at last Hope understood.

And she seemed to. She took a long, exasperated breath. "As I said—he doesn't always get it right. But it's funny. With most of his girlfriends, he's very accomplished, very suave, and there aren't enough O's in *smooooth* to describe him. It's obvious that if he's putting his foot so wrong with you, you're different. The one woman that matters to him." Hope stood and offered her hand. "We, all of us, would like him to have the life he desires. I hope to meet you again someday very soon."

Hannah took her hand and shook it. "That would be lovely."

"There'll be a car waiting for you when you wish to leave." Hope smiled kindly. "Goodbye, Hannah."

"Goodbye." Hannah watched Hope's exit. Then . . . she couldn't stand it anymore. She called, "His wound . . . has he had any more trouble with it?"

Hope came back. "He limps a little, but assures me it's getting better every day."

"Okay."

Hope took a step forward. "You know, if you marry

Gabriel, you'll get his whole family as part of the package deal. For someone who has no one, that might make it worth grabbing him."

"Do you really think that's a good thing for your brother? That he marry a woman who only wants him for his family?"

"I never said I thought you only wanted him for his family. I just thought it would be a convenient excuse for you." Hope smiled like a woman who understood face-saving gestures. "Certainly it's something to think about."

Hannah waited until Hope left, until the outer door opened and closed, until she knew without a doubt she was alone.

Then she seated herself. She wiped her suddenly sweating palms on the linen napkin. She took a deep, quivering breath. Pulling the photo album toward her, she opened it to the first page . . . and looked into a young Gabriel's deep green eyes.

THIRTY-NINE

"I think you'll want to see this." Gabriel's secretary placed a letter on his desk under his nose.

He glanced at the header, then looked up at Mrs. Martinez. "Why would I want to read some plea for money from the University of Texas?"

"It's not a plea for money. It's a request for a personal recommendation for one of their students."

He frowned. "A recommendation? For who?"

"Read it and see." Mrs. Martinez, normally stern and unsmiling, almost danced with glee. "This clever young lady has applied and been accepted to their master's program to become a physician's assistant."

Picking up the letter, he read. The words made sense, but he didn't dare believe the truth. So he read again. And for the first time in months, he took a full, deep breath. He looked up at his administrative assistant, a woman who had been with him for six years, who was old enough to be his grandmother, who had kept him on the straight and narrow for the last four months. With an intensity he usually reserved for difficult security situations, he said, "If you can tell me where she is right now, I'll double your salary."

"As I understand it, Miss Grey is moving into the Archwood Apartments on South Braeswood."

"Thank you." Standing, he whirled Mrs. Martinez in a wide circle, kissed her on both cheeks, grabbed his jacket off the back of the chair, and walked out the door. "Thank you!"

Hannah read the scrawl of the black Magic Marker—*kitchen*—took the moving box into the tiny efficiency, placed it on the counter, then headed back toward the truck parked downstairs at the curb. She'd been working for over an hour, wondering if she was doing the right thing, coming back to Houston, wondering whether Gabriel had received the letter from UT, wondering whether he'd even notice or if she'd have to actually screw up her courage, go to his office, and explain that he might be right, she might love him, but that it was unattractive for a man to take a thing like that for granted. . . .

Some guy was coming up the stairs, his face half hidden by the box in his arms.

She stopped. Stepped aside. Let him pass. Watched him climb. And realized that was *her* box, and he looked very familiar. *Very* familiar. Very dear. And very . . . hers.

So he'd received the letter, and this was his response. Thank God.

"Gabriel!" She followed him back up. "What are you doing here?"

"Helping you move in." He pushed her door open with his foot and headed into her apartment.

She stood in the doorway and lifted her chin at him, although he couldn't see her.

He looked good. Healthy. Really *good.*

He put the box down on the coffee table and started to turn toward her.

And she realized she was not ready for this confrontation yet. Not that she was a coward, but she needed a few minutes to gather her thoughts.

She turned and hurried back down to the truck. True, she had had months to gather her thoughts, but now that he was here, she was . . . not scared, exactly, but jumpy. Excited. Filled with hope when for so long, hope had been an expense she didn't dare purchase. Carrying boxes filled with her stuff had to be a better idea than racing up the stairs and kissing him until all she knew was his scent, his touch, the feel of his skin under her fingertips, the thrust of his body on hers. . . .

No. Don't think of that. Bad idea. Because they needed to talk first.

Gabriel had some explaining to do.

A massively built black guy was inside the moving van, carrying boxes and furniture toward the front.

"Daniel. I see Gabriel brought the whole crew." Hannah stood with her hands on her hips and viewed him with fake severity.

He wasn't impressed. "Hi, Miss Hannah. Welcome to Houston." He pointed at the box in front. "Take that one. It's linens. Unpack that and make the bed so you've got something to fall into tonight when you're done."

She glared at him.

"Trust me," he said. "You'll thank me."

Lifting the box, she headed back up. She passed Gabriel coming down.

He'd lost weight, probably fifteen pounds, in the hips and thighs, yet his shoulders looked bulkier. He looked as if he'd spent the time waiting for his leg to heal by lifting weights.

Made sense. She'd spent her time healing the break in her breastbone by walking five miles a day and eating her weight in burgers and fries. Consequently, she was both heavier and more muscular. Gabriel didn't know it, but she could crush a man between her thighs.

He probably would be fine with that.

She made the bed, not because she wanted to roll on the mattress with Gabriel, but because, like it or not, Daniel was right. When the moving day was over, she would be exhausted and in need of a place to sleep.

Before she could go down again, she had to wait while Daniel and Gabriel maneuvered her new Ikea table around the bend and over the railing on the stairway.

Gabriel was limping. Slightly. Almost imperceptibly. But still limping.

Stupid guy. He was such a stupid guy. Because if he was showing *any* sign of weakness, she knew he was in a lot of pain.

So she stopped in the kitchen, searched out her teakettle, and put it on to boil.

He stopped, too, in the doorway, and watched her. His sculpted face was familiar, more dear than she wanted to admit, and the hunger in his green eyes made her breath catch. But he sounded prosaic when he asked, "Are you making iced tea? Because I could kill for a good glass of iced tea."

She looked at the stove. She'd been planning on making a pot of hot tea, but . . . "I could make iced tea." She hadn't thought of it, but iced tea made more sense on this warm, muggy day in January.

Wearily, he sank down on the chair set against the cupboards. "Next time you make iced tea for me, you should use Luzianne. It's the best."

"Next time?"

"Next time," he repeated.

"I'll make sure I remember that."

"Thank you." If he noticed the sarcasm, he gave no indication.

She found the tea bags with no problem. A pitcher proved more elusive, and she finally dumped the bags into a quart glass measuring cup.

As she stared down at the tea, she realized the only sounds in the kitchen were the water as it started to heat and her own breathing.

Gabriel was watching her, and she felt his gaze as distinctly as those days at Balfour House when he'd spied on her with his video cameras. Intruded on her privacy. Learned her a little too well.

He was waiting and watching, and she was waiting, too. There was too much to say, and it was all so difficult, and they had to get it right. If they didn't, the penalty was too great to bear.

This was it. This was their chance.

"Listen—" she began.

"Here we are—" he said at the same time.

Their eyes met.

And she felt the magic sparkle like champagne in her blood. "You start," she said.

He inclined his head, and his voice was warm and deep. Earnest. And slightly hesitant. "Here we are at last. We've got nothing to do but talk. So . . . would you talk to me?"

"Only if you would please explain something to me." She hadn't meant to sound belligerent. But she had.

"You want to know why I would believe Carrick about you?" It was spooky how exactly he knew what irked her most.

"Yes. Yes!" Her irritation and bewilderment flooded back, and she turned on him. "Why did a man like you, who is so smart about people, take his word over mine?"

Gabriel stood and limped over to her. He looked down at her, insisting without words that she look back, and listen and hear. "I know what love is. I do. I've seen it. I've felt it. I have a foster family, and they love me and I love them. I see my sisters with their husbands and their children, and I can almost warm myself by their love. Almost. But it's not the kind of love I feel when I look at you, when I think about you. Do you know, the first time Carrick showed me your picture, I felt a punch to the gut. The woman he told me was a thief and a wh—" He stopped.

"Oh, don't stop now." Hannah waved grandly. "A whore. He told you I was a whore, and you believed him."

"Yes." Gabriel kept his voice low, giving his explanation without apology or insistence—and for that reason, she listened. "I believed him because he was my brother. I had spent my adult life focused on finding my father and my family, not because I was dissatisfied with my foster family and their love, but because I was haunted by the memory of my mother and how . . . awful . . . she was. Broken. She was broken. I thought . . . I dreamed that perhaps she had taken me away from a good man who would be glad to have me as a son. I thought if his family was good, there was a chance for me."

Aghast, Hannah asked, "What did you think was going to happen if you came from a *bad* family? Did you think you would suddenly go nuts and pick up an Uzi and shoot people?"

"It sounds stupid now, doesn't it?" He limped away again, to look out her window at the view of the next unit of brick apartments.

She followed him, getting angrier as she talked. "Think about this, Gabriel—how stupid is it to hire a nurse to care for you when you're critically wounded, a nurse who you believe killed one of her patients? One or more? *That* is the most ridiculous thing I've ever heard." She didn't know which idea infuriated her more—that he actually believed she'd killed Mrs. Manly, or that he'd been dumb enough to hire her while he believed it.

"I'm not normally a stupid man."

"You were stupid this time."

"Was I?" She never saw him move, but suddenly, he turned on her, towered over her. "Was I?"

"If you believed . . ."

"Did I?"

He'd trapped her. He made her face a fact she, in her anger, didn't want to face. Gabriel would never have hired her if he really believed she'd committed murder. He would have gotten her into his car, driven her to the police station, and turned her in.

Catching her wrist, he reeled her in to him. "No matter how often Carrick told me you were the villain, no matter how damning the evidence against you, I couldn't quite believe it. I saw you with Mrs. Manly. She wasn't a stupid woman, either, and I watched how you treated her, and how she treated you. And I saw how she despised her own son." He had Hannah completely enfolded in his arms now, and he looked down at her, so serious, struggling for redemption. "The first time I saw your photo, I knew I was looking at the woman of my dreams. Everything about you was perfect for me. But I've had my dreams broken to dust too many times, and I doubted. I looked at Carrick and saw what I wanted to see. My desire to have the perfect family tainted my instincts and observations."

"Don't forget to use the loss of my nursing license as an excuse, too." She mocked him, then realized she was convincing herself.

Being this close to him melted her irritation—and that would never do. She tried to jerk herself out of his arms.

He held her. "Let me finish. Then if you want me to go, I'll let you. But just . . . let me apologize."

"Men don't apologize," she stated flatly. "I've worked for and with enough men to know—a man doesn't apologize. No matter how wrong he is, or how big a jerk he's been."

"Then you should stay and watch and listen. This moment might never come again."

Damn. He was good. "Go on," she said grudgingly.

"You want a man who won't lie to you, and I've lied to you in every way possible. I've lied to you about who I am. I've lied about what I wanted from you. I've lied with my body and my words."

"How do you know what I want in a man?"

He didn't answer that. Of course not. He knew because he'd spied on her.

She flushed with fury once more.

He kept talking. "You want a man who won't use you for his own ends. I've done that. I used you to discover the truth, and I almost got you killed." His arms developed a fine tremor. He looked at her, his green eyes bleak with pain and remorse.

He didn't hurry his words. They came out slowly, carefully, as if he'd thought out this speech a thousand times, and the hint of a Texas drawl made her warm to the man . . . while being held close to him had made her warm enough. And flushed. And breathless.

"When Carrick shot you . . . I've spent my life thinking the anger inside me was an enemy to be controlled, to be purged. But at that moment, I realized my anger had been placed in me for a reason—so I could release it and kill the man who had murdered you."

Somewhere in the recesses of her unconscious mind,

she had heard the sound of Gabriel's fists striking Carrick's face, and now she flinched at the memory.

"He's not dead," Gabriel said, "and I'm sorry about that."

"He's your brother."

"I'm sorry about that, too." The tremor in his arms eased, yet still his eyes were tormented. "At night, I relive that moment when he raised the gun, and I tried to get between you, and every night, I'm not fast enough and you go down. . . ." His hands flexed against her ribs. "None of my nightmares compare to that. None of them even come close."

She hadn't thought that his nightmares would match hers. But hers were of a different shooting, on a street down from Wal-Mart, where the ligustrum hedge grew thick, and there a shot rang out, and she was never fast enough to save Gabriel. . . .

His hands slid around to grasp hers, and his deep voice was husky and warm as he said, "I wish, Hannah, that you would marry me, and let me spend my life making up for all the foolish things I've done."

"Is that a proposal?" Because it sounded frighteningly real.

"No, it's just a suggestion. When I really propose, I intend to grovel."

"I'll like that."

"I thought you would, and the practice, so my brothers tell me, will do me good."

Hannah laughed unsteadily and wondered if Gabriel was joking. "Your sisters told me to marry you for your money."

"My sisters are a bunch of busybodies." Leaning his nose into her hair, he took a long breath, as if he were relearning her scent after months of deprivation.

"They're very nice busybodies." She put her head on his shoulder, leaned her head into his neck, and took a deep breath of her own. He wasn't the only one deprived.

"Yes, and I do have a lot of money." Clearly, he didn't panic at the idea of being married for it, either.

"Hope also suggested that I marry you so I could be part of your large family."

"Sometimes a large family is nice. Sometimes . . . not so nice. Like when they're being busybodies." He sounded wryly humorous. "Do you want to know why I think you should marry me?"

She looked up sharply.

His hands flexed around hers, and he watched her with the simmering heat of the slowly boiling kettle.

"Why?" She only mouthed the word.

"Because when I pray, I say your name first, and I say your name last. When I breathe, I breathe for you. Every kind thing I say, every good thing I do, I do because I know you're in the world and I . . . I love you." He smiled at her with his mouth, his eyes . . . his soul.

He made her feel as if her heart had grown to fill her chest, warming her, healing her.

She lifted her head.

He leaned down.

Their lips touched. . . .

The kettle whistled shrilly.

They pulled apart, and Hannah wanted to shriek as loudly as the kettle.

"Don't bother yourself, Miss Hannah." She jumped at the sound of Daniel's voice in the doorway.

Gabriel tightened his grip on her, and glared at his employee and friend.

Daniel popped in so quickly and smirked so affably, it was obvious he'd been listening at the door. "I'll take care of that."

Gabriel watched him pour the water onto the tea. "Daniel's related to the busybody family."

"I can see that." Hannah was amused . . . and frustrated.

"Just wanting to catch the water before it boiled away." Daniel opened the freezer. It was empty. "I'll go to the store and get ice. Do you need anything else, Miss Hannah?"

"Milk," Hannah said promptly. "Bread. Bananas . . . Should I make you a list?"

"Might be a good idea." Daniel glanced at Gabriel and flinched. "Or maybe that can wait until later. Ice, milk, bread, bananas. Anything else I can think of that you'll need." He consulted his watch. "I'll be back in thirty minutes!"

"Don't hurry," Gabriel told him.

Daniel laughed and shut the door behind him.

"He's a good guy." Hannah relaxed into Gabriel's embrace.

"Even better, he doesn't hold a grudge."

"Hold a grudge?"

"He'll never hear the end of how you handcuffed

him. The other guards give him trouble about it all the time." Gabriel tightened his arms around her. "I encourage them."

"That was pretty kick-ass of me, wasn't it?" She looked into Gabriel's face, smoothed his hair away from his temples, wished she could kiss him right now.

"You're a legend." Pride sat on his broad cheekbones, shone from his black hair. Pride tugged at the corners of his mouth, glowed in his green eyes. "You handcuffed Daniel Howard, and you lassoed me."

"What is it with you Texans using that word?" She stiffened. "I did not lasso you!"

"Lassoed me like a long-legged calf." He wrapped his hand around her neck, and leaned his forehead against hers. "Luckily, when you hold the other end of the lasso, we're both caught tight. Right?"

She gave in. "Right."

"Because I love you and you . . . ?"

"I love you."

"Say it again."

She laughed a little and wiped away a mist of sentimental tears. "I love you."

He kissed her, warm and wet, a taste of all the passion in all the years to come. "And you'll marry me?"

She caught her breath, and caught at her rapidly vanishing good sense. "Sometime next year, after I settle into the master's program, we'll sneak off and get married—"

He kissed her and contradicted her. "You'll marry me this summer on the ranch with my whole family in attendance."

"You don't get your way about everything, you know." She scowled at him.

"Certainly not." He brushed her hair off her forehead. Kissed her cheek, her nose, her lips. "Once I'm married, I'll be a meek and obedient husband."

Remembering his brothers and their wives, Hannah didn't know whether to believe every word or snort in disbelief.

"Hey." Gabriel hugged her close. "I glanced in the bedroom. It appears you made the bed."

"Gabriel, I don't have time to fool around. I need to move in."

"My busybody relatives would be glad to help carry boxes. I'll call them . . . later." He walked her backward toward the bedroom, stopping only to kiss her and kiss her again.

"Gabriel," she yielded, and sighed, and kissed him back.

When Daniel arrived with his bag of groceries, he opened the front door very cautiously. He listened, then with a grin, closed it again, and took up guard duty.

Until that evening when the Prescott sisters and the Manly brothers, and all their spouses and children, arrived, Gabriel and Hannah were not disturbed.

New York Times *bestselling author Christina Dodd delivers a seductive new series about an ancient legend that lives in the world today. Read on for a sneak peek of the first book in* THE CHOSEN ONES *series on sale in August 2009,* STORM OF VISIONS, *and look for the second book in the series, one month later,* STORM OF SHADOWS, *on sale in September 2009 from Signet.*

STORM OF VISIONS

When the world was young, twins were born, a boy and a girl, marked with special signs and gifted with special powers. As the twins grew, one brought light to a dark world. One carried pestilence like a carrion crow. They gathered around others like them, men and women destined to use their powers in the battle between good and evil. Through the generations, they have been known as the Chosen Ones. . . .

All her life, Jacqueline Vargha has run away from her fate. Now Caleb D'Angelo forces his way into her life, demands his place as her lover, and insists she take her place as one of the Chosen. She flees, he pursues, but when their world explodes in flames, she must at last yield to her visions . . . or lose the man she loves. . . .

Napa Valley, California

Jacqueline pulled her backpack out of her employee locker and headed out the back door to her car, parked under the broad branches of the two-hundred-year-old blue oak that had given the winery its name. The little Civic started right up, and she headed south on Highway 29, the windows wide and the wind ripping through her hair.

The color was like the shimmer of moonlight . . . or so she'd been told. She realized now she should have cut it, and dyed it black, or brown, or purple, or any color besides this freakish platinum. The blond was too distinctive, too easy to spot. More than once, she glanced behind her, watching for a strange vehicle with the strange guy in it, but everything seemed normal. Then, as she pulled into the little town of San Michael, she spotted a black Mercedes SL550 with dark tinted windows, and that chill rippled through her.

Was it him? Was it Mr. Aggressive?

Not necessarily. There was money here, and a lot of people who drove cars like that.

But if it was . . . she couldn't outrun him. She had to outsmart him.

Rather than going to her apartment, she drove until she found a parking spot beside the old-fashioned town square. It was crowded here, part of the downtown renaissance. Quaint shops faced out on the park filled with grand live oaks and benches where tourists lolled in the shade. Directly across the way stood an old redbrick courthouse complete with white trim and a cupola. Jacqueline loved the courthouse, liked to imagine what this town, this wine-producing valley had been like a hundred years ago. When she talked about her decision to live in San Michael, she said the courthouse architecture and the styling of the town were the main reasons she'd chosen to stay in San Michael.

But of course, that wasn't true. The main reason she'd chosen to stay in San Michael was because it was as far away from New York City in culture and distance as she could be and still be in the continental United States.

Now she scanned the park, looking for Mr. Aggressive.

She saw nothing.

Plucking her cell out of her backpack, she called the winery.

Her coworker picked up on the first ring. "Blue Oak Winery, where the hell are you, Jacquie?"

"I didn't like that guy, and you did, so I left."

"Like I need you to leave before I have a chance with him?" Michelle was always crabby, and never more so than when she was offended.

"You got a date with him?"

"*No.* About the time I realized you hadn't come back from the back room, he put the glass down and walked out."

No wonder Michelle was offended.

Michelle continued. "All he did was ask questions about you, and he didn't even finish his tasting. Twenty dollars and he didn't take his second glass. What a loser."

And no wonder Jacqueline was uneasy. "Okay. Thank you." She hung up while Michelle was sputtering.

She got out of the car. Locked the doors. Slung her backpack over her shoulder. And started walking.

In Hills' sales window, a pair of red heels with diamond buckles caught her attention. She stopped, stared, and wondered if she could ever afford shoes like that again—and at that moment, she caught her first glimpse of him, a dark reflection in the glass. The other people on the sidewalk hurried past, but he stood still, a little to the side, and when she glanced at him—the way you do in a crowd, without really looking at him—he was watching her.

Tall. Lanky. Dark-haired. Blue, cold eyes, with the look of a hunter.

She turned quickly away from the window and hurried down the street, a cold draft on the back of her neck.

Okay. This wasn't her imagination. He *had* followed her. He *was* there, part of the impersonal crowd that gathered by the crosswalk. No one else was looking at her—that was for sure. Just him.

The light changed. The crowd surged forward. She surged with them.

The heat rose from the sidewalk and through the soles of her running shoes, and in the odor of the hot asphalt, she could almost smell the flames of hell.

Hell . . .

For a moment, the colors around her faded, turned pale and sepia-tinted, and the world stood still. . . .

She staggered and went down on one knee, and the pain brought her back.

Thank God. She couldn't afford to do this now. She *would not* allow herself to do this now.

Bending her head, she pretended to tie her shoe, and when she stood, Mr. Aggressive had moved on. She darted into the quilting shop and walked swiftly toward the back.

With a smile, the lone, elderly clerk said, "Hi, I'm Bernice. May I help you with your quilting needs?"

"I'm just passing through." Jacqueline paused, her attention captured by the long row of scissors hanging from hooks on the pegboard wall. "How much are those?"

"The scissors? It depends on the size and the quality, and what you intend to do with them." Bernice bustled forward, ready to have a long conversation.

Jacqueline scanned the selection, grabbed an eight-inch, fifteen-dollar pair, and flung it on the counter.

"That pair is good as all-around scissors, but if you're going to be cutting much material, you'd be happier with the slightly more expensive, chrome-plated Heritage Razor Sharpe shears."

Jacqueline dug out her wallet and flung a twenty on top of the scissors. "I'm going to stab somebody with them."

Bernice tittered; then as she stared into Jacqueline's face, her smile faded. "Well . . . then . . . I suppose they'll do."

She backed toward the counter and the cash register so slowly, Jacqueline knew she couldn't wait. She had about a minute before Mr. Aggressive realized he'd lost her, retraced his steps, and picked up on her trail again. Grabbing the scissors, she said, "Keep the change," and swerved around the sales counter and into the back room.

"Hey!" Bernice called. "You can't do that."

"Watch me," Jacqueline muttered. She slipped the scissors in her pocket, and was out the back door and into the alley before Bernice said another word.

Jacqueline took a left and ran hard for the next street. With a glance in either direction, she caught another wave of the crowd and headed away from the courthouse. At an opportune moment, she dashed across traffic and ducked into another alley. She hid behind the first Dumpster, a hot, filthy metal bin that smelled like rotting Mexican food. She opened zippers, dug down to the bottom of her backpack, looking for her baseball cap. She found it, gave a sigh of relief as she tucked up her hair, and ran again, away from the crowds, and toward home.

Her apartment was two blocks away on the town's former fashionable drive. If she could reach the old house, she'd be safe. Her stalker would be behind her. She'd have time to figure out what to do.

Like call the police? Not even.

Pack her bags and get out of town? No way.

Hide under the bed? Yeah, maybe.

She turned onto her quiet street, with its massive oaks and shady yards, slowed to a walk, and looked around, searching for any sign of *him*.

Nosy, retired Mr. Thomas stopped killing his weeds long enough to ask, "Hot enough for you?"

"Sure is," she said. "Have you seen anything interesting come down the street? Any strangers?"

Mr. Thomas leaned on his shovel. "No. Were you expecting someone?"

"No. Just asking!" She smiled at him.

Nothing or, rather, no *man* disturbed the even tenor of the neighborhood.

So she was hot and sweaty, but triumphant. Mr. Aggressive might be the world's all-time best tracker, but she'd lost him. That would teach him to terrorize young, single women.

She climbed the wooden steps onto the wide porch and checked her mailbox. A catalogue and a bill. She used her key to let herself in the side door and climbed the stairs to the second floor.

The old house had been divided into four apartments per floor, with a tiny kitchen and a living room, and a bedroom the size of a closet. She was one of the lucky ones; she had her own bathroom with a black-and-white ceramic tile floor, a pedestal sink, and a claw-foot tub.

Still cautious, she tried the knob; her apartment was locked.

She pulled the scissors out of her pocket and held them like a knife. She inserted her key, swung the door wide, and looked inside. The living room and kitchen were empty. Everything was as she had left it.

Damn him. He really did have her on edge.

But better safe than sorry. Swiftly now, she shut the door behind her. She slid her scissors back in her pocket, set the dead bolt and fastened the chain, then dropped her backpack and hat and, peeling off her T-shirt, headed for the bedroom. She kicked her shoes toward the closet—and paused.

She could hear water running. No big deal, because the lavatory upstairs was right over her head and the pipes ran down the wall. But this sounded like it was in *her* bathroom.

She walked through the door into the old-fashioned bathroom, and the steam hit her in the face.

She'd left the shower running.

Sure, this morning she'd been in a hurry, distracted by that sickening sepia world that hovered close to the edges of her consciousness. For the briefest second, she closed her eyes and touched the mark on her palm to the place on her forehead between her eyes.

Quickly, she took her hand away.

She didn't want to acknowledge the ache that plagued her there. If she could just ignore it, it would go away. It always had before. . . .

The shower. She'd left the shower running.

How could she have been so careless? She had her hand on the green plastic curtain when the word echoed in her mind.

Careless . . .

And she realized . . . someone was in there.

Flinging the plastic curtain open, he pulled her inside.